TRIUMPHANT

ACE BOOKS BY JACK CAMPBELL

THE GENESIS FLEET

Vanguard
Ascendant
Triumphant

THE LOST FLEET

The Lost Fleet: Dauntless
The Lost Fleet: Fearless
The Lost Fleet: Courageous
The Lost Fleet: Valiant
The Lost Fleet: Relentless
The Lost Fleet: Victorious
The Lost Fleet: Beyond the Frontier: Dreadnaught
The Lost Fleet: Beyond the Frontier: Invincible
The Lost Fleet: Beyond the Frontier: Guardian
The Lost Fleet: Beyond the Frontier: Steadfast
The Lost Fleet: Beyond the Frontier: Leviathan

THE LOST STARS

The Lost Stars: Tarnished Knight
The Lost Stars: Perilous Shield
The Lost Stars: Imperfect Sword
The Lost Stars: Shattered Spear

WRITTEN AS JOHN G. HEMRY

STARK'S WAR

Stark's War
Stark's Command
Stark's Crusade

PAUL SINCLAIR

A Just Determination
Burden of Proof
Rule of Evidence
Against All Enemies

TRIUMPHANT

JACK CAMPBELL

ACE
NEW YORK

ACE
Published by Berkley
An imprint of Penguin Random House LLC
1745 Broadway, New York, NY 10019

Copyright © 2019 by John G. Hemry

Library of Congress Cataloging-in-Publication Data

Names: Campbell, Jack (Naval officer), author.
Title: Triumphant / Jack Campbell.
Description: First edition. | New York, NY: Ace, 2019.
Identifiers: LCCN 2018053338 | ISBN 9781101988404 (hardback) | ISBN 9781101988411 (ebook)
Subjects: | BISAC: FICTION / Science Fiction / Military. | FICTION / Science Fiction / Adventure. | FICTION / War & Military. | GSAFD: Science fiction.
Classification: LCC PS3553.A4637 T75 2019 | DDC 813/.54—dc23
LC record available at https://lccn.loc.gov/2018053338

First Edition: May 2019

Printed in the United States of America
1   3   5   7   9   10   8   6   4   2

Jacket illustration by Jaime Jones
Jacket design by Katie Anderson
Book design by Laura K. Corless

To Robert R. "Bob" Chase, a gentleman of boundless goodwill and a writer of limitless imagination.

For S., as always.

ACKNOWLEDGMENTS

I remain indebted to my agent, Joshua Bilmes, for his ever-inspired suggestions and assistance, and to my editor, Anne Sowards, for her support and editing. Thanks also to Robert Chase, Kelly Dwyer, Carolyn Ives Gilman, J. G. (Huck) Huckenpohler, Simcha Kuritzky, Michael LaViolette, Aly Parsons, Bud Sparhawk, and Constance A. Warner for their suggestions, comments, and recommendations.

CHAPTER 1

The city of Ani, dead before it had been officially born, felt ghostlier than usual this night under the slowly shifting light of Kosatka's primary moon. Carmen Ochoa eased carefully among the deserted buildings constructed to house families and businesses that hadn't appeared before the foreign invaders who called themselves "rebels" infested the area.

She paused before entering an area scarred by war, the wide street half-blocked by the front portion of a tall structure that had collapsed when artillery fire tore into it. The rubble provided perfect cover for ambushers, while also forcing anyone traveling this way to divert their path into the open for a short space. Carmen knelt down in the shadow of an intact building, using the scope of her high-powered rifle to study the path ahead. Given time, the multispectral sensors in that scope could identify just about any threat.

The silent, empty city where unseen dangers lurked in the night reminded Carmen of a book she'd once read, a story set on a world called Barsoom that held many ancient, abandoned cities. It'd been a shock to realize that Barsoom was supposed to be Mars, Carmen's childhood home. The romantic, crumbling glory of Barsoom's lost cities had nothing in common with the squalid and ugly slums of Mars that Carmen had known, except perhaps for the fact that both contained endless threats to the life and freedom of anyone who lived there, and perhaps also that both were places where dreams of a brighter future had long since died.

Someone was trying to turn the recently settled world of Kosatka into such a place. Carmen wasn't going to allow that.

The invaders had been pushed out of the other two cities that Kosatka boasted, though both Lodz and Drava had taken a lot of damage as the price of that victory. The human cost had also been painful. But as long as the invaders continued to maintain a toehold on this world around and in Ani, the risk of the next attack succeeding remained too high, and no one knew if the star systems that had attacked Kosatka would return anytime soon with another invasion fleet. The more that could be learned about the military resources of Scatha, Apulu, and Turan Star Systems, and the more the area controlled by the remaining invaders could be shrunk and their numbers reduced, the better chance Kosatka would have.

Which was why she was here tonight, slinking through the shadows of an empty city, rather than back in Lodz with her new husband Dominic.

Satisfied that no dangers awaited, Carmen moved cautiously forward once more. The remaining invaders had lost a lot of equipment, especially the sort of sensors that could have spotted infiltrators such as her, and the sort of mines and automated defenses that could have threatened her. But Carmen kept her progress slow and careful as she flitted through empty buildings whose ground-floor doors and windows had been blown out or forced open during past fighting. She passed like a ghost through what would have been the large lobby of an apartment building, around the edges of what could have become a corner office or small shop, stepping over drifts of dirt on the floors in which weeds were striving to take root, past the empty maws of inner doorways and unfinished ventilation ducts. In the darkness those openings gaped with a deeper gloom that seemed somehow sinister, as if enemies lurked within, watching and waiting. But her sensors detected nothing, so Carmen kept moving.

Her first warning that she'd finally reached an enemy perimeter came when her scope alerted her to energy use and body heat ahead. Sentries, their gear battered enough that it could no longer offer the concealment it once had. The concealment that Carmen's outfit still had and kept them from detecting her.

Carmen waited, watching through her scope, long enough to spot the nearest sentries when they moved. Their camo clothing matched itself to the buildings and wreckage, but movement still showed against the otherwise deserted surroundings.

Finally, she slid warily through the nearest buildings and into a small park, the trees and bushes planted there nearly four years ago grown into a stunted and tangled mass. As Carmen had expected, the invaders had counted on anyone entering that to make enough noise to be heard, but she'd learned how to move slowly and cautiously enough to pass through such obstacles. She kept her eyes open and her scope active, spotting a single trip wire in time to avoid stumbling into it, and stepping carefully past it.

Finally, Carmen reached a position where she could lie next to a tree, gazing toward a building where several individuals were visible as shadows through the shattered windows. She focused on them, zooming in, but the features remained vague and the lips too ill defined for the scope to be able to read the words they spoke. There were enough other invaders present to make any attempt to get closer far too dangerous. The signal pickup on her scope remained quiet, showing that these invaders weren't using any electronic communications that didn't depend on fiber-optic landlines.

That left little chance of any intelligence collection. But she'd already pinpointed this enemy-held area. One more task and she could call in a strike. Carmen watched, patient and remorseless, until she could be sure which of the figures was in charge by the way the others acted.

Finally, she aimed her rifle up toward the satellites orbiting the planet, all controlled by Kosatka's own government, and used the high-gain transmitter in her scope to send a tight burst signal that identified the invaders' location, as well as a requested time for the strike.

Then she had to wait a little longer, the night quiet about her, occa-sional movements of enemy soldiers visible, the group inside the build-ing still talking, the timer on her scope counting down. As the numbers dwindled to less than a minute, Carmen zoomed in on the leader she'd identified, aimed with infinite care, and then fired, the noise of the shot shattering the calm of the night.

Her target jolted away and fell as the high-powered bullet slammed into them, the others around their leader scattering and diving for cover.

Carmen was already moving, no longer trying to remain silent, moving fast to put distance between herself and the invaders, hearing alerts sounding behind her, a few shots tearing through the bushes around her. As she had wanted, the invaders had all taken cover, lying low, their attention fixed on the buildings around them.

The strike came down.

It had been dropped by *Shark*, Kosatka's remaining destroyer. Streamlined, solid metal projectiles, released from low orbit on precise trajectories, falling for hundreds of kilometers, gaining energy as they fell. Carmen saw multiple sudden shadows spring to life in front of her as the projectiles drew bright lines of light through the night sky be-hind her, a display beautiful to anyone far enough away but terrifying to those at the aim points. The invaders, belatedly realizing the strike was inbound, might be springing to their feet to flee, or might be cow-ering helplessly on the ground.

It didn't matter what they were doing, because anything they did was too late now. Carmen felt her lips pulling back in a snarl of antici-pation as she ran, her breath rushing between her teeth.

The ground beneath Carmen shook as the projectiles slammed to the surface, releasing their accumulated energy, tearing apart anything they struck, cratering the soil, blowing apart buildings. In a moment of insane fury, a small portion of the dead city of Ani ceased to exist.

Carmen dropped to the ground as pieces of debris whipped past above her. A large piece of wreckage rocked the ground as it plummeted down a few meters to one side. She stared at it, feeling her heart pound in belated reaction to how close death had come that time. The roar of destruction blanketed all other sounds, momentarily deafening Carmen as she scrambled back to her feet and ran once more.

As the multiple roars of the impacting projectiles faded, Carmen heard the rumble of buildings collapsing and felt the rush of air and dust at her back.

Part of Ani was gone, but so were the invaders who'd sheltered there. A little more of Kosatka was free.

Carmen didn't linger near the site of the strike, moving a few kilometers through the dark and once-more-silent city before risking sending out a full report, her scope relaying the data and video it had recorded.

Eventually, she reached the building where the unit she was with had holed up. Outwardly, it looked as deserted and dead as the rest of the city. But sentries with weapons at the ready greeted Carmen in the outer rooms. A large inner room, shielded from the outside, held twenty men and women as well as their equipment. Inside, most wore only T-shirts and trousers, their camo, personal weapons, and body armor (if they had any) placed on the floor beside where they sat or lay. Officially, those twenty and the five sentries on watch outside made up the Third Company of the Second Regiment of the First Brigade of Kosatka's planetary militia. The unit had been one hundred strong before the invaders landed, made up mostly of people who'd come to Kosatka to start new lives in a wide variety of occupations but had found themselves forced to defend their new homes. Some of those hundred had been called back for critical jobs, others for family emergencies, others wounded. The rest had died. Those remaining wore the weary, fatalistic expressions of men and women who were going to see their job through but didn't expect to be there when victory finally came. If it ever did.

Carmen received nods of recognition as she entered, feeling a small rush of pleasure at being accepted as one of them. She'd spent a long time feeling alone. Carmen felt herself finally relaxing, exchanging greetings with her comrades, peeling off her camo, and gratefully accepting a cup of coffee.

"Kosatka is short on a lot of things, but they make sure we always have coffee," Captain Devish said as he crouched down beside her. "It's lousy coffee, but it's here."

"There's no more coffee in Drava or Lodz," Carmen told him. "What's left on the planet is being sent to the fighters here around Ani."

"I hope the planet gets more shipments in before it all runs out. You did a good job, Carmen."

"Thanks," she said. "What's the assessment?"

"No signs of life. The strike wiped out that invader strongpoint." Captain Devish, among the few professional soldiers in the unit, had come to Kosatka from Brahma, one of the Old Colonies. When asked, he always gave his reason for emigrating as "I was bored." He certainly wasn't bored now.

"Good." Carmen took a drink of the hot and bitter coffee, feeling exhausted. "Did my report make it through?"

"Yeah. Clean upload." Devish gave her a searching glance. "I heard you worked for Earth government once."

"Yeah. After I got off Mars." She didn't try to hide her origins anymore. People could accept her or reject her. Carmen no longer cared. "I worked in Albuquerque."

"Albuquerque? What was that like?"

"Better than Mars."

Devish grinned. "What'd you do?"

"I was in the Conflict Resolution Office," Carmen said. "Working to find legal and peaceful resolutions for conflicts and disputes on Earth and all settled worlds."

"You're kidding." Devish shook his head. "How effective was that?"

"It worked when people believed in it. When they stopped believing, stopped caring, it didn't work. I came out here to try to make people believe in that kind of thing again. Because what's happening to Kosatka shouldn't be happening anywhere." Carmen touched her rifle. "That's why I'm using this now. But someday we need to get back to depending on laws for our protection."

"That'd be nice," Devish said, not quite hiding his skepticism that such a day would ever come. "Anyway, you can relax. We've been ordered to stay under cover through daylight today, so there won't be any more action until nightfall."

Finishing the coffee, Carmen went into a side room for some privacy and uplinked to Kosatka's planetary net using landline relays to keep anyone from being able to tell where her signal was coming from. Fiber cables run to the roofs of other buildings linked them to antennas communicating to the satellites above.

This room, like most rooms in Ani, lacked furniture, so she sat on the floor, settling down with her back against the wall behind her. Carmen set her comm pad down long enough to comb her hands through her hair and rub her face so she wouldn't look like someone who'd just spent the night crawling through a dead city. Fixing a smile on her face, Carmen tapped a link.

After a long moment, the image of Dominic Desjani appeared. His face still bore signs of the strain of the injuries that kept him mostly confined to bed. "Hey, Red," he said, smiling. Red, the common slur aimed at those from Mars, had somehow become an affectionate nickname by Dominic for her, one she loved hearing from him. "How are you?"

"Working late," Carmen said. "Sorry."

"I never knew collecting intelligence was so stressful."

"Yeah, well, fieldwork. You know." She didn't want to lie to him, but she also didn't want to admit to all of the risks she was running. "How's the leg?"

"The one that's missing? Still gone." Dominic gestured vaguely. "I'm told maybe another month before I get a prosthetic. There's a big backup manufacturing them for all the wounded, and I'm sort of low on the priority scale."

"What about regeneration? Weren't they looking at a regrow for you?" Carmen asked.

"Still looking." Dominic smiled. "I can wait. There are others who need stuff grown back worse than I do."

"As long as you're okay," Carmen said.

"What have you actually been doing, Red?"

She sighed. "Collecting intelligence."

"That covers a lot of different ground. You look pretty worn-out."

"I'm doing my part, Domi."

He stayed silent, unhappy, his eyes on her.

"I'm going to be back in Lodz in a few days," Carmen added, trying to change the subject. "What do you want to do?"

Dominic shook his head, still gloomy. "Maybe have some more honeymoon."

"That'd be nice. Domi, I'm sorry. You know who I am. You knew what you were getting when you asked me to marry you. I'm a Red."

"You came from Mars. But you're not like those gangsters fighting for the invaders." Dominic looked away. "You are a fighter. I knew that, yeah. Maybe someday you'll tell me everything you did on Mars. Everything you did to get off that hellhole of a planet."

"You don't want to know, Domi." Carmen forced another smile. "What matters is that I made it here and found you. Hey, estimates are that the invaders are down to a couple of thousand in the areas of Ani they still occupy and the land just outside the city. They're short on everything, and they lost another senior leader tonight. They could crack at any time."

He nodded, not seeming happy at the news. "How'd you hear about them losing a leader?"

Stupid. Why had she said that? "Uh . . ."

"That's what I thought. Red—"

"Don't. Or I'll bring up the subject of you leaving your police job to become an officer in the militia."

Dominic eyed her, then smiled. "We're two of a kind, huh? Well motivated. Not too smart."

"Maybe too smart for our own good," Carmen admitted.

"Somebody has to do it. Any estimates on when the next invasion force will show up?"

"No. We have no idea what Scatha, Apulu, and Turan might have left."

"We know what we have left." Dominic pointed outward. "One warship, *Shark*. And a planetary militia that's low on supplies, weapons, and people."

Carmen nodded. "Lochan went for help, remember? And we're formally allied with Glenlyon now. Kosatka's not alone anymore."

"It still feels pretty alone," Dominic said. He laughed, the sound more bitter than humorous. "I was told that if another invasion fleet jumps into the star system, I'll be jumped up the priority list for a smart prosthetic so I'll be combat capable again. Nice of them, huh?"

"Yeah. Nice." Carmen had to look away this time, remembering seeing Dominic wounded, his lower leg gone, awaiting evacuation. For a moment her sight of the empty room about her was overlaid by her memories of the dimly lit basement where she'd found Dominic during the battle for Lodz, the stench of blood in the air, tired medics doing all they could, Domi himself sedated, her guts churning with fear that he might not make it. It took a major effort to wrench her thoughts away from that, to compose herself enough to smile at him once more. "I'll see you in a couple of days."

After the call ended she sat on the floor, gazing out at the vacant room, wondering what would happen and how long she and Dominic might have left together. *Please don't let us down, Lochan.*

L ochan Nakamura, who'd already escaped a few attempts to ensure he never reached Eire Star System, tried not to look nervous as the group he was with approached the security and customs screening at Eire's orbital facility. His attention on the people around them, Lochan twitched in nervous surprise when the security scanner chirped as Freya Morgan walked through it.

"Hold on." The security detail displayed a level of cautious wariness that had become normal in recent years. The days of casual security theater done as a matter of form had disappeared as threats multiplied on the frontiers of human expansion among the stars. One officer studied a display, frowning, as two others stood back, their weapons not drawn but their postures those of someone ready to react. "Freya Morgan?"

"That's the name," Freya confirmed.

"You're traveling alone?"

Lochan spoke before taking the time to think. "I'm with her. On business."

"So am I," Leigh Camagan said.

The officer gazed at them, his eyes flicking to the display and back again to focus on Lochan and Leigh. "Lochan Nakamura. From Kosatka. And Alice Mary Norton from Glenlyon."

Leigh shook her head, tapping her personal pad. "That's a false name to ensure I made it this far. Here's my real identification. Leigh Camagan, minister of the government of Glenlyon."

"I see," the officer replied in the tone of someone wishing that such a thing had happened on someone else's shift. "I'll have to ask you three to step aside," the security officer added in a voice whose politeness now held steel under the surface.

A fresh pair of security officers appeared to escort Lochan, Freya, and Leigh into a side room. The door locked behind them as the officers left them alone.

"Do they really think we're going to start talking freely just because we're the only ones in this room?" Leigh Camagan asked, sounding annoyed. Small, sharp, and fiery, she was identified by her false travel documents as a librarian on her way to Earth. Her ultimate destination was indeed Earth, but once there she'd be shopping not for novels but for surplus warships.

"You'd be surprised how stupid some folks can be," Freya replied. She appeared relaxed and calm, which reassured Lochan a great deal. Supposedly a straightforward trade representative from the world of Catalan, Freya Morgan had the outward appearance of an unconcerned traveler. Only someone who looked closely would notice the way her eyes kept constant watch on everyone else, and the way her every step kept her balanced and ready to react. Lochan hadn't learned everything that Freya was capable of, but she certainly knew a lot more about such things as improvised explosives and hacking into systems than the average trade representative.

Lochan looked around, seeing two displays on one wall, probably placed to encourage careless conversation among those waiting here. One showed an outside view of Eire's orbital station, including both the boxy shape of the freighter *Bruce Monroe* that Lochan and the others had arrived in, and farther off, the menacing barracuda-like shape of the destroyer *Caladbolg*. Like the other warships in the new colonies, *Caladbolg* had begun life in Earth Fleet, where she'd been the *Emperor Menelik*. But Earth, finally weary of war and tired of trying to police her unruly children on planets circling other stars, had been shutting down her legendary fleet and selling her former warships.

There had been similar destroyers among the forces of those attacking Kosatka.

"You'd think Earth would care who they were selling weapons to," he muttered.

"How can they tell?" Leigh asked. "From the distance of a few hundred light years and months of travel time, we all look the same."

Freya nodded. "All the authorities on Earth care about is whether buyers have enough cash or good credit."

Lochan shook his head, not sure what else to say, his eyes going to the other display, which showed a star chart of the local region. Humanity, exploding into this arm of the galaxy after the introduction of the jump drives that allowed travel between stars in a matter of weeks, had in the last few decades settled on Eire, as well as farther out on Kosatka, Glenlyon, and Catalan. Other stars, like Tantalus and Jatayu, lacked worlds suitable for humans, and remained simply waypoints to other places.

His eyes settled on a cluster of other stars. Scatha, Turan, and Apulu. Most people coming out here were seeking freedom of one kind or another. But the rulers of those star systems had wanted most of all the freedom to impose their will on others. With Earth far distant and uninterested in what happened on the borders of humanity's expansion, that freedom had meant war and other aggressions.

Lochan Nakamura's last sight of Kosatka had been of an invasion fleet closing in on a world with too few defenders. The end of Carmen Ochoa's last message to him echoed in his mind. *Get out of Kosatka. Go where you can find help for us. We'll hold out until you get back.*

"We'll bring back help," Freya said in a low voice, as if reading his thoughts.

"I haven't exactly been a success in life up to this point," Lochan said, trying to sound cynical rather than depressed. "I've failed at everything important."

"Not since you came out here, if half of what I've heard is true," she reassured him.

Leigh Camagan shook her head. "We've all come hundreds of light years from Earth or from the Old Colonies on stars near it, but our minds are still stuck there. All of us are still nursing grudges and fears born on the worlds of our ancestors instead of seeing clearly what's out here. If we're going to convince other star systems to help our worlds, we have to get their hearts and minds here and now, not mired in the past."

Lochan felt himself smiling, surprised that her words had gone home so well. "I'm going to steal that idea for my own speeches."

"You're supposed to call it 'research,' not 'stealing.' Instead, consider it a gift freely given," Leigh replied, smiling as well.

The door opened again to reveal another security officer, one whose looks were so unthreatening she resembled a generic loving grandmother.

But before the grandmother could begin lulling them into complacency and revealing statements, Freya spoke up. "About time you got here. Call Colonel Ryan. Tell him I'm here."

The grandmother blinked at Freya. "Colonel Ryan?"

"Your boss. Patrick Ryan. Tell him I said he's a gombeen and a bollix."

It took about ten minutes more of waiting before one of the display screens in the room changed to show an irritated but wary man in an Eire security uniform. "It *is* you, Freya," he said in a far-from-welcoming tone of voice.

Lochan was surprised to see Freya smile in response.

"Even a top criminal like me can't fool the likes of you, eh, Pat?"

The colonel didn't return the pleasantry. "Why are you trying to sneak into this star system?"

"It's nice seeing you again as well," Freya said. "I'm sneaking, am I? Traveling under my own name? As for why, I'm on official business for the government of Catalan. My companions are also on official business for their governments."

Colonel Ryan's gaze ran over Lochan and Leigh. "Two refugees from star systems at war."

"Diplomats," Leigh Camagan corrected him. "Two representatives of the governments of their star systems who are seeking allies against unprovoked aggression that has already endangered our worlds and if unchecked will reach your star system as well."

"Two diplomats from star systems at war," Colonel Ryan corrected himself. "One of them traveling under a false name."

"You know that Glenlyon is under blockade," Freya said. "How else was a representative of their government supposed to get through that?"

Ryan frowned, but nodded. "Fair enough. But what does Catalan have to do with Kosatka and Glenlyon?"

"Catalan's also under attack," Freya said. "Not military action, yet. Economic. The choke hold is being applied."

Ryan eyed her. "Anyone trying a choke hold on Eire will regret it."

"You with your two destroyers? Kosatka and Glenlyon both had two as well."

Freya's casual put-down of Eire's small fleet hung in the air for a moment. Colonel Ryan gave her a flat gaze before apparently deciding to avoid directly challenging the statement. "You're on a watch list, Freya."

She shook her head, apparently unfazed by the statement. "Official business. Government to government. Do you think I don't know the rules here?"

Ryan grimaced. "If you're here on official business for Catalan, I can't turn you back. But we've already received a warning regarding Nakamura."

"Anonymous, I'm guessing."

"That's right. You know me, Freya. I don't like anyone trying to pull my strings."

"*I'm* being open with you. Pat, this is something the government needs to deal with at a high level. There's a time to choose sides, and that time is now."

Colonel Ryan nodded. "I'm not going to stop any of you. Hold on and I'll have a couple of officers escort the three of you down."

"Make sure they're ready for trouble, Pat. There've already been a few tries to keep us from reaching Eire and talking to the government. If not for Lochan there, one of those attempts would've succeeded."

Lochan tried not to appear uncomfortable as Ryan's gaze bored into him once more. "So he's a dangerous one, is he?"

"Only to enemies of Kosatka," Freya said. "I can swear to that."

"That's good enough, then. I'll get you all down to the planet safely and let the government figure out what to do with you. That means notifying your father, Freya."

"Then do it. Thanks, Pat."

Colonel Ryan ended the call, leaving Lochan feeling embarrassed at being mistaken for "a dangerous one." "What was that about your father?"

Freya shrugged. "He's in the government."

Leigh Camagan's gaze on Freya sharpened. "In the government? And your father's last name is also Morgan?"

Lochan stared at Freya. "Your father is the prime minister of Eire?"

Another shrug. "His proper title is Taoiseach. But don't go thinking that means we've got an inside deal with Eire. I was disowned even before my brother. Mind you, my brother deserved it."

The two women who showed up to escort them down to the surface were both polite. But Lochan thought they acted more like guards for prisoners than escorts for guests as the small group headed for the shuttle loading area. Each shuttle dock had its own air lock, but the room facing the docks was long and fairly wide to accommodate both crowds and cargo. Lochan guessed there were about forty other people waiting there singly and in small groups as the guards escorted him, Leigh, and Freya into the room. Like most such waiting areas, it had only a few pieces of furniture near the walls, which featured large displays revealing either external views of space or status updates on shuttle flights.

The guards did such a smooth and expert job of herding Lochan and the others through those already in the room that Lochan half wondered if they'd been trained by watching corgis at work.

They were near the air lock for their intended shuttle when one of the guards jerked and fell against him. Lochan grabbed as she slumped, holding her up without thinking, ducking a little to catch her. The instinctive action saved his life as a second shot aimed at him also hit the woman, who was serving as an inadvertent shield.

A moment later, Lochan's feet were swept out from under him by Freya's leg as she dropped to the floor, Freya's hands also pulling down Leigh Camagan so all three fell to momentary safety out of the line of fire. Lochan kept his grip on the wounded guard, hearing her gasp with pain as they dropped. His thoughts and feelings were frozen, even fear not yet present as he tried to shake off the shock of the sudden attack. If not for Freya knocking him down, he'd still be standing there, paralyzed.

Some "dangerous one" he was.

The shots hadn't made any noise. Everyone else in the area either hadn't noticed the furor or were staring at Lochan's group, trying to understand why they were acting so oddly. He stared back at anyone facing them, trying to figure out who had fired those shots. Blood was spreading over part of the guard's abdomen, so Lochan pressed his hand hard on that spot to control the bleeding.

"Shooter!" the unhurt guard shouted, her voice cutting through the low buzz of conversation. *"Everyone down!"* Silence fell, people staring at the guard. "EVERYONE DOWN!" the guard repeated loudly enough for the command to echo.

The others in the room dropped to the floor in a flurry of movement.

"It's probably a rail pistol, completely silent," Freya snapped at the unhurt guard, who was crouching beside them and using her body to screen the others while she used one hand to call for help. The other hand held a weapon that swung back and forth in a futile hunt for a target. "Where's the shooter?"

"No idea," the guard said. "I've got nothing showing. All surveillance systems in here blanked. Looks like a worm in the network. Help's coming!"

A dozen guards ran into the room, their weapons out. With every exit sealed, they began searching everyone. Emergency medical personnel also arrived, kneeling beside the fallen guard, Lochan relinquishing his attempts to control her bleeding. He stood up, staring at the blood on his palm for a moment before a med tech used a wipe to swab it clean and disinfect his skin. "Is any of this yours?" the tech asked.

It took Lochan a moment to realize that the med tech meant the blood. "No."

The tech ran a scanner over Lochan, searching for any more blood on him or his clothing, before kneeling to clean up a few spots of blood on the floor.

"Whoever did it probably left right after their second shot," Freya was saying to the head of the guard force. "If any of your sensors can identify anyone who left here, that's probably our would-be assassin."

"The entire section went down," the supervisor muttered angrily, his eyes sweeping the room. "This was an inside job. The shooter must work up here." That hard gaze settled on Lochan. "Both shots were aimed at you. You're from Kosatka?"

"That's right," Lochan said, trying to sound calm, acutely aware of the blood that had been on his hand. He imagined that he could still feel it, wet and warm, someone else's life spilled onto him. "How is she?"

"The guard? I'm told she'll recover. The shots were aimed to kill you so they hit nonlethal spots on her when she blocked them."

"I'm sorry," Lochan mumbled, thinking of his friends Carmen and Mele, who might both at this instant be running the same risks under distant stars, perhaps suffering similar wounds. And counting on him to ensure their sacrifices weren't in vain.

"She was doing her job," the supervisor assured him. "Don't let it rattle you. You're safe now."

"It's not about me being safe," Lochan protested, stung by the idea that he was being protected while his friends faced danger. "I've got a job to do."

"I warned Colonel Ryan that there are people who do not want us to speak to Eire's government," Freya said. "The people who've attacked Kosatka and Glenlyon, and isolated Catalan, have been laying the groundwork to ensure no help comes to any of us."

"I don't care what their motives are," the supervisor said. "I do care about doing my job. Which shuttle were they going to take down?" he demanded of another guard.

"Drop Eleven Oh Six. Departing one hour from now."

"Anyone who could subvert our sensors would also know these passengers were scheduled for that drop and might have some backup plan for destroying that shuttle. Instead, these people are going on this drop. Right now. And I want Eleven Oh Six gone over with tech, fingertips, and eyeballs to ensure no one's planted any bombs on it or viruses in its systems."

"Bombs? Yes, sir!"

As the guard hastened off, Freya gave the supervisor an approving look. "You know your business."

He shrugged. "I learned it on Rhiannon Station, screening out the crazy Reds trying to come up from Mars. I thought I'd left that kind of thing behind when I came out here."

"We left nothing behind," Lochan said, thinking of what Leigh had said earlier. "We brought it all with us."

Anyone traveling by jump drive from Eire to the star that humans had named Glenlyon had to follow a crooked path. The jump drives could only enter and leave jump space at points where space-time itself had been stretched thin by objects as massive as stars, and the star jumped from and the star jumped to had to be within several light years of each other, forcing ships to jump from star to star on the way to their destination. From Eire a ship would jump across the five light years to Tantalus, where there were no good planets for humans, and then on to Kosatka, home to a nice enough world that it had already attracted the attentions of would-be conquerors. From Kosatka the ship would have to jump to Jatayu, another inhospitable star, before making a final jump to Glenlyon and proceeding onward to the planet of the same name as its star.

If, instead of going to Jatayu, the ship had jumped to Kappa, yet another star lacking suitable planets for humans, it would have then faced a choice of jumping either to Catalan or to a star named Hesta. Catalan, hemmed in by stars controlled by Apulu, Scatha, and Turan, had yet to be attacked, but had already found itself isolated. Hesta, supposedly still independent, had been the first target for aggression. Its puppet government had been under the control of foreign stars for two years.

But getting a ship to actually take you along those routes would be much more difficult than it had once been. Word was getting around that any star past Tantalus was in a war zone. If a ship didn't get caught in combat, it would likely fall prey to the pirates popping up in star systems like Kappa and Jatayu. The pirates, using freighters modified to carry a few weapons and a little more propulsion, were widely known to be privateers working for the aggressive star systems. Of course, freighters owned by Scatha, Apulu, or Turan still made the journeys, but at monopoly prices far higher than anywhere else. And traveling on one of their ships meant placing yourself under the control of stars who were looking for servants, not new citizens. Lochan, Leigh, and Freya had come from Kosatka on the *Bruce Monroe*, which for all they knew had been the last free ship to make that voyage after starting out from Glenlyon.

Light itself would take more than twenty years to cover the distance between Glenlyon and Eire. Scientists were still debating whether time was really uniform across such distances, or if humans were bringing their own perceptions of time with them. But then scientists were still debating what time *was*. Yet, if events in separate star systems could take place "at the same time," as Lochan Nakamura and his companions were arriving at Eire, his friend Mele Darcy was on the surface of the planet named Glenlyon orbiting the star of the same name. Wearing the uniform of Glenlyon's still-new Marine force, Mele stood facing Colonel Menziwa, the commander of Glenlyon's still-meager ground forces.

"What do you want, Captain Darcy?" Menziwa asked, as if she was equally annoyed and uncaring about the reason for Mele's visit. As usual, the ground forces colonel had a severely correct uniform, not a single thread out of place, and a matching hairstyle, not one hair daring to deviate from its proper position and placement. The colonel's desk was also as precisely laid out as a parade ground, without even a single stray paper clip to mar its order. Mele had wondered more than once if Menziwa's primary objection to the creation of a Marine force outside of her control was really about the existence of "soldiers" occupying the wrong organizational box.

"I wanted to propose some joint exercise activity," Mele said.

Menziwa frowned slightly before leaning back in her seat and giving Mele a closer look. "Joint exercise activity."

"Yes, Colonel." Mele tilted her head in the direction of the ground forces barracks. "Your people have been training by having mock engagements with each other. So have my Marines. But I think my people are falling into ruts, getting too used to each other and what they'll do. I'd like to shake them out of any training routines and confront them with new challenges."

Menziwa spent several long seconds gazing at Mele without speaking. "How large is your force?"

Like Glenlyon's ground forces, the Marines had been expanding, so Mele wasn't surprised that the colonel didn't know that number. "We're currently at forty Marines, Colonel. Forty-one, counting me."

"We need to count you," Menziwa said, her expression and voice leaving it unclear as to whether that was praise or a rebuke. The colonel fell silent again for a few seconds. "That's not a bad idea. I've never made it a secret that I see no need for a separate Marine force, but in this case it does offer some benefits in giving my people different opponents to face in training. Let my staff know I approve of the concept and want them to work out the details with you."

"Thank you, Colonel," Mele said, saluting.

Instead of returning the salute, Menziwa fixed her gaze on Mele again. "Captain Darcy, I've read all of the after-action reports from Kosatka."

Mele waited, holding herself at attention, wondering where this latest jab would lead.

"It's clear," Menziwa said, "that if not for your actions and those of Commodore Geary, the invasion of Kosatka would have succeeded. Our enemies know that as well as we do. What will those enemies do as a result, Captain Darcy?"

"Try to ensure that we can't intervene again the next time they try to conquer Kosatka," Mele said.

"Exactly. I don't particularly like you, Captain Darcy, but you've got a good head on your shoulders. We need to be prepared for whatever our enemies do to try to take us out preparatory to their next assault on Kosatka."

"I understand, Colonel." Mele paused. "Permission to speak freely?"

"Granted."

"I don't particularly like you, either, Colonel."

For the first time in Mele's experience with her, Menziwa smiled. "Your work at Kosatka earned you the right to say that. Now get out of here."

"Yes, Colonel." Mele saluted again, pivoted, and left the office, once more grateful that Menziwa wasn't in her chain of command.

The officers she needed to speak with about the training weren't available, being themselves out in the field on training exercises. Mele left messages for them to contact her, then headed back to the spaceport earlier than she'd anticipated for a lift back up to the orbital facility where Glenlyon's small Marine force was garrisoned.

Leaving headquarters required enduring a search of her driverless vehicle and a check of her ID by the gate sentries. Menziwa clearly was acting on her concerns, ensuring that no potential threat could easily pass in or out of her headquarters.

On the road leading away from ground forces headquarters, Mele's vehicle passed a truck lumbering toward that facility. A sign up front indicated the truck had no driver, fully automated as usual, and was one of the routine supply deliveries to the headquarters.

She hadn't gone more than a few kilometers when a flash of light behind her warned of the crash of an explosion that followed immediately after. Mele's vehicle swerved as the ground jumped beneath it in response to the shock wave from the blast.

Ordering her car to an emergency stop, Mele checked the radiation detector on her personal pad. There hadn't been a surge of radiation, so the blast hadn't been nuclear. Knowing there wasn't any risk of fallout, Mele got out of her vehicle and stared back toward ground forces headquarters. A mushroom-topped pillar of smoke was rising skyward, testimony to the amount of explosive in the blast, and pieces of debris were still falling back to the ground. The distant sound of emergency sirens wailing seemed faint after the noise of the blast.

Their enemies had struck again, just as the colonel had predicted.

She got back into the car and directed it to return to Menziwa's headquarters, wondering what she'd find there.

CHAPTER 2

The image of Mele Darcy on Commander Rob Geary's display had taken only a second traveling at the speed of light to reach the destroyer *Saber* where the ship rested in the repair dock at Glenlyon's orbital facility. Rob studied Mele as she talked, marveling at the way she could act and speak so calmly and coolly even after what she'd just witnessed and experienced. He knew Mele better than anyone else on Glenlyon, but even Rob couldn't be sure whether she was really that composed inside or if she was bottling it all up until it could be released in a night of drinking.

"The truck apparently tried to drive on through the gate when the sentries ordered it to stop for inspection," Mele told him. "Automated barriers stopped the truck, but then it blew up. Improvised explosives, but a lot of them, and very well screened from the sensors in the gate and along the road. The ground forces lost thirty men and women, including both sentries at the gate. Their base took some damage, but nothing like what would have happened if that truck had reached the main buildings before exploding. Colonel Menziwa is all right, but mad as hell."

"That sounds like a professional job," Rob said. "Not the work of amateur terrorists."

"Whoever did it was well trained. It looks like Old Earth is deporting its professional saboteurs to the stars. I guess the mother world is glad to have some distant places to dump all of its problems." Mele paused, her eyes clouded with thought. "Why didn't those saboteurs try to take out *Saber* and my Marines at the same time as they hit the ground forces base? Why warn us with one attack on one target?"

"Maybe they intended to hit *Saber*," Rob said. "One of the shuttles up here was taken off-line this morning when a systems check showed something odd in the autopilot software. When the autopilot was isolated and our code monkeys started a close look, whatever was in there ran a suicide subroutine that wiped the system clean."

"Software suicide?" Mele nodded. "What would've happened if that shuttle had suddenly gone to full autopilot, and then accelerated at *Saber*?"

"If the pilot aboard didn't manage to disable the autopilot in time, *Saber* would've been badly damaged," Rob said. "There's a chance it would've aimed at the facility, though. The enemy might have heard about the role you and your Marines played in stopping them at Kosatka."

Mele shrugged, as she usually did when someone tried to make a big deal out of her fight aboard Kosatka's orbital facility. "I think it would've gone after *Saber*. My guess is they still want to take Glenlyon's orbital facility intact, so they're willing to kill Marines one at a time to do that. But when it comes to you and *Saber*, I think they'll do all they can to blow you both to hell. Be careful, boss."

"Understood. They might be targeting you, personally, as well. Maybe they sent in that truck because they heard you were at the ground forces headquarters."

"I'm not that special," Mele said. "But I'm keeping my eyes out, and acting unpredictably. You know how good I am at the unpredictable thing."

"That's true. Still, I'm glad they didn't get you in that blast." Rob heard his voice waver a bit on the last words. *"You care about them too much,"* his wife's voice sounded in his memory. *"You can't afford to let it hurt you so badly when they die, because that's the business you're in. But you can't change that about yourself, can you?"*

Instead of showing any reaction to Rob's inadvertent display of emotion, Mele grinned. "Heaven won't take me and hell doesn't want me."

"That I can believe. How long until you're back up here?"

"As soon as they clear shuttles to lift again."

Rob Geary grimaced, and forwarded the message to his executive officer, Lieutenant Commander Vicki Shen. There wasn't anything else he could do.

Rob sat in the captain's stateroom, a grand name for a compartment about the size of a large closet in a building on the surface of a planet. In addition to being captain of *Saber*, he was also the Commodore in charge of all of Glenlyon's space defenses. Since those defenses consisted solely of *Saber*, and the small force of Marines commanded by Mele Darcy, the Commodore title was also a grand name for something fairly small in reality.

Victory at Kosatka had come at a price for *Saber*. The damage was still being repaired, even though the worst of it had been fixed. Trained personnel would have been harder to replace than equipment, if not for the survivors from *Saber*'s sister ship *Claymore*. Plenty of those experienced men and women had been eager to join *Saber*'s crew, most of them motivated by a desire to avenge shipmates lost in the destruction of *Claymore*.

"We can replace the people we lost in terms of skills," Rob had explained to his wife Lyn. He rarely called her by that name, since Lyn much preferred her professional software engineer nickname Ninja. "But it's a lot harder to replace the people as people. Those men and women we lost are gone, and every time I see one of the replacements I remember the people they replaced."

And Ninja, knowing that there were no words adequate to the need, would simply hold him until the darkness inside him faded.

The blare of an alarm shocked Rob out of his reverie. His desk display lit up, revealing an emergency alert. After an agonizing couple of seconds, the image of Council President Chisholm appeared. She had a grim set to her mouth, slightly tousled hair, and a red scrape along one cheekbone. "I am making this announcement in person to ensure that everyone knows the assassination attempt against me that took place a few minutes ago did not succeed thanks to the efforts of my bodyguards. The alleged attacker has been captured, and will be questioned. Rest assured that the government of Glenlyon remains strong and stable. Our enemies will not triumph. We will not fail."

Rob smiled as Lieutenant Commander Vicki Shen ran up to the stateroom hatch. "What do you want to bet Chisholm left that scrape untended until after she made that broadcast?" he said.

Shen raised her eyebrows at him. "Do you think she faked it?"

"No. Not for one moment. But our president knows how important image is." A soft ding announced the arrival of a high-priority message. Rob tapped "receive," reading rapidly. A tasking order for the Marines, sent to him because he was in overall command of them. "Like Chisholm said, they caught the would-be assassin alive."

"A Red." Shen, bending slightly to read Rob's display, didn't sound surprised. "Mars must have an inexhaustible supply of thugs and murderers for hire. Why do they want Corporal Oshiro to assist in interrogating the killer?"

Rob frowned in thought, tapping in a command that brought up a list of Mele's Marines to help jog his memory. "Oh. Yuri Oshiro. He came from Mars, too."

"One of our Marines is a Red?"

Shen looked ready to say more, so Rob forestalled her. "Mele and Gunnery Sergeant Moon approved Oshiro joining. It's possible for me to imagine someone fooling one of those two. I can't believe anyone could fool both of them." Since Mele was still down on the planet, he tapped the command to call the Gunnery Sergeant, and wasn't surprised when the call was answered almost instantly. "Gunny, Corporal

Oshiro's virtual presence is desired for the interrogation of President Chisholm's would-be assassin. Here's the link. Set that up, and let Captain Darcy know when she gets back."

"Yes, sir," Moon said, somehow appearing to look simultaneously both calm and alert for danger. "Do you know anything specific they want from Oshiro?"

Rob checked the message again. "The prisoner has gang tattoos. Torquas?"

Sergeant Moon nodded. "One of the three big gangs on Mars. Oshiro was a Thark before he got off the planet, so he might know what buttons to push on the Torquas guy."

Vicki Shen leaned closer so that Moon could see her. "What was Corporal Oshiro's position in that gang?"

"He was a Calot, ma'am. Entry-level strong arm. But instead of trying to get a spot on an enforcement team, he went for a low-prestige, low-chance-of-promotion assignment guarding warehouses." Moon grinned. "Because he was smart enough to know that'd let him get to know the people running the shuttles smuggling goods, so he could work out an escape from Mars."

"And keep his hands clean until he did get off-world?" Rob asked.

"Yes, sir. Believe me, we screened Yuri Oshiro so thoroughly that we could've spotted if his mother ever told a lie." Moon gave them both a reassuring smile. "Marines are rarely recruited from the ranks of angels, but it doesn't matter what they were before. We make 'em Marines, and then they're all equal. Well, equal to other Marines, that is."

Rob returned the smile. "Thank you, Gunnery Sergeant. Go ahead with setting up the link so Oshiro can assist in the interrogation, and either you or Captain Darcy let me know if there are any problems or concerns."

The call ended, Rob looked at Vicki Shen, who shook her head.

"It's hard to trust a Red," she said. "But the crews of the warships ranged against us include men and women hired from former Earth

Fleet personnel. Just like me. You'd have every reason not to trust me, wouldn't you?"

"That's what happened to Danielle Martel," Rob said. "She died fighting for Glenlyon, and even that didn't satisfy some people."

"Like President Chisholm?"

"President Chisholm," Rob said, choosing his words carefully, "took a while to make up her mind about Danielle. But she's ordered that Lieutenant Martel's name be included in the official histories. If you haven't figured this out about Glenlyon's president, she's both smart and determined. Smart enough to know that ethical behavior, treating people right, pays off in the long run. She'll make compromises when she thinks it's necessary, but I'm still in command of *Saber* because President Chisholm made the decision to overrule everyone who wanted to fire me for leaving Glenlyon undefended while we saved Kosatka."

"That's true," Vicki Shen said, smiling. "It's her fault *I'm* not in command of *Saber!*"

"Yeah. She owes you one." Rob glanced at his display, shifting to a wide view of the entire star system. "I wonder what's next? At Kosatka, they followed up their other attacks with a big strike."

"Hopefully they can't swing a big strike after their losses at Kosatka." Shen paused, her expression sober. "But even if they can't launch another invasion of Kosatka right away, they might have enough to hit us hard."

"See if we can get those final repairs done a little faster. If those terrorist attacks were a precursor to something else, we might need *Saber* at one hundred percent a lot sooner than we'd hoped."

Less than two hours later, Rob winced as another alarm sounded, this one from *Saber*'s own sensors. He stared at his display as more information accumulated from the sensors aboard both the ship and the orbital facility. "Damn."

As commander of Glenlyon's space forces he had a special link, direct to President Chisholm. Rob tapped the link and waited.

Chisholm's image appeared in a small box on one corner of his display. "What is it?"

"We've got company. About four and a half hours ago, two enemy warships arrived at the jump point from Jatayu."

"Two?" Chisholm paused, her expression fixed, but thoughts swirling behind her eyes. "You can hold off two, can't you?"

"If it was two destroyers like *Saber*, maybe," Rob said. "But one of the enemy ships is a light cruiser."

"A light cruiser?" Chisholm sighed. Rob noticed the background of her image. She was out in the open somewhere. He spotted the corner of a familiar-looking building, and realized she was visiting the ground forces headquarters in a show of support and resolve. "They're planning to bombard us. How much damage can they do?"

"If they have concentrated targets, a lot of damage. The bombardment projectiles will destroy anything they hit. But they can't do wide-area damage, so they'll aim for targets such as critical manufacturing sites, government offices, and groups of military forces. I'll do everything I can to disrupt their actions," Rob said.

"Disrupt. You can't stop it?"

"Barring a miracle, no. Not against those odds." Another alarm sounded. Rob watched a third symbol appear, that of a freighter, more data scrolling into place next to it. "A freighter arrived on the heels of the warships. It's modified to carry a lot of people."

"A troop carrier?" President Chisholm frowned. "Only one?"

"No more have shown up yet," Rob said.

"They used, what, a dozen troop ships to invade Kosatka?"

"Roughly, yes. One modified troop carrier can't be loaded with nearly enough soldiers to capture Glenlyon, even if both of the warships bombard the planet to support them." Rob paused. "Oh, hell. I know what they're planning. They want to eliminate *Saber*, and any chance that Glenlyon will interfere when they strike at Kosatka again. They want to force us to engage with them by threatening to eliminate our means to support a warship."

Chisholm's eyes widened. "The orbital facility. They're planning to capture it."

"Yes, I think so." Rob studied the images on his display of the enemy ships more than four billion kilometers from *Saber*. Empty space offered no obstacles to visual sensors that could spot objects even across such immense distances, though even they were limited by the speed of light. The images that Rob could see were of where those ships had been four hours ago. "With warships to provide support fire, there should be enough soldiers on that freighter to overwhelm any defenders of our orbital facility."

"Captain Darcy and her Marines saved Kosatka's orbital facility!"

"The situation wasn't the same," Rob said.

"You're right. Darcy only had six Marines at Kosatka." Chisholm nodded to Rob, her expression as hard as steel. "We can't afford to lose Glenlyon's link with space, Commander Geary. We will repel this attack, both the warships and any soldiers sent to capture the orbital facility."

"Those are my orders?" Rob said, feeling a heavy weight settling in his gut. "I'll do my best, but the price we'll pay is sure to be a high one."

Chisholm paused. Geary had to give her credit for that. She'd had a lot more experience in the last few years with sending people into life-or-death situations, and hadn't become jaded about what that meant. "Those are your orders," Chisholm finally said. "Regardless of the cost. You know why I have to demand that of you and the other defenders of Glenlyon. Commander Geary, you're to assume immediate command of everyone and everything on the orbital facility under terms of the planetary emergency authority. Evacuate everyone who won't be contributing to the defense of the facility and to keeping *Saber* able to fight. How long do we have until those enemy ships reach us?"

"We don't know yet what velocity they'll accelerate to, but the freighter is going to slow them down. It'll probably be ten days before they get here."

"Ten days. All right. Let me know what you need. Glenlyon is counting on you, Commander."

"I understand." The call ended, Rob sat, slumping in his seat, trying not to let despair overwhelm him. *What I need is an entire squadron of destroyers, and a couple of light cruisers. Hell, as long as I'm wishing, how about some heavy cruisers, and a thousand Marines?*

I don't know any way to win this. But I have to act and speak as if there is hope, because if the crew sees me despondent they'll lose hope, and our defeat will be quick and certain.

"Captain?" Lieutenant Commander Shen stood in the hatch to his stateroom, gazing at him with a somber expression. "I saw the new arrivals. What's the word for us?"

"Fight to the death to stop this attack," Rob said, straightening from his slouch. With Shen he could be candid, but he still didn't want to project despair.

Vicki Shen closed her eyes, took a slow breath, and then shrugged. "Fine. Our orders suck, but at least they make sense."

"Yeah."

"Where the hell did they get a light cruiser?"

Rob grimaced. "It's a Leader Class ship. So they got it from Earth Fleet."

"Decommissioned and disposed of as surplus," Shen added, her bitter gaze fixed on Rob's display. "Sold cheap to warlords many light years from Earth, so no one there has to feel guilty about fueling wars on the far frontiers."

"You'll have to let me know everything you can about Leader Class ships. Anything that might help us in a fight with one." He paused, thinking. "If Leigh Camagan can make it to Old Earth, she'll get us at least one light cruiser as well."

"It'll take her months, and months more for the trip back here," Shen said. "How are we going to cope with this threat we're facing now?"

"I don't know."

"We can't beat those odds, sir."

"Not in any way I know of," Rob agreed. "But we're going to go down fighting."

B eing commodore in charge of space defenses and being captain of the *Saber* had been more than enough work for Rob. Having control of the entire orbital facility handed to him could've been overwhelming.

Fortunately, he knew most of the important people on the facility from his years working in charge of the space dock. The officers in charge of Life Support and Structure Maintenance. The people running the space dock, who'd once worked for him. The warehouse managers. The company officials in charge of enterprises ranging from variable gravity manufacturing to nanomechs to the meager offerings of the small food court. The head of the station's school for the children in the families that lived up here. The local civilian representative of Glenlyon's government. Orbital facilities weren't ships. Once they were positioned near something, they tended to stay in about the same orbits. But they needed many of the same specialists as ships did, while also serving as the equivalent of small towns, bigger towns, and, in places like Old Earth and the Old Colonies, massive structures that could be considered cities in space.

Rob knew which of those people he needed to talk to. He also knew how to delegate, a task made easier since most of the people he talked to had to be given the same orders to carry out. Identify those critical to the operation of the facility, those who couldn't be spared until the last minute. Prepare everyone else for immediate evacuation down to the planet. Make sure families went first. Provide lists of anything that might help in defense of the facility. Get everything else that could be moved in the time available down to the surface. Request civilian volunteers with critical skills to stay on the station right up until the fighting started in order to keep things working as long as possible.

Once Mele Darcy had arrived at the facility, he put her in charge of planning and organizing the defenses, as well as maintaining order and commanding all security personnel. Since she'd run the facility's small police force for years Rob knew Mele could get that done without his worrying about any of it.

Messages started coming in from the planet below, where the government had begun the same process in the towns and one city that made up the human presence on the surface of that world. So far warships owned by Apulu, Scatha, or Turan hadn't been caught carrying out indiscriminate bombardment of towns and cities. They'd used the sort of small projectiles dropped from orbit that could annihilate whatever they hit, but weren't big enough to cause widespread damage. No one was supposed to use large projectiles that created massive destruction and could turn an entire city into a crater. Those sorts of weaponized meteors had done enough havoc at a few places on Old Earth to scare even violence-prone humanity enough to ban such weapons.

But legally banning something wasn't the same as getting rid of it. Someone had used weapons almost that bad at one settled world, employing an old Warrior Class destroyer, and just who had been responsible was never determined. As unthinkable as such an atrocity should be, Rob knew why the government had to consider the chance it might happen.

And Rob knew that in part the government had to think about it because as commander of space defenses he was supposed to prevent such a thing from happening, and could not. The guilt tore at him as he viewed the images from the planet below, a distraction when he needed to focus on what was happening and what needed to be done.

Vehicles were being mobilized, anything that could move overland and carry any people or cargo. Warehouses were being emptied out, and food supplies dispersed into the forests that would hinder any attempts to spot targets from orbit. News reports showed people preparing to evacuate, most looking worried. Rob wondered how long it would be before their resolve to stay free withered under hardship. The

Glenlyon Homeland Party that advocated "necessary compromises" with Apulu, Scatha, and Turan had been growing in support despite widespread rumors that it was being secretly funded by those enemy star systems. Would this give another boost to that group by bringing home the cost of continuing to resist a takeover?

Or would the resolve to keep fighting strengthen? From what he knew of Old Earth's history, people were often pretty irrational when attacked and bombarded. Instead of giving in, they became more determined to keep fighting.

But being determined to fight and succeeding in that fight could be two very different things.

Rob finally tore himself away from his other responsibilities to hasten through the facility to his living quarters.

He found Ninja sitting in front of her work screens, their daughter Dani, who only answered to Little Ninja, playing nearby. "Hey, sailor," Ninja greeted him.

Rob didn't waste time he didn't have. "The government has ordered—"

"I know," Ninja said, waving one hand at her displays. "It's still way too easy to crack into the government's comm systems."

"Why aren't you getting ready to go?"

She threw a flat look at him. "I'm essential personnel."

"This isn't the time to—!"

"Yes, it is!" Both noticed Little Ninja staring and lowered their voices. "I was in Alfar's fleet, Rob," Ninja continued. "Before you helped kick me out, remember? I can see what we're facing and I know what that means. Your chances of stopping those guys with *Saber* are pretty much zero, right?"

"Yeah," Rob admitted, feeling his guts tighten again.

"We have to even the odds, and the only additional weapon you have to do that with is me."

He shook his head. "I know you're the best hacker in this star system—"

"I'm the best *anywhere.*"

"Fine. It's still long odds that you'll be able to crack into the enemy systems. They've been strengthening those ever since you helped us capture *Squall.*"

She surprised him with a smile. "Oh, Rob, you still have no idea what I can do when I'm properly motivated."

Frustrated, Rob pointed to her swollen abdomen. "You're not much more than a month away from being due. And what about Little Ninja?"

"I can do a lot in a month. And the Parentis can take Little Ninja down with them. Sort of an extended sleepover for her with their daughter." She said it lightly, as if it were no big deal to send their daughter down to the planet without either of them while enemy warships approached, but Rob saw the fear Ninja was trying to hide.

He felt that same fear, magnified by his failed responsibility for preventing such things. "I don't have time—" Rob began, trying not to sound angry.

"Then why are you wasting time on an argument with me that you know you can't win?" The unspoken message behind her words couldn't be clearer. Ninja hated this, too, and didn't want to debate it. But she wouldn't give in.

He gazed at her, knowing who he'd married, grateful for that, but also at the moment extremely aggravated by his fears for her and their daughter. "I guess we're going to fight this battle together."

"Damn right we are. Get back to work. I'll let you know when Little Ninja is heading off on her long-term playdate so you can help send her off." Ninja let her facade drop for a moment, worry openly flashing in her eyes as she gazed at him. "Don't be a hero."

"You're telling me that? When you won't evacuate to the surface?"

"I'll go when they're getting close," Ninja conceded. "Mele already told me if I didn't she'd personally drag me onto the last shuttle down. Little Ninja won't be alone down there for very long."

Relieved, Rob headed back to *Saber,* wishing that Leigh Camagan had left months ago, and hoping that she was still all right.

There wasn't any way he knew of that Leigh could bring help in time to save him. But maybe she'd be able to bring help to someday avenge him and the others who'd very likely soon die trying to defend Glenlyon.

L ochan Nakamura nerved himself to walk onto a waiting shuttle at Eire's orbital facility. After the assassination attempts and the security officer's concerns about sabotage to shuttles, Lochan wasn't feeling particularly secure. Even worse, memories of the shuttle crash that he and Carmen had endured when first arriving at Kosatka kept jostling to the front of his mind.

"Nervous?" Freya Morgan asked Lochan as he strapped into his seat on the shuttle. They along with Leigh Camagan were the only ones in the passenger compartment, but none felt any urge to spread out, instead sitting close together.

"Yes," Lochan admitted.

"So am I. But the nice thing about shuttles is that if something goes seriously wrong we'll probably be dead before we have time to realize we're in trouble." Freya paused. "That's not really reassuring, is it?"

"Sometimes shuttles crash," Lochan said, gazing around the rows of empty seats. "That can take a while."

She eyed him curiously. "Are you speaking from experience?"

"Yes."

"Damn. And you still in one piece and all. You'll have to tell me about that."

Lochan forced a smile. "I will, if you'll tell me something. Why'd your father disown you?"

Freya frowned. "That's a personal question."

"I know," Lochan said. "But it bears on my mission, doesn't it? If I'm to get help from Eire for Kosatka."

"True. And I owe you for saving me from that freighter in league with the pirates." Freya leaned back, her brow furrowed in thought.

"Long story short, Dad likes people to do as he says. He likes being in charge and pulling all the strings. I'm not good at following orders without question. Maybe we're too much alike that way. When given the choice of following the path he'd laid out for me or finding my own, I walked. In my father's eyes, that was unforgivable."

"That does match what I've heard of Donal Morgan," Lochan said. "Do you have any advice for how to deal with him?"

"You're asking the girl he disowned?" Freya laughed. "Don't crawl. He needs to respect you. But acknowledge his power as well. Can you do both?"

"Maybe," Lochan said. "Maybe not. I haven't had a successful marriage yet."

She laughed again. "There's a good metaphor. Hey, *Alice Mary*," Freya said to Leigh, using the false name that she'd been traveling under. "How long are you staying on Eire?"

"Just long enough to say my piece and then on to Earth, where my mission is," Camagan said.

"Who represents Glenlyon while we try to get more allies for you?"

"I was hoping that Lochan would," Camagan admitted. "By now, Kosatka and Glenlyon should be formally allied at last."

"Assuming Kosatka is still free," Lochan said, his mind calling up a snapshot of the invasion fleet to temporarily shove aside memories of the shuttle crash. Between his experiences and the pictures created by his fears, his mind these days seemed to have an inexhaustible supply of horrific images to draw on.

"Assuming so," Leigh conceded. "Would you trust me to represent Kosatka if that was true?"

The question should have been a hard one to answer. But he'd had time to get to know Leigh Camagan, and more importantly his friend Mele Darcy had told him Leigh was trustworthy. So, instead, the answer came to him the moment the question was asked. "Yes." Lochan looked over at her. "I'll do my best. The fates of Kosatka and Glenlyon are linked by circumstance, but also by friendship."

Freya made a scoffing noise. "You're better off trusting in self-interest than friendship. Such as, Catalan is aware that Kosatka and Glenlyon are the only two star systems near us that won't stab us in the back."

"And here I thought we were friends," Lochan said, doing his best to sound disappointed.

"Oh, Lochan, if I stabbed you in the back, Brigit would never forgive me!"

The conversation had wandered into the ridiculous, but Lochan welcomed the distraction that offered from worrying about their flight to the surface. "Does Brigit know how much you think she likes me?"

The shuttle lurched away from the facility and began its controlled fall toward the planet below. Lochan stared at the display on the bulkhead facing his seat, momentarily distracted by the beauty of the view downward.

From orbit the planet named Eire seemed tranquil and impossibly green. As with any other place where humanity had found a home, the serenity was an illusion born of distance. But the color held truth in its emerald shades.

More of Eire's surface was land than on far-distant Earth, with vast continents sprawling among smaller oceans that on other worlds might be called seas, a weave of rivers and streams feeding them. Lochan knew the world had small axial tilt and thus little seasonal variation through the year, and it orbited its star at the right distance to receive the right amount of warmth. As a result, much of Eire basked in an endless summer, the grass ever green and the trees forever cloaked in their own verdant foliage.

Had the people who came here from an island nation on Earth chosen the planet before they'd known how it looked? A place that evoked the "cool, green hills of Earth," as an old story had put it? Remembering the brilliant green streaks that adorned the hair of Brigit Kelly, Lochan felt certain that they'd deliberately sought out a world like this.

He knew they'd also sought peace far from the ancient feuds that haunted Old Earth. But war had already found others, and would soon come here as well if Lochan couldn't convince Eire's people to join the apparently hopeless cause of the worlds of Kosatka and Glenlyon. "I hope Brigit is all right," he murmured.

"I know what you mean," Freya said. "There's someone on Catalan I'm worried about. How about you, Leigh?"

Leigh Camagan shook her head. "No one that close. I lost that person quite a few years ago. What I do have is a number of people whose fate I care about."

Their shuttle had made it only halfway to the surface when an alert tone sounded and the pilot called back. "Weren't you guys originally intended to come down on Eleven Oh Six?"

"Yes," Lochan said. "Your security chief changed that, though, so that shuttle could be thoroughly screened for problems."

"They launched it after us, loaded only with cargo and using un-crewed auto-descent even though the security search didn't turn up anything." A pause. "Turns out they did miss something. That shuttle blew up barely fifty kilometers from the facility."

A moment of silence was finally broken by a murmur from Leigh Camagan. "I need to buy that security chief a drink."

"A drink, hell," Freya said. "I'll buy the man a house if he asks for it."

On the surface of the planet, their shuttle was met by a strong force that included a couple of platoons of soldiers and several armored vehicles. As a curious crowd watched from a distance, Lochan, Freya, and Leigh were hustled from the shuttle's ramp to an armored limousine. Inside, four guards watched over them silently as the limo raced from the spaceport to the planetary government complex.

Another hasty movement from the limo to a side door of an impressive structure, and then Lochan and the others found themselves being led through the building until they reached a large reception room whose walls were lined with pictures and cases holding artifacts that appeared to be extremely old. Lochan stole glances at some of them, seeing ancient weapons including a long sword and a spear, a small harp whose wood bore the marks of exceptional age, and an old, squared-off stone that might have come from a home, a mansion, or a castle, one edge of the stone cracked and scorched by intense heat that must have been born of whatever destroyed the structure it had once been part of.

"Hi, Kyna," Freya greeted the older woman ensconced behind a large desk. "How's the old one?"

"It really is you," the woman replied with a disapproving shake of her head. "He'll be spitting fire when he hears."

"I'm here representing Catalan. Make sure he knows that."

"I can do my job without prompting from you," Kyna replied.

"Do you make friends like that everywhere you go?" Lochan asked.

"Only here," Freya replied. "There's no place like home. He'll keep us waiting awhile, by the way. Just to emphasize who holds the power here."

They stood in a group off to one side of the room. Lochan looked about again, realizing that there were no couches or chairs in the waiting room to make the waiting any easier. He recognized that tactic, a way of tiring out and making irritable those wanting to see the prime minister so that the visitors would start out at a disadvantage. It also emphasized in a very unsubtle manner that visitors forced to wait were not particularly welcome here.

But Lochan barely had time to become impatient before the same door they'd entered through opened again, this time to let in a group of five people who approached Kyna's desk and engaged in a low-volume conversation from which he could only hear occasional words such as "urgent," "regrets," and "unable."

The five newcomers stepped back from the desk, their carefully controlled expressions revealing little, but their movements carrying the jerkiness of frustration. As they turned to leave, one of the women in the group took a long look at Lochan and his friends. She spoke hurriedly to one of her male companions, who also studied Lochan before walking over and making a small bow from the waist to him, Freya, and Leigh. "You have recently arrived on Eire?"

"Yes," Lochan said.

"The emissaries from Kosatka, Glenlyon, and Catalan?"

"Word travels quickly," Leigh observed. "Where are you from?"

"Benten Star System," one of the women in the new group replied. "My name is Yukino Nakamura. This is Lawrence Sato. We're the leaders of our delegation."

"Nakamura?" Freya asked, amused. "Is she a cousin of yours, Lochan?"

"It's possible," Lochan said. "My ancestors immigrated to Brahma a long time ago, though."

"Most of us on Benten came from Old Earth and Amaterasu," Lawrence Sato said. "But perhaps your ancestors are the same and brought us together here. You have come seeking help for your worlds? Perhaps we can make common cause."

"Why does Benten need help?" Leigh Camagan asked.

"Benten," Yukino said, "can see farther than the orbits of our most distant planets. We see the dangers in the distance, and seek to prepare. But other star systems do not share our sense of urgency."

"They worry about giving up their freedom," Lawrence said.

"It's a lot easier to negotiate without giving up things when your back isn't against the wall," Lochan said.

"That is our reasoning. We seek agreements before crises force our hands."

A moment of silence was broken by Leigh Camagan. "What are the chances that Benten would consider lending aid to Glenlyon and Kosatka?"

"That would depend on many factors," Yukino Nakamura said.

"It's not out of the question?"

A long pause ended as Yukino spoke again. "If fighting is wise, then it is wiser to fight far from home than it is to fight at our front door. But whether fighting is wise remains to be determined."

"What could you bring?" Lochan asked, trying not to let his hopes get too high. "If you decide, I mean. Does Benten have any warships?"

"We came on a warship," Yukino said, gesturing upward. "The *Asahi*."

"We didn't see any foreign warships present in this star system when we came in," Lochan said, surprised.

She smiled. "When you see the stars through another's eyes, you see only what they wish you to see."

"Eire's systems screened out the *Asahi*?" Freya shook her head, transforming the gesture into a glare aimed at the door to her father's office. "He thinks if he doesn't want to see some things he can make those things go away."

"How many other warships does Benten have?" Lochan asked, trying to divert the discussion to a safer topic.

"*Asahi* is our only warship," Lawrence said. "We traveled on her to ensure that the seriousness of our work would be made clear. That does not appear to have impressed Eire, though," he added, a trace of bitterness entering his voice.

One of the other members of Benten's delegation murmured something that caused both Yukino and Lawrence to pause before shaking their heads. "We can't leave yet," Lawrence said. "We must make a few more attempts to present our proposals."

Lochan paused to think, realizing that if he could convince Benten to help, a star system still far enough from the conflict to not be in immediate danger, it would be a powerful example for others. They weren't here to speak with him, though, but with Eire. How could . . . ?

He glanced over at Kyna's desk as the secretary nodded in response to some message only she could hear.

"You can go in," Kyna said to Freya. She tapped something on her desk, causing the heavy wooden door adorned with carvings that led into the inner office to swing open.

Lochan felt something else opening, not a physical thing, but a possibility that hadn't existed a few moments earlier. A risky idea, something that could blow back on him and his mission to get help for Kosatka. Something that could kill his chances of getting aid from Eire. But, if it worked . . .

Make the big decisions. Mele Darcy had told him that just before they parted.

"Hold it," Lochan said, holding out a hand to keep Freya from moving, and drawing a startled and disapproving glare from the prime minister's secretary.

CHAPTER 3

"What did he say?" Lochan asked the secretary. "For just Freya to go in?"

Kyna eyed Lochan in a way that made it clear he'd been added to the category of troublemaker. "He said to send them in. Which includes you, sir."

"Them? That's what he said?"

"Are you questioning my competency, *sir*?"

"I'd never do that." It was now or never. Lochan looked around, including the delegation for Benten in his gesture, and seeing that both Leigh Camagan and Freya Morgan were waiting to see what he was up to. Apparently they really did trust him. "Let's all go in," he said.

Kyna stared in disbelief as Lochan led the entire group toward the door. She made a belated reach for her desk control, only to halt in midmotion as Freya leaned across it with an earnest look. "We're just doing as you said."

Lochan had learned that offices long occupied by a single individual tended to reflect many things about that person. He cast quick looks about as they were ushered into the office of Eire's prime minister, seeing a few landscape pictures on the walls, a couple of paintings showing dogs who were obviously valued pets, numerous framed documents, and several plaques representing awards. The desk was nearly empty but for a couple of displays whose screens couldn't be seen from this side. Conspicuously absent from the office were any pictures of people.

Donal Morgan sat behind his expansive desk, his expression revealing little about his feelings, though Lochan thought surprise and unhappiness flickered through his eyes as they saw the delegation from Benten coming in along with Lochan and his group. Prime Minister Morgan didn't get up in greeting when the others entered. "What brings you here?" he demanded of Freya.

Leigh Camagan answered before Freya could. "*I* am here as a representative of the free star system of Glenlyon. Is this the courtesy with which you treat diplomatic representatives?"

The prime minister eyed her, then slowly stood after apparently deciding that tangling with Leigh Camagan would be a mistake. "Forgive me. I let personal concerns override my responsibilities. Welcome to Eire."

"We're here seeking—" Lochan began.

"I know what it is *you* want, Lochan Nakamura. Our representative in Kosatka has sent many appeals on your behalf." Donal Morgan sat down again, pointedly ignoring the presence of those from Benten. "But if the latest reports are to be believed, the time for help has passed. Why should Eire join a fight already lost?"

Lochan thought of Carmen, doubtless fighting at this moment on Kosatka, anger rising in him at such callous words from an arrogant man facing no immediate threat to his own world. Rather than rein in that anger, Lochan let his words come out without trying to censor them. "It's my dearest wish at the moment that someday you send for help to others as invaders close in on your home, and that they give you the same answer you just gave me." He locked eyes with Morgan, who glared back for a long moment before a trace of a smile appeared.

"I admit that's a good answer." The prime minister shifted his gaze to Leigh Camagan. "I imagine yours is the same."

"Not entirely," Leigh said. "Because Glenlyon has twice risked everything, leaving itself unprotected, to aid Kosatka. We know that if we don't aid our friends, we'll have no friends when we need aid. And we have put ourselves in danger more than once as proof that we live by such commitments."

"Have you?" Morgan's eyes went to Freya. "You'd have a stronger argument if you were traveling in better company."

"Catalan needs help, too," Lochan said.

"And is willing to contribute to mutual defense in proportion to its ability," Freya added.

"They'd have been wiser to send someone more reliable to offer such a deal," the prime minister said.

"Sir," Lawrence Sato said, his body as stiff as his tone of voice, "we have come to discuss the same matter with your government."

Donal Morgan frowned at his desk. "Benten is a valued trading partner. Of course we recognize that. However, we're not ready to listen to demands made of us."

"Demands?"

"I'm aware of discussions among Benten's government to levy a special tax on shipments transiting through your star system en route to Eire! I'll not have my arm twisted by those claiming friendship!"

The silence in the room felt heavy enough for Lochan to imagine it pressing down upon him. So that explained Donal Morgan's treatment of the delegation from Benten. Oddly enough, though, the delegation from Benten appeared to be trying to hide not guilt, but surprise at the accusation.

Lochan cleared his throat softly. "This is a situation that our star systems have already faced," he said, keeping his voice calm and low. "What happens when traffic for your star system has to go through another star system? There aren't any laws enforced by Earth out here.

There aren't any rules. I hear your unhappiness at the thought that Benten might tax shipments heading to Eire, sir, but what recourse would you have if they did? Would you go to war?"

Donal Morgan glared at Lochan. "If necessary."

"What would that cost you? What if Benten simply blocked all traffic from continuing on to Eire? What would you do then?"

"Bring it through Adowa, the longer way around!"

"And if Adowa joined Benten?" Before Donal Morgan could answer, Lochan leaned forward, his hands planted on the front of the desk. "That's what we're facing at home. That's what you'll face if we lose. That's what you will face someday even if we win. If there are no agreed-upon rules, then sooner or later everyone starts doing whatever they can get away with!"

Yukino Nakamura spoke firmly. "Benten has no desire to aggress against any other star system."

"The people of Benten are human!" Lochan said. "*If men were angels, no government would be necessary.* Have you heard that? It was said long ago by a man named Madison who was arguing for a system of laws to govern both his country and the government itself to keep it from exceeding its given powers." He'd been reading a lot about such things in recent months, trying to learn more about the difficult work of attempting to keep human beings from acting all too human toward each other. "None of us here are angels. All of our worlds were settled by men and women who wanted to be free. But the absence of rules isn't freedom. It's an anarchy waiting to be filled by the strongest arm and the most ruthless tactics. That is what Kosatka faces today, and what you'll all face someday if we do not find a means to resolve any differences and support each other against common foes!"

"You're talking about more than a military alliance," Lawrence Sato said.

"Of course I am! What would be the purpose of an alliance? The same sort of thing that Apulu, Scatha, and Turan are doing? No, such an alliance would have to be based on principles, rules, and laws that we all agree upon. The military cart, the defense cart, should not be set before the horse of our interests and needs as free people!"

Donal Morgan shook his head slowly. "Tell me, what was the situation in Kosatka when you left?"

"When we jumped out?" Lochan took a deep breath, knowing that Morgan already knew the answer and wanted to see how the truth would be presented to him. "An invasion fleet was closing on our primary world. It was opposed by a single destroyer from Glenlyon while Kosatka worked to get its remaining destroyer back into fighting shape."

"Is Kosatka still free? Tell me that."

"I don't know," Lochan said. "I do know the people of Kosatka won't stop fighting. Right now even a single warship can make a huge difference! Glenlyon's destroyer is giving Kosatka a chance."

Another pause, Donal Morgan's eyes on his desk, the others waiting.

"There is no fate but what we make for ourselves," Freya said. "Lochan has the right of it. We're all out here pretending we don't need anything to do with anyone else, but we're as tied to what everyone does as if we were still on Old Earth. If we don't talk," she added, emphasizing her words with a look at the delegation from Benten, "then what happens won't be to the advantage of any of us in the long run."

"What's in it for Eire?" Donal Morgan demanded, each word falling with the weight of a hammer blow.

"To be part of it," Lochan said, "rather than being on the outside, looking in. We've got representatives of five star systems in this room. Those from four of those star systems are willing to talk about working together, about mutual defense and rules for trade. How would it benefit Eire if it's on the outside when such deals are made? Doesn't Eire want a voice when decisions are made?"

Donal Morgan gazed at Lochan, his glare slowly changing to a thoughtful look. "Brigit Kelly didn't tell me you were that good. You don't even know if the world you represent still has its own government! But you come here, with me expecting you to beg for help, and instead you talk as if from a position of strength." His eyes went across those facing his desk. "Without Eire, such an alliance would be much weakened. You all know that."

"That is why we seek your partnership in an agreement," Lawrence Sato said.

"It would've been better if you hadn't come also threatening trade sanctions."

Sato and Yukino Nakamura exchanged looks. "Prime Minister," Yukino said, "we have no knowledge of any such trade sanctions or tax discussions."

Donal Morgan narrowed his eyes at her. "You deny knowledge of such matters?"

"I tell you that none of us have been informed of such matters."

"You do not carry a list of demands?" Donal Morgan leaned back in his chair, his eyes hooded in thought. "So. There are people responsible for keeping me informed of the secrets of others. It seems those people have failed in their task. I was told that such was your mission."

"Perhaps," Leigh Camagan said, "someone fed your people that information, and sought to sway your actions with lies aimed at potential allies."

"Perhaps."

"Eire has already been attacked," Freya said, as if sensing that her father was wavering. "An assassination attempt against us, which I'm sure you've been told of, that took place on the orbital station that is legally part of Eire. And a shuttle destroyed. When last I checked, a shuttle was a valuable resource. And if not for the wisdom of your security chief on that facility, a good number of Eire's citizens might have died on that shuttle. Yet our enemies did not hesitate to attack Eire in their attempt to get at us. Those enemies respect no borders. They respect no other worlds. And their attacks on Eire are a slap in the face to Eire's government, are they not?"

Lochan watched Freya's words strike home in the prime minister and realized she was hitting Donal Morgan in the one place he was most vulnerable, his own pride.

The prime minister's face darkened with anger, his breaths coming deeper and faster like a man preparing for a fight. Donal Morgan snorted, bringing to Lochan's mind an angry bull facing a challenge. "I already know of spending from mysterious sources flowing to a couple of minor political parties on Eire," the prime minister said. "And now this. Eire will not be treated in such a way! Not as long as I am the leader of this world." His gaze focused on Freya, fierce and demanding. "Say it, then."

"I was right," Freya said. "Eire needs allies. It shouldn't stand apart."

"And I didn't listen, accepting the reassurances of those doing business with Scatha and Apulu that those star systems would respect us out of desire not to cause trouble with trade. They let their greed taint their advice to me. As for Turan, I've not dealt with the leaders of that star system directly, but it seems they've already tried to deal with me by means of a knife in my back. Destroying one of Eire's shuttles and endangering her people! Who would be held to blame? Me! I'll not stand for it! But how can I know your star systems will not do the same if given the chance? Why should I make deals with you?"

"Because we're not them," Lochan said. "Worlds sometimes make deals with dictators, because they must. But they make common cause, alliance, with those who share the same interests and values, because it's smart."

He wondered for a moment, as the prime minister glared at him, whether his point had been too subtle. Whether Donal Morgan would pick up on the implication that someone who was smart would make deals with other star systems like Kosatka, while someone who wasn't smart would refuse such opportunities.

After a long moment, Donal Morgan nodded to the delegation from Benten, and then to Lochan. "Yes. That's what those who are smart will do. I'll call a cabinet meeting for tomorrow. There's much for us to discuss, and many details to work out."

"I can't stay long," Leigh Camagan said. "I must continue on to Earth without delay. However, Lochan Nakamura can speak for me and Glenlyon."

"Can he? Why does Glenlyon trust this man so?"

Leigh smiled slightly. "A Marine vouched for him."

Donal Morgan nodded a bit in return. "I've risked more on less. You stand with Catalan, though. Glenlyon and Kosatka would have a better chance of closing a deal if they stood apart from Catalan."

"I have my faults," Lochan said. "But abandoning my friends isn't one of them."

"You call yourself a diplomat?" Donal Morgan asked. "You apparently don't know the first rule of diplomacy. Countries and worlds don't have friends. They have interests. If interests coincide, countries and worlds can make deals to their mutual benefit. But everywhere those interests diverge, those same governments have a duty to look after their own."

Leigh Camagan shook her head. "Just how much could you trust Glenlyon or Kosatka if we so quickly abandoned another star system in need? If you're talking about interests, it seems to me your best interests are served by making deals with those who stand by them rather than breaking faith at the first opportunity."

The prime minister frowned in a manner calculated to quail the stoutest political opponent. "So you stand with Catalan regardless?"

The implication was clear. The potential deal might be canceled here and now unless he disowned any ties with Catalan. Donal Morgan was just the sort of man to place his dislike of an individual ahead of the good of many, and he didn't want to deal with his daughter. A lot of lives rested on whatever Lochan said and did. Could he risk the fates of his friends on taking a stand now?

But if he caved, if he tossed away Catalan as a matter of expediency when the people of Catalan needed help as well, wouldn't he poison everything? Sacrificing innocents to protect his own? What kind of bargain would that be?

He wouldn't pay such a price. Perhaps he couldn't. Some things mattered more than self-interest. If that wasn't true, the likes of Apulu and Scatha had already won. "Yes," Lochan said, "Kosatka stands with Catalan."

"As does Glenlyon," Leigh added.

The prime minister's frown deepened. Perhaps he was angered by the stand made by Lochan Nakamura and Leigh Camagan. Or perhaps he had trouble understanding why they wouldn't trade Freya and Catalan for the help they so desperately needed. "And what of you?" Donal Morgan asked Freya. "Would you step aside if I demanded it as a condition of aid to Catalan?"

Freya nodded without hesitation. "In a heartbeat."

"You've found something you'll fight for, have you? Something you won't run away from?"

Lochan saw the anger that flared in Freya's eyes but her voice stayed level. "That's right."

"I see."

Lochan watched Donal Morgan, seeing the hooded eyes and tight jaw that spoke of the prime minister's internal debate. Morgan knew that Eire needed to be part of this group, but he didn't want to appear to have caved to the demands of others. Which left only one option.

To pretend that his demands had been only tests. Tests that the others had passed, making them worthy to deal with.

Prime Minister Morgan stood again, smiling approvingly at Lochan and the others. "Despite appearances, and my error regarding our friends from Benten, I'm not a fool. Nor, Lochan Nakamura, am I eager to find Eire begging for help against enemies who've grown stronger while we watched them conquer others. You cut to the heart of it with your first words. The day might come when it's us facing bad odds. Our trade is already being hurt, because the traffic beyond Eire to star systems such as your own has already fallen, and what remains are monopolies controlled by the likes of Turan. There are many on this world who argue for neutrality, because the people of Eire have no wish to surrender their fates to foreigners. But if you can offer proposals that do not compromise that, that respect Eire, and that other star systems will sign on to, we may be able to reach agreement. My own trade office has been urging an agreement with nearby star systems, for just the reasons you cited. Madison, was it? No, none of us are angels. I ask the patience of all of you for a short while longer while the cabinet meeting is arranged. You'll be notified soon."

Lochan nodded politely, trying to hide his elation. He knew full well that when Donal Morgan spoke of "respecting Eire," the prime minister really meant "respecting me." Freya had shown him that weak spot in Donal Morgan's armor. Lochan had every intention of exploiting it by framing his arguments in ways that flattered the prime minister without sounding servile, and by letting the prime minister claim victory for himself when the result had been what others wanted.

As they left the office, Lawrence Sato and Yukino Nakamura stopped Lochan and offered quick bows from the waist. "Thank you," Sato said. "You've helped Benten with a crisis we did not realize existed."

"There are people who don't want us talking to each other," Yukino said, her eyes dark with anger. "We must bend every effort to find common ground."

"I agree," Lochan said.

"There's a representative from Adowa on this world. We'll try to get him added to the cabinet meeting."

Donal Morgan's secretary Kyna harrumphed loudly, plainly still put out by having been outmaneuvered by Lochan. "Citizen Camagan, I've been asked to expedite your return to the orbital station for transport onward toward Earth. An escort for you is assembling to ensure your safe departure from Eire."

"Be careful, Leigh," Freya said. "We're going to need every warship you can acquire."

"We need them now," Leigh said, sighing. "But time and space won't yield to our needs. Glenlyon, Kosatka, and Catalan must hold out a little longer."

Lochan nodded, not trusting himself to speak as he thought of what might be happening right now at those other stars. Was his home still free? Was Glenlyon? And, if so, how much longer could they hold out?

The three ships approaching the world of Glenlyon all claimed to be from Hesta, a supposedly still-independent star system that had in fact been taken over by the Scatha-Apulu-Turan coalition. Hesta's puppet government answered to its foreign masters, not its own people.

Hesta had lacked any warships before surrendering. Of course the days were long past when the origin of a warship or its crew could be determined by sight. Everyone was using warships cast off by Earth Fleet or the Old Colonies, and humanity had moved and mixed enough that even places like Eire and Kosatka had a blend of ethnicities and origins in their people. But Rob Geary felt confident that these warships and their crews had no real ties to Hesta.

The commander of "Hesta's" flotilla, in fact, had the look of the sort of bland bureaucrat who'd be at home in any place where obedience to the demands of the boss took priority over lesser matters like justice and humanity. His attitude carried the confidence of the uncaring who was certain of superior muscle at his back to protect against personal consequences for his actions.

"As a result of its unprovoked and repeated, unjustified aggression against its neighbors, we have a legal order requiring Glenlyon to surrender control of its orbital facility to independent monitors who will ensure that no further violations occur. Your warship is required to power down all weapons and reduce shields to minimum, and all forces aboard Glenlyon's orbital facility are required to surrender all weapons to our peacekeepers. Failure to comply with our diplomatic and humanitarian measures to avoid further conflict will force us to employ any necessary means to ensure a lawful resolution to this situation. You are directed to communicate your compliance immediately upon receipt of this message."

Lieutenant Commander Vicki Shen shook her head in disbelief as the message from the commander of the enemy force ended. "It's like one of those distortion fields that flips everything inside out. Do you think they actually believe what they're saying?"

"I doubt it." Rob Geary rubbed his forehead, feeling the furrows that anger had carved into it. "They're playing a game, lying as if truth doesn't matter, as if this is some stage play to impress outside observers and not something that will decide the freedom of others, and the deaths of any who oppose them. We can't let people like that win."

He reached for the reply command. *Saber* had moved away from the orbital facility and the world it served, heading to intercept the oncoming foes, but the enemy ships were still more than two light hours distant. The enemy demand that had just arrived had been sent over two hours before, and Rob's reply would take more than another two hours to be received. There wasn't any need for a quick response, and maybe he should wait until the government sent its own formal answer. At the least, maybe he should take time to craft a careful response of his own.

Or not.

Rob tapped the reply command. "We'll see you in hell first."

Bold words. They'd help inspire the crew of *Saber*. Maybe they'd even inspire others. But they were no substitute for the firepower Glenlyon needed. And words alone wouldn't stop those enemy ships from reaching the orbital facility with their no doubt heavily armed "peacekeepers."

"You saved Kosatka's orbital facility! If anyone can save ours, it's you!"

Mele Darcy stifled a sigh of resignation as the message from President Chisholm ended. "The problem with overachieving," she said to Gunnery Sergeant Moon, "is that everyone expects you to keep doing it."

"Your life would be a lot easier right now if you'd just died at Kosatka, Captain," Moon said sympathetically.

"Thanks, Gunny. Why didn't that occur to me at the time?" Mele called up on her display the schematics of the orbital facility. "How are the preps going?"

"Everybody's working like mad. I understand," Sergeant Moon said, "that we have to assume the attackers will have close-in heavy fire support."

"Commodore Geary told me he can't stop them," Mele said as she studied the schematics. "Not unless they do something really stupid that he can exploit. We have to assume one of those warships will try to park itself near this facility to provide fire support to their soldiers."

Sergeant Moon frowned. "Permission to speak freely?"

"Granted. And don't ask me that again. I want your candid opinions."

"Yes, Captain. How much can we count on the destroyer? *Saber*, I mean. How hard will they push to support us against the odds they're facing?"

Mele gave Moon a sidelong look. "You're asking if we can count on the fleet? Gunny, that's Rob Geary commanding *Saber*. If there's any way to do it, he will. Even if the risks are awful."

"Captain, I heard at Kosatka you were pretty much on your own."

"*Saber* was dealing with the invasion fleet," Mele said, "and still managed to take out some of the shuttles sending troops against us at Kosatka, and kept their warships busy. I knew going in that we'd be on our own most of the time, but I also knew that if I'd yelled for him, the Commodore would've pushed space and time itself to get there for me. We can count on him to do everything possible, and maybe a few things that anyone else would know was impossible."

"That's good to know." Moon pointed out places on the schematics.

"Barricades are going in here, here, and here. We've got people cutting new accesses and installing new hatches where they weren't before, putting armored partitions in place where open passages are supposed to be, and other modifications to the station so when those attackers come in using schematics based on the original plans they'll get real lost real fast. These other passages and access tubes are going to be completely plugged."

"We're booby-trapping the plugs?"

"Yes, Captain. Anyone trying to blast or cut through them fast is going to get some nasty surprises."

"Good." Mele indicated an access tube that wasn't marked for barricading. "How about the modifications here?"

Sergeant Moon grinned. "I'm overseeing those myself. The modifications to these paths are designed so that anyone who finds them and tries to head inward will get easily confused and think they're running into multiple dead ends, while also running into a lot of traps oriented toward anyone coming from that direction. You need to know the specific tricks to get through all that on each path. But any counterattacks we send heading outward through those paths won't have any trouble moving fast."

"What did you say they call them?"

"Diode routes," Moon explained. "Because a diode only allows a circuit to flow in one direction. I personally think it's a misleading name. The paths are more like transistors, which are optimized for current to travel in one direction but can allow current through the other way, though not nearly as—"

"Got it," Mele said. "You know what one of the hardest parts of an officer's job is, Gunny?"

"Figuring out what to do with all of your free time?"

"That's not the part I was thinking about." Senior enlisted had always insisted that officers didn't actually do anything, leaving the real work to the senior enlisted. "No. Figuring out how much I need to know about something to make decisions, and then moving on to the next thing instead of focusing on details my people should be handling."

Sergeant Moon nodded. "I'd noticed that you seem to have a handle on that, Captain. With all due respect, not all officers figure that out."

"Yeah. Grant Duncan helped me understand that kind of thing when we were throwing together troops to take down Scatha's illegal settlement on Glenlyon."

Moon nodded again, this time respectfully. "From all I hear, Grant Duncan was a great soldier."

"He was. I wish you'd had a chance to meet him." Mele gazed at the schematics of the facility, her thoughts going to places she usually tried to avoid visiting. "But even being the greatest won't save you if you happen to be in the wrong place when a chunk of metal goes through it really fast." She paused, trying to rally her mood.

"Are you okay, Captain?" Moon asked.

"Yeah. I'm okay. Absent friends, you know." The ping of another incoming message provided a welcome distraction for Mele. She read it, feeling her spirits lift. "We're getting reinforcements. Colonel Menziwa is, um, *lending* us her reconnaissance company and a heavy weapons platoon."

"The recon company?" Moon asked, surprised. "That's her best. How'd you convince the colonel to send them up here?"

Mele shrugged. "I might've mentioned to someone who could mention to someone who could give orders to Menziwa about how much I could use those particular soldiers."

"Oh, man. Colonel Menziwa must be . . . very unhappy."

She responded with only a slight nod this time, feeling a grim satisfaction for not just the physical reinforcements but for what those reinforcements represented in a broader sense. The government wouldn't have decided to send those soldiers up to the facility unless it really intended to try to successfully defend it. Mele wouldn't have to worry about her Marines being sacrificed in a symbolic and hopeless last stand. They'd be fighting a battle that Glenlyon was determined to win.

When he arrived at the orbital facility the next day, the commander of the recon company, Captain Batra, seemed as unhappy as Colonel Menziwa must be. He rendered Mele a salute as stiff and formal as his posture and tone of voice. "I understand we need to work out coordination procedures, Captain Darcy."

"Coordination procedures?" Mele asked, her own voice calm but unyielding.

"Since our units will be operating in the same area," Captain Batra added. About ten years older than Mele and physically a bit larger, Batra leaned in slightly, trying to get her to back off.

Mele didn't budge. She'd played that sort of game before. "You've seen your orders, Captain Batra. Your unit won't be simply operating in the same area as my Marines. Your orders place your unit, and you, under my command."

Batra barely hesitated. "Colonel Menziwa informed me that she was seeking to have that corrected."

"Colonel Menziwa can seek all she wants," Mele said, not giving a millimeter in the argument. "As of now, you're under my command. Will you follow your orders?"

Captain Batra eyed her, his mouth a thin, hard line, before finally nodding. "Yes, Captain Darcy. I will follow my orders."

"Good. You know what we're facing."

"I have one question," Batra said, anger still dancing in his eyes. "Is this a forlorn hope? Or do we have any chance? I ask not for myself, but for the men and women in my company."

Mele gave him a brief nod in return. "We have a chance. I'm not eager to see my Marines sacrificed, either. If we can hold out long enough, those enemy warships will have to withdraw to resupply themselves."

"What if the enemy sends new supplies?" Batra pressed.

"Commodore Geary believes he can frustrate any attempt at re-supply."

Captain Batra paused, thinking, then nodded. "I understand. Our goal is to prevent the enemy from winning before they run low on supplies and are forced to withdraw. A classic siege defense situation. What is your plan?"

Mele nodded toward a display with a schematic of the facility on it. "To hide our strike groups in the core of this place, where the weapons on those enemy warships can't target us, while launching frequent and unpredictable counterattacks against areas of the facility the enemy has occupied."

"I see." Batra studied the layout. "You think the initial attack will come in that area?"

"Commodore Geary thinks they'll be worried that we might have antiorbital weapons mounted on the surface of the planet, so they'll come in from an angle that puts the facility between their ships and the surface of Glenlyon. I had the facility tilted in orbit so the enemy will come in at the best place for us and the hardest places for them."

"I see. I wouldn't have thought of adjusting the battlefield that way," Batra admitted.

"It's a Marine thing," Mele said. "We're trained to think that way."

"I see," Batra said again. "Why don't we have any antiorbital weapons?"

"Limited resources," Mele said. "Didn't Colonel Menziwa brief you on that? The government had to decide where to allocate limited amounts of construction capacity and raw materials. Up-to-date battle armor and hand weapons got priority."

Batra had the grace to look slightly embarrassed. "Equipment that went to expanding the ground forces."

"And my Marines," Mele conceded. "It wasn't necessarily a bad decision, even now. A single antiorbital weapon would have eaten up a lot of resources, and would have been in danger of being itself destroyed by something like a light cruiser. Now, get your people settled and your equipment off-loaded. We'll work out the best combat positions for your company and my Marines to greet the enemy. I welcome your input on the best placement for your heavy weapons platoon. We'll need to run a lot of training in the days left to us so your people can get accustomed to the facility and learn the ways around it."

"I concur," Batra said, which sounded far too much like the words of an equal rather than a subordinate.

Mele knew why he was doing that. She also knew she couldn't permit it.

"One other thing, Captain Batra." Mele paused a moment, fixing Batra with a look as cold as she could make it. "You don't have to like me. You don't have to like the orders I give or the situation we're in. But if you fail to obey my orders, fail to properly understand my orders, or fail to carry out your duties to the utmost, I will relieve you of your command and personally rip a hole in you big enough for your entire company to march through line abreast. Is that clear?"

Batra nodded, his expression as impassive as if carved from stone. "Yes, Captain Darcy."

"If you have anything you need to get off your chest, say it *now*."

"I've been doing this a lot longer than you have . . . Captain. I know how recently you were promoted from enlisted to officer ranks." Batra took a deep breath before continuing. "There's a lot you don't know yet."

Mele smiled at Batra in a way that made the other hesitate as if he'd been threatened. "Do you think that you're telling me something that I don't know?"

"If you're aware—"

"I'm not finished. Captain Batra, how much of your time in the ground forces includes combat experience?"

Batra didn't answer for a long moment, his eyes fixed on the wall behind Mele. "As I am sure you are already aware, I did not experience combat while in the Old Colonies, and have not yet done so here."

"Count your blessings, Captain Batra," Mele said, her voice hard. "It's ugly. You've spent your life training to do it. That's important. I'm not fool enough to think I know everything. But I've trained and led forces in combat engagements. I've won every one of those engagements. When *you* can say the same we can discuss *my* experience. Is that clear?"

"Yes, Captain," Batra replied in a voice that carried a wealth of suppressed emotion.

"Then that's all for now. After all of your people are settled, you should personally familiarize yourself with the layout of this facility. That layout is changing as we speak, so don't depend on any schematics you brought with you."

Batra saluted once more, the gesture rigid, then pivoted and walked out.

Mele studied the schematics again, but her thoughts were focused on Batra. His attitude would very likely be repeated among his junior officers and senior enlisted.

She needed those ground forces soldiers if this facility was going to be successfully defended. But their leaders were likely to be a real pain the butt.

What was it that Clausewitz had called stuff like this in that old book on military strategy? Friction. The junk that made everything really complicated even though it ought to be easy.

Not that winning the fight for this orbital facility would be easy by any definition of the word. If she had to fight the ground forces leaders as well as the enemy, it'd be even harder.

But no matter what, the outcome would be her responsibility, any failures her fault. Because she was in command here. *"When troops flee, are insubordinate, distressed, collapse in disorder or are routed, it is the fault of the general."*

Sometimes the words of Sun Tzu, another writer of ancient military advice, were no comfort at all.

CHAPTER 4

"You're wrong."

Once more in the city of Ani at Kosatka, Carmen Ochoa bit back her first response, trying to come up with a more diplomatic one. "My assessment is based on—"

"Your assessment is wrong," Jayne Redman said as if correcting a child.

Carmen counted to ten inside before saying anything else. "I'm on the scene. I'm collecting the intelligence."

"You're too close to it all," Redman said. "My office is far enough back to have the necessary perspective. And, if you'll pardon my being blunt, we have actual trained intelligence analysts here to evaluate the available information. Analysts such as myself. Your experience is . . . self-taught. Amateur."

Feeling heat in her face and the muscles in her jaw tightening, Carmen sat silent. She'd learned long ago that tactic could throw off people like Redman.

Outside, the morning was far enough along that sunbeams were surely spearing through the open sky between the empty buildings of

Ani. But the dim illumination here in a bare inner room was mainly provided by the light from the screen of Carmen's comm pad. Most of the soldiers in the unit she was with were sleeping in other rooms, so she'd chosen a separate place where any conversation wouldn't bother them. Carmen wasn't sure whether this room had been intended as a small office or a large closet, but it answered her need for privacy.

After a long pause, Redman frowned at her. "We're in the process of professionalizing this office so we can ensure the best possible support for decision makers by maximizing group dynamics, effective interaction, and synergy in analysis. If you want to be part of that process, you need to integrate yourself into the team mind-set, embrace positive priorities, and adopt positions that resonate with those reached by your colleagues."

Carmen shook her head. "Have you forgotten that I worked in Earth gov? I know exactly what all of those words mean. Or rather, what they don't mean. Please don't waste my time with meaningless phrases that sound important." She saw that jab go home in a way that telegraphed that Jayne Redman hadn't bothered learning much about Carmen's past before trying to browbeat her. "My job is to give the military commander in Ani the best information I can, and the best assessment I can of what it means."

"Your job is what I say it is."

"Perhaps you should inform General Edelman of that," Carmen said. "He thinks I'm working for him."

"He's wrong, and we're going to correct that. You're to return to Lodz immediately for reassignment."

Carmen shook her head again. "Only General Edelman can give me that order."

"I won't tolerate loose cannons," Redman insisted. "Analysis will be centralized in Lodz, and individual assessments in the field will conform to central office guidance. Do you understand?"

"I understand what you said," Carmen replied, deliberately not adding whether or not she'd comply with the order.

Redman glared at her wordlessly before abruptly ending the call.

As her screen blanked, Carmen sighed and covered her face with one hand, wondering why she didn't simply quit and go back to Domi.

Someone cleared their throat softly. Carmen looked toward the darkened doorway, hardly lit by the low lights set up in the inner hallways, and saw Captain Devish. "I couldn't help overhearing," Devish said.

"Really?" Carmen said, hearing weariness in her voice instead of annoyance. "You mean you couldn't help overhearing because you stood by that doorway while I talked?"

"Exactly." Devish walked into the room a couple of steps, lowering himself to sit against the wall opposite Carmen. "What's going on?"

She thought about how much to tell him, deciding that political games didn't deserve any protection from her. "That was the head of Kosatka's new Integrated Intelligence Service. Her name's Jayne Redman. She got the ear of some people high in the government and got herself appointed to the job."

"Does she know what she's doing?"

"Supposedly." Carmen leaned her head back against the wall behind her, feeling the cold, rough, unfinished neocrete through her hair. "She worked in an office for some big intelligence outfit on Old Earth. Exactly which one I don't know."

"You don't know the outfit or the office she worked in?"

"Neither one. I'm not sure anyone does since when asked Redman always asserts secrecy and nondisclosure agreements that supposedly keep her from providing any details. She claims to be a skilled intelligence operative, but as far as I can tell, her main talent is empire building."

Captain Devish nodded. "I know the type. She wants to control the whole ship, but you're rocking the boat."

"I'm not sure whether you're mixing metaphors there or not," Carmen said. "Yeah. Basically. You know what I've been telling General Edelman. The enemy forces left in Ani are on their last legs. They're running low on every kind of supply, they know they're trapped, and a lot of them are just soldiers for hire, not dedicated fanatics. They're going to crack soon."

"I agree with you. But the new central office in Lodz disagrees?"

Carmen shrugged to pretend the dispute didn't anger her as much as it did. "They think the enemy will keep digging in, improving their hold on the parts of Ani they still occupy, and that the enemy retains the resolve and the means for offensive operations."

Devish raised both eyebrows in surprise. "That's not at all what we're seeing."

"Thank you!"

"They're not even staging limited counterattacks. The argument that they're strong enough to launch big attacks is so obviously wrong, why do you have to fight Redman over the issue? Why not just let her eventually be proven wrong?"

"Because," Carmen said. She met Devish's gaze with her own. "If the government believes that assessment, believes that the enemy is capable of holding out for a long time, will only keep improving their defenses, and could counterattack, what will the government order General Edelman to do?"

Devish hesitated, his mouth tightening. "Attack. Not just the constant pressure we're putting on the enemy, but a major effort."

"Advancing building by building," Carmen said. "As fast as we can. Against a desperate enemy. How many more people will we lose?"

"A lot. We don't have a lot left, but what's left will be used up fast if we're forced to make those kind of attacks." Devish looked around him. "And building by building, more of Ani will get turned into rubble. What are you going to do?"

"Keep telling anyone who'll listen what I think based on what we're seeing here."

"Can that Redman really recall you to Lodz?"

Carmen spread her hands in the age-old gesture of uncertainty. "You know how many things have been improvised to deal with the invasion.

Including my exact status and my exact chain of command. Nothing has been written down anywhere saying who I have to listen to."

Devish grinned. "I wish I could say that. Does the general know what's going on?"

"I'm telling him what I think," Carmen repeated. "And I've met a few people high in the government, people I got to know when Lochan Nakamura and I first came to Kosatka. I'm letting them see my reports, though technically I'm probably breaking some security rules there."

"Technically?"

"Probably. I don't know for sure."

Another grin from Devish. "And you're not fool enough to ask. May I offer some advice?"

"Sure. I'm better at listening to advice than I am at listening to orders," Carmen said.

"Good." Devish glanced out the doorway. "If I were you, with my status and chain of command a bit blurry, I'd be working to focus things the way I wanted them to be. Before someone else focused things the way they wanted."

Carmen frowned. "Meaning I should ask the general to formalize my status as working for him?"

"Why is that hard? Word is he respects you."

"Yeah, but . . ." Carmen felt the reason behind her reluctance, knowing its origins rested far from this world. "One of the lessons I learned on Mars was to stay under the radar of powerful people. Once they knew who I was, they'd try to use me."

"Maybe not every lesson learned on Mars is applicable to Kosatka," Devish suggested. "Listen. I'm not giving you this advice out of charity. It's self-interest. You know what the situation is for our side in this fight. We've taken plenty of hits, lost a lot of people, we're short on everything. Sure, we're stumbling toward a win, but we're not that far from collapsing. The only reason we're winning is because the other guys are worse off than we are. It wouldn't take much in the way of stupidity to lose this fight. Stupidity like ordering us to charge in and dig out the enemy fast instead of wearing them down. It wouldn't take much of that to crack what we've got left, and then the enemy would have a chance to break out and spread through the unpopulated areas of this continent, where they'd be able to hide and regroup and launch raids. I want the general listening to you, because you listen to people like me, and you know from personal experience what things are like for us and for the enemy."

"I can understand self-interest," Carmen said.

"Then factor in your self-interest in as well," Captain Devish said, his expression grim. "There are rumors going around that the government is planning to get us reinforcements from an untapped reserve. That reserve being previously wounded men and women whose prosthetics or other aids are sufficient to allow them to function on the front lines."

She stared at him in shock. "That's crazy. Even if the prosthetics are one hundred percent effective replacements for whatever was lost, it creates a whole set of problems with logistics, with keeping the prosthetics in repair and their power supplies and . . . and that creates problems with shielding the prosthetic materials and energy use from enemy sensors, and . . . and smart prosthetics can be hacked, or rendered useless by EMP weapons . . . and . . . the rumors can't be true."

"Can't they?" Devish ran the tips of his fingers through the dust that had accumulated on the floor. "What do you think? We need warm bodies to carry on the fight. Kosatka is effectively blockaded, so no new immigrants can arrive to help. That means drawing on what's available. Trained, experienced soldiers. Even if those men and women have already, and literally, given up parts of themselves to the fight."

"Damn." Carmen ran one hand through her hair, her thoughts darker than the shadows lurking in the deserted buildings of Ani. "The last time we talked, Dominic told me that he'd been moved up in priority for a new leg. No new invasion fleet sighted, no other explanation, just 'congratulations, you'll have the prosthetic a lot sooner than expected.'" Events had just become extremely personal again.

"Surprise," Devish murmured.

"Yeah. Okay. Thanks." She tapped a command to bring up a list of addresses. "I'll take it from here."

Captain Devish stood up, moving carefully in the limited space available. "Let me know if there's anything I can do to help."

She looked up at him. "What if you get orders to send me under guard to Lodz?"

Devish shrugged. "Orders often get garbled, or misdirected. You know how it is. And I have a lot of other things to be dealing with, as well as no soldiers to spare on some bureaucratic squabble. If it gets to the point where I can't stall any longer, then you'll become invisible to me and every soldier in this unit. Sorry, she's not here. Haven't seen her. It's not my problem if Lodz lost one of their volunteers."

"Thanks."

"It's not like you haven't earned it." Captain Devish sketched a brief salute in her direction before walking out into the hallway and out of sight.

Carmen felt an almost overwhelming urge to do something. Do it now. But she'd felt that before. One of the things that Mars had taught her was that impatient people died.

So she'd be patient. Make preparations. Until it got dark and she could do what needed to be done.

"I'll be out for a while," Carmen told Captain Devish.

He glanced at her, taking in her camos and the rifle. "Do you know tonight's password?"

"Yeah. Holo."

"Countersign?"

"Wolf," Carmen said.

"Good," Devish said. "You've got a plan?"

"Of course I have a plan."

"Good. Try not to get your sorry butt shot off."

The night wasn't perfect for what she was doing. Too bright, the stars shining down unhindered by any cloud cover, and too quiet, only the barest breeze drifting along the silent streets. Carmen heard the soft scuttling of small creatures moving through the darkness, and knew any sounds she made would also be too easily heard. Maybe she should wait for another night.

Domi had been moved up in priority for a new leg.

She wouldn't wait.

The building where Devish's unit had been staying for the last few days was only half a kilometer from the current front line. In daylight, in peace, it would have required only a few minutes of walking to cover that distance.

But this was night in an unlit city where enemies lurked. She figured that traveling alone and trying to remain unseen it would take her about an hour to safely reach the front.

Carmen had been making slow, patient, and nerve-racking progress for about half an hour when somewhere not far away from her a pebble rattled down a short drop, the last click as it came to rest seeming to echo through the city.

Carmen, one leg raised for another cautious step, froze. She stood, breathing as softly as possible through her mouth, straining her ears for any more sounds. Had it been part of the slow shifting of debris in the empty city? Or had the pebble been dislodged by an insect moving about? A small animal? Or had it been the result of a misstep by larger creatures, of the same species as Carmen, carrying weapons of their own and a lethal intent toward anyone they found?

Even if it was a friendly patrol she'd still be in terrible danger if spotted. This close to the enemy positions, a figure in the dark would be assumed to be one of those enemies. She'd likely be dead before she could speak the password or countersign for the night. And if they were enemies the password wouldn't do her any good.

She heard nothing else except vague, faint sounds that might be born of her own blood rushing in her veins or the breath coming in and out of her. Her eyes searched the night but saw no sign of movement. The sound of the pebble falling seemed to have paralyzed the entire city. After holding herself motionless for at least half a minute, Carmen slowly lowered her leg, looking down to try to ensure she wasn't stepping on anything that might make a sound.

Moving with infinite care, she eased closer to the nearest wall, pausing often to listen.

Memories crowded into her mind, distracting her. The darkness, the need for silence, the fear of discovery. How many times on Mars had she hidden in closets or cabinets or small spaces, a young girl waiting to learn if this time she'd be discovered? Once she had been, by a big man who didn't realize in time that a small girl could be carrying a large knife.

Carmen could almost taste the ever-present red dust of Mars in her mouth as she waited, watching, her weapon ready.

The soft scurry of an animal sounded off to her left.

Carmen dared to relax slightly. If they felt in danger, animals wouldn't move. If one felt safe enough to scurry, any danger that might have been here had probably passed.

But she still took her time studying her surroundings through the smart scope on her rifle, looking for any traces of danger. A small blob of heat briefly appeared, moving fast and low, as the sound of another small creature running from cover to cover came to her. Otherwise the city once more appeared to be empty and dead.

It took another half an hour of cautiously moving through the night and a succession of vacant buildings before Carmen reached the place she'd been heading for. Intended to be a small store or office, the room faced across a deserted street where similar mixed-use buildings loomed in the dark, stores on the ground floors and apartments above them.

She settled down to one side of a window that hadn't been blown out or broken. Set against the wall and just above the floor, a thumb-size fiber terminal rested where she'd left it a week before.

Carmen unspooled a connector from her rifle and plugged it into the terminal, also pulling out an earbud that she stuck into one of her ears. Her scope lit up with data, showing that all six bugs she'd planted in rooms across the street were still connected. She sighed with relief. Listening devices that used wireless transmissions were too easily detected these days, so only something linked to a fiber-optic cable and activated only when someone like Carmen plugged in could remain hidden from sweeps for bugs. The transparent threadlike cables were very hard to see even under the best of conditions, but she'd still done as well as she could to hide the cables that ran across the empty street. Fortunately, nothing had cut any of them by accident or design.

The only question left was whether she'd lucked out by bugging a room some of the enemy would be in tonight. Places a little distant from the front line where Kosatka's defenders faced the invaders could be safely occupied for days and even weeks as long as care was taken not to present external signs of the people within the apparently deserted buildings. But here, where the two sides faced each other, the soldiers on each side would change positions every day or so to avoid having their positions spotted. Carmen had planted her bugs a week ago, choosing offices facing the street that she could tell weren't occupied, hoping that she'd picked one that would be a temporary enemy position on some future date.

Carmen couldn't quite suppress a gasp as one of the lines lit up. Conversation. Across the street, some of the enemy were watching for Kosatka's defenders, and as soldiers often did were whispering among themselves even when standing orders required silence.

"—shot Falchion," a woman was saying, her voice barely audible even with the enhancements provided by Carmen's listening gear. She thought the voice might carry the distinctive accent of Reds from the area around Olympus Mons, but couldn't be sure.

"What'd he do?" a man asked, his own Olymons accent clear enough to confirm Carmen's suspicions.

"Don't know."

"Falchion was an idiot. Didn't know when to shut up."

"Yeah."

A third voice joined in, too faint for Carmen to tell if it was a man or a woman speaking. "Dibs on his share of rations."

"Rations, hell, I'd have eaten Falchion if they'd left the body."

"There wasn't a lot of meat left on him," the woman said.

"There's not much left on any of us," the third person said. "How much longer—"

"Shut up. You want to end up like Falchion?"

"Sooner or later, we'll all—" The whispered voice cut off abruptly. "Hey. We got a ping."

Faint rustling sounds probably marked the enemy fighters readying themselves and their weapons. "Where?" the woman asked.

"One of the places we rigged across the street. I'm only seeing one hit, though."

"A scout? Or point for a patrol?"

"I dunno. It's not moving. Probably trying to spot us."

Carmen spent only a single second berating herself for carelessness. Of course the enemy had done the same thing that she had, covertly seeding sensors in some of the places their foes might occupy. They knew she was here, perhaps even where in the room she was.

And if they'd planted sensors here, they might have planted other, more lethal, things as well.

She turned her head slowly, studying the dark-shrouded back of the office, deciding on a path to take. A door hung open invitingly, offering refuge deeper in the building and arousing her suspicions. That was just where she'd put a booby trap, to catch anyone seeking safety. No. The same for the sturdy-looking solid wall to her right. Exactly the place someone would go if they were worried about danger from the street. Carmen raised her rifle enough to examine that wall through the scope, seeing a patch of newer work on that wall where a mini-mine had probably been hidden.

All right, then. Go hard left, past the floor-to-ceiling window where no one in their right mind would seek shelter or expose themselves. They wouldn't have planted a trap there. Keep on, out into the side alley, and keep running away from the main street.

"How long we gonna wait?" one of the enemy whispered to his companions, the sound ghostly through Carmen's earbud. "If that one's point for a patrol, shouldn't they have shown up by now?"

"They might be targeting us for a strike," the woman said. "Right now as we're talking. Why else would they just be sitting there?"

"Yeah," the third enemy agreed. "Take 'em out now."

Carmen yanked the rifle cord free from the fiber terminal and leapt into motion, hurling herself to the left past the floor-to-ceiling window, feeling horribly exposed in that moment as the darkened street beyond was briefly visible, nothing between her and the weapons of the enemy but a few layers of insulated glass. She hit the side door to the alley as chaos roared behind her, the force of the explosion at her back hurling Carmen out of the office and into the alley. Scrambling to her feet but staying in a crouch, Carmen ran only a few meters before spotting a blown-out window to her right and leaping through it, landing on a litter of glass fragments inside that building and somehow avoiding any serious cuts.

She got to her feet again, limping slightly as her right ankle protested, pausing for only a moment to check the hallway outside the room before heading down it, away from the street that here marked the front line. Behind her, shots rang out as soldiers from both sides traded fire, but the flurry of action quickly subsided. Neither side could afford to waste ammunition, though at least Kosatka's forces could still get power packs for pulse weapons.

With at least two blocks between her and the site of her near disaster, Carmen finally stopped in the pitch dark of an inner room, breathing heavily, her heart pounding from exertion and fear. Had it been worth it? She'd only gotten a few words of conversation between the enemy soldiers. Those words supported her own arguments, but having worked with bureaucrats in Earth gov, Carmen knew how Jayne Redman and her new agency would react to them. Fragmentary conversation, open to interpretation, and at best anecdotal data. Something easily dismissed from the lofty perspective of comfortable offices in Lodz.

She'd write it up anyway, and send it to General Edelman's staff, along with a not-so-veiled plea for the general to formalize her status as someone who worked for him. And hope that worked.

And also hope that Domi never heard about tonight. She'd never hear the end of it from him.

Carmen was woken from a restless sleep by a messenger who said headquarters wanted to talk to her. Trying to blink away drowsiness, she checked the time. Late afternoon. A call from headquarters wasn't normal. This probably meant that Jayne Redman had already acted on her threats.

She ran her hands through her hair to order it, hastily braided it back, straightened her camos, and after opening her comm pad clicked the callback link.

It took a few minutes before the image of a worn-out-looking colonel appeared on her pad. "Citizen Ochoa," he greeted her. "I hear you were out collecting intelligence last night."

"Yes, sir," Carmen said.

"General Edelman wants me to tell you he values your reporting," the colonel continued, while Carmen wondered if the apparent praise was the lead-in to bad news. "Are you aware that your security clearances have been pulled?"

"What?" Of course. She should have realized that Redman would do that. "What was the justification?"

The colonel frowned slightly as he read something off to the side. "Unresolved questions regarding past activities in regions of extensive enemy recruitment."

Carmen gasped a derisive laugh. "Why didn't they just say they were doing it because I'm from Mars?"

"Because discrimination on the basis of place of origin is illegal under the laws of Kosatka," the colonel said. "Yeah, that's obviously what they mean and why they're doing it, but they can't say that. The message telling us your clearances had been yanked also directed us to send you back to Lodz by the first available means."

All of that was what she'd expected. "What is the general going to do?"

"General Edelman doesn't like getting directives from agencies that are supposed to be supporting him." The colonel smiled. "And General Edelman is authorized to issue security clearances for anyone he thinks needs access. Normally, that's for people on his staff. He directed me to issue you a new clearance. Your job description on the clearance is special intelligence support to the field commander, which means you officially work for the general now. Which in turn means he won't be sending you back to Lodz, because he wants you here. Are you good with that?"

"I'm very good with that." Carmen let out a relieved breath. "Please thank the general for me."

"Just keep doing what you've been doing."

"Do I need to pay attention to directives from the Integrated Intelligence Service?"

The colonel responded with an intrigued look. "Have you been paying attention to those directives up to now?"

"No," Carmen said.

"Then I will repeat the general's instructions. Keep doing what you've been doing."

Carmen grinned. "Thank you. I will."

A couple of hours later, as the sun dipped toward setting and the nocturnal defenders of Ani began rousing themselves for another night of cat and mouse against the invaders, Carmen checked her mail and saw another callback request.

This one was from her former boss Loren Yeresh, so she clicked on it.

Loren answered immediately. He gazed at her with such obvious worry that she shook her head defensively. "I'm fine," Carmen said.

"You're fine." Loren sighed, looking haggard. "Do you have any idea what the atmosphere was like at work today?"

"Work? Did you get sucked into the Integrated Intelligence Service nonsense?"

Loren nodded. He was seated at a desk, and paused to reach and take a drink of what looked like coffee but surely wasn't. As far as Carmen knew there wasn't any coffee left in Lodz. "Everybody is getting sucked into it, whether they like it or not."

"I'm not," Carmen said.

"No, because you're Our Lady of Perpetual Chaos," Loren said. "Have you thought about maybe changing your approach?"

Carmen settled back, fighting her own instinctive resistance to such a question. "Why?"

"Because the goal for all of us is a free and safe Kosatka. If you're working at IIS, you can influence the analysis and make sure your viewpoints are heard."

"Are you also forgetting that I worked for Earth gov? That's the oldest argument in the book," Carmen said. "That's how you get coopted. That's how your voice gets silenced. Because they don't listen, Loren. You know they don't. People like Jayne Redman want the perks and the big offices and the ability to tell other people what to do. They don't want disagreement or initiative or thinking outside the boundaries of the box they've built. Tell me I'm wrong, that your experience with this IIS is different than what I think."

Loren hesitated, frowning.

"You never did lie to me," Carmen said. "Don't start now."

He sighed again. "You know what she'll do, Carmen. Redman and her loyal followers. They'll fight you every step of the way, try to discredit everything you say and do, and if you turn out to be right, which you probably are, they'll then claim credit for that themselves."

That stung. But Carmen shook her head. "You're right, and I won't pretend that doesn't make me angry, but the alternative is to let them silence me by editing out or changing everything that conflicts with their own, official view of things."

"Integrated," Loren said. "It's not the official view, which implies we're being told what to say, it's the integrated view." He laughed scornfully and took another drink. "Which implies we have real input into the final product."

"You're too good to end up like this," Carmen said. "Has the IIS really sucked up every part of the intelligence collection and analysis biz on Kosatka?"

"Either it already has or soon will," Loren said.

"Really?"

Loren paused, eyeing her. "What are you thinking?"

"I'm thinking that if there's only one source of intelligence collection and analysis on this world, that places a huge amount of power in the hands of whoever is in charge of that."

"Sure." Loren nodded. "I'm sure Jayne Redman has thought of that."

"Has the First Minister? Has the House of the People's Representatives?"

This time Loren Yeresh paused for several seconds. "I don't know. Carmen, people like me can't just walk into the First Minister's office and talk about stuff like that."

"I know First Minister Hofer," Carmen said. "Remember?"

"Are you . . . ?" Loren exhaled slowly. "Should I know anything more about what you're going to do?"

"Who said I'm going to do anything?"

"That's right, you didn't. You just mentioned someone you knew from when you first arrived on Kosatka." Loren gave her a level look. "Be careful."

"Loren, have you heard they might start sending soldiers with prosthetics back to the front?"

He hesitated. "There are rumors."

"You don't know anything else?"

"Your clearance was pulled, Carmen."

"General Edelman gave me a new one," she told him.

"That's right. I heard of some very loud, um, discussions about that going on in the IIS front office." Loren grimaced as if in pain. "Someone in a position to know told me that preparations are being made for mobilizing the so-called combat-capable injured. Supposedly it's just an emergency plan to be implemented if another invasion force lands. That's what they're being told, anyway."

"Does your someone in a position to know believe that?"

"No, he doesn't. The need already exists, and too many of the details seem focused on the near future, not on some future contingency." Loren nodded to her. "Okay. I understand your personal motivation. This isn't about you or getting credit or kicking Redman in the butt."

"You know who it's about," Carmen said. "Dominic is not going to the front again with a prosthetic if I can stop it. And this single-source control for all intelligence and related activities is not a good idea. It gives too much power to whoever runs that agency. I need to get people to see that."

"I'm not stupid enough to get in your way," Loren said, giving her another concerned look. "Be careful," he repeated. "If you do anything. Which I don't know anything about."

After the call ended, Carmen spent a while gazing at the screen of her comm pad, wondering if some of the things being done in the name of preserving Kosatka's freedom would turn out to be as dangerous to that freedom as the invaders she and the other soldiers were fighting.

CHAPTER 5

Rob Geary had the destroyer *Saber* on an intercept with the three attacking ships. He didn't have the luxury of waiting until the enemy commander made a mistake on his own. Hopefully the commander could be nudged into a mistake.

The three enemy ships, the light cruiser, the destroyer, and the freighter, were moving through space at a crawl, only about a thousand meters per second. That was to accommodate the freighter carrying the invading troops, which couldn't accelerate or brake at anything like the rate a warship could. Freighters were designed to move a lot of cargo at efficient speeds, and refitting them with life support in the cargo areas so they could carry a lot of soldiers instead of cargo didn't change that. Fortunately for Rob and the people of Glenlyon Star System, Old Earth hadn't yet sold to the aggressors out here any surplus military ships designed for moving troops quickly through space.

Saber was approaching the three enemy ships from below and to the left as seen using the human conventions that allowed people to orient themselves in space, where no real up or down existed. Humans defined the plane in which a star's planets orbited as a basis for "up" and "down," and the star itself for deciding if something was to their left (away from the star) or right (toward the star). It was rough and simple, but it worked to give common references in space. Instead of coming in with a swift stroke befitting her name, *Saber* was moving at a moderate velocity for a warship, only point zero one light speed, or about three thousand kilometers per second. There had been plenty of time to accelerate up to point zero two light speed, but Rob hadn't wanted to burn the fuel necessary to do that since he had no idea when he'd be able to refuel *Saber*, and the slower velocity allowed better accuracy. "If we get a shot," Rob told his bridge crew, "I want to make sure we get as many hits as possible."

The officers on the bridge, all of them Earth Fleet veterans, understood how tough the situation was, how bad the odds were. But, because of how well things had gone during the fighting at Kosatka a few months ago, they had an amount of confidence in him that Rob found worrisome. Overconfidence could lose battles at least as surely as a lack of confidence. That's what Mele Darcy had told him during one of her rambling discussions of military theory and history, and Rob had no reason to doubt her. Not on that matter, anyway. Some of Mele's stories about her own experiences in life seemed a little . . . exaggerated, but then Mele was a Marine, and she never told stories about what she'd done in combat except to offer an occasional learning lesson.

"Half an hour to intercept, Captain," Lieutenant Cameron reported.

"Very well," Rob said. He magnified the image of the enemy ships on his own display, seeing they remained in the same triangular formation, the destroyer and light cruiser positioned so that they could hit *Saber* before *Saber* could get in any shots at the freighter carrying the enemy troops. Rob had lined up the intercept course to offer an apparent chance for the enemy to better concentrate fire on *Saber* by moving the light cruiser "down" and to one side, in hopes that the enemy commander would take advantage of that without noticing that it would offer a chance for *Saber* to make a last-minute change of course to hit the freighter, with lower odds of being hit herself. But so far the enemy hadn't changed anything about their approach.

Lieutenant Commander Vicki Shen, who was already in engineering in anticipation of the upcoming fight, called him. "He's not going to bite, sir."

Rob nodded as much to himself as to her words. "He spotted the trick."

"No, I doubt that," she replied. "I've gone back over every maneuver that guy in command of the enemy force has made since they arrived at this star system. Every single move, every single formation shift, has been by the book. Exactly by the book."

"We guessed he was an Earth Fleet veteran," Rob said. "It's not surprising that he'd still be using Earth Fleet procedures."

"I think this is more than that. I worked for a few people like this guy. They couldn't even spell 'imagination' because they didn't think they'd ever need it." Shen shook her head. "I don't think he saw the possible opportunity we offered. He's not looking for that. He's got his ships arranged by the book. Anything we do, he'll counter by the book."

"Hell." Rob leaned his head back, staring at the tangle of wiring and piping and ducts attached to the overhead of the bridge. "If we had superiority, or even odds, we'd be able to take him apart if he's that predictable. But when he has this much superiority, we can't use that predictability against him. We need him to make a mistake, and you're telling me that he's not going to do that."

"I don't think so, no." Shen paused. "The combat simulation system estimates that if we continue this intercept, we have a two percent chance of inflicting significant damage on the freighter, and a ninety percent chance of our own ship suffering serious damage when both enemy ships hit us. As second in command, I feel obligated to advise you against making this attack."

"Thank you," Rob said, feeling as if acid were eating at his insides. "You're right. Is there anything we can do? You know Earth Fleet procedures better than I do. Even if all we can do is force him to use more fuel, that's something."

"I don't think—" She paused, her brow lowering in thought. "Leader Class light cruisers have a single missile launcher. We don't know if that ship has any missiles aboard. But if it does, Earth Fleet manuals spell out exactly when to fire."

"How are you thinking we can use that?"

"Maybe we can trick him into using up some of his missiles by knowing when he'd fire and being ready to evade them."

He took a moment to think. His own, limited, experience had been in the small fleet that the Old Colony star system Alfar had maintained. If Vicki Shen saw something in the enemy commander's actions that her Earth Fleet experience could identify, he'd be a fool to disregard that. "That's not much, but it's something. And lessening the threat from the missiles on that cruiser will help our odds when we do close to a fight." Rob turned to look at the officers at their watch stations aligned along the back of the bridge, focusing on the weapons officer. "Ensign Reichert, what do you know about Earth Fleet parameters for firing missiles?"

Reichert, concentrating on her weapons display, jerked with surprise at the question. "Missiles? I haven't employed any, sir, but I've still got the manual loaded into the combat systems for reference. That was required by Earth Fleet regulations, but by your orders the combat system is no longer slaved to the manual to govern when to fire."

"Good. The executive officer tells me the enemy commander is doing everything exactly as Earth Fleet manuals dictate," Rob said. "I want to know under what conditions he'll fire a missile at us, and then I want to know how we can evade that missile."

Reichert nodded, her eyes intent. "It'll be based on probability of a hit. I'm sure of that."

"Get me what I need to know, because I needed to know it five minutes ago."

"Yes, sir! Do I assume we continue on this approach vector to intercept?"

"Yes. Lieutenant Cameron, work with Ensign Reichert on the evasive maneuvers."

"Yes, Captain. Uh . . . twenty-five minutes to intercept, sir," Cameron added. "We should have an answer to you well before then."

Sitting, watching his display, and not interrupting proved to be one of the hardest things Rob had done. He had to keep fighting himself to avoid demanding progress updates from Reichert and Cameron, because he knew those disturbances in their work would slow them down. He'd seen enough of both Reichert and Cameron to be sure they'd get the job done, but it was still hard as hell to wait it out while they worked as the timer on his display kept counting down the seconds and minutes until the intercept.

Twenty minutes prior to the intercept the general quarters alarm sounded, calling everyone aboard *Saber* to their battle stations. There wasn't any rush of sailors through the ship in response to the alarm, which wasn't a surprise. Rob wondered if there was anyone on the ship who wasn't already in position, ready for battle.

He pulled out the survival suit stored at his seat and put it on in case *Saber* took a hit bad enough to open this part of the ship to space. He kept the helmet unsealed to make it easier to talk with everyone else and to conserve the suit's oxygen recirc system. The familiar routine momentarily took his mind off of the welter of worries about what to do if the answer couldn't be found in time.

"We've got it, Captain," Ensign Reichert announced breathlessly. "The exact circumstances of when to fire are determined by the situation. Since we have the same Earth Fleet manuals as the enemy does, we know what they call for in this exact situation. If he follows the engagement rules in the manual, he'll fire when the combat systems estimate a seventy-five percent chance of a hit regardless of whatever evasive maneuvers we carry out."

"We can determine exactly when that will be on our approach to intercept," Lieutenant Cameron said.

"Seventy-five percent?" Rob said. "No matter how we evade?" He tried to keep the disappointment out of his voice. How could he take that kind of risk?

"Yes, sir," Cameron said. "But, as Ensign Reichert pointed out to me, that's assuming the targeted ship doesn't know in advance when that missile will be fired at it. If we do know that, and we initiate an evasive maneuver based on that rather than waiting to detect the launch of the missile before we try to dodge, that buys us at least a couple of seconds, and our chances of evading the missile will be very good."

"That's the best news I've heard in a while," Rob said. "Good work, you two. What does 'very good' mean in terms of us not getting hit by a missile?"

"Pretty close to a hundred percent, sir," Reichert said. "The probability of hit calculations assumes the targeted warship will continue its vector at least until missile launch is detected. At the velocities we're traveling, even a tiny shift in vector a couple of seconds earlier than that will be more than a missile can compensate for."

"Let's set it up," Rob said. "We don't have a lot of good options, but if this allows us a means to deplete his supply of missiles, it'll help the odds we're facing. We've got less than ten minutes left to intercept."

"The maneuver will be sometime in the last minute," Lieutenant Cameron predicted confidently. "We'll have it for you before then, sir."

Rob felt himself relaxing as he watched his display. Physics ruled in space. Go fast enough and relativity started to really mess with things, but Newton's old rules governed most matters that humans had to deal with. Anything like this, the movements of ships in space, their curving tracks through the emptiness and their velocity and the time when they'd pass close enough to each other to exchange fire, could all be calculated precisely, down to the last decimal place. The math, as complicated as it could get, was easy and predictable.

What wasn't predictable were the actions of humans. Which was why Rob was in command of *Saber* instead of some artificial intelligence program. "There are two basic problems with AIs in command of weapons," one of Rob's instructors back at Alfar had told the class. "The first is that, from the point of view of the enemy, an AI is too predictable. It has to operate by the rules written into its code, even if that code is supposed to be mimicking human thought process. The second problem, though, is that from the point of view of our own side, an AI is unpredictable in all the worst ways. Think of every time your comparatively simple home computer systems have malfunctioned or glitched or done the wrong thing, even when no malware was involved, and imagine that in charge of weapons that can kill you. That's why humans remain in the loop for critical systems. Each of you has to decide whether the AIs assisting your actions and decision making are giving you the best advice, or even good advice. Don't default to letting them decide for you, or you won't know how to decide for yourself when you need to."

That wasn't how Earth Fleet had worked, though. They'd been wedded to checklists and procedures that made decisions for them. If Vicki Shen was right, the commander of the enemy force had no practice in making his own decisions because he always did what the book said. And Rob finally had a way to use that weakness.

"He'll launch at fifteen seconds before intercept," Ensign Reichert reported. "If he follows the Earth Fleet combat rules programmed into his weapon controls."

"And if he has missiles," Lieutenant Cameron added.

"All right," Rob said. "I want to set up a maneuver to evade the missile, and then . . . come back around for another intercept." That return maneuver would require enough time for him to figure out what to do next.

"Yes, sir." Cameron's hands flew across his display. "Sending to you, Captain."

Rob's display lit up with the proposed maneuver, a wide swing up and around, making the most efficient use possible of *Saber*'s existing momentum. He checked the time left, seeing that it was just less than two minutes, then approved the maneuver. "I'm putting this one on automatic to make sure we shift vector at just the right moment," he told Cameron.

Touching the glowing control marked "confirm," Rob let out a slow breath to calm his voice before activating *Saber*'s internal communications. "All hands," he said. "This is the captain. We're less than two minutes to intercept. We're going to try to fool the enemy into expending some of his missiles on this run, so stand by for last-moment evasive maneuvers."

One minute left.

A Leader Class light cruiser could carry only four missiles because of their size and mass. The missiles had to be big enough to carry enough thrust and fuel to engage a target, as well as the necessary sensors to track the target, and the warhead itself, which was big enough that a single missile hit would have a good chance of inflicting damage on a destroyer like *Saber*. Reduce how many missiles the enemy had, or confirm that the enemy hadn't purchased missiles along with the cruiser, and the odds against *Saber* would go from impossible to only extremely bad.

But if he was wrong, if Vicki Shen and he had misjudged the actions of the enemy commander, and that missile was fired a second earlier at, say, a fifty percent chance of a hit, then *Saber* might very soon be in serious danger. This wasn't a sure thing. But it was the best he had.

In the final seconds before the evasive maneuver, as *Saber* and the enemy warships rushed through the final thousands of kilometers that had separated them, Rob had a moment to wonder which Leader the light cruiser had originally been named for. Whoever it was, how would they feel if they could know that the ship once named in their honor was now being used by those intent on conquering nearby star systems? Or had the leader themselves once been a conqueror who was crowned by success into someone to be admired by people many generations removed from the carnage?

The maneuvering warning alarm blared.

Five seconds later, as the automated command activated, *Saber's* thrusters kicked in hard, pitching the destroyer up onto a higher vector that would carry her past the three enemy ships at too great a distance for an engagement. Some of the force of the sudden change in her path leaked past the ship's inertial dampers that kept the stress from tearing apart *Saber* and her crew. Rob heard *Saber's* hull protest with a prolonged groan of metallic pain as he felt that force push him down into his seat.

The thrusters had just begun firing when another alarm sounded, high-pitched and urgent. "Missile launch detected from the light cruiser!" Ensign Reichert called out, her own voice strained by the effort of dealing with the stress of the vector change. "The launch was exactly when predicted."

Rob kept his gaze on his display as the symbol representing the missile fired from the light cruiser leapt out and raced toward an intercept with *Saber*. The ships were moving so fast that the destroyer was past the enemy in an instant, the enemy warships just out of range of *Saber's* weapons. Rob's display showed him what had happened in those moments of time during which human reflexes were too slow to cope, the missile's path jerking as it tried to compensate for *Saber's* course change, the violent stress of the necessary maneuver shattering the missile into a shower of fragments that raced off into space.

He let out a breath he hadn't realized he was holding. *Saber* was still coming up and around, her course bending in an immense curve that would steady out on a vector to once again intercept the enemy, though this time the destroyer would be approaching from above and to the right of the invaders. The stress of the maneuver had lessened, though, as the ship bent on a more leisurely change of its course. "Okay," he said, trying to sound confident rather than shaken. "That worked."

"Captain?" Vicki Shen said, calling once more from engineering. "Do it again."

"What?" Rob glanced from the display to the image of his executive officer. "That'd be a waste of fuel, wouldn't it? He saw what we did. He has to assume we'll do the same thing on the next approach."

"It doesn't matter," Shen said. "I went through I don't know how many evaluation drills in Earth Fleet that all came down to whether or not you did what the checklists and the procedures said. It didn't matter whether or not it worked. What mattered was that you followed the procedures. That guy we're fighting is a successful product of that system. He got his rank by doing exactly what the procedures told him to do. I think if we make another run at him, he'll do exactly what procedures say, and fire another missile when the hit probability reaches the right number."

"Even though he knows we'll dodge it?"

"Even though. I worked for guys like him, sir. He knows what the book says to do, and that's what he'll keep doing."

Rob rubbed his face with both hands, trying to decide whether or not to risk it.

Would the enemy expect him to do the same thing? That'd be a stupid thing for Rob to do. But . . . the enemy commander didn't know the dodge had been deliberate. He might convince himself it had been a lucky coincidence.

"All right," Rob said. "It's worth the risk if we can get rid of another one of his missiles. Lieutenant Cameron, Ensign Reichert, I want the same thing worked up. Figure out exactly when he'll fire a missile at us and how we need to evade it."

The two officers bent to their tasks while *Saber* continued around through space. Despite her velocity, immense by the standards of any world, to the humans inside her she seemed to be motionless. Even the nearest references, the three enemy ships, were so far distant at this point in the turn that they were mere specks of light against the star-spangled darkness.

With *Saber* approaching this time from behind and above the enemy, and the relative speed at which the destroyer closed on the enemy slower than when all the ships were heading toward each other, the point at which the light cruiser would hopefully fire another missile was at a different place along the intercept curve. Still, it was just math.

"Got it, Captain," Ensign Reichert said. "He'll fire when we reach this point, which will be at this time."

On Rob's display, a point along the projected intercept route glowed, showing him the place and time Reichert had worked out. "Excellent. Lieutenant Cameron, can we manage a good evasion from there?"

"Yes, sir," Cameron said. "If we break upward again at the moment he fires, we should have a one hundred percent chance of getting clear."

"We broke upward last time," Rob said. Repeating the same tactic twice in a row was worrisome enough, but doing it in exactly the same way? "And that'll require a more intense maneuver than steepening our turn and diving faster, won't it? More stress on the ship and the crew."

"Yes, sir. Captain, you said to do the same thing, so . . ."

"So you laid out the same thing." Rob waved an apologetic hand. "Sorry. You did what I said. Can we evade the missile by diving instead of bending our course up?"

"I need to run that, sir."

"But we can evade by turning upward if we need to."

"Yes, sir. But, as you said, it's a more intense maneuver. More stress on the ship and crew. We'd be at least in the yellow stress zone, and might shade into the red." He paused as one of his hands danced over his display. "Yes, sir, we can ensure successful evasion of the missile by diving."

"All right. We'll dive. Give me the maneuver."

"Yes, sir." Lieutenant Cameron worked quickly, reminding Rob that while Earth Fleet hadn't valued imagination or initiative it had trained its people extremely well in carrying out tasks. "Then . . . twenty-two minutes until we evade."

"Enter the maneuver into the system and I'll set it to take place automatically again," Rob said.

"Yes, sir."

The maneuver command popped up on Rob's display. He authorized it, then once again had nothing to do but wait.

Once more, time counted down at what seemed a very slow pace.

As the moment of the maneuver approached, Rob felt himself tensing. If the enemy commander ordered a missile launch earlier than the book dictated, it might put *Saber* at risk of being hit.

He silently counted off the last seconds before the maneuvering alarm sounded, followed by *Saber's* thrusters firing, and once again a report from Ensign Reichert.

"Missile launch detected, exactly when predicted."

Saber tore past the enemy once more, this time diving under the three warships. Rob watched the missile race above *Saber*, too far off to engage the destroyer, and continue on into empty space. "When will it self-destruct?"

"About now," Ensign Reichert said, just as an alert appeared on Rob's display showing the detonation of the missile's warhead. "Damn, I'm good."

"What was that, Ensign?"

"Nothing, sir."

Rob called Lieutenant Commander Shen. "Do you think he'll do it again?"

"Maybe."

"'Maybe' isn't a recommendation. You can get inside this guy's head better than I can."

She paused, thinking, then slowly nodded. "Yes, sir, I think he will."

"What if he anticipates our evasion maneuver this time and fires early?"

"He won't do that."

"Why not?" Rob asked. "It's a logical response to what we've been doing."

"Because," Shen said, "he doesn't have any guidance on how to do that. There's nothing in the manual about what to do in this situation.

I'll guarantee you that he's looking for such guidance right now and finding nothing. That leaves him only two choices. Either fire exactly when the book says to fire, or don't."

Rob sat back, trying to decide if this was worth the risk. "I find it hard to believe a commander would find it that hard to think for themselves."

"Sir, you saw the after-action reports from the survivors of *Claymore*."

Shen didn't add anything else. She didn't have to. Rob recalled his disbelief as he read those reports, wondering why the commanding officer of *Claymore* and the Commodore had kept looking for answers in their checklists rather than doing something, anything. "All right. Lieutenant Cameron, let's bring her around for a third pass. Ensign Reichert, as soon as we have that maneuver worked out, I want to know when he'll fire at us."

Rob waited for any sign of worry or skepticism from his crew as they prepared to do the same thing for a third time. The approach vectors had been different the first two times, and would be different again this time, but it was still the same tactic. It worried him that he saw no concern in his officers as they worked. Did they trust him that much? Or was this a product of their Earth Fleet training, where doing what you were told mattered much more than the results of whatever you did?

Once again *Saber* swooped in, the enemy warships repositioning in another by-the-book maneuver so they could hit her before Rob could get in any shots at the freighter. Once again, Rob waited, tense, until the maneuvering warning sounded and *Saber* altered vector, followed by the report of an enemy missile fired from the light cruiser. This time the enemy missile tried another radical maneuver to catch *Saber*, breaking into two large pieces from the stress. The front portion self-destructed, while the stern part of the missile spiraled off into space, heading "up" on a path that would take it into the endless dark between stars.

"One more time?" Lieutenant Cameron asked.

"Yeah," Rob said.

Barely ten seconds later Ensign Reichert called out, "Captain! Problem!"

He swung to look at her. "What is it?"

Reichert was studying something on her display, her eyes intent. "Sir, a Leader Class light cruiser carries four missiles. He's fired three. The manual seems to say he should fire again on our next pass, but I've been running a simulation of the enemy cruiser alongside our own actions as a check, and a warning just popped up on it. I tagged it, and the combat manual says since the cruiser is down to one missile, it should reserve firing it until hit probability exceeds ninety percent."

"Ninety percent?" Rob looked at his display, which showed the long, projected path of *Saber* curving toward a fourth intercept with the cruiser. "Lieutenant Cameron, what are our chances of successfully evading if he waits for a ninety percent hit probability before firing?"

"Working it, sir." Cameron paused, finally looking distressed. "Captain, that'd require us to hold our approach longer, making evasion harder. That leaves such a short time to change vector . . . the system is estimating something less than fifty percent chance of evading the missile."

"Less than fifty percent?"

"Yes, Captain. Possibly as low as twenty percent depending on how the missile reacts."

Rob rested one hand over his eyes, thinking, but almost immediately lowered it. "Give me a vector to place *Saber* in a position above and slightly forward of the enemy formation at a distance of one light second."

Three hundred thousand kilometers. Close enough to menace the enemy, and to pounce if the enemy made a mistake, but far enough off that if the enemy warships suddenly turned to charge *Saber* he'd have time to react. Only a few minutes, but Rob had confidence that his crew could respond that quickly.

Feeling an obligation to explain what was happening, Rob tapped the ship's general announcing system. "All hands, this is the Captain. We've tricked the enemy into expending most of their missiles, but any further attempts are too likely to result in damage to *Saber*. Our presence here is the only thing hindering the enemy's ability to act, so we will maintain a close watch on them, waiting for an opportunity to strike. We'll be standing down from full combat alert, but everyone has to be prepared for action on only a few minutes' notice. That is all."

This was the point, Rob Geary thought, at which his ship was supposed to charge into battle and defeat the invaders of Glenlyon, overcoming impossible odds. After all, he'd done that before.

But that wasn't happening this time.

Saber took up position shadowing the enemy force.

Unless something changed the odds, there wasn't much else he could do.

This conference room on the orbital facility had been stripped of valuable equipment, but the chairs and big table hadn't been worth hauling down to the surface in the time available. Mele sat at one end of the table, looking down its length at the Marine and ground forces officers and senior enlisted. Aside from her, the only other Marine officer was newly promoted Lieutenant Shahid Nasir. Shahid had been an easy pick for the lieutenant job since he'd been in officer training on Luxor when that Old Colony followed along with the others and drastically cut back the already small military force it had maintained. Almost completely qualified in a job for which there was no longer local demand, he had, like many others, looked outward to where humanity was rapidly expanding deeper into the galaxy.

For Mele the deciding factor had been that when Shahid was approached by recruiters for Apulu he'd balked at their terms of service and demands for obedience to all orders. "History shows the dangers of such things," he had explained to Mele. "Demanding that all orders be obeyed regardless of legality or humanity. Any government that fears the consciences of its own soldiers is not a government to be trusted."

"You do understand," Mele had replied, "that you need to have a really good reason for refusing to obey an order, right?"

"I hope never to have to disobey an order," Shahid said. "But if you do not trust me to know when an order is illegal, or when such an extreme circumstance exists, perhaps you should not entrust me with an officer position on which the lives of others rest."

"Good point."

Lieutenant Nasir sat next to Gunnery Sergeant Moon. Opposite them sat Captain Batra, along with Lieutenant Keith Paratnam, Lieutenant Jana Killian, and Master Sergeant Teri Savak. They all looked worn-out. Mele imagined she looked at least as bad. "We've got twenty hours before the enemy arrives if they maintain their current velocity," she said. "I want to ensure everyone gets some rest before then. We're not going to have many opportunities for rest after that."

Mele gestured toward the display still mounted on one wall. "The enemy ships started braking velocity exactly when expected. They're maintaining a vector to bring them next to this facility, with the facility between them and the planet below."

"It's too bad we don't actually have any antiorbital weapons on the surface," Lieutenant Killian commented, her eyes somber.

"We do have fakes," Mele said, drawing surprised looks. "Colonel Menziwa briefed me on them. This information does not go outside this room. The government has set up decoys in a dozen places. The decoys generate the same passive and active signals as real concealed antiorbital weapons sites would. From orbit they'll look like actual hidden weapon locations. Aside from keeping the enemy ships nervous, we're hoping they'll expend their bombardment projectiles on those sites so every other place will be safe."

Captain Batra smiled. "It would take a half dozen standard projectiles to eliminate each suspected site. At the least, that would use up a lot of their supply."

"But why would the enemy believe we really have such sites?" Killian asked. "Aren't we fairly sure they have spies on the planet who would've spotted something like that?"

Mele nodded. "At least one of those spies has been identified, and deliberately allowed access to details on the top-secret antiorbital weapons program."

"Nice," Killian admitted. "It's good to know we've been punching back on the covert junk."

"The goal of the deception was to discourage the enemy from attacking the planet again," Mele said. "It failed in that. Hopefully it'll work better as a way to soak up the enemy bombardment capabilities."

"How close do the enemy ships have to get before they launch a bombardment?"

"I was told the soonest they'd probably launch would be ten hours from now. By then they'll be close enough to be fairly sure of accurate drops on their rocks. But it's possible they won't bombard if they think they can capture this facility. They probably want to capture intact as much weaponry and industry on the planet as they can."

Lieutenant Paratnam rubbed his eyes. "Do we have any better estimate for how long we'll need to hold out once they get here?"

"No," Mele said. "There are too many variables with unknown quantities. Especially the fuel supplies on the enemy warships. The more damage we do, the more we force them to use energy, the sooner they'll have to withdraw."

"A death grapple," Captain Batra grumbled. "I wish we knew exactly who we were up against."

"It's unlikely to be Reds," Sergeant Moon said. "The enemy knows they need well-trained troops to take a facility like this."

"Maybe Red shock troops to take the damage from our initial defense," Lieutenant Killian suggested. She nodded as if confirming her own words. "Use them to wear us down, and limit the losses to their good troops."

Mele was about to reply when a high-priority message alert sounded.

"Ninja? Not a great time." From what could be seen in the image on Mele's pad, Rob's wife was sending this message from inside a tent.

"This is business," Ninja snapped in reply. "Here," she added as a pop-up window appeared. "A network on the enemy freighter lit off, probably somebody testing the gear just before action who hit the wireless command by accident when they were supposed to be using only physical links. Before it went off I was able to ping it and get it to send back identification. Here are who some of the people you're facing used to be."

Mele stared at the ID. "Perfect timing. Any luck getting into that network?"

"Not yet. It shut down before I could make a serious try. As soon as they activate again I'll see what I can do."

"Thanks, Lyn. You're a wonder."

The others stared at their pads as Mele forwarded the message. "Old Earth military," Captain Batra said. "These guys are good."

Master Sergeant Savak cleared her throat. "Sir, most of those units were only maintained as cadres," she said. "Officers and senior enlisted, but very few junior enlisted. They were expected to fill out their ranks if needed using activated reserve forces."

"Reserves." Batra pondered that. "People with their own jobs, and lives outside the military. Far less likely to have felt cut loose and be lacking for employment when militaries were drastically cut back."

"And far more likely to have stayed at home," Sergeant Savak said. "We'll be facing really good leaders, and whatever rankers they've been able to sign up. Taking out the leaders will be even more important than usual." Savak didn't seem to be particularly worked up over that, but then from what Mele had seen, Sergeant Savak didn't get particularly worked up over anything.

"You said most units like that were organized that way," Mele said. "Some were all professionals?"

Savak hesitated, then nodded. "That's right, Captain. It is possible that we'll face an outfit like that."

"We'll have to assume the worst until we find out otherwise," Gunny Moon said.

Captain Batra aimed a sharp look at Savak. "Master Sergeant, somebody on the other side got careless and gave us some very important information. Let's be very sure that none of our people make a similar mistake."

"They all know I'll use their guts to decorate the outside of this facility if any of them screw up like that, sir," Sergeant Savak said with a smile.

"Perhaps one of them should," Gunnery Sergeant Moon said in the way of someone who'd just had a thought. He grinned at the surprised looks sent his way. "I mean, let something *false* out that gives them a misleading impression of us."

"Disinformation?" Batra said. "They should know who we are, Sergeant Moon. Our unit came to Glenlyon some time ago."

"Yes, Captain," Moon agreed. "But they don't know who is up here, and what our readiness is or our morale."

"I see. Make them think we're scared or sloppy? Ready to crumble?" Batra asked.

"Maybe this leak to us was also deliberate," Killian suggested.

"If so, they were trying to impress us. To scare us." Batra frowned. "Captain Darcy, how do we want the enemy to approach us?"

"Do you mean as a threat?" Mele asked. "If they overestimate us, they'll be more cautious, and employ more firepower straight off regardless of the damage it does to the facility."

"But," Sergeant Moon said, "if they underestimate us, they might come charging in hard and fast, hoping we'll break easy and let them capture this place almost intact."

Sergeant Savak smiled in an unnervingly serene manner. "If they come in hard and fast, with little preparation, we can have a very impressive reception waiting for them."

Captain Batra nodded. "Captain Darcy, with your permission I'd like to have my hack-and-cracks create some false identities who sneak messages past security protocols to lament to their friends about the very sad state of the defending forces here."

"Go ahead," Mele said. "Give the impression that we have too few people and too little in the way of weapons, that we're a sacrificial force left in a hopeless position to make it look like the government didn't simply abandon this facility." She paused, realizing that she'd just described the situation that she'd been in at Kosatka. But if any of the others noticed, none of them reacted. "Sergeant Moon, make sure Glitch provides any assistance Captain Batra's people need to carry this off. We want the enemy to think our Marines are shaky, too."

"Yes, Captain." Moon gave her a speculative look. "Maybe Sergeant Giddings can add in some information about the Marine commander being so severely impacted by post-traumatic stress suffered at Kosatka that she's walking wounded."

"Anything that causes the enemy to underestimate me is fine." Mele noticed the ground forces soldiers trying to hide smirks. "Is there a joke I missed?"

The smirks disappeared. Over the last week all of the ground forces leaders had learned what happened when they messed with Captain Darcy. There had been more than one tense "instructional moment," but at this point open disagreement at least was a thing of the past.

"Good," Mele said. "Because I was thinking that if this deception works, when will we find out?"

A pause, then Lieutenant Killian answered as cautiously as someone worried about a trick question. "When they attack."

Captain Batra nodded. "If they expect heavy resistance, their warships will conduct heavy fire support before they land, hitting anyplace they think might be a strongpoint. If they think we're going to cave, they'll risk doing without a heavy pre-assault in order to limit damage to the facility."

"Right," Mele said. "Which means we have to be ready to shift our defense on the spur of the moment. We won't know which type of attack we're going to face until we see it coming at us."

Captain Batra waved aside Mele's concern. "We're force reconnaissance. My soldiers are trained to move fast and often. That is exactly the type of battle we're best suited for."

"What about the heavy weapons platoon?"

"They also move fast and often," Lieutenant Paratnam said. "If they stay in one place for any length of time, the enemy can fix their position and hit them. They won't have any trouble shifting position after every couple of shots. It's what they do anyway."

"Our Marines are light infantry," Sergeant Moon said. "So the same is true of them. We're actually better off in a mobile fight than if we all dug in and fought from fixed positions."

Captain Batra fixed Mele with a sharp look. "You planned for that kind of fight all along."

"Of course I did," Mele said. "It offers us the best chance."

"What if the enemy had come in preparing for a different kind of fight?"

Mele grinned. "This is our battlefield. We get to choose how we fight. If they're not prepared for that kind of fight, it'll hurt them."

"Captain Darcy," Lieutenant Killian said, "what if they decide the fight is too tough, withdraw their troops, and set off charges to shove this facility into a decaying orbit? That'd deny them use of the facility, but it would also eliminate Glenlyon's ability to use it. And of course none of us would survive that."

"That's a possibility," Mele conceded. "If that happens, we'll react in the best manner we can given the exact circumstances."

"What could we do?" Captain Pradesh asked. "If it comes to that?"

"That'll depend on exactly what's happening." What Mele thought was a simple, common-sense recognition that it was impossible to predict exactly what would be the best thing to do was met with concerned frowns from the ground forces officers. "If they're losing badly enough to give up on capturing this place," she added, "that'll mean we have the ability to mess with anything else they try to do. The enemy may outnumber and outgun us, but that doesn't mean we can't make them dance to our tune."

This time Captain Batra nodded along with encouraging looks at his subordinates. "Captain Darcy is right. If we keep the enemy off-balance, he'll have a hard time acting as he wishes."

"All right," Mele said. "Company's coming. Let's get the final preps done for a nice, warm welcome when they get here."

Once the ground forces soldiers had left, she gestured to Lieutenant Nasir and Sergeant Moon. "Get going on that disinformation. The more we can make the enemy complacent about what they'll find here, the more we can knock them back hard when they get here. Gunny, is Sergeant Giddings working with Ninja?"

"Lyn Geary?" Moon asked. "Are you asking if Glitch is officially or unofficially working with her?"

"Officially, from this point on," Mele said. "On my authority. I want Ninja to know what the ground forces code monkeys are doing so our efforts don't stumble over each other."

"I'll notify Glitch immediately," Moon said.

"Good. Lieutenant," Mele added, "can you check on the modifications to the exterior surface of this facility on the side where we expect the attack to come in?"

"Yes, Captain. I'll get you a complete status report."

As she left the conference room, Mele stood aside for several soldiers and a civilian worker who tromped into the room and hefted up the table and a few of the chairs. "These are going into the barricades," the worker told Mele. "They won't stop those guys, but they'll slow 'em down. That's the idea, right? We're gonna rope-a-dope these guys?"

That was a new one on her. "'Rope-a-dope'?"

"Yeah." The worker paused to answer her, setting down the two chairs he was carrying. "Back on Old Earth that's what we called backing up and protecting yourself while the bad guys wear themselves out throwing useless punches. Isn't that what we're gonna do?"

"That's exactly what we're gonna do," Mele said. Rope-a-dope. Maybe the great military theorists like Sun Tzu and Clausewitz hadn't come up with that term, but it was exactly the tactic and the strategy she was planning on. "Why is it called that?"

The worker shrugged as he hefted the chairs again. "I don't know. Something to do with boxing, I think. Or wrestling? They've both got ropes around the ring."

"Thanks. Are you heading down soon?"

"I guess." The worker paused, looking conflicted. "I hate to leave you guys. I mean, I might be able to help if I stay up here."

Mele gripped his shoulder. "Head for the surface. We'll handle the fighting. People like you are going to be needed to put this place back together after we finish saving it."

He smiled, perhaps relieved to have his offer rejected. "Try not to trash it too bad when you kick their butts."

"I'll do my best." Mele watched the worker head away from her, hoping that when the fight was done there'd be a facility left for him to fix.

CHAPTER 6

Carmen Ochoa woke up as the transport set down at the main spaceport serving the city of Lodz. Yawning, she hoisted her rifle and headed out onto the tarmac, where the morning's rising sun had barely begun to warm the air and surface beneath her feet. She walked to the terminal, avoiding looking toward where a raid aimed at this spaceport had once been stopped dead.

Once upon a time, wearing a uniform on public transport and carrying her weapon would've made her stand out. But now Carmen was only one of those like that. A team of soldiers in full combat gear, their weapons at the ready, looked Carmen over as part of their security duties. She offered her ID without being asked, then exchanged nods of mutual respect with the guards.

As usual, Carmen felt conflicted about such things. She didn't like the sense of oppression that armed guards brought with them. The way they made open places feel confined just by being there. But she'd grown up on Mars, where the only armed guards were thugs answering to gangs and warlords. These guards on Kosatka were here to prevent such people from working their will on the helpless. That made their presence comforting.

She didn't bother trying to reconcile the conflicting feelings. There probably wasn't any way to do that, anyhow.

Parts of Lodz looked like a city where a big invasion had been fought and repulsed, while other sections were unmarked by violence. That felt weird, too.

First Minister Hofer's office was in the large collection of buildings known as the government complex. Many of those buildings had been damaged during the recent invasion and still bore the scars of battle. But Hofer had moved everyone back as soon as the enemy was driven out, insisting that Kosatka's government would not be displaced by the actions of foreign foes. It made for some difficult working conditions, but the decision had been popular with the people of Kosatka, who were tired of being pushed around and needed some strong imagery.

There were more guards here, of course, but Carmen had the necessary access pass. She did have to leave her rifle with the security post at the main entry.

Hofer's private secretary looked up as she entered the outer office. "Good morning," he said, polite and deferential without being servile in any way.

"Hey, Palmer," Carmen said.

AI assistants were cheap and common, and always in danger of being hacked and revealing everything they knew. Human assistants cost a lot more, but weren't nearly so easily subverted. An assistant like Palmer, loyal, discreet, and reliable, could command a salary almost as high as whomever they worked for. Because, also unlike AI assistants, such men and women couldn't be manufactured on demand.

Palmer smiled at her. They'd become acquainted when Carmen first reached Kosatka. The older man had judged her at that time and been her ally ever since. "Welcome back, Citizen Ochoa."

For her part, Carmen had quickly learned to admire the sheer professionalism and courtesy with which Palmer handled the job of being the gatekeeper for the First Minister. She smiled in return. "You were able to set up a meeting for me?"

"Yes. Fifteen minutes from now. Coffee?" Palmer made an apologetic grimace. "It's not really coffee."

She looked at the dark liquid, sniffing. "What is it?"

"A mix of a native nut and Earth-origin wheat, ground and roasted."

"Is there any caffeine in it?"

"No," Palmer admitted.

"Why drink it?" Carmen wondered. She took a cautious taste and winced.

"I'm not sure," Palmer said. "I guess it gives a semblance of normalcy. That's important, isn't it? To remember that the current state of affairs is not normal, and to believe that it will not be permanent."

"You're right. How's the First Minister holding up?"

"Well, considering the pressure on him." Palmer eyed her. "You rarely express open concern as you did when asking for this meeting."

Carmen looked down at the foul liquid that passed for coffee in Lodz these days. "As you said, we have to ensure that the current conditions don't become regarded as normal."

"You know that you have been cited as a problem by a certain government office?"

"Let's say I'm not surprised. How has the First Minister responded?"

"With skepticism," Palmer said. "But I think you're wise to come here and make your case in person."

"You've entered this meeting into Hofer's schedule?"

"Yes. Of course. Half an hour ago."

"Have you notified anyone of it?"

"Only the First Minister." Palmer raised an eyebrow at her. "What are you up to?"

"Setting a trap. I'm the bait." Carmen tried another taste of the fake coffee before setting it aside with a shudder. "Maybe we should send that to the enemy troops holding out around Ani. A few drinks of it and they'll probably surrender."

"Perhaps Lochan Nakamura will return aboard a ship loaded with coffee, chocolate, and other off-world necessities."

Despite her nervousness, Carmen let out a short laugh. "That'd make Lochan the most popular person on Kosatka, wouldn't it?"

Palmer looked upward toward the ceiling. It was funny how everyone did that, Carmen thought. Whenever they thought of events on other worlds or in space or in other star systems, they looked up as if those things would somehow be visible to their gaze even though the odds that they were looking in anything like the right direction were vanishingly small. But, still, people looked up. "Did Nakamura make it to Eire, do you think?"

She nodded. "Lochan is surprisingly resourceful when it's needed."

"Brigit Kelly asked if we had any news of him."

"Kelly would know faster than we would." Carmen looked a question at Palmer. "Why was she asking?"

Palmer smiled. "For professional reasons, she said, her being Eire's representative on Kosatka. But I believe there may be personal reasons for her interest as well."

"Oh? Lochan hasn't told me there was anything going on with Kelly." Carmen felt her protective instincts kick in. "I'll need to find out more about her."

"From what I know of her, you don't need to worry." Palmer looked up, his smile fading into a look of bland politeness as Jayne Redman entered the office. "Citizen Redman?"

The head of the Integrated Intelligence Service offered a perfunctory nod to Palmer, ignoring Carmen. "I need to see the First Minister."

Carmen, noting that the words were given as a command rather than a request, watched Palmer, admiring how well he concealed his annoyance. "The First Minister will be available after meeting with Citizen Ochoa."

"The meeting is why I'm here. Is there any reason why I shouldn't be present during that meeting?" Redman asked, her eyes finally resting on Carmen.

Carmen feigned a look of not-quite-suppressed confusion and guilt. "No reason at all." Inside, she felt her heart leap with jubilation. She'd been right in her guess of some of what the IIS would be up to, and Redman had taken the bait as eagerly as a starving fish leaping for a worm.

She couldn't always predict what one person would do, but predicting what a certain type of person would do in a certain situation was becoming easier all the time.

"Coffee?" Palmer offered.

"No," Redman said. She pulled out her comm pad and made a show out of working on it as she waited.

It was, Carmen thought, an ostentatious display of importance, as well as a way to dismiss the presence of the others in the room. Again, just what she'd have expected from Redman.

At the appointed time, Palmer opened the door to the First Minister's office. "Citizen Ochoa is here to see you, sir. As well as Citizen Redman."

The First Minister sat behind a large but not fancy desk whose surfaces bore the scars of rough searches when enemy forces had occupied this building. Carmen had no doubt that Hofer had continued using that desk not in spite of the damage but because of it, as one more sign of what Kosatka had endured and overcome. When Carmen entered, she got a quick smile from Hofer, followed by a quizzical look as Hofer's eyes rested on Redman. "What's this about?" he asked Carmen.

"I hoped to be able to discuss some matters that are concerning me," Carmen said, using her most formal manner of speaking, and realizing how that contrasted with her worn battle uniform.

"That's why I'm here as well," Redman chimed in. "First Minister, there are—"

"Hold on. Since this is supposed to be a meeting with Citizen Ochoa, I'll let her go first."

Carmen took care not to look triumphant. "I'm worried about two issues. One is the ongoing effort to eliminate alternate perspectives in the information you and other leaders receive, and the other is the concentration of power in certain offices."

"I see." Hofer's gaze went to Redman, giving no clue as to what he thought of what Carmen had said. "Those issues do seem to involve you, Citizen Redman."

"First Minister, I've been discussing with you the problems with a few unassimilated intelligence assets," Redman said. "This offers a good opportunity to address that issue."

Hofer gave her a skeptical look. "Are you saying that Citizen Ochoa is one of those . . . what did you call them?"

"Unassimilated assets."

"I see. And why is that a problem in the case of Citizen Ochoa?"

Redman sighed as if reluctant to say more. "First Minister, she's providing personal, untrained impressions of the intelligence picture to portions of Kosatka's defensive infrastructure. That's leading to erroneous impressions of enemy capabilities and intentions, which imperil not only the safety and security of our world, but also the lives of our brave defenders."

First Minister Hofer pursed his lips as if considering Redman's words. "You are aware that Citizen Ochoa has been working on the front lines in Ani? That she is one of Kosatka's brave defenders?"

Redman smiled apologetically. "I didn't mean to impugn the bravery of Citizen Ochoa. This is about her judgment, her training, and her uncontrolled, autonomous actions that endanger other defenders of our world."

"That's a reasonable concern," Hofer said. "Citizen Ochoa, Palmer tells me that General Edelman recently assigned you to a formal position on his staff. Why was that done?"

"To protect me," Carmen said. "Citizen Redman wants to . . . assimilate me, place me under her control."

Hofer held up a restraining hand as Redman began to speak. "Citizen Ochoa, why did General Edelman wish to protect you?"

"Because he trusts my assessments of the enemy forces."

"Which differ from those of the Integrated Intelligence Service?"

"Yes, sir," Carmen said.

"First Minister," Jayne Redman said, speaking sharply. She saw Hofer's unhappy reaction to her tone and moderated it quickly. "I can show you our assessments, and the data, sources, and material that went into those assessments, which are being made by trained individuals without any personal axes to grind."

"What would you say to that?" Hofer asked Carmen.

She knew what he was doing, giving both her and Redman plenty of rope to see if one of them would hang themselves with it. So Carmen chose her words carefully and kept her voice calm and respectful. "I'd say that the data, sources, and material chosen to make those assessments were very carefully chosen to support a predetermined judgment. What you should be concerned with are the data, sources, and material that do not support the assessments of the IIS, and which you will not be told of because the purpose of the IIS is to produce a single point of view."

Redman snorted in derision. "Why are you afraid of the First Minister, and General Edelman, being provided with a single, correct picture?"

Carmen shook her head. "I said the IIS has the purpose of producing a single point of view. I never said it was a correct picture. That's the problem. The First Minister, and others in the government, have no way of knowing what you're not telling them. There is no agency or service independent of the IIS serving as a devil's advocate for the assessments the IIS makes. Based on my experience, I believe that's a serious mistake."

"First Minister Hofer," Redman said, her voice and posture now stiff with outrage, "I must object to being accused of professional misconduct."

The emotional reaction and claim that Carmen was attacking her were both predictable reactions, ones that Carmen had expected and didn't let rattle her. "Undetected errors and unquestioned assumptions," Carmen said. "That's what I'm warning of."

"That's exactly—!"

"All right." Hofer wasn't a large or physically dominating man, but he'd learned to use his voice to accomplish the same purpose. He leaned forward, resting his elbows on the desk. "If I understand your concern, Citizen Ochoa, it's that you think the entire concept of the IIS is a mistake."

"Yes, sir."

"But you realize as well as anyone that Kosatka has extremely limited resources." Hofer paused, his eyes clouded with unpleasant thoughts. "I have to constantly balance what goes where, and there's never enough. The IIS eliminates duplication and waste, doesn't it?"

"My argument, sir," Carmen said, "is that in this case, the efficiencies created by combining everything into one service controlled by one individual could well lead to far greater costs to Kosatka than any extra spending required for an independent check on the intelligence you and other decision makers are provided." At times like this she was grateful for the practice in diplomatic speech her time at the Earth government offices in Albuquerque had provided.

"That is an accusation and a personal attack on me," Jayne Redman insisted.

"It is not," Carmen said, sure that she'd phrased her words to avoid justifying Redman's claim. "First Minister, no one in a free system of government should operate without independent oversight. People are entrusted with power, but they are never trusted to use that power without someone else watching them. That is a principle enshrined in the ideals of Earth government. I have personally seen, on Mars, what happens when powerful people do not have independent checks on their actions."

Hofer frowned again, this time plainly uncomfortable with her words. "That is tantamount to a warning that Citizen Redman will misuse her authority. I'd need to see some examples of such a thing before making any decision."

Carmen sighed to cover her nervousness as the vital moment

approached. "First Minister, one of the serious flaws with the IIS is that any such examples would be known only to the IIS. How would you ever know if their powers had been abused? Fortunately, I can provide an example of what I'm concerned about. Sir, did you tell Citizen Redman that I'd be meeting with you?"

"No."

"Yet she appeared in your outer office a few minutes before the meeting, insisting that she should also be present."

Redman, suddenly realizing what Carmen had done, hesitated before speaking quickly. "I didn't know—"

"Palmer can tell you what was said, First Minister."

Hofer's frown deepened considerably as he realized the meaning behind Carmen's words. "Did Palmer notify you of the meeting?" he asked Redman.

Redman hesitated again. "I . . ."

"He did not," Carmen said. "I asked. Citizen Palmer entered the information about the meeting in your private schedule, and in about half an hour, before the time of the meeting, Citizen Redman arrived saying she was there to join the meeting."

Hofer's frown was now directed exclusively at Jayne Redman. "My private schedule. How were you aware of the change in that schedule without being notified, Citizen Redman?"

Carmen waited, watching Redman, who had recovered her balance enough to frown slightly as if puzzled.

"I received an update. I'll look into how that information was acquired," Redman said.

"You'll look into how you or someone else in IIS immediately knew of a change to the First Minister's private schedule?" Carmen asked. "Are you saying you're unaware that the IIS has been reading the First Minister's mail?"

It was the sort of question that the head of the IIS couldn't answer either yes or no to without getting into trouble. Backed into a corner, Redman shifted her approach even as she cast Carmen a look that promised a dire fate. "Monitoring the expected movements of the First Minister is a vital component in ensuring his security. We have to be sure anywhere he goes is safe before he gets there, and ensure anyone he plans to meet with is not . . . dangerous."

"Citizen Redman," Hofer said, his voice harsh, "I thought I had clearly stated that my private scheduling information should not be shared beyond my personal security detail."

"First Minister, your safety—"

"My safety is the responsibility of the Public Security Coordinator. Does he know you're monitoring my private schedule and intruding on his work? Should I call him in and ask?"

Redman paused. "Sir, you approved consolidating intelligence resources formerly scattered throughout Public Security—"

"I didn't approve changing their tasking! I made my wishes clear, those wishes were disregarded, and if not for this incident I'd never have known." Hofer sat back, still frowning. "This does illustrate the point that Citizen Ochoa is making. It's a concern our own history back on Old Earth should have warned us of, where autocratic governments gathered information on anything they pleased. There's no longer anyone outside the IIS who could have told me the IIS was monitoring my future schedule despite my clearly stated wishes to the contrary. If not for this meeting . . ." Hofer paused this time, his frown slowly shifting into an appraising gaze as he looked over at Carmen.

She kept a straight face as she nodded once in reply to the unspoken comment.

"First Minister—" Redman began.

"I'll discuss this matter further with the Public Security Coordinator," Hofer said, his tone making it clear that this meeting was over. "And, Citizen Redman, I want any taps on my private schedule to cease immediately. Is that clear?"

"Yes, First Minister. I deeply regret any misunderstanding that led to inadvertent—"

"Yes, yes." Hofer waved off Redman's words and not-really-an-apology. "Thank you for stopping by, Citizen Ochoa. You've always been an invaluable aid to Kosatka. Will you be in Lodz for long?"

"I was going to surprise Dominic and then head back to Ani first thing tomorrow," Carmen said.

"Please give my best wishes to your husband!"

As soon as the door closed behind them, Jayne Redman blocked Carmen from walking farther. "I underestimated you," Redman said, her gaze boring into Carmen.

Carmen smiled slightly in reply. "People do that."

"I won't make the same mistake again. Next time we fight, you'll lose."

"That's your problem, isn't it?" Carmen heard how cold her voice had gone, and wondered how her face looked as Redman stared at her. "You think I'm the enemy. You want to fight *me*. You claim to be able to control all of the intelligence assets on Kosatka, and you don't even know that the enemy is in Ani, not in this room. You're not really focused on fighting the people who threaten us, but on fighting anyone who threatens the little bureaucratic empire you're striving to create. That's not acceptable in my book."

Jayne Redman inhaled sharply before replying. "How dare you threaten me."

"You think that was a threat?" Carmen leaned in a little closer, her eyes fixed on Redman's. "This is a threat. If I decide you're a danger to the future of Kosatka, that you're harming our efforts to defend this world and keep it free and safe, I will deal with you."

"You're nothing but a Red!" Redman spat the last word, giving it all the force of the ugly insult it was back on Old Earth.

"That's right," Carmen said. She smiled, seeing how that rattled Redman. "I love Kosatka, but I grew up on Mars. Deep down inside, I'll always be a Red. You should remember that if ever you get the urge to once again threaten *me*."

Redman turned and walked out, her back stiff.

"Always nice to see you," Palmer said as Carmen walked past his desk. "Don't be a stranger."

"I've been sort of busy," Carmen said.

"Yes." Palmer cast a speculative eye in the direction that Redman had gone. "Does she realize that you saved the life of the First Minister soon after you arrived on Kosatka?"

"I imagine she bothered to find out about that before this meeting, yes."

"I wonder why she still tried to undercut you so blatantly."

Carmen smiled, though the expression held no humor. "Jayne Redman came here from Old Earth, where people from Mars are looked down upon. To her, I'm a Red, and that's all I am. Anything I accomplish is luck, or should be credited to someone else, or is part of a small-time plot to further my own petty criminal desires."

"I see." Palmer nodded. "I've always thought that the oddest thing about prejudice is that it causes those who adhere to it to underestimate the abilities of the people they fear."

"That doesn't seem very smart, does it?" Carmen said. "I wonder how many times in history that sort of thing has bitten people in the butt? Oh, do you know if there's an official file on Brigit Kelly?"

"I'm sure there is," Palmer said. "Since she's the representative of another star system."

"Any chance I can get a copy?"

"For what purpose?"

"You know perfectly well for what purpose! Lochan and I have been looking out for each other since before we even got to Kosatka. I just want to make sure this Brigit person can be trusted with him. Lochan is . . . important to Kosatka."

Palmer looked as if he were thinking it over. "As long as the purpose is related to the security of Kosatka—"

"Yes. That. Absolutely."

"And not some sisterly-like interest in protecting Nakamura—"

"How could you think such a thing?"

"Then I'll see what I can do."

"Thanks." As she left the building, Carmen looked up, wondering how Lochan Nakamura was doing.

L ochan pressed the palms of his hands against his eyes, trying to block a headache that kept threatening to turn into a migraine. "Why are we arguing over trivia when lives are on the line? My home is under attack! It's as if a neighbor's house is burning down, and instead of rushing to put out the fire we're all debating what to call the person who's going to hold the hose."

"I'm tempted to just say Catalan agrees to everything so we can get moving," Freya said. "Except that I know Catalan would reject that out of hand. No one trusts anyone."

They were sitting in two chairs at a circular table in a secure conference room whose walls, bare but for a star chart of this region of space, spoke to its serious purpose. Four other chairs at the table sat empty at the moment as the other star system representatives took a break. Lochan looked over at Freya and saw the lines on her face born of weariness and worry. "Even if we both said we agreed to everything, Eire, Benten, and Adowa would probably start arguing about what 'agree' means." Lochan shook his head, looking at the chairs the others would once more soon occupy. "It's like when I was talking to a lawyer once. We were speaking the exact same language, I thought. But then I suddenly realized that while we were using the same words, I thought the words meant different things than the lawyer did. Using the same words just concealed the fact that the language was in many ways different."

"Maybe that's an idea," Freya said. "Let the different star systems use the words they want, and footnote every one to say the meaning of the words or phrases will be subject to future clarification."

Lochan paused, thinking. "Could we do that?"

"You mean, for serious?" Freya hesitated. "Maybe we could. I think Eire and Benten are itching for reasons to get going, and Adowa wants to have reasons to be part of it but doesn't trust what the rest of us might be trying to get them to agree to. If we say this is just a preliminary agreement whose exact terms are, um, subject to future refinement, maybe that'll give everyone the cover they need to say yes right now."

"Would your father buy that?"

"Of course he would. It gives him a chance to mess with everybody else for a long time over the exact meaning of something like *debhrioch*."

"*Devf-ree-ah?*"

"It means ambiguous," Freya explained with a grin.

"Okay." Lochan looked upward, his thoughts far beyond the ceiling. "How soon do you think one of those warships could go help if Eire agrees?"

"If I know my father, he's got one ready to go, just so he can jump whichever way he wants when he wants." Freya sighed as the other negotiators returned. "Let's try again to convince these others to act now while there's still a chance to help your world, and play with the meanings of words later."

Half an hour later, though, the others were still balking. "The problem is," Lawrence Sato remarked, "that while those of you representing Catalan, Kosatka, and Glenlyon were sent to reach some sort of military assistance agreement, we from Benten were not. You see how that limits what we can agree to."

"And there is no greater matter than the sending of warships to fight," Yukino Nakamura added.

"This is my problem as well," Ato Elias said. "Adowa empowered me to discuss trade matters, not matters of war."

"War has a major impact on trade," Freya said. "I've shown you all how my home star system is being choked by what amounts to a blockade. The same will happen to your own star systems in time."

"We don't dispute that," Lawrence said. "But at this time we can't commit Benten to matters beyond the authority we were given."

"At this time lives are being lost!"

"I took a risk for you," Lochan said. "Joining the fate of my mission to yours so you could be heard. Try to imagine my position. And Freya's. Catalan is surrounded by hostile star systems. For all we know her home has also come under attack by now."

"If we make a commitment that we know Benten will not honor," Lawrence said, "we would be doing nothing, only pretending to help!"

Lochan sat back, grimacing. "Am I right that we all want to do something that will benefit us all? All that's holding us back is . . . what to call it! An action that your worlds will see as in their interests as well as those of Kosatka, Glenlyon, and Catalan."

Colonel Patrick Ryan, appointed to be Eire's representative to the discussions and not appearing the least bit happy about that, drummed the fingers of one hand on the table. "If it's the right words you're looking for, the term 'self-defense' covers a lot of ground, doesn't it?"

"Sending our only warship many light years to fight an enemy seems to stretch the definition of self-defense," Yukino said.

"A light year is a long way," Ryan said. "Yet, strangely, war seems close when it's hitting star systems light years away but not that far off in terms of travel time." He leaned forward, giving the others a stern look. "Like the rest of you, we've no wish to surrender a hint of sovereignty to anyone else. But the war is here. Eire has already been attacked. Low-level strikes such as the destruction of a shuttle, but the intent is clear. Which means war is not that far from your homes, either. Eire has already decided on what measures it will take. It's up to the rest of you whether you're playing as well or watching from the side."

"What measures are you speaking of, Pat?" Freya asked him. "Can you tell us? Has the old one already decided to send one of Eire's destroyers to help others?"

"To defend Eire," Ryan said. "And to defend the trade interests of Eire. He'll send both."

Momentary silence fell.

"Both?" Lochan said, wondering why he wasn't feeling elated at the news.

"What is it?" Freya said. "Something's bothering you, Lochan."

"Yes," he said, trying to nail down that elusive feeling. Two warships from Eire arriving at Kosatka. Surely they'd be greeted joyously. Or would they?

"I know what you're thinking," Elias said. "Because it's what Adowa would think. Why are these so-called friends here? To drive off these other enemies perhaps. But what then? What prevents the liberators from becoming a new set of overlords when they control all space in your star system?"

"Eire's offer is meant generously," Ryan said, looking affronted.

"But you know what concern I speak of," Elias said.

Patrick Ryan paused a moment, before nodding. "Yes. All of us or our ancestors came from Old Earth, where history is full of wars in which countries simply traded one foreign master for another."

"That didn't always happen, though," Lochan said. "Sometimes the countries that freed others didn't try to maintain control afterward."

"Sometimes," Elias said, letting the single word carry a wealth of meaning.

"And now that history threatens to bind our hands," Lawrence said. "What rules our decisions? Fear of the worst that has happened, or hope for the best?"

"We came out here for hope, didn't we?" Lochan said, deciding that turning down Eire's offer would be foolish. Donal Morgan was no saint, but Eire had nothing in common with the star systems that had attacked Kosatka. "So let's commit to hope. Let's say anything we agree to here is bound to a basic foundation that all star systems should be free, and any actions against any other star system in this . . . uh . . . alliance are prohibited unless that star system violates that principle."

"Would Kosatka take that as sufficient protection against conquest by supposed friends?" Elias asked.

Lochan took a moment to answer, aware that his reply would carry a lot of weight. "Yes. There's a basic reality we can't escape. That I can't escape. I'm representing Kosatka, and Glenlyon. They're a test case, right? A test of trust. If forces are sent to aid Kosatka and Glenlyon, and then stay on to themselves try to conquer those star systems, from what I know neither Kosatka nor Glenlyon will have the means to resist. If I agree to your worlds sending assistance, I am risking that. The government of Kosatka that sent me here knew I'd have to take such a chance, and because of our extreme duress left that decision up to me."

He paused, thinking, looking at the surface of the table, the polished wood smooth and bright. "If I'm wrong, the best I can hope to be remembered as is a fool. At worst I'll be labeled a traitor. But . . . Freya is somewhat aware of my past, before I came to Kosatka." Lochan looked up at the others. "I failed at a lot of things. But I learned something very important from those failures. When you're in great need of help and someone eagerly offers everything you could ask for, there's a good chance they're out to take advantage of your need. But if you need help, and those who can help seek to find ways to do it but also express real concerns and reluctance, they probably do want to help you, not themselves."

Freya nodded. "As those of us here are approaching this. We're all reluctant to agree to what seems the best course of action."

"For good reason," Lawrence said. "It was the same for all of us, wasn't it? Leave Old Earth or one of the Old Colonies, and also leave behind the ills that have plagued us in the past. Why did we think we could? Has anywhere humanity been ever known only peace? No place has been immune to troubles. Back on Old Earth, Canada was hailed as one of the quietest, nicest places on the planet, and even Canada had the Clown Riots."

"Did you have to mention those?" Freya asked. "Now my dreams tonight will be troubled. But, I think there's an important point there. Those who have sought to impose their will on others have often done so in the name of peace and law and order, arguing that freedom must be given up to accomplish those aims. We know that's false. That's why we balk at giving up even a little of our freedom even when we see danger at our doors. But perhaps we should be thinking of it as if all of us were in a fight, and standing back-to-back to protect each other. We'd have given up some freedom of movement, but nothing that matters compared to knowing we can't be stabbed in the back."

"There is truth there," Lawrence said. "Let me discuss this in private with my colleague." He and Yukino Nakamura stood up, going to one side of the room to speak very quietly to each other.

"Pat," Freya said, beckoning to Eire's representative. Patrick Ryan stood as well, coming over beside her. "I've an idea."

Ryan stopped by her seat. "Let's hear it, then. If you want this one to hear it as well," he added, gesturing toward Lochan.

"I can move," Lochan said, beginning to get up.

"No," Freya said. "I want you to know what I'm advising." She glanced at Ato Elias, who was pretending to be unaware of what the others were doing as he checked data on his personal pad, before lowering her voice to a whisper. "Pat, I know what game my father is playing. He sees this happening, and if it does, he wants Eire to have bragging rights as the biggest wolf in the pack. That's why he's sending both of Eire's warships."

"You're only part right," Ryan said. "I'm sure he also wants to be certain the effort succeeds. He wants Eire to get credit for being part of a victorious force, not tagged as having participated in a failure."

"Ah," Freya said, nodding. "I'm sure you have the right of that. But as you see, Benten is balking. If the old one really wants this to happen, I know of a way to get Benten to agree."

"And what would that be?" Patrick Ryan asked with a skeptical glance at Lochan.

"Offer to place Benten's ship in command of the force. Put Eire's two destroyers under the combat authority of *Asahi*'s captain."

Ryan frowned. "That's a big step to take."

"A big step that speaks of confidence," Freya said. "Of Eire having such a big heart and such a strong heart that it does not fear to place its forces under the command of another, trusted, friend. A trusted friend who will, naturally enough, feel obligated to repay that trust at some future time, and in the current circumstances feel a need to match the generosity of Eire. And how to match that generosity except by agreeing to send their ship to this fight?"

"That's so," Ryan said, nodding. "Clever. You really are Donal Morgan's daughter, aren't you? Why'd you leave Eire, Freya?"

"Because I'm his daughter. Eire couldn't hold both of us."

This time Ryan laughed. "There's truth. All right. I'll ask the old one." He hesitated, though, appearing uncertain. "Freya, why'd your brother leave? The same reason? Too much like his old man?"

Freya looked away, her jaw tight, finally shaking her head. "No. Marcus never stopped thinking he was smarter by far than our father."

"Don't we all go through that phase? Most outgrow that, though," Ryan said.

"Most do. Marcus didn't." Freya shifted her gaze back to him, glancing at Lochan as well. "He always had to be the smartest. In his own eyes. Every failure was the fault of others. Never his own."

"That's one flaw I eventually outgrew," Lochan said.

"Lucky you were smart enough to avoid a dire fate before then. When I warned my brother about taking employment with that colony group heading far into the dark to get away from what they called government interference, he boasted that he expected them not to live up to their promises, but that mattered not, because he would be on top of one of those corporations within a few years. Then he'd be the one able to do whatever he wanted, with no interference, and he'd finally show the hosts of humanity what he could do."

"That eejit." Ryan shook his head slowly, like someone viewing the aftermath of an awful accident. "How'd he make it far enough in life to make that big a mistake?"

"The old one bailed him out," Freya said. "More than once. Marcus was his son and the baby of the family. If Mum had lived, I think she'd have laid down the law on him, but when we lost her, Marcus probably lost his chance to get hit upside the head hard enough for reality to intrude on his illusions."

"He'll get that hit now, I'm guessing. And I suppose it's one he earned, but I still feel sorry for him, wherever he ended up among the stars."

Freya looked over and up toward the ceiling. "Him and those with him. Some were doubtless desperate, seeking a way to make a life and a future. Others perhaps foolish, and still others greedy or true believers in everyone for himself. But what of their children? And their children's children? They chose a fate for themselves, but their descendants will live with that choice. We increasingly praise our ancestors these days, but I wonder if someday those whose ancestors took the path like that of my brother will curse those who put them there."

"I'm determined that my descendants will have no cause to curse me for anything other than their looks," Ryan said, nodding to her once more. "I'll go talk to the prime minister."

In orbit well above where Lochan, Freya, and the others sat debating the meaning of words and the symbolism of actions, Commander Bard Hubbard paused on the way to the bridge of the destroyer once named the *Jose Silva* in Earth Fleet. Now the ship was the *Caladbolg*, and she and her officers and crew followed the orders of the government of Eire. When the *Jose Silva* was decommissioned as part of the general shutdown of Earth Fleet, it hadn't been a hard decision to accept an offer of employment from a far-off new colony. Jobs weren't easy to find on tired, crowded Old Earth, especially in specialties like those of fleet sailors, whereas places such as Eire promised new worlds, fresh air and land and water, and countless opportunities for the future.

No, it hadn't been a difficult decision to come out here and bring his family with him to live on the beautiful, green world the *Caladbolg* orbited. Even at times like this when the government of Eire was demanding the destroyer be ready for instant action, but not betray any signs of being ready for instant action.

He'd spoken a few times with Commander Miko Sori on Benten's destroyer *Asahi*, catching up on personal as well as professional matters. Even though they'd known each other in Earth Fleet, she hadn't revealed much of whatever her orders were, but he had the sense her ship had also recently been told to be ready for anything.

It had something to do with the battles raging deeper into space, Hubbard guessed. He wondered if his ship would finally see the combat it had been designed for. The idea both excited and worried him, because for all the confidence he had in his crew, he knew all too well how easily even the simplest things could go wrong.

"Captain Hubbard, please contact the bridge."

Hubbard tapped the nearest wall comm. "What's up?"

"Sir, the Chief Engineer wanted us to inform you that a major software update for the power core is being uploaded. She's not anticipating any problems but there may be some minor power fluctuations."

"Understood," Hubbard said. "Keep me informed if—"

An alarm blared, cutting off his last words. *Caladbolg* shuddered as pumps, fans, and other equipment abruptly jolted all over the ship. Hubbard heard the subsiding whine of fans shutting down and knew circuit breakers had tripped. "Bridge! What the hell's going on?"

"Major power core fluctuations, sir! Chief Engineer thinks the software was sabotaged! She's initiating emergency manual shutdown!"

Hubbard heard another sound, a vibration running through the structure of his ship like the spasms of a badly wounded animal. The power core, running out of control. If the Chief Engineer didn't manage a shutdown within the next few seconds, *Caladbolg* and her entire crew would die a spectacular death.

CHAPTER 7

Under the light of Glenlyon's star, the barracuda shape of the destroyer *Saber* moved through space a mere light second from the three enemy ships heading for the planet's orbital facility. The enemy ships would reach that facility in two more hours. And *Saber* couldn't stop them.

"We managed to trick the enemy light cruiser into expending three of its four missiles, but that's all we could do," Rob Geary said. He was in his stateroom, sending a private update to the government on a situation that he couldn't change for the better but could easily make even worse. "We've run all feasible attacks through simulations. Under every possible outcome we might manage to score some damage on the freighter, but the odds of causing enough damage to prevent it from continuing on are extremely small. Measured against that, *Saber* would take fire from both enemy warships, and would almost certainly suffer serious damage as a result. If *Saber* is eliminated, the enemy warships could remain at Glenlyon indefinitely, receiving new supplies of fuel cells and food. If *Saber* remains a threat, we can prevent any resupply from being carried out. The only way to maintain the chance of a better outcome is to avoid combat at this time, await a possible mistake by the enemy, and hope that our defenders on the orbital facility can hold out until the enemy is forced to withdraw in order to resupply. I make this decision with great difficulty, but it is the only decision I believe offers any hope under the current circumstances." Rob hesitated. "If ordered to attack regardless, I will do so, but I must be sure the government understands the very small chance of success and the very high probability that will result in the loss of *Saber* and the loss of any chance to save our orbital facility. Pending further orders I will maintain my ship close enough to the enemy warships to hinder their freedom of action and to be able to strike if a favorable opportunity arises. Geary, out."

The message ended, he sat back, staring at the tangle of conduits, ducts, and wiring attached to the overhead.

The ping announcing the arrival of an incoming message broke through his dark thoughts.

Ninja gazed out of his display, looking haggard and doing nothing for his peace of mind. "Hey, love. Not a lot of progress yet. The bad guys are staying tight, not offering me any new openings. That's going to change once they start assaulting the orbital facility. They'll have to start firing up a lot of networks then, and that'll give me the shots I need."

His wife grimaced. "We're doing okay down here. Hiding in the woods like we were kids playing Robin Hood. The kids think that's great. The teens are old enough to know how serious the game is, though, and they've been stepping up. Little Ninja is doing fine. She thinks it's the best camping trip ever, especially since I told her she gets to play sys admin and jump on anyone using anything but landline links."

Despite everything, Rob smiled. Trust Ninja to teach their little girl to monitor system security. Little Ninja was already probably better at it than most of the adult hackers on the planet.

"Rob, I know you're going to think of some crazy idea to save the day. Don't do it." Lyn sighed, shaking her head. "We need you. So . . . come home safe. See you later. Bye for now."

That was depressing.

"Captain?" Lieutenant Commander Vicki Shen stuck her head around the corner of the hatch. "Anything new?"

"No," Rob said. "Just some personal mail. How's the crew doing?"

"Same as before. Itching to do something, despite knowing it'd be suicide." Shen leaned against the side of the hatch. "Don't worry about that. I'm the executive officer, so I get to tell the crew they have to keep working and not have any fun."

"Just out of curiosity, what's Earth Fleet doctrine in this situation?"

"You're doing it," she said.

"I am? Seriously?" In Rob's experience, Earth Fleet doctrine had been both rigid and rarely useful in any practical circumstances.

"Yeah." Shen jogged her head in the general direction of the enemy. "We can't win if we exchange fire with those guys, so Earth Fleet doctrine would call for avoiding such a fight and waiting until the enemy is either forced to retire or reinforcements arrive to help you out. Captain, I know just hanging here in the same relative position while they close on Glenlyon is tough, but we've done what we can. You know that if we burn through our fuel cells making more feints at them in the hopes they'll react in a really stupid way, we'll run out of fuel before they do. And then our people on that facility won't have any chance at all."

Rob brought up an outside image on his display. At a light second's distance, or about three hundred thousand kilometers, the three enemy warships were just tiny dots on an unmagnified view. They were still on a curving path through the star system, heading for an intercept with the planet Glenlyon as it swept in orbit about its star. "Even if we win," he murmured, "I'm going to be the guy who didn't do anything while the enemy ships attacked the orbital facility."

"Sir?" Shen shook her head. "You're doing the right thing. The *only* right thing. Anything else would be a mistake."

"That's not how it'll look, is it?" Rob exhaled heavily. "I wonder how many commanders in similar circumstances throughout history have staged a hopeless attack simply to show they were doing something? Because it would make them look better, even though what they were doing would make things worse?"

"You're not going to—"

"No," Rob assured his executive officer. "I'm not going to sacrifice *Saber* and her crew and Glenlyon's chance of winning this fight just to make myself look better. But I never realized how hard something like this could be, to have to sit and wait, knowing how that'll look to everyone who *doesn't* have the responsibility that I have."

Shen frowned, running one hand through her hair. "Every officer on this ship will testify that you did the only thing that could've saved the situation."

"That won't matter," Rob said. "Thanks, though."

"It's not right that you have to choose between sacrificing yourself and your career or failing in your duty!" Vicki Shen looked away, her jaw tight. "If some important equipment breaks, you wouldn't be able to attack no matter how much you wanted to."

"Giving me a perfect excuse for not acting that everyone could understand? No," Rob said. "We're not going to fake that. Everything I'm doing now is right and legal. Lying about the material state of the ship would be misconduct. This is my job. My responsibility. I'm going to accept whatever consequences come from doing what I should do."

She didn't answer for several seconds, her gaze still averted. "Are you trying to get fired?"

After Shen had left, Rob stared at his display. Was he trying to get fired? This wasn't a job he wanted, after all. He hated having lives riding on his decisions. He hated being away from his family while they faced danger.

But he wasn't doing anything wrong. He was doing this damned job as best he could. He was trying to salvage a nearly hopeless situation, knowing that he'd probably get a medal for doing any number of wrong things, and probably catch hell for doing what seemed the only right thing.

If they wanted to fire him for that he could walk off this ship with a clear conscience.

Yet as Rob looked at the enemy ships closing steadily on their intercept with the world of Glenlyon and its orbital facility, he didn't feel either right or happy. Angry, frustrated, impotent. All those. But not happy with the only choice he felt he could make and still keep faith with those he commanded and his own duty.

The light of the sun that shone on the world of Kosatka felt blinding to Carmen Ochoa after so many days spent in inner rooms, venturing forth only in the dark. The last time she'd spent any time outside during the day had been during her visit to see the First Minister, and even most of that trip had involved being indoors either with the First Minister or later with Dominic. The idea that she'd become a creature of the night both amused and upset her.

Being out during the day did remind her of that trip, though. Of the long periods in which she and Domi had avoided asking each other questions whose answers were likely to be unpleasant. He'd heard the rumors about men and women with prosthetics being sent into combat, and though he laughed off the way he'd jumped up the priority list for a new leg, Carmen had seen the anger and worries that Dominic tried to hide. She'd gone back to Ani more determined to bring about an end to the fighting there, but had no idea how to get that done any faster without spending the lives of others who like Dominic had those who loved them.

But despite the discomfort the sunlight brought, Carmen had no choice but to be out in it. The high-priority summons from General Edelman had demanded her immediate presence, and parts of the journey to his headquarters had to be made outside due to cave-ins and mines or booby traps planted by both sides in belowground passages intended for transit and maintenance. Avoiding roads and streets where she'd be easy to spot, Carmen slunk through bright sunlight that illuminated tall weeds in courtyards and alleys where the only sign of human presence was the dirt trails wending through the underbrush. In the never-occupied city of Ani, humans lived like rats, and weeds flourished along with real rats.

Someday it would be different. Someday people would live here in peace.

The rodents making up most of the population of Ani these days weren't technically real rats. Humanity hadn't brought that life-form with them, and hadn't had to bring it. Every world that developed its own life and ecology had also evolved things that filled the role of a rat. On every such planet people called them rats, to the despair of bioscientists who had given each species its own highly specific name that usually included some variation on *pseudorattus*.

What hadn't been found anywhere humanity had yet gone were any traces of another intelligent species on a par with humans. The reasons for this were being hotly debated, with some saying it was proof of how special an intelligent species was, and others pointing out that it could simply mean that worlds needed rats much more than they needed something like humans. Tied in with those debates were theories that missing deep space exploration missions might have been victims of peaceful aliens wishing to remain undiscovered by the likes of human beings.

As Carmen cautiously picked her way along the last portions of her route through the empty, war-torn city, she thought that last theory might have some merit.

On the other hand, she had long ago realized the possibility that, just as rats everywhere were basically rats, other intelligent species might be as dangerous as humans.

But maybe there were friends out there. Or at least someone

humans could live with. It was a very big galaxy, one that humanity had barely explored a tiny fraction of so far.

She paused before making the final move toward the building holding the command center, carefully looking over the area. A series of paths shielded from the sun (and observers) by lightweight panels, which had been whimsically designed to look like very large cards being scattered by the wind, had so far survived the fighting and offered covered routes to her destination. Someone had chosen this location well. From the outside, the building appeared to be completely unoccupied, just another multiuse structure that had been empty since it was built.

She made the last stretch moving quickly, but not so fast that she seemed to be rushing the place. Someone in that building would be watching her approach, and Carmen didn't want to look like an attacker.

It wasn't until Carmen was inside the entrance that she saw the sentries with weapons aimed at her. Any enemy going from the bright day to the dim interior would lose a precious few seconds while their eyes adjusted and their bodies stood out sharply against the day behind them. Most of the soldiers fighting for Kosatka were amateurs called to defend their world, but those who'd survived this long had learned their lessons the hard way, and they'd learned them quickly.

Carmen waited patiently as her identity was confirmed, then followed the guards' directions through a maintenance door and to an access stairway heading down. As she took the steps, Carmen saw portable sensors stuck on the walls, scanning everyone who passed.

Another sentry stood by the door at the bottom of the stairs. "I was ordered to report to General Edelman," Carmen told her. She'd never actually met the officer in charge of retaking Ani, though she had participated in a number of remote conferences in which Edelman had been present. That made it easy to recognize the general when she was directed his way.

The lights strung up on the ceiling of the underground command center lacked the glare of the sun, being set dim enough not to hinder reading displays. The command center still looked mostly like the sub-surface parking garage it had been intended as, with bare walls of gray neocrete and broad, unadorned structural pillars standing at regular intervals. Displays had been mounted on two walls, and other equipment set on desks that looked like they'd been looted from a college or high school, bundles of fiber-optic lines and solar-linked power lines snaking across the dusty floor and out doorways like the roots of some bizarre plant grown from the manufactured devices of humanity.

General Edelman, a man past middle age who'd been a major in an Old Earth military, greeted Carmen. "Ochoa. Good. We're going to need you. You used to work in Earth gov, right? Conflict Resolution Office?"

Carmen nodded. "That was a while ago."

"I assume you remember a few things about negotiations. You know the military situation in and around Ani as well as I do." Edelman smiled. "Perhaps better than I do. I greatly value the intelligence reports and assessments from you that I've received. You've been saying the enemy situation is desperate, that they may crack at any time. You know that older and wiser heads back in Lodz disagree with that. They believe that the enemy will continue fighting for all they're worth until the last one is dead."

"Yes, sir," Carmen said, wondering if she'd been called in to justify her judgment in person. Hadn't Edelman agreed with her? "I've been made aware that my assessment differs from that of the IIS. But I stand by it. Most of our opponents aren't elite troops fighting for a cause they believe in. And the ones who are so highly motivated are also the ones who've been fighting the hardest and dying at the highest rate as we keep shrinking the area held by the enemy."

"The IIS is very unhappy with you."

"Yes, sir," Carmen repeated. Was she about to be raked over the coals? "But I need to inform you of what I believe the evidence here at the front shows."

General Edelman grinned at her. "As it turns out, your assessment has been proven right. We've been contacted by two leaders of the enemy forces who want to discuss surrender. Good job sticking to your guns, Citizen Ochoa."

"Thank you," Carmen said, trying not to look relieved. "I appreciate you backing me up and giving me a position on your staff to protect me."

"That's my job, isn't it? Now, your job is this. I want you observing while we negotiate with those two commanders, and assist in working out a deal if we can. Beyond that I expect you to speak up at any time if you see something I need to know about."

"I'll do what I can," Carmen promised.

"I know." Edelman smiled. "Back on Earth, I saw your name on some of the messages that resolved a border dispute going back a thousand years."

"I actually did some good?" Carmen asked.

"Yes. There, and here. You also have some experience on Mars, I understand."

She nodded again to give herself time to phrase her answer carefully. "I'm a Red, General."

"Did you think that was a secret from anyone?" He smiled again, surprising her. "I've never trusted any way of placing humans into categories based on where they're from or what their ancestry is. It divides all of us into our little boxes, doesn't it? But humans aren't made to fit into boxes. What matters with you is the work you've done up until now, and that is why I want you here for this."

"Yes, General." Pleased to know that she'd earned his trust, Carmen followed General Edelman to a side passage, where they met a dozen other officers. The general stopped, facing one wall where a display had been set up. Those viewing the command group that Carmen was now part of would see nothing else but a bare wall behind them that would offer no clue to their location.

Carmen stood behind and to one side of Edelman. Not certain what to do with her rifle, she rested the butt of the weapon on her foot, canting the barrel to one side as it pointed toward the ceiling. She didn't feel like a diplomat, and not quite like an intelligence officer, either. But, despite the sentiments of General Edelman, she also wasn't like the others gathered here. Carmen felt as if Kosatka was home now, the sort of home she'd never had before, but this morning she didn't feel like everyone else. Maybe she never would.

The display activated. Carmen saw a man and a woman, both wearing the sort of nondescript camouflage fatigues that could have marked soldiers from just about anywhere in human-occupied space. Neither wore any kind of rank insignia, or any identifying patches indicating their allegiance. But she saw a small tattoo on the woman, just beneath the left ear, that Carmen recognized. She fought down a wave of hatred at the sight. That woman had been one of those feeding off the misery of countless other inhabitants of Mars. "General," she said before the call was accepted, "that woman has the tattoo of an executive in one of the cartels that control the businesses that exist on Mars. She must be in charge of many if not all of the Reds recruited to serve with the invaders."

"It's a small tattoo," a colonel observed. "Does that mean she's a minor executive?"

"No," Carmen said. "The saying on Mars is 'the bigger the dog, the smaller the tattoo.' It's a way for the elite to boast that they don't need to try impressing anyone with large tattoo displays. The highest of the warlords, gang leaders, and cartel bosses only have a single mark tattooed on one earlobe."

"Then this person is of high rank despite her lack of insignia?" Edelman asked Carmen.

"Yes, General."

Another staff officer chimed in. "From the way they're standing, the man is of roughly equal rank to her. Neither one is displaying dominance over the other."

"All right. Accept the call." An officer tapped the command, and the call went live and real time. "I understand you have an offer to make. Talk to me," General Edelman told the two without any polite exchange of greetings.

The man spoke with a formal cadence that betrayed his own origins with some Old Earth or Old Colony military. "We are prepared to surrender our forces in exchange for certain guarantees."

"You're in command of all of the invading forces?" Edelman demanded.

"Yes."

Carmen had spotted the barest hesitation before that reply and saw the way the woman's eyes looked slightly aside. "That's not true," she said, drawing measured looks. "They're throwing dust at their own."

That statement brought the attention of the woman executive fully on Carmen. "Throwing dust at their own" was a distinctly Martian term for betraying your own side, born of the way the ever-present red dust of Mars could be used to blind anyone and cover secretive movements.

Edelman nodded once in reply to Carmen before turning a flat look back on the enemy officers. "I'll ask again, and if the response this time doesn't satisfy me this negotiation will be over. Are you in command of all of the invading forces?"

The enemy officer aimed an angry gaze at Carmen as he replied. "Between us we command more than three-quarters of the remaining forces, *and* control all of the remaining ammunition stockpiles and power supply reserves. If we surrender our troops, you won't have any trouble finishing off what remains."

"What are your terms?"

"Freedom and safe passage for ourselves and selected members of our staffs."

General Edelman gazed back at the other for a long moment. "Freedom and safety for you? And the other soldiers, those you are surrendering?"

The man smiled, a thin and humorless expression. "We are sure they will be treated in accordance with the laws of war. We are looking out for them, ensuring they won't die in senseless fighting."

Carmen glanced at the general, but he had obviously picked up on his own the insincerity in those last words.

Edelman grimaced like someone tasting something foul before replying. "When are you willing to surrender?"

"Tomorrow morning."

"Wait." Edelman gestured to an aide who entered a command that caused a "mute" symbol to appear on the display. He and the others turned away from the screen so their faces and lips couldn't be seen as they talked. "They're willing to throw their own soldiers under the bus to save themselves."

One of Edelman's senior assistants scowled. "I hate to see people like that walk away free."

"But . . . ?" the general prompted.

"But," the assistant said reluctantly, "if they surrender their forces and those ammo supplies, we'll be able to roll up the rest quickly. It'll save lives on our side, and prevent having to destroy any more of Kosatka to end this."

"Why are they willing to betray their comrades, though?" another officer wondered.

Carmen answered. "They're mercenaries. They got hired to fight for our enemies, so they're not motivated by any causes or beliefs beyond their own personal profit. That woman is an executive from a Red cartel. She doesn't care about what happens to the people she's in charge of any more than farmers care about what happens to the stalks of grain that they're harvesting and selling. What she does care about is looking out for herself."

"If they're that dishonorable," the first officer to speak suggested, "why can't we agree to their terms and then arrest and try them anyway?"

"Because then," Carmen said, "we'd have let them dictate our actions, let them turn us into the same kind of people they are."

General Edelman nodded. "Exactly. We'd know we did that, and others would hear of it. Who'd trust Kosatka after that?"

"But we shouldn't be expected to honor agreements with people like that!" another protested.

Edelman shook his head, his eyes briefly closing as if with pain. "I suppose not. But if we don't honor agreements with them, why should we be trusted to honor agreements with others? It's all reduced to self-interest, isn't it? But what's the measure of a people? Whether they act honorably toward their friends? Or whether they act honorably toward their enemies? Let me tell you something. I only made major back on Old Earth because I thought there were more important things than pursuing my next promotion. Out here, you made me a general. But I'm still the same man. Until this world decides to demote me again, I'm going to do what I think is right. Because you need that. This is a young world. What we do will form the foundation for all that comes after. And that foundation needs to be one that you can all be proud of. Not like those two, pretending they're doing this to save the lives of their own when all they care about is themselves. No. We're not like those two. That's why we're fighting them."

"But do we have to agree to this deal?" a colonel asked.

General Edelman paused. "I think we must. We don't know how long we have until the next attack comes from Apulu, Scatha, or Turan. The sooner we end this fight, the longer we'll have to prepare for the next one. We must assume there will be another invasion of the world that has become our home. And we must do all we can to assure that invasion is also defeated."

Carmen saw those around the general nod in silent agreement, and realized she was doing the same.

Edelman turned back to face the display and gestured for the sound to be activated again. "Let's talk the specifics of this deal."

Much of what followed was predictable, details of Where and When and How, until the two turncoat commanders both looked at Carmen. "We want a guarantee," the woman from Mars announced.

"Guarantee?" General Edelman asked.

"A hostage," Carmen explained.

"Her," the male enemy commander emphasized, pointing at Carmen. "She proceeds to a designated spot, we meet her there, and she escorts us out. Once we're clear, we'll send the surrender commands to every unit under our control."

Edelman gave Carmen a troubled look. "I can't demand this of you. If anything goes wrong . . ."

"I understand," Carmen said, her eyes on the female Red. "But, as you said, many lives can be saved if this goes through. I won't be the cause for it to fail."

The general frowned before turning a dark look on the two enemy officers. "If anything happens to her, neither of you will leave this world alive."

C armen sat in an isolated corner, breathing slowly, trying to sort through words she didn't want to say. Despite being encouraged to sleep and being given an unusually good dinner that had felt uncomfortably like a last meal, she hadn't gotten much rest. During the negotiations it had become obvious that the enemy forces were splintering, some following the orders of officers who remained loyal to the overall enemy commander, while others were listening to the two who were preparing to surrender. With the enemy forces breaking into factions, an already hazardous mission for her could become even more dangerous. Little wonder she'd had trouble sleeping.

Now morning had come and she could no longer put off what she had to do.

Starting with this. She activated her personal pad, looking into it as she spoke. "Hi, Domi. If you receive this, it'll be because something happened and I didn't survive. I . . . I can't ask you to understand. I saw so much suffering as a child. I'll do anything to stop that from happening again. I have to do what I can, no matter how worried I am. I can't stop trying. I'm sorry. I love you. But I have to do this if I'm to live with myself. I left some eggs frozen, so if the worst happens we can have children still, and hopefully they won't be as stubborn and set on doing what they must as I am. But there have to be good things worth dying for, Domi. Not things worth killing other people over, but things worth our own sacrifices. I won't live believing that what happened to Mars is acceptable. I can't. I hope you never see this message, that I come back and we have a full life together. But if I don't come back, tell our children I did it for them. And for you. I love you."

She ended the recording, breathing deeply. Tagging Dominic Desjani, she set the message to transmit in forty-eight hours if not canceled. Wiping her eyes, Carmen stood, grasped her rifle, and walked through the dimly lit underground garage to where the soldiers waited who would escort her part of the way to the place where she was to meet the enemy commanders.

C armen left her escort in what would've been the lobby of a hotel, and might someday become one. For now, it was a large, open, and bare space with shattered windows looking out on a stretch of what should have been a strip of parkland but was currently a scorched band of bare soil punctuated by the broken stumps of dead saplings.

"This'll be a nice town once it gets rebuilt," Carmen commented to one of the soldiers as she handed over her rifle. "Take care of this for me."

Her escort stayed behind as Carmen stepped outside into the light of morning, her skin crawling with the feeling of unseen weapons aimed at her from the enemy on the other side of the dead parkland. No camouflage or armor protected her, just the fabric of her fatigues. Holding her arms slightly out and her empty hands clearly visible, she walked at a steady pace across the street, through the strip of dirt, and on across the street beyond toward the buildings on the other side. She couldn't see any enemy soldiers in those apparently vacant buildings, but she knew they were there. Knew they were aiming weapons at her.

Carmen concentrated on keeping her breathing slow, deep, and steady, trying to counter the hard and fast beating of her heart. She'd seen what the invaders had done on Kosatka, had seen what those of them from Mars had done on that world. And she was placing herself at their mercy, counting on the good faith of people who were betraying their own comrades.

No, not the good faith of such people. The self-interest they had, the desire to survive the disaster that the invasion of Kosatka had become for these invaders.

"Halt."

Carmen jerked herself to a stop at the command hissed in a low voice. She stood, trying not to let her extended arms shake badly enough for it to be visible.

"Come ahead. Slow and steady."

She found it surprisingly hard to get her feet moving, only her own stubbornness and rising temper countering the instinct for self-preservation that threatened to paralyze her. Carmen walked onward, saw a hand gesture beside a doorway with two shattered doors offering open access, and stepped through.

Inside, a half dozen men and women stared at her like a pack of wolves ready to strike. Their faces bore the marks of too little food for too long and nearly constant stress, wide eyes set amid bones standing out prominently. "Rainbow," Carmen whispered through a throat that suddenly felt very dry.

For a moment she wondered if these enemy soldiers recognized the password she'd been given. This position was supposed to be occupied by soldiers loyal to the two commanders who wanted to surrender, but what if that had changed and she'd just become a prisoner of hard-liners? Carmen's mind was already racing through possible ways to escape when one of the enemy soldiers answered in a whisper, "Mountain."

The countersign. Carmen relaxed a little as an enemy soldier stepped forward, patting her down in a rough search for weapons, while another scanned her with a handheld.

Carmen studied the enemy soldiers who stood back as the search proceeded, their weapons ready for use. Wolves, yes, but wolves who'd been run to the edges of their endurance, whose eyes were those of trapped creatures waiting for the end. She saw the way they watched her in return, both wary and hopeful. Backed into a corner, desperate, wolves could attack someone trying to help them.

Someone like her.

Satisfied that she had no weapons or tracking devices on her, the searchers stepped back and a man with the air of command gestured to Carmen. "Come."

They walked through dark, empty halls inside the building, the sound of their footsteps echoing softly. Carmen guessed at least two of the enemy soldiers were following behind her as she walked in the wake of the man in charge.

One of those guards behind her startled Carmen by calling out to the officer in the lead, "Lieutenant? Who is she again?"

"A guarantee," the lieutenant said, his voice sharp. "The defenders have agreed to let us surrender and promised humane treatment. All we have to do is get her to Alternate Command Center Gamma and turn her over to the brass there."

"But this morning we got another message from the top saying to hold out because reinforcements would be here anytime now."

The lieutenant's voice grew harsher. "Things have changed."

"But—"

"There aren't any reinforcements coming for you," Carmen said, trying to keep her voice calm. "The ships in the invasion fleet you came on were destroyed or captured. Only one warship escaped, and it was badly damaged. Kosatka's warship controls space in this star system. You're alone. No help is coming for you."

"She's lying," the other soldier behind Carmen said.

"No, she's not!" the lieutenant snarled. "We've all been lied to! To hell with Marshal Lopez and his orders. General Idris and Colonel Liu have made a deal with the defenders. We don't have to die here!"

After a pause, one of the soldiers replied in a hushed voice, "I don't want to die here. But what if the Field Marshal hears about this?"

"Or some soldiers who are still listening to his orders," the second soldier said. "What'll we do if we run into somebody like that?"

"Get through them," the lieutenant said, his tone now grim. "We get through them and we get her to Alternate Command Center Gamma. Listen up. I explained this earlier. The chain of command is falling apart. You have to trust *me*. We might run into other people on our side who want to stop us because they're too stupid to see what's happening or too scared of going against orders from Lopez. If we let them stop us, all of us die within another few weeks when our ammo supplies run out and the rest of our positions are overrun. Because the defenders won't have to offer us mercy then. Today we've still got a little leverage, still got a little time. As long as we get this woman to Alternate Command Center Gamma, we'll be okay. Understood?"

"Yes, sir," the two soldiers behind Carmen said.

"If some from our side start shooting at us, shoot back," the lieutenant emphasized. "That's our only chance. From this point on, the enemy is whoever is trying to stop us or kill us."

They left the building through an intact side door, moving quickly across the street there, feeling horribly exposed in the light of day, and then inside what was meant to be a covered shopping arcade. As they walked through the never-occupied arcade, dimly lit by dirty skylights, down wide aisles between rows of empty shops, Carmen watched her guides, seeing their nervousness increasing the farther they got into what should be friendly territory for them. Obviously the talk about their own side shooting at them had been real and not some theater meant to mislead her.

The arcade ended, the corridor opening into a wide courtyard with tall buildings looking down at it from all sides. Hallways stretched out to either side until ending at doors that hung agape. In front of Carmen's group, high openings intended to hold windows looked out onto the courtyard. The commander of Carmen's escort stopped. Visibly worried, the lieutenant knelt to study the patchwork of weeds and paving they'd have to cross to reach the other side. "Where's Cortez?" he whispered irritably.

"He oughta be over there," one of the other enemy soldiers whispered in reply, gesturing straight across the courtyard.

"He knows he's supposed to show himself, right?"

"Yessir."

"Damn."

Before the lieutenant could say anything else, a low call sounded across the open area. "In the building. Come on out."

"Damn, damn, damn." The lieutenant gestured silently to the other two enemy soldiers to take up positions looking each way down the hallway. Only when they were ready did the enemy officer reply to the hail, his hands clenching his rifle nervously. "Who's out there?"

"Captain Perion. I know it's you, Lieutenant Haldane. Come on out."

Lieutenant Haldane glanced back at Carmen, then faced the courtyard again. "How do I know you're Perion?"

The reply sounded impatient. "We know what you're doing. If you want to live, turn over the hostage."

Carmen heard a very low gasp that sounded like despair and laughter mixed come from Lieutenant Haldane.

The lieutenant licked his lips before calling an answer. "How about if *you* want to live, Captain? How much longer do you think it'll be before they close in on the last of us?"

"That's not my call, Lieutenant. Not yours, either. We hold out until the reinforcements get here."

"There aren't any reinforcements coming! Do the soldiers with you know that, Captain Perion?" Haldane called louder. "Do they know that we've got only a couple of weeks max before we're all out of ammo and the locals have us at their mercy?"

"Shut up, Lieutenant! If you turn traitor you'll die a traitor's death!"

"I'd rather fight for a chance to live! Why are you so eager to die for the bosses on Apulu who left us hanging here? Don't you want a chance at life?"

"The locals don't take prisoners, you fool! It's fight or die."

"Yes, they do!" Haldane shouted back. "The bosses lied!"

"Last chance, Lieutenant Haldane!"

"Go to the bottom of Marineris and rot there!" Haldane yelled, his voice echoing through the empty courtyard. "I'm taking my last chance, and anyone with you should do the same! All of you! Shoot Captain Perion, come with me, and you'll have a chance at life!"

Carmen went flat on the dirty floor, expecting the eruption of shots that tore across the courtyard toward Haldane. The enemy lieutenant and his two soldiers fired back, fighting with the desperation of people who knew there was no place for them to run to.

All she could do was lie there as shots tore holes in the walls, hoping that no one would fire grenades. There weren't any energy bursts, confirming the reports of how low the invaders were on the power supplies for that kind of weapon. But a metal slug could kill just as surely, so Carmen found small comfort in that.

One of the enemy soldiers near her jerked and fell, lying limp.

Haldane cursed as his weapon clicked on an empty magazine.

The other soldier with them dropped his weapon and stood up, arms spread wide, as several other enemy soldiers came charging down the hallway, their weapons covering Lieutenant Haldane, the surviving soldier, and Carmen.

The man who must be Captain Perion walked forward, holding a pistol. He shot Haldane's surviving soldier who'd surrendered, then raised the weapon toward Haldane.

Carmen, knowing that she'd be next, snarled at the captain, "Idiots! If you kill him and me, you'll all die! You're being given a chance to surrender! Don't throw it away!"

Captain Perion's arm swung so his pistol centered on Carmen. "You lie. And you'll be dead before we are."

CHAPTER 8

The crash of a shot made Carmen flinch. It took her a moment that seemed much longer to realize that no slug had torn into her, that the shot hadn't come from Captain Perion's pistol, that it was Perion who staggered sideways with an expression born of fury and then fell as more shots fired by some of the captain's own soldiers rang out and slammed into him.

Carmen inhaled a ragged breath, waiting as Lieutenant Haldane and the enemy soldiers looked at each other.

"Your orders, sir," one of the new soldiers finally said.

Haldane grinned, baring his canines. "Come on. We have to get her to the rendezvous site."

"There're blocking forces set up between here and Command Bunker Sigma."

Lieutenant Haldane smiled wider. "They heard that, did they? That was disinformation. We're taking her to Alternate Command Center Gamma."

"Gamma?"

"I know where it is. Just follow me."

"Lieutenant," Carmen said, "how do we know this isn't a trick, too? To get you to take them and me to where the general and the colonel are waiting?"

Haldane hesitated before holding out his hand. "Give me your weapon," he told one of the new soldiers.

That man hesitated as well, but then handed over the rifle.

Lieutenant Haldane checked it, nodded, and then looked around. "Here's what we're doing. The hostage and me will bring up the rear so I can cover you. I'll tell you where to go. Does anyone have any problems with that?" The glare that accompanied his challenge went to both the soldiers and Carmen.

No one objected.

The dead were left lying behind them. Lieutenant Haldane moved the group much faster now, almost running. Nobody objected to that, either, since they all knew the importance of getting clear of the area before anyone came to investigate the sound of a fight well inside enemy-held territory. Carmen did her best not to stumble, not to hesitate or lag or make any move that might cause nervous and rebellious enemy soldiers to twitch fingers on triggers of weapons.

By the time the group halted at a heavy doorway, everyone was gasping for breath. Lieutenant Haldane had to take several deep breaths before he rapped at the door in a careful pattern of three, two, and three again.

The door opened a slit. Nothing could be seen through the narrow opening but there was a sense of weapons at the ready just beyond, like the prickly feeling of danger surrounding a rickety stairway descending into darkness.

Haldane gestured to Carmen.

She nodded, wet her mouth, and spoke as calmly as she could. "Rainbow."

"Mountain," someone said from behind the door.

Carmen relaxed slightly as the door to the grandly named Alternate Command Center Gamma swung open. The building had been designed as some sort of secure facility, with strong walls and electronic shielding, the interior bare of decoration. Perhaps, ironically, it had been intended to service Kosatka's government. What little portable equipment Carmen could see appeared to be military models of various ages and styles. She also saw more than a dozen enemy soldiers, including the male and female commanders who'd negotiated with General Edelman. "What happened?" General Idris demanded of Haldane.

"Captain Perion almost nailed us," Haldane explained in a rush. "These soldiers were with him, but turned on him."

"Then they're with us," the woman named Colonel Liu said. In person she was even more obviously a Red like Carmen, the executive tattoo under one ear standing out in the harsh light inside the command center. She looked Carmen over, eyes narrowed. "What mob were you?"

"Eat dust and die," Carmen spat in reply.

Colonel Liu studied Carmen. "That accent. You're not from anywhere near Mons."

"I'm from Shandakar," Carmen said, knowing that would sting another Martian's pride.

"Shanda?" The female executive laughed mockingly. "I'm in debt to a Shanda!"

"You were beaten by a Shanda," Carmen said.

The other's eyes flashed with anger. "You still might not survive this."

"If I don't, you don't."

General Idris intervened. "We don't have time for this. Lopez almost caught her before she got to us. He's probably realizing that she didn't try to reach Sigma and is trying to figure out where we really are. Let's get going before he finds us."

The entire group started off at a rush, Carmen noticing that among those waiting in the command bunker were several hoisting expensive-looking luggage. The entire situation might be crumbling into chaos and their own troops shooting at each other, but these enemy commanders were going to make sure their personal baggage made it out safe.

Outside, their route angled away from the path that Carmen and Haldane had come, Lieutenant Haldane staying close to Carmen as the group flitted through overgrown or barren spaces between empty buildings. At first she thought that was because he was afraid there'd be another attempt by loyal soldiers to stop her, but it gradually became apparent that Haldane was hoping she'd protect him.

Maybe she would. If he hadn't committed any war crimes. It was much easier to kill the enemy when they didn't have faces, when they were just vague figures without individuality. But she'd been around Haldane enough in just a short time to see him as a person.

The group reached another enemy outpost, nearly twenty soldiers occupying it, those men and women gazing anxiously at their commanders who were clearly intent on leaving them behind. "We'll transmit the surrender command when we've personally confirmed that it's safe," Colonel Liu assured them. "You'll all be taken care of."

She turned to Carmen with a sadistic smile. "You first."

Carmen resisted the urge to slug the woman, instead turning to face outside, toward where Kosatka's defenders were hidden among the buildings. Visible across the street was the elaborate entrance to the shell of a future large restaurant, the agreed-upon place for the two enemy officers to turn themselves over to Kosatka's forces. Carmen couldn't see any defenders, but she knew a lot of them were in place, concealed and wary of a last-minute betrayal from the enemy who had promised to surrender. Once she went into the open, she'd be between the itchy trigger fingers of friends ahead and enemies behind.

Nerving herself, she stepped out, standing a moment with her arms held high and wide, taking a deep, calming breath, before beginning a slow walk toward where she knew her friends waited. Her heart hammered in her ears as she walked, making it hard to listen for faint sounds.

The surrendering enemy came out behind her, crowding Carmen as they tried to push the pace, but she knew anything that looked like a rush might cause the nervous defenders to open fire. Carmen held her own steady walk despite the pressure she felt behind her, despite the growing fear that other "loyal" enemy soldiers might show up and open fire on those who were trying to surrender.

Oddly, she also felt sick at betraying the enemy soldiers at that last strongpoint. They were being abandoned by their leaders, but didn't know that yet. It felt strange to care more about the fate of those enemy fighters than their own leaders did.

Carmen led the group through the ornate gateway and into an open plaza surrounded on three sides by galleries that were supposed to someday hold happy diners. Defenders finally showed themselves, weapons leveled. Carmen came to a halt as an officer called to those behind her, "Put down all of your weapons."

For a moment everything once again hung precariously balanced on the narrowest edge of trust and hope for survival. Lieutenant Haldane crouched to gently set down his rifle, before standing up again. The others followed in a rush until the plaza was littered with discarded weapons.

"Follow me single file," the officer ordered, heading for the main entrance to the building.

Lieutenant Haldane gave Carmen an anxious look, so she nodded to him to do as he'd been told. "They won't kill you," she said. Holding his empty hands out, Haldane began following the Kosatkan officer.

Carmen waited until all of the enemy soldiers had passed her, then went as well. Inside, more of Kosatka's soldiers waited to search the surrendering enemy for weapons or taps or beacons before moving them on into an empty ballroom.

General Edelman nodded in greeting to Carmen as she followed the last of the enemy soldiers into the ballroom. "Well done. Any problems?"

"A few," Carmen said. "But it all worked out."

"Transmit the surrender orders," Edelman demanded of the two enemy commanders. "And give us the location where the remaining commanders of the enemy forces are."

"We'll be happy to give you the coordinates of Field Marshal Lopez's bunker. But first, are you guaranteeing our deal?" Colonel Liu demanded in turn.

"You'll be given good quarters and at the first opportunity allowed safe passage home," Edelman said. "As agreed to. You know that we cannot guarantee how long it will be before a transport arrives in this star system again. But when it does, you'll have priority to board it."

As the two commanders called in the surrender, Carmen slumped back against a wall, feeling her nerves jumping in reaction to the stresses so far this day.

General Edelman came to stand beside her. "We've saved a few lives today, Captain Ochoa."

Apparently the general had decided to reward her with a formal military title. "It's Citizen Ochoa, sir. Too bad saving other lives came at the cost of saving those two lives," Carmen grumbled, glaring at the enemy commanders.

"Maybe." Edelman leaned close to whisper. "According to the intelligence reports I've seen, Apulu, Scatha, and Turan have agents in all the nearest star systems, working undercover."

"That's right," Carmen said. "We found out a lot about them in files we've captured from the invading forces. They're at Catalan, and Eire, and other places."

"And those agents engage in what I believe are called active measures?"

"Yes, General. The files indicate those agents engage in missions up to and including assassinations to further the interests of their star systems. What does that have to do with those two officers?"

Edelman smiled, a thin, humorless expression. "I didn't promise that what those two did, betraying their employers, wouldn't be communicated to anyone along the routes of whatever transport they get toward their homes. What do you think those agents of our enemies will do if they learn two turncoat officers are passing through their star systems?"

Carmen realized that she was also smiling, her teeth clamped tightly together. "That's not too hard to imagine, General."

"I trust that Kosatka's intelligence officers can put together proper messages using what is known about those enemy agents? Good. Those two may *think* they're escaping from what they've done, but it's going to follow them for as far as they manage to run. We promised not to imprison or prosecute them for war crimes. We made no promises to keep their actions secret from anyone else."

"You can be pretty merciless when you want to be, can't you, General?" Carmen said.

"I have no love for those who break faith with the men and women under their command."

Carmen saw Lieutenant Haldane watching her anxiously from across the room. "Are the others going to get humane treatment, sir?"

"Yes. I promised that and I'm going to see to it." Edelman sighed. "Who knows. Maybe some of them will decide this world is worth fighting for, instead of fighting against."

"Could we ever trust them?"

He glanced at her. "Somebody asked me that about Reds. What do you think?"

Carmen shrugged. "It depends on the Red."

"Exactly." Edelman looked over everyone in the room. "When the history of Kosatka is written, these moments won't have to be glossed over or hidden. Our descendants will be able to take pride in them. That's important to me."

"I guess everyone worries about how they'll be remembered."

"Not everyone," the general said. "Those two who surrendered their troops to us? They're not looking past their own deaths. They don't care about the future, Captain Ochoa, because they won't be there."

"You're right," Carmen said.

"Oh? So sometimes you agree with your superiors?"

She couldn't help a short laugh. "Only when I have to. But, sir, it's just Citizen Ochoa."

"If I want to call you a captain, I can," Edelman corrected her. "I may call you Major Ochoa tomorrow, and if so, you are to accept it as your due."

"Yes, sir."

An officer came over to speak with the general, so Carmen walked to where Lieutenant Haldane sat against one wall, gazing ahead as if viewing a short and ugly future. He looked up when she stopped in front of him, gazing at her with wordless hope.

She knelt down to look into Haldane's eyes. "Why did you help this surrender happen?"

"I don't want to die," Haldane said, weariness, fear, and sorrow mixed together in his voice.

"Where are you from?"

"Brahma. Are you really from Mars?"

"Yeah."

"Well . . ." Haldane blinked, shuddering for a moment. "Thank you. I'd heard that Reds . . . I'm sorry. Um, you guys could've just wiped us out."

"Were you in Lodz?"

"Huh? No. My unit landed near here. We were supposed to secure this city, so we've been here the whole time." Haldane gasped a pained laugh. "We were worried we wouldn't see any fighting. Stupid, huh?"

"Yeah. Listen," Carmen said. "We keep our promises. The troops who are surrendering will be treated humanely. You can help with that. Those troops will be looking for officers of their own to tell them what to do and reassure them that if they behave well they'll be treated well. You can be one of those officers, you can help ensure no more of those you once led die uselessly, but you'll have to get up and think about the men and women who are about to walk in here and will need leaders they trust."

Haldane looked at her, startled, before nodding. He got up, moving more slowly as his sudden action attracted the interest of Kosatkan guards, whose weapons swung toward him.

Carmen saw a colonel she knew and waved him over. "This officer," she said, indicating Haldane, "can help you handle the enemy soldiers who are surrendering."

"Can he?" The colonel looked over Haldane with cold eyes. "Are we sure he's clean?"

Meaning had Haldane committed any atrocities. "He's been in Ani the whole time."

"Okay. Come on, you." The colonel gestured to Haldane, who followed quickly.

Carmen went to a quiet corner and linked in to her messages, pausing as she looked at the unsent message to Dominic.

Instead of pushing "delete," she sent the message into her drafts file, waiting in case it would be needed again.

She felt the ground tremble as an orbital strike dropped from *Shark* fell onto the far-off site of Field Marshal Lopez's bunker, wiping out the remaining enemy leadership. Outside, in the distance, she heard the desperate rattle of scattered gunfire as the remaining enemy resistance in Ani rapidly collapsed.

All of Kosatka was once more free.

Carmen thought of those who had died to stop the invasion, and wondered if this world could afford such a price a second time.

"This is absurd," Captain Batra snapped. "We've been watching the enemy charge at us for weeks!"

"They had a long way to go," Mele Darcy replied. She was in a location separate from the ground forces officer, the defenders having already been broken into eleven separate groups that were positioned throughout the orbital facility. As long as any of the many fiber links run through the facility remained intact, it would be possible for them to remain in contact at least occasionally. "Captain, I'm worried about your group commanders. We've done a lot of work, but they're still not thinking in terms of this being space rather than a planet's surface."

"My soldiers will not disappoint you," Batra insisted.

"That's not what I'm talking about! They're brave and they're well trained, but they've been trained in a very different environment. When they're inside the facility it's easy for them to forget this is space and rules are different in important ways."

"We understand that."

"Do you? I think you and your lieutenants have grasped it, but I'm worried about your senior enlisted. They still seem to be way too sure of themselves." It could always be a problem with senior enlisted, who could be so good at what they did that the idea something could trip them up didn't even occur to them. And the ground forces sergeants were, as far as Mele could tell, very good at what they did. "Tell them again, Captain. We're in space. The rules are different in important ways."

"Yes, Captain Darcy. I will remind them."

Mele decided she'd pressed the point as much as she could. "I hope they listen. The enemy is too close now for preparations to continue. Depending on how fast they make their final approach they'll probably be here in about an hour. I'm going to place all units on full-combat status." She shifted her comms to speak to the commanders of every individual group, some of them officers and some sergeants. "All personnel, we are now in a combat situation. Prepare for action within approximately one hour. You all know the plan. Wait for my command to go weapons free. After that, we have to assume the enemy will be doing his best to jam, trace, and interrupt all comms. Are there any last-minute questions?"

Of course, Lieutenant Killian had a question. "Major, what if the enemy succeeds in jamming you before you can give the command to fire?"

Which was actually not a bad question. "If enemy soldiers physically reach the facility and you haven't heard the fire command yet, that moment will serve as your authorization to fire. I want to emphasize," Mele added, "that everyone will have to use a lot of individual thinking and initiative to keep the enemy off-balance and unable to predict our actions. We've deliberately avoided drawing up detailed action plans for after the enemy boards this facility so that each of your groups will act independently. Keep moving and stay unpredictable. Any more questions? Then prepare for battle."

With nothing else to do now but wait, Mele Darcy leaned against one bulkhead in what had once been a closet in a storage room deep inside Glenlyon's orbital facility. The facility, a blocky thing constructed in space, looked a lot like a section of a city in which every building had been squashed together into one structure and then hoisted into orbit. It had been designed to be home to industry and services and the people who worked in those areas and their families. It had also been designed to ease the movement of people and equipment and other items through the facility, because it was the orbiting link between the planet below and all of space beyond.

Those people were gone, the offices and factories and other facilities empty. The men and women remaining were all Marines or soldiers, and all were in their battle armor, designed not just to protect against combat but also to serve as space suits once the helmets were donned and sealed. It was a certainty that the atmosphere inside the facility wouldn't last long once the fighting started, and then everyone would be living in their sealed battle armor for the duration.

Mele glanced inside her battle armor helmet that she still held in one hand, seeing the schematic displayed on the inside of the face shield. It bore little resemblance to the original layout. The entire facility had been converted as much as could be done in the time allowed into a three-dimensional maze filled with hidden compartments and paths. Any route that offered easy movement had been blocked at as many places as possible using everything available. Which was why she was leaning against a bulkhead instead of sitting down. Every chair had been securely fastened into the barricades and barriers.

Markers glowed at apparently random places on the schematic, showing the locations of small, well-hidden stockpiles of food, water, ammunition, and other necessities. Other markers, shining a deadly red, marked numerous booby traps and mines.

Mele bit her lip, wondering if her decision to limit copies of the new schematics to the armor systems of officers and noncommissioned officers had been the right thing to do. Any rank-and-file Marines or soldiers who got separated from their leaders would be unable to find their way around any better than the enemy could. But she didn't want to risk any more than she had to the chance that that schematic might get captured. If the enemy got their hands on it, Mele's Marines and Batra's soldiers wouldn't last long.

She double-checked the software suicide command on the schematic to ensure it could be easily triggered and would take place automatically if the armor detected serious harm to the human wearing it. Even if officers got captured, the schematic loaded into their armor shouldn't be.

A high-priority incoming call diverted Mele from thoughts that were darker than she cared for. "Darcy here."

Her faceplate screen lit with an image of President Chisholm. What Mele could see of the background didn't seem all that different from Chisholm's usual office in the capital, but Mele knew that at the moment Chisholm was in a newly constructed underground facility a good ways from the city. "I wanted to wish you luck," the president said. "You know how important it is that Glenlyon hold on to that facility."

"We'll do our best," Mele replied.

"I also wanted to inform you of your promotion to major. Congratulations."

"I'm a major again?" She tried to suppress a laugh that would surely sound inappropriate.

President Chisholm's smile remained polite and encouraging. "Permanently this time. In recognition of your service to Glenlyon, and your dedication to your adopted world. I hope you will have many more years of service in Glenlyon's Marines."

"Me, too," Mele said. "Thank you, Madam President. We're expecting the enemy to hit us in about an hour. After that, comms are going to be intermittent at best."

"I understand. Good luck." Chisholm hesitated, and Mele saw her real feelings show in her eyes. "I'm sorry we couldn't have given you more resources. We gave you our best, though, and Commodore Geary has been authorized to take any actions he feels are necessary or appropriate to support your defense of the facility. Please believe that our hopes are with you."

"I do believe that," Mele said. "Like I said, I'll do my best, and I know every other man and woman up here will do the same. We'll hold on to this facility."

"Thank you, Major. Um . . . good luck," Chisholm repeated awkwardly, as if uncertain how to properly end what might be her last conversation with Mele. The president's image vanished as the call ended.

Mele surprised herself with a laugh. A promotion. At this time.

She had an obligation to inform those under her command. "All groups, this is . . . Major Darcy. I've just been informed by President Chisholm that I've been promoted. I'm afraid the promotion party will have to wait until after this battle is over, though."

A moment later a call came in from Captain Batra, his image revealing surprise. "They really promoted you on the very eve of the battle?"

"They really did."

Batra grimaced. "I'm sorry. You know what . . . I mean . . . traditionally . . ."

"Yes, I know my history," Mele said. "Commanders in hopeless positions are promoted to encourage them. But, you see, I have a plan regarding this promotion."

"What is that?"

Mele gave him one of those grins that always earned her worried looks from Rob Geary. "I intend on winning this fight, and surviving it, so the government will be forced to live with me as a major."

After a moment, Captain Batra nodded. "Then I congratulate you, Major, and wish you a long career."

"Thanks. Make sure you come to the promotion party when this fight is done."

"I will," Batra said.

Mele made one more call, to Lieutenant Nasir and Gunnery Sergeant Moon. "I'm counting on you guys in particular."

Nasir's tight smile betrayed his nervousness prior to his first battle, but nothing else did. "I will not let you down."

"Don't let down the Marines under your command," Mele said. "That's the priority. Be the leader they need you to be."

"Yes, Major Darcy. I will."

"We'll get it done, Major," Moon assured her. "Don't let Giddings or Lamar slack off. They've been pulling that 'I'm a veteran of Kosatka' stuff on the newcomers. I told 'em they better live up to that."

"Good. Get your final preps done," Mele said.

She left the cramped compartment through a new access that was pretty close to invisible when closed, entering a larger one where a dozen Marines waited. "How's it look, Glitch?"

Sergeant Giddings gestured around him. "It's as ready as we can make it, Captain."

"Major," Mele said.

"Oh. Right. Sorry, ma'am." Giddings looked down toward the deck, which was something people on orbiting facilities tended to do when thinking of people on the world the facilities were orbiting. "Ninja hasn't been able to get into the enemy networks, though. She says these guys are really good. No telling if she'll be able to make any useful penetrations of their systems."

"We'll play it as if she won't, so if she does it'll be a bonus," Mele said. "Corporal Lamar, Sergeant Giddings is going to be handling comms and net matters for me. That means for most matters you're my leading noncommissioned officer."

"Yes, ma'am," Penny Lamar said.

"You seem pretty relaxed."

"Been there, done that, Major Darcy," Lamar said with a slight smile.

"This is going to be different from Kosatka in some ways," Mele warned. She looked around at the other Marines, eight privates and another corporal. "Since we're the command element, we're going to focus on staying uncaught rather than trying to hit the enemy whenever we can. That doesn't mean we'll be safe. The enemy is going to be trying to get us in particular in hopes that taking out our command element will cripple the defense. Every indication we have says that these guys are pros, and will give us a tough fight. Stay sharp. You're Marines. I wouldn't want anyone else here with me right now."

So much for the pep talk. Mele beckoned to Giddings. "Glitch, give me links to everything we've got."

Giddings touched one command. "That's already set up, Cap— Major. You've got access to all sensor feeds and comm links. As soon as the enemy gets onto this station, they're going to tap into physical links and force-feed jamming and malware at us, so those links might autosever without warning if they detect anything bad coming their way."

"Understood." She checked the time. Maybe half an hour left until the enemy reached the facility. "Let's armor up, everyone." Mele took a deep breath before putting on her battle armor helmet, knowing that it might be days or longer before she'd have a chance to take it off again since even if air remained, life support on the facility would be cut off as soon as the power supply was shut down. Without fans to circulate the air, unseen and deadly concentrations of carbon dioxide could accumulate and knock out or kill.

Her helmet sealed, she called up a view of the outside of the facility, seeing the stars and the endless night, and the symbols marking the three enemy warships getting closer with every moment. The systems tied into the sensors did the math and informed her that the enemy ships were twenty-six minutes from intercepting the facility in its orbit about the planet. "Sergeant Major Savak, prepare to carry out a destructive shutdown of the facility's primary power systems in about twenty minutes. I want enough damage to the power handling and distribution systems that the enemy will need more than a week to bring anything back online."

"Understand, Major. We are standing by to break the facility power systems twenty minutes from now. We'll receive an order to carry out the action at that time?"

"Yes. Wait for the order. I want to make sure the enemy approach doesn't turn into a feint designed to make us react too soon."

"Understood, Major. Standing by."

"All units, enemy forces are on final approach," Mele announced to the defenders. "Maintain full cover until ordered to charge weapons and fire."

The destroyer was holding back, covering against *Saber*, but the light cruiser was swooping in close, the freighter just beyond it. As expected, they were coming in from an angle toward one side of the facility that faced away from the world it orbited, so the bulk of the facility itself protected them from any antiorbital weapons on the planet's surface.

"They don't have to come in that close to fire, do they?" Lieutenant Nasir asked, his voice hushed as if the enemy could potentially overhear. The approaching ships were now close enough for their shapes to be visible, the blocky outlines of the big freighter dwarfing the lean mako shark–like lines of the light cruiser. Appearances were deceiving, though, since the larger freighter would be helpless if a warship like the cruiser attacked it.

"No," Mele said. "What they're doing is coming close to look for defenses and maybe lure some of the defenders into firing at them. That'd let the cruiser take out the defenders with targeted shots."

"We can't match them," Nasir said, sounding regretful this time.

"Not a chance," Mele agreed. "We don't have anything heavy enough to knock down that cruiser's shields. So instead we stay quiet until they give the go-ahead for the freighter to move in close and launch its attack."

"If that ship stays close, they'll be able to spot some of the preparations, won't they? And engage any of our forces that open fire on the attack force?"

"The cruiser? Yeah. They've got visual sensors designed to examine details on objects millions of kilometers away. This close they'll be able to spot the tiniest hint of our preparations on the areas they're examining." Mele stared at her display, trying to will the enemy commander to get bored with examining the facility. The freighter, coming in more slowly, was still about a hundred kilometers out, probably waiting for the cruiser to give the all clear.

"They're not making any mistakes, are they?" Captain Batra said over the command circuit.

"No," Mele said. "Commodore Geary said these guys were doing everything by the book, and their book doesn't seem to have any stupid parts. We'll have to do this the hard way. Hold on."

The cruiser had suddenly fired thrusters, pitching upward and over. A moment later its main propulsion lit off in a blinding flare of light as the cruiser began accelerating fast, back the way it had approached.

"What's he doing?" Batra asked.

Mele shifted her display and saw the answer. "*Saber* is coming in. It looks like an attack run against the freighter."

"The freighter would be a perfect target right now, wouldn't it? Moving so slowly?"

"As far as I know." Mele watched the curving paths of the warships steadying out and saw the pattern. "The enemy destroyer alone couldn't stop *Saber* from getting through to the freighter, so the cruiser is moving to reinforce it. *Saber* won't have a chance of reaching the freighter now without taking heavy damage, but I bet it breaks off before engaging the enemy warships."

"He pulled away the enemy cruiser," Batra said. "That was a well-timed move."

"Yeah. I told you we could count on Rob Geary. Now—what the hell is the heavy weapons platoon doing?"

Her armor had alerted her to movement, highlighting the actions of the ground forces heavy weapons platoon as they burst from cover and began setting up to engage the freighter, which was now only about twenty kilometers away and steadily getting closer. "I haven't ordered them into action! Get them under cover! Immediately!"

"Yes, Major."

"They're still up there! Get 'em inside!"

"Major, the platoon sergeant says with the enemy warship thousands of kilometers away and opening the range at a rapid rate—"

"This is space! We're in a fixed orbit so the fire control solution is easy for a warship, they're still in firing range, and they can see that part of the facility! Thousands of kilometers is nothing to a particle beam traveling at nearly the speed of light! Get those idiots—"

The particle beams from the light cruiser had spread out somewhat in their long path from the cruiser to their target, but still carried plenty of energy against individual battle armor. The beams clipped the portion of the facility where the heavy weapons platoon had emerged onto the outer surface. Invisible, the beams could be seen only by the havoc they wrought, slicing through soldiers and equipment as well as the outer edges of the facility at that site. But explosions erupted as the particle beams ruptured energy storage cells for some of the heavy weapons, adding to the destruction.

Mele heard her breath going in and out as she stared at the annihilation of the heavy weapons platoon, unable to speak for a moment. Finally getting her voice back, she spoke with forced calm. "Captain Batra, get any survivors back under cover, and let me know if any of their weapons are still usable."

Batra, for the first time in her experience with him, sounded badly shaken. "Yes, Major. Major, I . . ."

"It's done. It won't happen again, will it?"

"No, Major."

"Make sure all of your soldiers know exactly what happened," Mele ordered, her tone merciless. "Tell your sergeants that I will shoot them the next time any of them hesitate for even a second in doing what I say. We can't afford to let overconfidence kill any more of your soldiers."

"Yes, Major." Stunned, Batra didn't try to defend his soldiers this time. "I agree."

"Major?"

Mele looked over to see Corporal Lamar watching her anxiously.

"Our armor reported some explosions on the facility, ma'am."

Inhaling slowly, Mele tried to speak normally. "The heavy weapons platoon has been wiped out. They broke cover while the enemy light cruiser could still engage them." Lamar gazed back at her wordlessly. "Corporal, they were overconfident. I know you're a combat veteran, but don't you be overconfident. This isn't Kosatka. I don't want to lose a single Marine because you thought you had it solid."

"Yes, ma'am. I understand. It won't happen."

"Good."

As hard as it was to focus back on the fight, Mele wrenched her mind away from the massacre of the heavy weapons platoon and back to the oncoming freighter.

The freighter carrying the enemy troops came in slowly, ponderously, unable to match the swift, graceful maneuvers of the warships. But given enough time big freighters had no trouble matching vectors with something like the orbital facility. The enemy troops wouldn't be delivered fast or with flair, but they would be delivered.

The facility's navigation systems estimated the freighter was ten minutes from docking. She doubted the enemy soldiers would wait for the ship to dock. The first wave, at least, would come sooner than that. "Sergeant Major Savak, disable the power system. Take it down hard."

"Yes, Major," Savak said. In the aftermath of the heavy weapons platoon's destruction, even Savak sounded less like her usual imperturbable self. "Taking down facility power system now. All personnel, the power system is going off-line."

A few seconds later power loss alerts rippled across the display on Mele's face shield. The light overhead in the compartment where she was went out, leaving only the dim glow of an emergency lantern in one upper corner. The soft, ever-present background noise of fans circulating air halted.

Her sensor readings stayed steady thanks to battery backups for those systems on the facility. Mele could see in a virtual window on her face shield the freighter sidling closer, growing slowly in size now that it was less than a kilometer from the facility and gently slowing its mass the small remaining amount needed to match orbits. Numerous small objects scattered on the side of the freighter facing her were now easily seen to be enemy soldiers in battle armor. They were clinging to the side of the freighter, preparing to leap across the remaining gap.

"I'm seeing warnings from our facility's sensors," Captain Batra said. "They look like weapon alerts."

"I see the alerts," Mele replied. "I think they're preparing to fire a chaff screen."

"Chaff? Yes. Those tubes match some disposable chaff launchers I've seen."

"Here we go," Mele said. No sound of firing carried through the emptiness of space, but she saw objects hurled at very low velocity from the mouths of the tubes, objects that burst into swarms of small bits and pieces that merged into a curtain suspended in space and moving at a steady pace toward the facility. Small strips of metal chaff glittered in the light of the star as they drifted, blocking any active radar or communications, and hindering the firing of any laser-type weapons through it. A moment later the active elements of the chaff field lit off, hundreds of tiny thermite flares whose brilliant light blinded visual sensors and whose intense heat blinded infrared systems. Mele's vision of the freighter and the attacking soldiers vanished behind that wall of light and heat and tiny metal strips as the sensors viewing it frantically filtered out the glare.

She let out a slow breath to calm herself. The enemy, even if they'd intercepted the faked messages about shaky morale on the facility, were coming in with full preparations. They weren't giving her any mistakes to exploit. In fact, the only mistake so far had been that of the heavy weapons platoon.

This was going to be as tough a fight as she'd feared. "All units, charge weapons and prepare to fire. The chaff curtain is heading toward us. The first wave of attacking soldiers will be right behind it."

No one could aim through that mess. But there were surprises embedded in the surface of the facility they were approaching, surprises that had taken into account the possibility of a chaff curtain like this and that didn't require precise aim.

"Major," Lieutenant Nasir called, "can we estimate when the flares will burn out?"

"It depends what they're set for," Mele said. "They might've been set to burn out just before they reach the facility so their thermite won't eat into the outer skin of this place. But there's a good chance they're going to keep burning until they hit the facility so the enemy can use them to knock out sensors and any defenses on the surface facing them."

"Won't that set off—?"

"Sure will."

Her display predicted the chaff screen would reach the surface of the facility in ten seconds. She switched back to the command circuit. "All units, weapons free. Fire when you have targets. Remain in protected positions."

Five seconds to contact.

CHAPTER 9

The burning curtain drifted into contact, and Mele felt a faint shudder through the structure of the orbital facility as the burning thermite triggered the mines concealed on the outside of the facility.

The claymore mine was a very old concept, a weapon designed to hurl a blast of projectiles in one direction like a giant shotgun. Very old, but still very effective. The mines the Marines had planted could've been set off one by one by remote command or by contact, but the thermite had set them all off at once. The barrage of metal balls from all of the mines filled space between the facility and the freighter, the space where Mele expected the first wave of the enemy assault to be located, concealed just behind the chaff curtain.

The explosions of the mines also scattered the remaining chaff barrier a bit. Using a few surviving pinhole visual sensors, Mele got a look at the aftermath.

Dozens of enemy soldiers in that first wave had been hit as they flew through space toward the facility, the impacts of the balls from the mines knocking them back toward the freighter, or if the soldiers were really unlucky, pitching them outward either toward empty space or down toward the planet. The arms and legs of those killed by the mines dangled motionless or swayed with the rolling of their bodies. Those only wounded were triggering emergency thrusters on their armor to get back to the freighter, or to reach the facility where their luckier uninjured comrades were alighting on the dock and advancing toward the side of the facility. Mele watched the smooth, professional movements of the enemy soldiers, some standing and aiming their weapons to cover their comrades who rushed to breach the bulkheads facing them. The first wave of attackers had lost a lot of soldiers to the mines, but they knew what they were doing, and they were doing it well.

She wanted to be there, to be among the forces concealed a little ways back from the bulkheads that were about to be blown open. She wanted to be able to fight, to let her fears and worries be forgotten in the rush of battle. But that wasn't her job. She had to stay back from the fight, had to remain functioning and overseeing everyone else as they fought, giving the orders that would allow the defense of the facility to be as coordinated as possible while communications were still easy.

Sensors viewing the outer bulkheads from the inside showed the holes being blown into existence by enemy breaching charges, the atmosphere in the adjacent areas venting into space, the enemy soldiers tossing in EMP grenades to disable automated defenses, then coming through in a rush of battle-armored shapes.

A rush that almost immediately faltered as the enemy soldiers found themselves facing the barriers and blocked passages that the defenders had created in place of the original plans that the enemy had expected to reliably guide them in this attack.

But they found ways ahead and charged into them, ways that had been designed as traps. Mines implanted along the apparently clear routes detonated, dead ends suddenly appeared, and in three places groups of defenders opened fire on enemy soldiers trapped in tight hallways.

The enemy tried to hold their advanced positions, but as their numbers melted away under fire they finally fell back to where the second wave of attackers was arriving on the facility. Reinforced, the enemy attack surged forward again, once more running into the defensive maze, more mines detonating, and in several places defenders adding their fire to that of the booby traps. This time, with greater numbers, the attackers held on, pushing ahead stubbornly despite their losses.

Mele checked the situation on the dock, seeing another wave of attackers landing. Oddly, though, they didn't surge forward to join the push against the defenders. Why not?

Maybe because of something happening that she hadn't noticed yet.

She pulled out the scale on her display, taking in what could be seen of the situation in space. *Saber* had been forced to break off her attack run, leaving the light cruiser room to pivot and charge back toward the facility. As the light cruiser once again drew close, Mele saw the enemy soldiers exchanging fire with the defenders begin to fall back, breaking contact. "All units, the light cruiser is returning to provide fire support to the attackers. Lieutenant Killian, Lieutenant Nasir, Gunnery Sergeant Moon, reposition. The enemy knows enough about the location of your forces for the light cruiser to target them."

No one hesitated carrying out her orders this time. Mele watched her units repositioning, moving to different defensive locations within the deadly maze. The information flowing into her battle armor flickered, symbols and warnings freezing for a moment before suddenly updating.

"They're hacking into all of the cables and circuits they've located," Sergeant Giddings reported. "I'm blocking, but we might have to sever links soon."

"If you need to drop a link, do it," Mele said.

Alerts appeared on the schematic where new holes were appearing in the facility, particle beams from the light cruiser punching through the structure and through the areas where Mele's defenders had been before they moved. Because the beams had to pass through other parts of the structure, and anything else in the way, they damaged equipment and opened holes, allowing more atmosphere to escape into space.

The barrage over, the enemy forces surged forward again, Mele's defenders hitting them from new positions.

What odds were they facing? The information flowing in from many sensors offered only fragments of data. How many soldiers were attacking? How many had Mele's forces already taken out? She couldn't be sure, couldn't even come up with a reasonably close estimate, but it seemed the guess that they'd face at least three-to-one odds had been unfortunately accurate. And the enemy had that damned light cruiser to offer fire support, as well as whatever they'd brought on the freighter.

Her data flow hesitated again, for a couple of seconds this time, and when it updated a lot of the current information was gone, replaced by last-known-data markers.

"They're sending jamming through our lines," Giddings said. "I'm blocking their malware but the jamming is just noise that keeps any other signals from getting through. All I can do about it is try to hop my own signal frequencies and modulations fast enough to get something through."

"—status," Mele heard.

"Say again," she called in reply.

"—pressure is . . . req . . . ov . . ."

She'd known that this moment would come, but it happened earlier than she'd hoped. "All units, this is Major Darcy. Comms are seriously disrupted. All groups operate independently. I say again, comms are disrupted, all groups operate independently. Darcy, over."

A few replies came back. "This is Sergeant Major Savak, roger, out." "This is Lieutenant Paratnam, roger, out." "This is Gunnery Sergeant Moon, roger, out."

The rest knew what to do if comms were lost, though. Mele watched her picture of the situation evaporating like a chalk drawing on a sidewalk being hit by heavy rain as sensor links were severed or jammed, and heard wavering blasts of static on the comm frequencies. It was up to the other group commanders now, to keep hitting and keep moving, avoid staying in one place long enough to be trapped by the superior numbers and firepower of the enemy.

"Major," Sergeant Giddings said, "there's a chance the enemy localized us based on data flows. I recommend that we shift locations as well."

"Good idea," she replied. "Corporal Lamar, head for our first alternate hide hole. I'm sending you the route."

"Yes, ma'am. On your feet!" Lamar ordered the other enlisted. "Relaying the route to each of you now. Got it? Ford, take point!"

"Which Ford?"

"Sean Ford! Use your heads, people," Lamar said. "Ford Okubo is our medic. I'm not putting him on point. If I say Ford, I mean Private Ford. Got it? Good. Why are you standing around?"

Private Ford went to the access door, darted through in a rush, and headed for an apparently solid barrier. Once there he paused, studying the route information sent to his armor, found the hidden lock that allowed a section of the barrier to open, and led the way through.

As Mele followed in the center of the group, emergency lighting giving a weird cast to the otherwise dark hallway they were in, her armor reported the faint vibrations caused by explosions elsewhere in the facility. She looked in the direction that the fighting was in as the flurry of destruction ended, wanting to head that way and knowing that she couldn't.

Stay alive. Stay free. For as long as possible, while the other groups tried to wear down the enemy faster than the enemy wore them down, and the enemy sought to gain control of this facility so they could dominate Glenlyon's inhabited world from orbit.

She had no illusions. They had to survive until the enemy was forced to withdraw. If they couldn't do that, and nothing else changed, Glenlyon would lose this battle and probably the entire conflict.

JACK CAMPBELL

So they'd have to keep fighting and hiding as long as they could, and pray that would be long enough.

A day and a half later, Mele sat in a long, narrow access tunnel that was barely tall enough for her Marines to sit upright in. The voice of Lieutenant Nasir wavered in volume over the link that Giddings had managed to establish. "Lieutenant Killian is dead, along with most of her group, I think. I was speaking with a group of two survivors when we lost our link to them."

"Do you have any idea what happened?" Mele said, trying not to think about how much the loss of that group diminished the firepower available to her defenders.

"An ambush, they said. No warning. It must have been in an area where the enemy had managed to map out everything."

"If you contact anyone else, warn them of that. We can't assume the enemy is lost in all portions of this facility."

"But, Major, we cannot know which areas the enemy has been in long enough to map them," Nasir said.

"That's true," Mele said. "Which means we have to assume the enemy has mapped out anywhere we go. How's your group?"

"We have been chased, and we have made those who chase us unhappy when they have caught up with us."

"Good. How are *you* doing, Shahid?"

"I am fine, Major. I try to give my Marines hope in my words and my actions. I believe I have been successful so far."

Mele hesitated, surprised by how calm Shahid Nasir sounded. "Good. Try to remain positive, but don't forget to stay scared enough to be alert for the threats we're facing."

"I have not forgotten the danger. But I remember what my father told me. Those filled with fear see only their fears," Nasir said. "Those filled with hope see what they fear, but also a path onward that leads to what they hope for."

She looked along the dark tunnel at the tired shapes of the Marines in her group, slumping as they rested. Her Marines. "Yeah. I see hope, too."

"Major, someone's trying to trace this link," Sergeant Giddings said.

"Got to go, Lieutenant," she said. "Good luck. Darcy, out."

Choosing a route to another hiding spot, Mele passed it to Corporal Lamar.

"Got it," Lamar said. "Ford—"

"Take point," Private Ford said, sounding resigned.

"Don't anticipate commands," Lamar chided him.

"Yes, Corporal."

"Take point."

"Yes, Corporal."

They dropped through a hatch into a small room that led to a stairwell.

Private Ford had taken only four steps down the stairs when he froze, his weapon aimed downward.

"What is it?" Lamar asked.

"I don't know," Ford said, his voice wary. "Something doesn't feel right."

"Nothing's showing on sensors," Lamar said.

"I know. But it's wrong."

"Major?"

Darcy gazed down into the darkness, weighing the need to move against the instinct of a single private. Was Ford spooked, or was there some danger up ahead?

She had maybe two seconds more to decide. If there really was trouble ahead, it might not give her any more time than that to make up her mind.

And right now her mind urged her to order Ford forward. Just go. Don't hesitate.

But she did hesitate.

Damn.

Why?

The voice of her old sergeant echoed in her memory. *"You're not as smart as you think you are, Darcy. And even smart people can be stupid. Try not to forget that in case anyone's lives ever depend on you."*

"Fall back," Mele ordered. "Everyone cover Ford."

Ford retreated backward, one cautious step up the stairs, like someone moving through a minefield.

Warning alerts flared on Mele's battle armor display. "Move!"

She fired as explosions rippled up the stairway, the rest of her group joining in, Private Ford jolting backward as at least one shot struck him, then being hauled along as they retreated up through the hatch, enemy fire chasing them and wounding another Marine.

"Get it sealed!" Lamar ordered.

"Not yet!" Mele shouted, grabbing grenades from other Marines, priming three, and pitching them in a group down through the hatch into the projectiles and energy bolts flaying the hatch. "Now!"

Two Marines got the hatch closed, another pouring liquid weld onto the seam to seal it solid. They hadn't finished when the surroundings rocked from all three grenades detonating.

Mele calmed herself, studying the schematics, choosing a new route, and relaying it to Lamar.

"Ford!" Lamar called.

"He's wounded," Corporal Okubo said. "So's Kusinko."

"Can they move?"

"K's going to need to be carried. Ford can only use one arm until I get him patched up."

"That's a yes," Mele said. "Let's get moving, Lamar."

"Mac! On point!"

Private MacKinder moved out, his weapon ready, threading through the maze along the path displayed on his helmet's face shield. The others followed, Mele staying in the middle of the group along with the wounded. She studied the layout as they went, guessing what the enemy might be doing, where they might be going to try to catch

Mele's group as it fled. "Sergeant Giddings, are you picking up anything?"

"There's some signal traffic flying," Giddings replied. "Just random hits on my sensors. But a lot of it. I can't tell anything else."

"They're being sloppy with transmissions," Mele said. "That means they're in a rush, trying to box us in. Lamar, I'm shifting the route. Got it?"

"Yes, Major."

"See that segment to the left with the access running past it?"

"Yeah."

"I'm certain that some of them are going to be coming along there to cut us off. We're going to wait and give them a welcome."

"Got it, Major."

They headed to the left, the Marines pausing and dispersing along the short hallway, Lamar and Mele positioning them with hand signals to avoid tipping off enemy sensors scanning for even the weakest transmissions. The Marines readied themselves, aiming toward the doorway to the access tunnel, Mele preparing two more grenades.

Vibration through the structure. She felt it a moment before her sensors warned of approaching movement. As she expected, they were moving fast, trying to seal off some of the routes that Mele's group would need to use to escape. Urged on by commanders eager to ensure their prey didn't escape. Moving too fast to spot unexpected trouble before they ran into it.

As the shaking caused by the footfalls of heavily laden soldiers in battle armor grew very close, Mele pitched the two grenades in rapid succession through the access, bouncing them off the far wall so they rebounded down the hallway into the approaching enemy. The soldiers who appeared as they ran past the opening were cut down by fire from Lamar and the other Marines, the grenades detonating among their comrades who would at that moment be piling up just short of the access.

Mac led the charge through the access, firing down it as his shoulder hit the far wall, the other Marines following and shooting into the surprised and already battered enemy force.

By the time Mele had readied her rifle and followed, the shooting had stopped.

She spent only a moment evaluating the situation, seeing the bodies of the enemy sprawled about, ensuring this enemy force had been wiped out. Fifteen fewer enemy soldiers to worry about.

No, fourteen. One of the enemy was wounded, breathing heavily, staring at the Marines. Mele kicked the soldier's weapon away before speaking to Lamar again. "New route. Go."

"What about—"

"They'll have picked up our attack here and be coming to this location. They'll find their wounded and take care of him. Now get going!"

"Yes, ma'am. Mac, point!"

Mac grumbled as Lamar designated him point again, but went ahead.

Without the schematics in their battle armor the group would've been quickly lost as they threaded through apparent dead ends and actual tight spots until finally reaching a compartment where they could stop. "Post two on sentry," Mele told Lamar. "Glitch, how's it look?"

Sergeant Giddings took a moment to reply. "If they're still talking, it's too far off from us to pick anything up through the structure. I can't see any signs they're close."

"We lost them," Lamar said.

"Maybe," Mele said. "One hour here while Doc Okubo fixes up our wounded, then we move."

"Major?" Giddings said. "If you want my opinion—"

"Damn, Glitch, don't you know better than to say that to an officer? Fine. What's your opinion?"

Sergeant Giddings gestured outside the compartment. "When we move, we make noise. We have to move sometimes, because they're going to be searching everywhere, but if we move too much, we'll make too much noise."

"Making it easier to find us?" Mele thought about that, looking toward where two Marines on guard duty watched the entry to this place. "That's a good point. Have you got any feel for how long we should stay in one place before we move?"

"I'm guessing three or four hours minimum between moves, Major. Unless we hear them coming and have to move sooner. Six hours if we can stay in one place that long. They want us to bolt, like rabbits, because we're easier to spot when we run."

"Yeah," Mele said. "We just got a demonstration of that, didn't we? All right. Five hours. But I want some portable sensors planted out there with independent fiber feeds back to here."

Corporal Lamar nodded. "On it, Major."

Mele finally let herself relax again for a moment, trying to rest, wishing she knew how much longer this contest would last. "How're Ford and K?"

"They'll live," Corporal Okubo said. "Ford'll be able to use his arm again in a little while. But K's not going to be walking for some time."

She let out a long breath, staring into space, trying to decide. "Does he need hospitalization?"

"No, Major," Okubo said, knowing what she meant. "We don't have to leave K to be picked up by the enemy. I'll let you know if it comes to that."

"Do we know these guys will treat prisoners right?" Corporal Lamar asked.

Mele nodded. "If they're a pro outfit, they should play by the rules when it comes to prisoners. It's stupid to kill prisoners when they might spill something under interrogation, or provide leverage in negotiations. For all they know, K is a knucklehead with a grudge against his officers who'll tell them lots of stuff if they treat him nice. If we have to leave K, or anyone else, they'll be all right. But for now we keep him with us."

"Major?" one of the other Marines said. "Kusinko really is a knucklehead."

"But I love our officers!" Kusinko added from where he lay as the others laughed.

"Sure you do," Mele said. "Doc, is Ford going to be well enough to work point again?"

"In five hours? Yes, ma'am," Okubo said.

"Good. Lamar, I want Ford on point when we move."

"Major, I'm wounded!" Private Ford protested.

"If Doc says you can handle the job, you get the job," Mele said. "Because you're so good at it. I'm going to be counting on you to sniff out any more ambushes. Congratulations, Private Ford."

"But . . ."

"No good deed goes unpunished," Corporal Lamar reminded him.

R ob Geary, frustrated with sitting on the bridge while not able to do anything to help the defense of the orbital facility, had retreated to his stateroom. "Me being there was just making everyone else as tense as I was," he told his wife.

The image of Ninja on his stateroom display gave a nod, her eyes shadowed by fatigue. "You're not the only one who wishes they could do more."

"No luck?"

"Not much." She gestured around vaguely, the motion sharpened by anger. "They're keeping everything tight. Good discipline. About all I've been able to do was break into their comms long enough to find out they're really unhappy about the resistance they've run into."

"But nothing we can exploit?"

"Not yet. At least we know Mele's people are still fighting."

Rob grimaced. "That just reminds me that I can't help her."

"You're helping, Rob. You're keeping those warships off her back."

"Is that how everyone is seeing it?" he asked. Her hesitation provided the answer without words. "Okay. I knew how this would look."

"They know better than to say anything around me," Ninja said.

"Have you heard anything from the enemy warships?" Rob said, deliberately changing the subject. "Any clues to their supplies or fuel cell levels?"

"Not yet. Promise me you won't do anything crazy."

"I already did."

"Promise again."

"I promise." Rob sat forward, looking down at his hands. Hands that could do nothing. "I've never let Mele down before. I've never let you down. But this time . . ."

"The chance will come. Leigh Camagan went to get help. That woman is tough. She'll get us help. And when it gets here, you will kick the butts of those guys."

"I hope you're right."

His tone must have made clear how he felt, because his wife's gaze and voice grew fierce. "Hey, Rob. You're a hero to me. Never forget that."

He couldn't help a small smile as he looked back at her. "I hope I never do. But I still want to save those people on the facility."

"Well, duh, why do you think you're my hero?"

"**M**ine." Private Ford breathed the single word, freezing in place as another Marine slid forward cautiously to disable the enemy trap.

"Got a sensor over there, too," Sergeant Giddings said, pointing. "We need to disable it."

"Where?" Corporal Lamar asked, checking the spot. "Oh. I got it." She used an EMP pen to send a kill charge through the sensor the enemy had planted. "They'll know we just took that out."

"By the time they get here we'll be long gone," Mele said. "Is the mine disarmed?"

"Yes, Major."

"Move it over there, and reset it to explode on any target. When they come looking for that sensor, their own mine will be waiting for them."

They were about fifty meters farther on, Mele guessed, when she felt the shock of the mine's detonation.

Ten meters beyond that, Ford stopped moving again. "I'm picking up movement!"

"Me, too," Lamar said. "On the right and below us."

"Move straight on," Mele said. "They might be trying to herd us."

As the group moved through a large compartment subdivided by improvised barricades, a place that Mele belatedly realized had been part of her favorite bar up here, a flurry of enemy fire suddenly came from their left.

One of the Marines carrying Private Kusinko fell, and so did Kusinko. The two nearest Marines hesitated.

"Get out of here!" Kusinko yelled, rolling onto his stomach to fire. "I'll cover!"

"Move up and straight!" Mele ordered Lamar.

They scrambled through the barricades, heading for a spot Mele knew, through what had been a door behind the bar and through a storage area that held crates of mixer too cheap to bother taking down to the surface. She heard Kusinko's fire cease abruptly, and hoped that meant he'd been captured rather than killed.

Private MacKinder paused long enough to slap a small mine next to the exit as they went out.

Ford dropped through an access, ran over a couple of meters, and then pulled open a concealed access visible on the helmet schematics. Everyone followed as he dropped through again.

By the time they reached another hiding place, everyone was breathing heavily, their battle armor life support laboring to process their exhaled carbon dioxide back into oxygen.

Mele gritted her teeth, trying not to think about Kusinko.

"Major?"

"Yeah, Doc," she said.

Okubo waved in roughly the direction they'd come. "I was still getting Kusinko's life support readings when they cut off. He didn't register as killed before his armor systems stopped transmitting. Maybe they killed his armor systems and him at the same time, but there's a good chance K was taken alive and his suit systems wiped themselves."

"Thanks," Mele said. "Corporal Lamar, who'd we lose?"

"Yuri was carrying Kusinko," Lamar said. "I think he bought it. Where's Carlita? Did anyone see what happened to Carlita?"

"I think she got hit right before we got away from where we left K," Mac offered. "I didn't see her after that."

"Son of a . . ." Lamar muttered. "That's it, Major. We lost Privates Josh Kusinko, Carlita Indra, and Yuri Chen."

"Thank you," Mele said, feeling personal responsibility for the dead and injured Marines, trying not to let her rage and sorrow at the losses show to the others. They needed an officer who was calm and in charge, not one overwhelmed by emotion or beating herself up with guilt. "Inventory the power supplies and ammunition before we move on from here. Glitch, see if you can get any picture of the enemy's movements, and see if you can contact any of our other groups. I need to know how many effectives they have left."

"Do you want locations, Major?" Sergeant Giddings asked.

"Hell, no. If they tell us that, the enemy might intercept it. All that's important is knowing which of our groups are still active and how many people they've got left."

Mele slumped against a bulkhead, closing her eyes, thinking about K and Indra and Chen. And wondering how many more of her Marines, and the ground forces soldiers fighting alongside them, had also been lost already.

The unwelcome sound of a high-priority incoming message awoke Carmen from a deep sleep filled with clashing images of Mars, Old Earth, and Kosatka. She bolted awake, breathing heavily as she fumbled for her pad. Had a second invasion fleet arrived in this star system? "Ochoa."

The image of her old boss Loren Yeresh gazed at her. "You're needed, Carmen."

Carmen glared at him. "I'm needed? In the middle of the night after the day I finally got back to Lodz again? Has another invasion fleet arrived? Because if it's anything less than that, I'm not going to be happy." She glanced over to the other side of the bed, seeing Dominic watching her with concern mingled with curiosity.

"Sorry!" Yeresh said, not looking the least bit contrite. "But when the office of the First Minister tells me to find you and get you to a meeting there right now, I have to do what I'm told."

"The First Minister's office? Right now?" She felt a chill that didn't come from the night air. "Another attack really has arrived?"

"Something big is up, but nobody is saying anything." Yeresh grimaced. "For what it's worth, no military alert has been sent out. But I can't access space status reports. No one can. They're blocked."

Carmen tried to fight off a wave of despair. Again? So soon? "What about *Shark*? What's our destroyer saying?"

"I tried pinging her," Yeresh said, "but *Shark*'s gone silent. I assume she's still up there because there wasn't anything that could take her out, but nobody's saying anything to me or anybody else except get Carmen Ochoa to the First Minister's office *now*."

"What about Redman?"

Yeresh shook his head. "She gave me the 'shut up you'll be told anything you need to know when you need to know it.' That's all I've got. Are you going to get to the First Minister? Because I think if I say you're not heading that way they'll send the cops for you."

"It's that bad?" Carmen took a moment to breathe in and out slowly, trying to quell panic before it rose in her. Another invasion? Already? Some of the signs seemed to be pointing to that, but others didn't. Why alert her personally and not the entire defense system? "You tell them that I'll be at the First Minister's office as soon as I can."

CHAPTER 10

Carmen jumped out of bed, hesitated as she reached for her camos, reluctant to don the garments of war again, then grabbed the uniform and started getting dressed while Dominic watched her with somber eyes.

"Any idea what it is?" Dominic asked her.

Carmen managed to shrug while getting her outfit on. "It might be another invasion. But if it was another invasion arriving, the military should've been alerted first off. Why else would access to information about the space in this star system be blocked, though? Something has arrived, I think, but what I don't know."

"Maybe Nakamura is back."

She paused to stare at Dominic. "Lochan? But why would that scare the First Minister's office? Domi, I'm sorry I have to—"

"Let's just hope it turns out to be good news for once." He forced a smile. "It's about time for good news, right? Let me know what you can when you can."

"I will." Leaning over the bed, she kissed him. "Thanks."

"I knew what I was getting. Fix your hair before you go."

"Right."

The streets of Lodz were eerily quiet at this hour, long after midnight but well before dawn. The nighttime curfew on movement had been lifted only yesterday, so even workers who in normal times would be on the streets were still absent. She snagged a parked drop car, her ID overriding the curfew limits still in its software. The drive to the government complex was swift, going from an undamaged section of the city to a badly torn-up area in just a few blocks.

One of the sentries recognized her and waved Carmen through.

Palmer was at his desk. Of course Palmer was at his desk. The sheer normalcy of that calmed Carmen a bit. "What's up?"

"An important event," Palmer said. "I don't believe that it's bad news, but that's for the First Minister to speak of."

Carmen entered the office to find First Minister Hofer at his desk. Minister of Public Security Kowalski was standing, gazing at one of the office display screens even though it was showing nothing. The sight of him still jarred Carmen. The former Public Security Minister, Sarkozy, had been assassinated a year ago, not long after the title of her job was changed to that more assertive name from the previous peacetime title of Safety Coordinator, but somehow Carmen still always expected to see her. Seated on the office couch was the Leader of the House of the People's Representatives, Lisa Nowak, who'd replaced Ottone after the last election.

Carmen moved to one side as Jayne Redman hustled in, giving Carmen a glare before smiling politely to Hofer.

"We're all here," Hofer said, neither his face nor his voice revealing anything about his feelings. "There's one more participant, though. Palmer! Link in Derian!" One of the display screens on the wall flared to life, showing the bridge of a ship and an officer in the command seat. "You all know Commander Derian on the *Shark*," Hofer added. "Do we have a good link?"

Derian nodded. "Yes, sir."

"Something very important has happened," Hofer told the others.

"Commander Derian notified me of it. I need a read from the rest of you on this before it becomes public. Commander?"

Derian gestured to one side of where he sat. "Three warships have arrived at the jump point from Tantalus. Two are destroyers of the same type as *Shark*. The other is a slightly larger destroyer of a different class."

"Warships? Destroyers?" Nowak asked, shocked.

"From Tantalus?" Kowalski said. "Why would our enemies be coming from there?"

"Apparently they're not enemies," Hofer said. "At least, that's what we're being told." He touched a control on a repaired section of his desk.

The display lit up, showing what was identified as a message received half an hour ago.

Carmen gasped as Lochan Nakamura's image appeared. His face bore signs of long-term strain, but otherwise he looked all right.

"This is Lochan Nakamura, special representative of the government of Kosatka," he said, "calling for First Minister Hofer and the House of the People's Representatives. I need to—excuse me. Straight off, these warships are not here to attack Kosatka. They are friends."

Tension that had suddenly ramped up in the office subsided just as quickly. Nowak gasped with relief, but everyone else stayed silent as Nakamura continued.

"The star systems of Eire, Benten, and Adowa have provisionally agreed to form a protective alliance with Kosatka, Catalan, and Glenlyon. These warships are from Eire and Benten. Eire made the final decision to commit both of its warships because agents linked to our enemies tried to destroy both of them with malware, an attack that came close to succeeding. That also helped convince Benten to act now. They're here to deal with the invasion fleet, which we discovered upon arrival has apparently already been defeated. The commander of this force, Captain Miko Sori on this ship, the *Asahi*, wants permission to proceed through Kosatka's space. She and the other commanders are currently discussing whether to proceed onward to Glenlyon to ensure that star system isn't being attacked."

Lochan Nakamura sharpened his gaze as if he were actually looking at those viewing this message. "I understand that this is a sudden development, but I strongly urge the government of Kosatka to formally embrace this new alliance. The more who join it, the stronger it will be, and the less chance that anyone will risk messing with any star system who's a part of it. But, at the least, this group of ships needs approval from the government to transit this star system. Unless I receive orders to the contrary, I intend accompanying them to Glenlyon if they go there. In about six hours you should be seeing a freighter also arriving from the jump point for Tantalus. That freighter is from Adowa. Adowa did not have a warship to contribute, but did redirect a freighter whose cargo was intended to be sold at Eire. That cargo will be donated to Kosatka as a sign of Adowa's commitment to the alliance." Lochan paused, squinting as he read something slightly to one side. "The cargo . . . Adowa has a lot of land suitable for farming luxury crops like coffee and chocolate, so much of the cargo will be made up of that and similar products. I'm sorry it's not something more useful under current circumstances. Please advise me of the government's preferred course of action from here on. Nakamura, out."

Carmen sat back, realizing that her jaw was hanging loose. "He brought three destroyers to help us. He got Eire, and Benten, and Adowa, and Catalan, to ally with us and Glenlyon. And he's showing up with a freighter full of coffee and chocolate."

First Minister Hofer nodded. "If he runs for my job he'll probably win."

"Lochan doesn't want your job," Carmen said.

"Good thing," Nowak said, her voice still a little faint. "Can we trust this? Is Nakamura telling the truth? Or is he a hostage reciting lines designed to lull us into complacency before they pounce on *Shark* and eliminate our last defense in space?"

All eyes went to Carmen.

She nodded. "Yes, we can trust it. I could tell if Nakamura was lying or under duress."

"He looks stressed," Nowak said.

"I agree. But not fearful or worried. If he was under duress, he'd communicate that somehow. There are things he could have said that would've tipped me off."

Redman spoke up, her voice sharp. "That personal judgment is a very thin reed to cling to under these circumstances. The security and safety of the entire star system is at stake."

Minister of Public Security Kowalski's voice sounded harsh. "What are you suggesting, Citizen Redman?"

"That Nakamura could've been drugged, or might've made some sign that Citizen Ochoa did not spot, or—"

"I know Lochan Nakamura," First Minister Hofer broke in. "I agree with Carmen. He looks like himself, and gives no sign of duress. If he's been fooled, he hasn't realized it yet."

"It's not as if we could fight them even if Nakamura is lying," Kowalski said. "Commander Derian, what would be our chances against that force?"

"If we fought them?" Derian asked. He shook his head. "Three-to-one odds, and the one identifying itself as *Asahi* is a bit stronger than *Shark*. It's an Island Class destroyer. *Shark* still needs a full overhaul after the damage we sustained earlier, but even if my ship was in top shape I wouldn't see any chance of beating them."

"Why are we even discussing fighting them?" Nowak asked. "They're here as allies!"

"Are they?" Jayne Redman asked. "Or is this a Trojan Horse situation?"

"It's not," Carmen said, directing her answer to Hofer rather than Redman. "Lochan Nakamura wouldn't be a part of that."

Commander Derian spoke up again. "If I'm given permission to speak directly with the new ships, I can see if I know any of their commanding officers from my time in Earth Fleet. If we talk, I can probably get a feel for their sincerity, even if we're not acquainted from our earlier careers."

"Two of those warships are from Eire!" Redman pointed out. "Who here is prepared to accept the good intentions of Prime Minister Donal Morgan? It's not like him to act unless he expects to gain from it."

"What could he get from Kosatka?" Nowak asked.

"The same thing the earlier attackers want. Another star system whose population and resources are at their disposal."

"Lochan Nakamura would not be a part of that!" Carmen said.

"Could they have promised one thing to Nakamura while intending to betray him, and us?" Nowak said, looking about anxiously.

"Why would Benten assist in that?" Kowalski asked. "Or Adowa?"

"Why would they ally with us?" Redman demanded.

"We can ask," Carmen said. "Lochan can tell us the details of whatever negotiations went on."

"That's true," Hofer said.

"We have no chance of success if they choose to attack," Kowalski said, "but if these new ships are here for the reason Nakamura gave, what will we do? How will we respond?"

Hofer looked around the room. "It's an offer to join an alliance that already includes at least three other star systems. Can we afford to say no?"

"Is it an offer, though?" Kowalski said. "Or is it an offer we can't refuse? Perhaps an offer made in good faith, but one that will require us to relinquish more rights and sovereignty than we care to?"

"That's a good question," Redman agreed.

"Excuse me," Carmen said. "We're on the verge of losing all rights and all sovereignty, and there's concern that agreeing to this alliance might cost us too much?"

"We came out here to be free," Kowalski said.

Carmen heard the silence stretching in response to that statement, and realized she had another answer. "They're requesting permission to travel through our star system," she pointed out. "They *don't* have to do that."

"They're supposed to request such permission," Kowalski said.

"But they don't have to. If they wanted to send a message that we'd better play along, that we had to agree to whatever deal they offered, then they could have just told us they were going to pass through Kosatka's star system. We'd understand what that meant, wouldn't we?"

"That's right," Commander Derian said. "They could've flexed their muscles just by acting as if they had every right to do whatever they wanted. The message sent by that action would've been unmistakable. Instead, they're acting like someone who wants to work with us."

"They're playing by the rules, even though they don't have to," Carmen said.

The First Minister slowly nodded, then fixed his gaze on Nowak. "Actions, not words. As Citizen Ochoa pointed out, these new warships are showing us their intentions toward Kosatka. If I call a vote on formally agreeing to join this alliance, what will the House of the People's Representatives do?"

Nowak laughed in disbelief. "I can't be certain! It's not a question I've canvassed anyone on because it's not a question anyone thought we'd need an answer to." She lowered her head in thought. "There'll be some questions. What motivated these other star systems to help us? Did Nakamura make promises that the government won't want to honor? Um . . . how did Catalan agree? What does Eire expect from this? Things like that, which we've already brought up here."

"We can ask Kelly about Eire's motivations," Kowalski said. "It's Brigit Kelly, right?"

"A coded diplomatic message was sent from one of those ships to Kelly," Redman said, checking her comm. "She should have received it already."

"There's nothing suspicious about that," Carmen said. "Kelly is Eire's representative to Kosatka, and these ships are the first contact from Eire in a while. It's natural that they'd carry any diplomatic communications for her."

"Not suspicious, no," Hofer agreed. "But we should find out what we can about it. Palmer! Please send someone to invite Brigit Kelly to this office. I'd like her here as soon as possible. Make sure whoever is sent knows this is an invitation, not an order for her to appear."

"We should make sure she comes here," Kowalski said.

"There are two warships from Eire in this star system," Hofer replied. "We'll fight them if we have to, hopeless or not, but I'm not going to go out of my way to offend Eire if they've truly come to help us. Palmer! Ensure Kelly receives an *invitation*."

"I'll word the request to ensure that's clear, First Minister," Palmer called back.

"We can break Eire's diplomatic code," Redman said.

"Maybe," Kowalski said with a skeptical snort. "Unless they're using a book code or something similar."

"Wouldn't breaking that diplomatic message be an unfriendly act?" Nowak asked.

"Let's wait and see what Kelly tells us," First Minister Hofer ordered. "I'm going to respond to Nakamura, asking for whatever he can tell us about the agreement for this alliance and what demands it may make of Kosatka. But I want everyone to understand that we may not have the luxury of turning down this opportunity. Not if those other star systems can help prevent another attack on us."

"Sir," Carmen said, "we know what the governments of Eire, Benten, and Adowa are like. Unless they've changed radically, none of them would've agreed to a deal that would infringe too much on their own rights to govern themselves."

"That's true," Kowalski said. "The same goes for Catalan."

"Eire could've strong-armed the others," Redman said. "I wouldn't put it past their prime minister from what we know of him."

"Eire doesn't have that much power," Kowalski said. "Unless

they've picked up a lot of new military capability since our last reports from there."

Carmen looked at the display where Lochan Nakamura's message had played. "Lochan said the overall commander of the force was the captain of the warship from Benten."

Kowalski ran one hand through his hair, appearing frustrated. "That would imply either Benten is the senior partner, or that Eire is treating this as an alliance of equals. I don't see how Benten could've forced its will on Eire that way."

"An alliance of equals," Nowak said. "That I could sell to the House of the People's Representatives. *If* that's what we're dealing with and being offered a part of."

First Minister Hofer glanced at the display that showed Commander Derian. "If these ships represent a hostile force, one aimed at dominating Kosatka, that would mean we're trapped between Scatha, Apulu, and Turan on one side and Eire, Benten, and Adowa on the other. Our only meaningful action would be deciding which side to surrender to."

"But why would they go on to Glenlyon?" Redman asked. "Do they know something we don't?"

Commander Derian answered. "I can easily guess. It's been quiet here, in space I mean, since we dealt with that invasion fleet. It's possible that our quiet period has been bought at the price of Glenlyon facing attack as our enemies shift targets."

"Even if Glenlyon is safe," Carmen said, "those warships arriving there would be a powerful symbol that Glenlyon has strong friends."

Hofer nodded. "There's nothing suspicious about that."

"Sir," Commander Derian said, "I'd like to propose a course of action. If those warships continue on to Glenlyon, I'd like for *Shark* to accompany them."

A moment of surprised silence was broken by Leader of the House of the People's Representatives Nowak. "Leaving Kosatka defenseless? That's out of the question! Isn't it?" she added, looking at the others.

Hofer looked at the Minister of Public Security, who instead of replying directly looked in turn at Carmen. "Citizen Ochoa," Kowalski said, "you've spent a lot of time with our forces at Ani. What's your candid assessment of their emotional state?"

Carmen took a moment to reply as she considered the best answer. "I think they could be characterized as happy for the victory, but also tired. Exhausted . . . and . . . bracing themselves for the next attack. Everyone expects another hammer to fall, so there's a . . . a fatalism there. They'll fight, but they're tired, and they're waiting for the next blow."

Kowalski nodded, glancing at Hofer. "I agree, First Minister. Our people have fought very well, especially considering that many were volunteers who never expected to have to defend their new home this way. But they've paid a price for the victories we've won. They think all we can hope for is to wait for the next attack, and try to survive it. If that attitude hardens, our eventual defeat will be certain."

Hofer rubbed his chin as he gazed back at Kowalski. "Are you saying you agree with Commander Derian? That *Shark* should go to Glenlyon?"

"Yes. I think that Kosatka needs to strike back, needs to take the fight to the enemy. It's important to keep the enemy off-balance, but it's equally important to show our own people that we aren't just a punching bag. We can hit those who attack us, and we can aid others in need of help."

"As Glenlyon aided us," Carmen said. "They sent their only destroyer to help us, leaving themselves unprotected."

"Exactly," Kowalski said. "Who would we be if we accepted such aid and then denied it to those who helped us? These actions, these decisions, will define what Kosatka is and who we are. I urge you to accept Commander Derian's suggestion."

"We're getting a little ahead of things, aren't we?" Nowak asked, sounding plaintive. "We haven't even decided if we're going to be part of this new alliance. Shouldn't we—"

"Excuse me, sir." Palmer stood at the door. "Citizen Kelly has arrived."

"This quickly?" Hofer asked.

"I was on my way here when I received your invitation," Kelly said, stepping into view behind Palmer. "I have a personal message from the Prime Minister of Eire for First Minister Hofer."

"Please come in," Hofer said, rising from his chair to greet her. "I'm anxious to hear your message."

Kelly stopped before his desk, nodding politely to the others in the room. "First Minister, a copy of the message is on this pad," she said, offering it to Hofer.

"Can you summarize the message for me and the others here?" Hofer asked.

Brigit Kelly looked around her, evaluating the audience, before replying. "Yes. In short, the Prime Minister of Eire wants you to know that Eire agreed to join this alliance partly as a result of a malware attack that nearly resulted in the destruction of both of Eire's warships. If not for the prompt actions of their crews, both destroyers would've been lost. Eire wants other star systems, friendly star systems, to be aware of that danger. The source of the malware was traced to a Scathan agent on Eire. It's not known whether this attack on Eire was an attempt to soften us up in anticipation of their victory here at Kosatka, or if it was merely aimed at preventing Eire from being able to intervene. But, regardless of the exact motive, the Prime Minister will not tolerate such an unprovoked stab in the back. He sees it in Eire's best interest to join now with others threatened by Scatha and its allies."

"I see." Hofer exchanged glances with the Security Minister and the Leader of the House of the People's Representatives. "That matches what we were told by Lochan Nakamura, and answers one of the important questions we had. Is that Eire's only motive?"

Brigit Kelly shook her head. "There are also issues of trade, some that have developed as certain star systems attempt to seize control of trade routes in this region. Eire would like to develop shared agreements on trade just as we share values as people. The Prime Minister also wanted you to know that while Eire's government has formally accepted the proposal of alliance, the governments of the other star systems have only done so on the basis of commitments from representatives. And that so far only general principles have been agreed upon. Nonetheless, the Prime Minister believes that with agreement on general principles we will all be able to reach agreement as well on details after necessary negotiations."

"Eire is extending a helping hand to Kosatka," Carmen said.

"Yes," Brigit Kelly said. "For that, the Prime Minister wishes it to be known that the words and actions of Lochan Nakamura played a significant role in Eire's decision. Apparently, and I don't have details on how this happened, Nakamura was also representing Glenlyon during the negotiations for the alliance."

"What?" Nowak said, looking around at the others once more. "Who approved that?"

Hofer made a face. "We did grant him considerable freedom of action since we had no way of knowing what he might encounter."

"He was supposed to be representing Kosatka!"

"Which is allied with Glenlyon," Carmen said, trying to sound reasonable. "When it comes to defense, our interests are joined. Any aid to Kosatka would be bound up in defending Glenlyon as well."

"Kosatka has agreed to that," Security Minister Kowalski said. "We already have a formal alliance with Glenlyon, as Citizen Ochoa says."

"That's one more thing I'll ask Nakamura about," First Minister Hofer said. "Citizen Kelly, would you mind waiting outside for a few minutes while we discuss this in confidence?"

"Of course not."

As the door closed behind her, Hofer pointed to Nowak. "I'm going to send questions to Nakamura, but the ship he's on is so far off that we won't be able to get a reply until nearly noon. We can't afford to wait for that. This morning I want the People's Representatives canvassed for votes, with an eye to making a formal acceptance of the proposed alliance before the end of this day."

Nowak gazed back in disbelief. "Today? There hasn't been any groundwork laid. I have no idea how the representatives will react, especially when we don't have a detailed agreement to vote on yet."

"All we'd be accepting is the general principles that Eire's Prime Minister alluded to," Hofer said. "Details can follow. We can work an escape clause into the acceptance, something along the lines of not being bound beyond a certain point if negotiations cannot resolve fundamental matters. You know how to word it. Think about the impact of this on our people. We're not going to be able to keep it quiet much longer that there are three new warships in this star system. We have to tell our citizens what is going on. And when we do that, we'll have to tell them either that we've accepted the help of neighbors who have come to our aid, or that we're thinking about the offer of help and haven't decided whether to accept. Which option do you think will generate the most enthusiasm from our people?"

"I'm worried about what Nakamura might have agreed to!"

"So am I. I'll get details of that before the actual vote," Hofer said. "But we do know that whatever Nakamura agreed to was also agreed to by the representatives of Benten, Eire, Adowa, and apparently Catalan and Glenlyon."

"Glenlyon's representative," Kowalski pointed out, "was apparently our representative. That might have simplified gaining Glenlyon's agreement to a deal benefiting Kosatka."

First Minister Hofer laughed. "Yes. Nakamura might have managed a lot using that leverage, as long as it's something that Glenlyon could also agree to."

"Lochan has a close friend at Glenlyon," Carmen said. "The head of their Marines, Mele Darcy. He would not betray her interests."

"We *all* owe Darcy," Kowalski said. "I think you're right."

"Do we have representatives of Benten or Adowa on Kosatka?" Hofer asked.

"Not that I know of."

"Not officially," Jayne Redman said. "Sir, we have to consider whatever motives the Prime Minister of Eire might have. He's not known as a very charitable individual. Just why he agreed to this—"

"Eire was attacked," Kowalski said. "In an attempt to lay the groundwork for their next conquests, our enemies overreached."

"That's what he's claiming. What proof do we have?"

"We have Lochan Nakamura's word," Carmen said.

"And on that we're going to risk the future of Kosatka?"

Carmen felt words rising in her and clenched her teeth to block them. "Lochan risked his life getting to Eire," she finally said.

"That doesn't—"

Hofer interrupted. "Lochan Nakamura helped save *my* life. And he has offered invaluable service to Kosatka. I'm going to listen to what he has to say."

Lisa Nowak rubbed her neck, looking uncomfortable. "I can't understand why Scatha would've attacked Eire at this point, though. Why gather more enemies while they were still fighting us?"

"Overconfidence," Kowalski said. "They must have seen victory here as all but certain. And if they somehow lost, they'd have even more reason to make sure Eire's warships were out of the picture. Commander Derian, if that malware attack had succeeded in destroying both ships, would Eire have been able to trace its origin?"

Derian thought before shaking his head. "It would probably have greatly hindered finding out what had happened and how."

"Overconfidence," Kowalski repeated. "History is full of similar cases, with aggressive governments seeking out new enemies before dealing with the ones they've got. Somebody called that . . . committing suicide out of fear of death."

"We certainly don't want to do the same," Hofer agreed. "I don't find it that implausible that Scatha did such a thing. We're politicians here. We know that stupid actions are common among people who ought to have more sense."

"First Minister—" Redman began.

"I understand your concerns. See if you can find out anything else. We need this help, though. And if Nakamura has managed to bring it at a price Kosatka can live with, he'll deserve every reward we can give him."

"First Minister," Kowalski said, "if there's a possibility that Commander Derian's ship might accompany these new ships to Glenlyon, preparations will have to be made as soon as possible. That's right, isn't it, Commander?"

Derian nodded. "We'll need supplies. Food, and fuel cells. I wish we could wait for some of the coffee that freighter from Adowa is bringing, but that'd probably take too long."

"We'll make sure you get coffee," Hofer promised. "Security Minister . . . damn. I thought I'd decided but it scares me to think of sending our last warship away." He hesitated while the others watched. "But, Glenlyon did that. We'd have lost but for them. We have to . . . let me think on it . . . but make preparations. Get the supplies you need, Commander Derian."

"First Minister," Lisa Nowak said, "when the People's Representatives hear we're sending away our warship—"

"To attack the people who attacked us," Kowalski said. "We're hitting back. That's not just spin. It's the truth."

"Yes," Hofer said, nodding quickly. "That would be the reason. Citizen Nowak, notify the People's Representatives and get the legislative logs rolling. Citizen Redman, let me know if any more signals are sent from those ships to anyone else on Kosatka—"

"One already has been," Redman said, looking at Carmen. "Addressed to Citizen Ochoa." The last sentence sounded like that of a prosecutor laying out the final, damning bit of evidence against a suspect.

But before Carmen could respond, Hofer did. "Is it from Nakamura?"

"Yes. Yes, sir."

"They're friends. They came to Kosatka together. He probably wants to ensure she's all right. I'd be worried about how my friends were doing if I'd been gone while my home was invaded." Hofer dismissed Redman's worries with a wave of his hand. "Citizen Ochoa, let me know if there's anything in Nakamura's message to you that I should know of. Citizen Redman, let us know if any *other* messages are sent to people on Kosatka. Oh, and someone should escort Citizen Kelly home."

"I can do that," Carmen volunteered.

She left the room alongside Security Minister Kowalski, who laughed softly. "This will give you a chance to plot with Eire's representative," he commented. "That's probably what Citizen Redman is warning the First Minister about in there."

"I am a Red," Carmen said, making sure she sounded like she was playing to the joke.

"Are you? I always think of you as Kosatkan." Kowalski nodded farewells to Carmen, Kelly, and Palmer before heading for his own office.

Smiling, Carmen watched him go, then turned to Kelly. "I'll escort you home, if that's all right with you."

The streets outside were still deserted, but the sky had just begun to pale as the dawn intruded on night's domain. Carmen walked alongside Brigit Kelly for a ways before speaking again. "So . . . Lochan Nakamura is back. Safe."

"Yes," Kelly said. "You must be happy."

"Are you?"

"That's an odd question."

"Is it?"

Kelly turned a questioning look her way. "What business is it of yours?"

"Lochan and I are friends," Carmen said, feeling defensive.

"Friends?" Kelly laughed briefly. "He speaks of you fairly often, and always in the tones of a proud father or a loving brother."

"I just don't want Lochan to be hurt," Carmen said.

"Then we're in agreement." Kelly smiled. "You've no grounds for worry on my account. He's a good man. But whether he and I become more than friends is yet to be seen. And I only tell you that much because I know how much Lochan values you."

"Thank you." Carmen looked up at the stars. "I guess soon we're probably going to be allies. As many as six star systems. Maybe more will join."

"That's been your dream, hasn't it?"

Carmen felt her face warm. "Lochan told you, huh? Yes. I wanted to make sure these new star systems didn't turn into a vastly larger version of Mars. I wanted people to be safe in their homes. I'm not ashamed of that."

"You shouldn't be." Kelly laughed again. "I came out here like so many others, wanting to be left alone. Which is all well and good until you stumble and fall. When that happens, it's nice to have someone around to help catch you." She sobered, looking about them. "I've seen firsthand what war has done to Kosatka. I hope it never reaches Eire."

"We're in agreement on that, too," Carmen said. "Um, do you mind if we stop for a moment? Lochan sent me a message."

"No problem," Kelly said.

They stopped while Carmen pulled out her pad and popped a bud into her ear before calling up the message. Lochan's image appeared, surprising her with how good it made her feel to see him safe. "Hi, Carmen. I really hope you're okay. We were shocked to get here and find out that the invasion force had been defeated, but I guess I shouldn't have been surprised since Kosatka had you. I'm fine, despite a few, uh, adventures along the way. Please let me know you're all right. And, uh, if you have a chance, can you check up on Brigit Kelly, Eire's representative? I'd like to know if she's okay, too. I have to keep this short, so, I'll wait to hear back from you, and when I finally get back on Kosatka we'll have a long talk to bring each other up to date. I think . . . I think your dream might have a chance of coming true, Carmen. I'm glad I was able to help make that happen." Lochan glanced to the side as if someone else was speaking to him. "Oh, and tell Brigit that Freya says hi and she hopes that . . . I'm not going to tell her that. What? Freya says hi to you, too. Nakamura, out."

Carmen frowned at her pad after the message ended. "Freya? Who the hell is Freya?"

"Freya?" Kelly nodded to herself. "Oh. Freya."

"She says hi. Who the hell is Freya?"

"She's a dangerous one. That's who she is. Lochan met up with her, eh? That's excellent."

Carmen looked at Kelly. "Not a rival, I take it?"

"No. Someone I knew on Eire before she went to Catalan. I sent word to her to help him. If Lochan did run into danger she probably helped ensure he survived it."

"I'll have to thank her, then. Lochan asked me to check on you."

"Did he now?" Kelly smiled again.

"Should I tell him you're okay?"

Brigit Kelly smiled wider. "Tell him I'm at death's door and whispering his name over and over again."

"I'm not going to do that to Lochan!" But Carmen found herself laughing.

As soon as she dropped off Kelly, Carmen made another call. "Domi? Good news. Really good news."

But as she spoke to Dominic, Carmen thought about how long it would take those warships to reach the jump point for Jatayu and beyond that Glenlyon. She hoped that Glenlyon wasn't already in dire need of help.

Time didn't mean much inside the facility, where every compartment was either pitch black but for minimal lights on the battle armor, or dimly illuminated by emergency lanterns whose batteries hadn't quite given out yet. Days meant nothing. Life was divided into too-short periods of rest, longer periods of watching and waiting, and short, tense times spent moving from one hiding place to another.

"You ever think about home, ma'am?"

Mele shrugged despite knowing the gesture would be invisible inside her armor and in the gloom that filled the compartment they were in. "Not really. You mean the place or the people?"

"The people, I guess," Corporal Lamar said. "I mean, I knew when I left I might never make it back, but I guess I didn't understand it. Does that make sense?"

"Sure it does," Mele said. "Where was home?"

"Old Earth." Lamar sounded wistful, and sad. "Where I grew up it was really hot and dry, and not much to see except some mountains in the distance. A lot of nothing as far as the eye can see, my dad used to say. And there was nothing there for me. Just sit around on your butt all day because there weren't enough jobs. My mom and dad didn't want me to leave, but they also wanted me to have a chance to do something, you know? I thought about staying, and then someday realizing on the day I died that I'd never really done anything. So I left."

"I guess a lot of people left home for reasons like that," Mele said.

"I guess. New worlds, new chances. But I still miss the old. I wonder what time it is back home? It could be night and they could be sleeping, or they could be eating breakfast. I wish you could taste the hash my mom could make. Or maybe right now they're standing in the afternoon sun and looking up at the sky. Wouldn't that be funny?" Lamar said. "If they was looking up thinking about me at the same moment I was here thinking about them?"

"Maybe they are," Mele said. She always felt a little uncomfortable when her people needed to unburden themselves and sought her out, but that was part of the job. If they were willing to risk death at her orders, the least she could do was listen to them when they got homesick.

"I wrote them," Lamar said. "It takes months for ships to carry a message home, doesn't it?"

"Three or four months from here, I think," Mele said.

"I told them I was a Marine now. I bet that'll surprise them! Attached some pictures of me in uniform and everything. And some pictures of the planet from orbit. Planets sure look nice from orbit, huh?"

"I've seen some that didn't look too nice even from that far off," Mele said.

"But this one looks nice. Beautiful. Worth fighting for," Lamar said. "Right?"

"Right. Did you tell them about the fight at Kosatka?" Mele asked.

"Just a little. Like, we fought, and it was kind of rough, but we won. And what it was like on the ship and all."

"You did real good there. And here. I might have to make you a sergeant."

Lamar laughed. "Thanks. But I didn't . . . I didn't say much about it. It's kind of hard to talk about."

"That's true for a lot of people," Mele said, feeling the unyielding metal against the back of her armor and remembering similar sensations on the orbital facility at Kosatka.

"But I can talk to you about it. Or Glitch."

"We were there. It's like a special club that you get into by surviving and getting the hell scared out of you and watching stuff that you don't want to remember." Mele reached over to pat the armor over Lamar's shoulders. "Your mom and dad won't get it. And that's good. Because it means what you went through mattered. They'll never have to face the same thing."

"I guess. Thanks, Major. Have you got anybody? In another star system, maybe?"

"I've got you apes," Mele said. "That's enough trouble and responsibility for anyone."

"Are we going to make it, Major? Seems like it's been forever we've been doing this, fighting and running and picking up new ammo and power supplies where we hid them."

"We don't have to hold out forever," Mele said. "Just until they get low on supplies or until help arrives for us."

"If help is coming, I hope it gets here soon," Lamar said. "I'd kinda like to tell my parents I survived this fight, too."

"You and me both," Mele said. "We'll make it. Don't let any of the others see you doubting that. If you don't believe we can win this, they won't believe it."

"Do you believe it, Major?"

"Sure I do."

Mele wondered when she'd gotten so good at lying that she even sounded sincere to herself.

CHAPTER 11

"**M**ajor?"

Mele Darcy grabbed for her rifle as she woke from a nap so deep and dark it had held no dreams. Her heart abruptly pounding, Mele focused on Sergeant Giddings, calming her breathing as she realized that no immediate danger threatened. "What's up?"

"I got a link with Captain Batra."

"Tie me in." A moment later her comm status light glowed green. At this point in the fight for the facility the link was voice only, of course. Images took up a lot more bandwidth, and were that much harder to get through enemy jamming and that much easier to trace. "Darcy here."

"Batra here," he replied. From his voice, Captain Batra was feeling the strain. Not that she could fault him for that. "I'm still active, with seven surviving soldiers in my group. Nine hours ago I made contact with Lieutenant Nasir's group. He still had eight with him."

"Good," Mele said.

"We decided against merging groups. But about fifteen minutes after we separated, my group detected fighting in the general direction that Lieutenant Nasir's group had gone. I haven't been able to reestablish contact since then."

Damn. Her momentary relief at knowing Nasir was all right dwindled into nothing, because she couldn't afford to feel despair. "Okay. Thanks for the update. Continue operations." There weren't any other orders she could give.

"Under—"

Mele's comm status light went red.

"We lost the link," Sergeant Giddings said.

"I saw. Glitch, have you heard anything from Lieutenant Nasir's group in the last nine hours? Even a momentary connection?"

"No, Major. Nothing. I had really short comms with Savak's group and Gunny Moon's, but not Lieutenant Nasir's. You want me to try to link with them?"

"Yes. See if you can find them. Captain Batra reported detecting a fight near where Lieutenant Nasir's group would have been, and he hasn't been able to contact them again since then."

"Oh." Sergeant Giddings nodded, the gesture tired. "I hope they're okay. He's a decent officer. We need people like that now."

"We always need people like that," Mele said. "And there are never enough of them."

"Corporal Yoshida was with the Lieutenant," Giddings said. "If something happened to the Lieutenant, Yoshi will get through to us."

"Right. See if you can get ahold of him or Lieutenant Nasir." If Nasir and Yoshi were both gone, the entire group might have been wiped out, like Lieutenant Killian's. Mele shook her head, trying to dislodge the dark thoughts gathering there. Maintaining hope was hard here, buried inside the facility, surrounded by metal and composites and the ever-present gloom, wearing battle armor that'd become uncomfortable days ago, breathing air and drinking water recycled by the armor from your own waste. She checked their location, wondering if she dared move her group to some spot next to the exterior of the facility. That'd be dangerous, exposing them to possible detection if an enemy warship was watching that location, but she really wanted to see the stars, to know that something else still existed outside of this dark, claustrophobic maze that she'd doomed the people under her command to endure. And to die in.

Time didn't exist in jump space, they said. In order for time to exist, something had to exist to create it. Entropy, maybe. And there was nothing in jump space. Nothing that humans could measure. But maybe the moment even a single human entered jump space then time also sprang into existence there. Because humans measured time within them, in the actions of cells and organs and thoughts. "What is time?" some philosopher had asked on one of the Old Colonies, and then answered himself. "We are." Scientists laughed at that, but they'd yet to come up with a better, provable answer.

What time was it now? Lochan Nakamura wondered. What time was this moment back on Old Earth where humans had first looked up at the stars and wondered what lay among them? What time was it back at Kosatka, and what time would it be when they arrived at Glenlyon?

Once they saw what awaited them at Glenlyon, would time be defined in only two ways that mattered, "soon enough" or "too late"?

In contrast to the apparently limitless nothing of jump space outside, there wasn't all that much room on the bridge of a destroyer, and just about every square centimeter of the bulkheads and overhead seemed to be covered with something important. Lochan did his best to find a spot that didn't seem to be blocking anything or in anyone's way, waiting uncomfortably for the inevitable moment when someone would need something that he was standing in front of.

Freya Morgan stood by him, apparently unconcerned about being in anyone's way. From the confidence with which she looked about her, she might have been an admiral in command of the entire force, waiting for the moment to declare her authority.

"You don't have any secret orders about this, do you?" Lochan muttered to Freya.

She grinned. "I'm just keeping them on their toes, wondering exactly who I am and what I'm up to. It's good tactics to surprise people who don't realize what's under what they see. But who am I lecturing to? You're better at it than I am."

"Me?" Was she serious? Lochan's thoughts and the conversation were interrupted before he could say more.

"Leaving jump space in ten minutes," one of the watch standers on the *Asahi* reported to the captain. "Ship is at full combat readiness."

"Very well," Commander Miko Sori replied.

Benten's commanding officer had impressed Lochan as a nononsense sort, almost severe in her attitude, who'd surprised him with flashes of sudden dry humor. There was no doubt who she was underneath it all. She was the captain and she knew her job. Just like most of the rest aboard *Asahi*, Sori had gained her training and experience in either Earth Fleet or one of the much smaller fleets once maintained by the individual Old Colonies.

Lochan glanced at the nearest display, one showing the external view, which in jump space was nothing except formless gray. He'd asked many people, some crew members of civilian ships and some sailors on warships and some scientists of various sorts, just what that gray nothingness was, and the answer was always the same. Nothing. As far as human science could tell, jump space contained nothing. "Do you ever wonder," he asked Freya in a low voice, "why the nothing in jump space looks gray? Shouldn't it look black?"

"Black is something, though," Freya said. "Our brains know that. Maybe that's why we see nothing as gray."

Lochan didn't reply, startled into silence. But he heard gasps from several of those on the bridge as two lights suddenly flared amid the gray nothingness of jump space. The lights blazed brilliantly for a moment, then faded as quickly as they'd appeared.

"Twin lights?" one of *Asahi's* officers asked, amazed. "Has anyone ever reported seeing two lights at once?"

Commander Sori replied, her intrigued gaze on her own display. "Not that I know of. Make sure all data concerning those lights is compiled. We'll want to forward this sighting to scientific institutions."

"Yes, Captain, but . . ." The officer hesitated. "There are no data. Nothing except the lights themselves."

Frowning, Sori touched her display, activating commands. Her frown remained as she read the results. "Nothing."

"I don't understand," Lochan said. "We saw lights. Those lights had to be made by something."

Commander Sori turned to look at him. "That's what you'd think, wouldn't you? But you can view the data yourself. Our sensors recorded the lights that our eyes saw. But there's nothing else. No source. No energy. The light simply existed."

"I'd heard," Freya said, "that the first trips into jump space didn't see any lights at all, but that they started to appear and have become more frequent as more human ships traveled jump space."

"That's correct." Commander Sori gazed intently at her display. "Whatever they are, their appearance may be linked to human presence. But how? To know that, we'd have to know what they are. And there is no clue to that at all."

"Perhaps the lack of clues is a clue," Freya said. "Perhaps they point to the lights being something that has no origin in the science we know."

"If so, there are no answers there that can be confirmed by the science we know." Sori raised an eyebrow at Freya. "And, if so, what about this ship would inspire *two* such spirits to escort it?"

Freya smiled. "Perhaps my father sent them to keep an eye on us."

"I do not think even Donal Morgan has that much clout with the angels and spirits."

"I assure you, he thinks he does."

Sori smiled only slightly, maintaining a carefully diplomatic expression rather than openly laughing at the prime minister of Eire. "And what of you, Lochan Nakamura? I'm told that you're a wise man."

"Who said that?" Lochan asked, startled again.

"You don't think it's true?"

"I'd never call myself wise," he said.

"Perhaps it is true, then," Commander Sori said. "What do you think of the lights?"

Lochan made a face. "I've learned that when you don't understand what something is, it's a big mistake to assume you can be certain what it isn't. All you know is what you don't know."

"Ah, you're a follower of Zen?"

"I . . . don't really know anything about that," Lochan said.

"And you admit it?" another officer said. "You must be a master of Zen!"

The laughter that followed was interrupted by an alert. "Leaving jump space in two minutes, Captain."

"Everyone, focus on your tasks," Sori ordered. "We don't know what awaits us at Glenlyon."

R ob Geary had been making another failed attempt to get some sleep when an urgent alert sounded in his stateroom, the noise echoing like a herald of doom. "Captain! Four destroyers have arrived at the jump point from Jatayu," Ensign Reichert reported, her voice remarkably level for someone conveying such terrible news.

Four destroyers.

They couldn't possibly be new forces from Glenlyon purchased by Leigh Camagan. There hadn't been time for her to get to Old Earth and those ships to return here. Camagan was probably a long ways from even reaching Old Earth yet.

And Kosatka had only one destroyer, with no prospects of gaining more anytime in the near future.

Which meant the new arrivals were almost certainly enemy.

In the few seconds it took him to reach the bridge, Rob thought about what these new threats meant. Four more warships, each equal to *Saber*. Survival was no longer an option. There was no way *Saber* could outrun and outdodge that many opponents. The only question remaining was how much longer *Saber* would survive.

He wouldn't surrender her. He'd get as much of the crew off as possible before the last fight, but *Saber* wouldn't become an enemy prize to be used against other worlds. Rob felt an emptiness inside him as he realized what that resolve might well mean, that he would never see his wife and family again, that the new child born to Ninja would never know their father.

And yet, somehow, he kept a calm and steady demeanor as he walked onto the bridge. Perhaps he'd gone numb inside, overwhelmed emotions shutting down to avoid running out of control. "What do we have on them?"

"None of the destroyers are broadcasting identification," Lieutenant Cameron said.

That wasn't a surprise. Enemy ships had been doing that sometimes in recent battles like that at Kosatka. "How long until they get here?" Rob asked.

"We're . . . Captain?" Lieutenant Cameron's voice broke like that of a startled teenager.

"What?" Rob tried not to snap at Cameron, who had every right to be rattled at the moment.

"Sir, our sensors are giving a tentative ID on one of the destroyers as the *Shark* from Kosatka."

"The *Shark*?" How could the enemy have captured Kosatka's remaining warship? "How good is that ID?"

"Eighty percent, Captain. Just upped to ninety-two percent."

Lieutenant Commander Shen dashed onto the bridge and dropped into the executive officer's chair beside Geary's command chair. "Give me the data."

"On its way, XO."

Shen spent a long moment staring at her display. "I think the ID is right, Captain. It's based on the repairs visible around *Shark*'s stern. Those repairs sure as hell look like what I remember. But there's no sign of new battle damage on her."

"Kosatka surrendered?" Rob asked, rage appearing inside him. "After all we sacrificed to help them, they gave up and turned their ship over to—"

"Captain! Incoming message from one of the new warships! It was sent tight beam to us so only we'd see it."

Rob had to inhale slowly, wondering what sort of surrender demand this would be. "Send it to me."

A window opened on his display, revealing a woman seated in the command chair on a bridge nearly identical to the one on *Saber*. "Commodore Robert Geary, this is Captain Miko Sori, commanding officer of the *Asahi*, flagship of Benten Star System. I am in command of this task force, which has been assembled to assist Glenlyon and Kosatka against external aggression."

Rob's hand twitched, hitting the pause command as he stared at the image.

"Captain?" Vicki Shen asked, her expression somber.

"You need to hear this." Rob's hand shook so he had trouble touching the right controls, sending it to Shen's display and reversing the message to play the first part again.

"—this is Captain Miko Sori, commanding officer of the *Asahi*, flagship of Benten Star System. I am in command of this task force, which has been assembled to assist Glenlyon and Kosatka against external aggression. We will proceed on a course to meet up with your ship, and then deal with the invaders."

"Can we believe this?" Shen asked, her mouth hanging open. "Have our prayers been answered?"

The image of Captain Sori kept speaking, as if replying to Shen's question. "To provide you reassurance that I am who I say and that we are here to assist Glenlyon, Commander Derian on *Shark* will be contacting you as well." Sori gestured to one side of her. "I am told that this individual is also known to you and can confirm that our mission here is a friendly one to Glenlyon."

The middle-aged man who appeared was indeed familiar to Rob. "Commodore, I'm Lochan Nakamura, special representative of Kosatka Star System. You know me, and I hope you trust me. I've been asked to let you know that Eire, Adowa, and Benten Star Systems have entered into an alliance to halt aggression in this region. Catalan has made a preliminary commitment to join as well. Kosatka has formally agreed to join that alliance, and we hope that Glenlyon will also do so. I, uh, made a preliminary commitment to the alliance on Glenlyon's behalf because your Leigh Camagan empowered me to do so before she continued on toward Old Earth. I realize that doesn't bind Glenlyon, but I assure you that I did my best to represent your interests as well as that of Kosatka. Please pass on my respects to Mele Darcy, who I hope is somewhere safe at the moment."

The image switched back to Captain Sori. "I will await your reply on how our forces can coordinate their efforts to defend this star system. Just as our ancestors stood together in the past, so we stand together now. Sori, out."

Rob buried his face in his hands, momentarily unable to speak.

"Captain?" Lieutenant Commander Shen asked, her voice shaking. "This is real? Not a trick?"

"It's real," Rob said, raising his head to look around the bridge. "I've never met Nakamura in person, but I've talked to him on calls like this, and Mele Darcy knows him. She's told me I can trust him."

"Sir?" Ensign Reichert said. "Are these new ships on our side?"

"Yes," Rob said. "It seems so. It looks like we'll be denied a heroic, doomed last stand against overwhelming odds."

"I'm good with that, Captain."

"Me, too," Lieutenant Cameron said. "Sir, there's another message incoming."

This time the image was of a man Geary knew well, the commanding officer of the *Shark*. "Greetings, Commodore!" Commander Derian said. "It looks like we get to return the favor you did for Kosatka, and the favor your Marines and Commander Shen did for me personally and for my ship. I didn't know Miko Sori in Earth Fleet, but I did know Bard Hubbard on *Caladbolg*. He says this is the real deal. The two ships from Eire are the *Caladbolg* and the *Gae Bulg*. I can attest that they have good crews and good commanding officers. I can't imagine Glenlyon rejecting this alliance, but if anyone questions whether we can be trusted . . . well, you know the answer. I wouldn't help anything that would hurt Glenlyon, not after how you guys helped us deal with that invasion fleet. And we haven't finished avenging the loss of *Piranha* and Captain Salomon.

"Let me know if you still have any questions. Our task force commander on *Asahi* says all ships can contact *Saber*, so if you want to talk to Bard on *Caladbolg* or Tanya the Wicked on *Gae Bulg*, feel free. Derian, out."

"Tanya the Wicked?" Rob repeated.

Shen grinned. "They've got Tanya the Wicked with them."

"She's commanding one of the destroyers. How'd she get that nickname?"

"Allegedly it's because her record is absolutely spotless. Never a mark or a demerit. Earth Fleet used to gossip that meant she was so good at hiding the bodies that nobody'd ever been able to catch her working her evil plans."

"What's she like at commanding a ship?" Rob asked, wondering just how rigid a person would be who'd never been caught doing anything wrong.

"That's the funny thing," Vicki Shen said. "Because her record was so clean, because she never broke a rule, she could *bend* the rules more than anyone else, because her superiors assumed Tanya the Wicked would do no wrong."

"She sounds like a good person to have on our side. I can't . . ." Rob tried to get his head around what had happened, the sudden shift in odds, the unexpected help, the chance to finally engage the enemy again with *Saber*. He realized that his first priority would be passing on this news and getting approval to act with Glenlyon's new allies. "I need to make a private call in my stateroom. Get me President Chisholm and link the call to there."

It took ten minutes after Rob reached his stateroom before the image of Chisholm appeared. The president, who looked like she'd been awoken from the sort of miserable attempt at sleep that Rob had also been enduring, had apparently been briefed on the probable reason for the call. It took her two tries to get the necessary words out. "Is this as bad as it looks? I'm told that four more enemy warships have arrived."

"No," Rob said. "It's very good news. The four destroyers that arrived from Jatayu came from Kosatka. They're here to help us."

Saber was far enough from the planet for a tiny delay in communications, but Chisholm took much longer to reply than that would account for. "They're friendly?" she finally got out. "Are these ships hired by Leigh Camagan?"

"No. She probably hasn't even reached Old Earth yet. These ships are allies from Kosatka, Eire, and Benten. Eire provided two of them."

"Allies? We've only signed an agreement with Kosatka."

"Yes, Kosatka sent *Shark*, their surviving warship, and—"

"Eire and Benten? Why are Eire and Benten helping us?"

"Apparently Kosatka's special representative Lochan Nakamura convinced them that would be a smart thing for them to do." Rob spread his hands. "That's all I know so far. I can attest that really is Nakamura aboard the Benten destroyer, and that Commander Derian on the *Shark* is genuine as well. I have to no reason to doubt their claim that they're here to help. But I need, as soon as possible, approval from the government to reply to their messages and to work with them to defeat the ships attacking our orbital facility."

President Chisholm frowned in thought. "What do they want in exchange for this help? Have they said?"

"No," Rob said, startled. In his exhilaration over the arrival of help, the question of possible costs or trade-offs hadn't even occurred to him. "There hasn't been any mention of a quid pro quo, but Nakamura did say that Benten, Eire, and, um, Adowa have already formed an alliance that Kosatka has joined, and Catalan may have joined. They're hoping we'll join, too."

Chisholm sighed, looking older than her years. "At least they're asking us to join their group. That's an improvement on the threats and demands we've gotten from Apulu, Turan, and Scatha. But we're going to need to know a lot more before we commit to an alliance with that many other star systems. Who's in charge of these ships? This Nakamura?"

"No. He's a representative of Kosatka's government. Captain Miko Sori on Benten's destroyer *Asahi* is in command of the four destroyers," Rob said. "Nakamura said he also attempted to represent Glenlyon at whatever negotiations took place to form this alliance because Leigh Camagan asked him to."

"That's—! Wait. What?" Chisholm shook her head, grimacing. "Nakamura was empowered by Camagan to represent Glenlyon? She didn't have the authority to do that."

"She must trust him," Rob said.

"That doesn't matter. Nothing he said or did will bind the government of Glenlyon. Especially when command of this group was given to—" Chisholm halted in midsentence, staring into space before focusing back on Rob. "The ship from Benten is in command of this group? Didn't you say two of the warships are from Eire?"

"Yes. The *Caladbolg* and the *Gae Bulg*."

"Doesn't the larger group normally provide the commander in a case like that?"

"I . . . think so," Rob said.

Chisholm chewed her lip. "There's a lot of symbolic meaning in giving that command to Benten. Yet Donal Morgan of Eire agreed to it. From all I've heard, Donal Morgan can be a total rocket when he feels like it, and he feels like it fairly often. Why did he agree to this? And how can we learn the truth?"

The implications of the president's words bothered Rob. "From what Mele Darcy has said of Nakamura, I think he'll be open with us about whatever agreements were reached."

"Darcy knows Nakamura? Has she vouched for him?"

"She has to me, yes," Rob said. "If it comes to that, trust him with your life, she said."

The president rubbed her temples as if fighting a headache. "Trusting our lives is one thing. But this is about trusting our world and our star system and everyone in it to the word of this Nakamura. How long do we have until the new ships are close enough to this world to attack either our enemies or us?"

"At this point in our orbit, they came in three point eight light hours from us. They're accelerating, but we don't know how fast they're going to ramp up their velocity. If they stick to point zero two light, it'll be about eight days. If they go up as high as point zero four, only about four days."

"No sooner than that, though? Can you find out more about their plans?"

"If I'm permitted to talk to them," Rob said. "It sounds like they want to develop plans together with us."

"That may be what they're saying, but . . ." Chisholm looked pained. "All right. If you could have everything you wanted at this moment, what would it be?"

Rob didn't have to take any time to think about that. "Permission to both communicate freely with the new arrivals, and to coordinate the actions of *Saber* with them to ensure those attacking our star system are wiped out."

"Coordinate? Are you talking about placing *Saber* under the command of the officer on Benten's warship?"

Rob realized that hadn't occurred to him. "No. I guess I assumed the government wouldn't agree to that. I'm talking about acting with each other, making sure the actions of our warships support each other, as we did at Kosatka."

President Chisholm squinted as she thought. "Is there any chance they'd agree to be under your command? Since they're in our star system?"

"My command?" Rob hesitated, then shook his head again. "I can't imagine that either Benten's Captain Sori or the officers on Eire's ships would agree to that. They probably have orders not to do anything like that. *Shark* might agree to it, depending on their orders from Kosatka's government."

"Then maybe we should do that. Even up the forces."

Rob looked at his display, wondering why he felt a vast reluctance to agree, and finally realizing why. "That'd be splitting the alliance, wouldn't it? An alliance forms to come help us, and our first act when they get here would be trying to split it by breaking Kosatka's warship away from the others."

"That's not what I'm talking about."

"With all due respect, Madam President, that is what you're talking about," Rob said. "Four ships arrive under unified command of an alliance formed to help us against aggression, and our response is to try to get one of those ships to answer to us instead of to the alliance commander. How would you interpret that other than as a deliberate act to split the force and undermine the new alliance?"

Chisholm grimaced in frustration. "Maybe that's what we should be doing."

"Someone is offering their hand to us and our response is to slap them?" Rob demanded, the frustrations and fears of the last weeks boiling over inside him. "I've been waiting for the moment when my ship had to enter a hopeless battle. For the moment when my crew had to die trying to make a difference for the future and the freedom of this star system that's our home now. And when instead I learn that my crew can live and we can all strike a blow to win this fight as long as we cooperate with those who've come to help us I'm supposed to say, 'Hell no, we won't trust anybody but ourselves'?"

"I have to think of the future of everyone in Glenlyon! My responsibilities are far greater than yours!" Chisholm sat back, fuming.

Rob considered his next words carefully, knowing that he'd never be able to take them back. "I will not continue in command if this offer of help is rejected, or if the government refuses to commit to accepting the help."

"You're threatening the government with your resignation?"

"It's not a threat," he said. "It's what I will do. If all Glenlyon sees around us is enemies out to take our freedom, then that's all we'll ever have. Enemies. But I know Kosatka can be trusted. I know Lochan Nakamura would not lie, because Mele Darcy told me that. Whatever price this alliance requests . . . and we haven't even asked what price before talking about breaking that alliance or rejecting its help . . . whatever price it *asks* must be a lot less than that *demanded* of us by those attacking us at this moment."

President Chisholm glared at him. "We came out here to be free of obligations and commitments and control."

He returned the glare. "If Glenlyon insists on a wall to keep out everyone else so we won't have any obligations or commitments or any infringement on our own actions, then that wall will actually be a cage. A cage we built ourselves, to hide inside. A cage that limits everything we do. That's not freedom. It's self-imprisonment. I can't tell the government what to do, but I can refuse to lead men and women to their deaths in support of a policy I believe will poison the future of this star system."

She eyed him for several seconds without replying. "I see. I can't deny your right to make such a decision. You feel this strongly about it?"

"Yes," Rob said. "I'm not trying to dictate government policy, but I think approaching this opportunity as if it was simply another threat would be fundamentally wrong, and disastrous to our hopes for real freedom."

"Do you think I'm unaware of the need for rules and laws and mutual agreements?" Chisholm demanded. "I wouldn't be president if I wasn't willing to work within such a system. But these are rules and laws and agreements that we made, without anyone holding a gun to our heads. Don't you want to protect Glenlyon's people from foreign coercion?"

"Yes," Rob said. "I do. I think I've proven that by my actions. But . . . we've been attacked repeatedly. Almost since the day we arrived in this star system. We've come to see any approach from the outside as a danger. Is that how we want to view everyone who comes here? Do we want to let the actions of places like Scatha dictate how we respond to the actions of places like Benten and Eire and Adowa?"

"That's a point worth considering," Chisholm said. "Coercion can take a variety of forms, and poison can spread beyond its source. I admit . . . yes . . . my first thought when they arrived was that this had to be another attack. We've already been conditioned to see things that way. But that doesn't mean such a view is wrong."

"Madam President, if this force is here to coerce us, to make us do something, then Glenlyon might as well give up now. There is no chance of us winning that fight. We can't wait too long to decide. Those new ships will arrive here in a few days. And even sooner than that, the enemy ships already attacking our orbital facility are going to figure out these new people are not their friends. They'll act, whether we've made up our minds regarding this alliance or not."

Another long pause as Chisholm thought, then her eyes sought Rob's. "I'll be contacting those ships directly for more information. You also have permission to communicate with the new arrivals."

"Am I allowed to coordinate actions with them?"

"You already have authority to take necessary actions in space to defend this star system. Use it."

"I'm to interpret my orders that broadly?" Rob asked.

She smiled, a cold, hard expression that carried a message of expectations as well as conditional support. "You've shown that you can interpret orders broadly, and make the right decisions when doing so. Act as you think you should, Commodore Geary. If the government decides that your orders need to be modified, they will be. Understand?"

He nodded. "I'm free to act until I do the wrong thing. I understand. I assure you that every action I take will be with the long-term safety, security, and freedom of Glenlyon foremost in my mind."

"I've never doubted that, Commodore. That's why I keep coming back to you when Glenlyon is in trouble. Keep me informed."

The call ended, Rob sighed, got up, and walked back to the bridge, where Lieutenant Commander Shen waited along with the watch standers.

"What's the word?" Vicki Shen asked.

He shrugged as he took the command seat. "The ball just got dropped into my lap again. I was pretty much told to decide what I should do."

Shen let out a sigh. "Freedom of action offers you a lot of chances to do the right thing, and a lot of chances to screw up. What're we going to do?"

"I'm going to send a message back to the new ships, offering to coordinate *Saber's* actions with theirs. Because I think that's necessary for the defense of this star system," Rob added, speaking loudly so he'd be overheard by others on the bridge. He wanted this decision, and his reasons, to be on the record. "At this point, the enemy warships won't know who those four new ships are. They'll wait to be contacted, and when that doesn't happen they'll send a message. Minimum time for a message to be sent and received will be about eight hours."

Lieutenant Commander Shen nodded. "I'm guessing four hours before they send a challenge. That is, excuse me, that *was* the usual interval to wait for a reply in Earth Fleet. Then eight hours for messages to fly both ways at the speed of light. That's half a day. After that . . ." She paused, thinking. "This guy we're fighting will send another message. He has time, and will be thinking that will cover his butt if he makes a wrong decision. Another half day, maybe. It'll be at least a day before the enemy seriously starts considering the fact that these new arrivals are not friendly. After that, the enemy reaction will depend on how long he has to run before the approaching force can intercept him on his way to a jump point out of Glenlyon."

"We need to keep him guessing as long as possible," Rob said. "I wonder if there's any way to get a message to the defenders on the facility that help is here, but that won't tip off the attackers if they intercept it?"

"Any code might be broken," Shen said, thinking. "Unless . . . Darcy knows this Nakamura guy?"

"Yeah. She knows he's settled on Kosatka."

"So if she knew he was here . . ."

Rob grinned. "Yes. That's it. Ensign Torres, give me a link to any remaining friendly receivers on the orbital facility."

"Done, sir!"

"Major Darcy," Rob said, "this is Commodore Geary. Nakamura says hello. Geary, out."

CHAPTER 12

"**M**ajor?"

"Yeah, Glitch." Darcy blinked herself awake from a cat-nap, hoping this wasn't even worse news. "What's up?"

"We've received a message. It was sent in the clear, but it's some kind of code. I don't know what it means."

"Relay it to me." She listened to Rob Geary's voice.

"Nakamura says hello."

Nakamura? As in Lochan? But he was at Kosatka.

Unless he'd arrived at Glenlyon. Why would Lochan come here?

For only one reason. He'd brought help. Good old Lochan, the guy who thought of himself as a failure at everything, but had a way of coming through when it mattered. Mele smiled with relief. "Glitch, try to get through to the other commanders. Tell them help has arrived." Why hadn't Rob Geary just said that? Because the enemy might not realize yet that whatever had shown up was on Glenlyon's side? "The enemy apparently doesn't know help for us has shown up. When they figure it out, we may see a burst of activity, either a sudden last-ditch attack or a sudden pullback. Got that?"

"Help is here," Glitch recited, "the enemy may not know, sudden enemy activity possible when they figure it out."

"Right. After you get that out see if you can get me a decent link to Captain Batra."

She finally checked the "local" time on the facility, which was slaved to that of the primary (and still only) city on the planet below. 0500. Five in the morning. Mele let out a gasp of exhausted laughter. Normally 0500 would be when reveille sounded, time to get out of your bunk, hit the deck, and get ready for a new working day. This was probably the first time in several days that she'd actually woken up at about the "normal" time.

Mele moved carefully through the cramped compartment they were huddled in, the darkness barely illuminated by a nightglow setting on a small light on the side of her armored glove. The medic, Corporal Okubo, was already awake and on sentry, eyeing a sensor screen whose glow marked his face with the distorted reflections of warning symbols. Mele lightly touched each Marine still asleep. Corporal Penny Lamar and four privates. All that were left in this group after a few more encounters with enemy patrols. "Up and at 'em. It's another glorious day in the Marines."

"Oo-rah," Corporal Lamar grumbled in a whisper.

Sergeant Giddings was still working on getting the message out. Mele waited until all of the other Marines left with her were awake, sitting up and yawning, bleary-eyed with fatigue that the rest period hadn't done nearly enough to fix. "Here's some news before breakfast. The space squids got word to me that help has arrived." Everyone's eyes jerked to greater alertness, sharpening their gaze on her. "I don't know how much, or how long it'll be before it gets here. But sooner or later those apes we're fighting will also get the word. We need to be ready for whatever they do, and need to keep them distracted as much as we can."

"Major?" Sergeant Giddings held up a fiber link. "I've got Lieutenant Paratnam. He says he needs to talk to you about Captain Batra."

"You guys eat while I handle this." Mele took the link and plugged it in, the green light that would mark a solid connection flickering instead of staying steady. "What's up? Where's Batra?"

"I haven't been able to contact him for the last eight hours," Paratnam said. "Not even momentary burst signals. I'm assessing that he's . . . no longer active."

She heard enough in Paratnam's voice, the weariness, the anger, the stubborn determination, for an image of his haggard face to appear in her mind's eye. "How many did Batra have with him?"

"Nine, last I knew. We've had no contact with any of them. According to Captain Batra's orders, since we can't—"

Mele waited as the comm status light flickered red, yellow, and then green again, the tiny illumination casting shades of color on the Marines huddled in the dark compartment. "Say again all after 'Batra's orders.' I lost you."

"Um . . . per Captain Batra's orders I'm assuming command of the ground forces element."

"Okay." She resisted the urge to add "congratulations." That'd be humor too dark for even a situation like this. "You got the word that help's on the way?"

"Yes. Any details on that?" Paratnam pleaded.

"That's what I'm trying to get. Do you have anyone able to tap into surviving navigational systems on the facility or see *Saber* directly?"

"Sergeant Savak's group was close to the outer edge last I knew."

"Try to contact her and see if she can call *Saber*. I need any details Savak can get about whatever help has arrived and when it's going to get close enough to help us kill stuff."

"Understood," Paratnam said. "I hope it's a lot and I hope it's soon."

"Agreed. Wait." Mele looked over at Corporal Okubo, still on sentry duty, who gestured urgently at his sensor readouts.

"Company heading this way," Okubo whispered. "We're getting hits on movement. Estimated ten to fifteen hostiles."

"Got it. Lieutenant Paratnam, I gotta go. I'll try to reconnect as soon as a local threat situation is resolved. Darcy, out." Mele looked at her Marines, who were hastily shoveling the last crumbs of food bars into the feed ports on their lower helmets and readying their weapons. "Anybody got any mines left? No? How about grenades?" Everyone shook their heads.

Ten to fifteen enemies, and she had eight counting herself. The odds weren't too bad.

Unless the estimate was too low.

Mele rubbed her forehead, tired, very tired, of running, and feeling reluctant to avoid a fight that would help wear down the enemy a little more. But she was in command of this entire battle. Choosing to risk an engagement that didn't have to be fought would be both reckless and irresponsible. "Glitch, Lamar, we need a new hide hole that isn't where that patrol will find us."

The sergeant and the corporal huddled over Giddings's schematics of the facility near their location while Mele conducted a count of the ammunition everyone had left. That wasn't great, either. The last supply cache they'd tried to use had been emptied out earlier, probably by another group of defenders since the location hadn't been booby-trapped the way it would be if the enemy had found it. "If we get into a fight, don't waste rounds," she cautioned her Marines. "If I catch anybody spraying shots without aiming I'll make you regret the day you joined the Marines."

Private Ford raised his hand. "Major, with all due respect, the last few weeks I've kind of already been regretting that."

She laughed along with the others. As long as they could still make jokes they'd still be able to fight.

Sergeant Giddings pointed to his right. "There's a spot about a hundred meters that way."

"It looks okay, Major," Corporal Lamar agreed.

"Let's get going, Lamar. Glitch, stay with me."

Corporal Lamar eased cautiously out into the hallway, gazing around before beckoning the others to follow. "Ford, take point."

"Ford, take point," Ford grumbled. "I think I'll let myself get shot again."

"Is it malingering if you let the enemy shoot you instead of shooting yourself?" Private MacKinder wondered.

"Yes," Corporal Lamar said. "Now shut up. Mac, you take the rear." Lamar followed Ford as he headed along the hall away from where their sensors warned that the enemy patrol was approaching.

"Are we still tracking them?" Mele asked Corporal Okubo, who was just in front of her, while Giddings was just behind.

"Yes, Major, they're—wait. It looks like they just changed their path. They're moving fast."

"Toward us?" Mele demanded, peering down the darkened hallway. "Talk to me!"

"No! Sort of right angles to us."

A sudden change of route. Moving fast. "They might've spotted some of our other people. Lamar! Change the route to get closer to that patrol. Keep it careful."

"Yes, ma'am. Ford, have you got readings on them?"

"Uh . . . yeah. Now we're trying to catch them?"

"Yes. Go." Ford eased up to a corner, then edged around it, the others following.

Less than two minutes later, sudden crashes erupted ahead along the path the enemy patrol had taken, the sounds of shots echoing and rebounding from walls, ceilings, and floors. "That's less than twenty meters off. Let's go!" Mele said. "Our guys probably need help."

Much faster now, running up a stair, out into a hall blocked only a few meters down, into a room, the sound of shots growing louder but the exact locations still hard to grasp because of the echoing, out the second door into another hall, and—

Ford jerked to a halt, waving to the others to take cover. Mele kept going until she could see what the lead Marine had spotted.

Two enemy soldiers, crouched at a corner, leaning out to fire carefully to their left. Concentrating on whomever they were fighting, their backs to Mele's small group, the enemy hadn't yet noticed the danger behind them. "Lamar, you're my best shot. Pick the second best. Take out those two fast and clean."

"Got it, ma'am. Mac, you take the shorter one. Fire on three." Lamar and Mac aimed carefully. "One . . . two . . . three." Both weapons barked. One enemy soldier fell limply to the floor, while the other staggered and began to turn. Lamar and Mac both fired again, the shots knocking the soldier back into the hallway.

The other firing nearby paused.

"Get down," Mele ordered.

Lamar was already moving, snagging a grenade off the closest enemy soldier.

Holes appeared in the wall to their left as someone fired through it, the shots dancing up and down and over, but not going low enough to hit the Marines prone on the deck.

Enemy soldiers suddenly boiled out behind the Marines.

Lamar pitched the grenade into them as Mele and her Marines fired back. An enemy grenade went off too close to Mele for comfort, but her armor stopped the shrapnel. Steadying her aim, she put a shot through the faceplate of a soldier charging at the Marines.

Firing ceased as the Marines searched in vain for more targets, the sensors on their battle armor no longer warning of movement except for that of an enemy soldier twitching, unable to rise. Studying the remnants of the fight, Mele saw one of her Marines lying limp where the grenade had tossed him. "Medic!"

"On it," Corporal Okubo said.

As the medic scrambled over to the injured private, Lamar positioned the remaining three Marines to cover against any more enemy soldiers showing up.

In the aftermath of the noise of battle, the sudden silence felt strange. The dark interior of the facility was pitch black once more except where the light Corporal Okubo was using cast some illumination. Infrared sight only made the darkness and the battered walls around them seem stranger and more alien. Mele checked the sensor displays on her armor, spotting fading vibrations that spoke of heavy footsteps, soldiers in battle armor, retreating rapidly. "Those ground apes were shooting at somebody." Despite the risk of the transmission being detected by other enemy forces, she boosted power and called on the command circuit. "Any Marines out there?"

"I've got something to the left," Sergeant Giddings said, checking his own readings. "I think it's friendly ID transmissions. Real low power. Close by."

"Anybody out there," Mele sent again. "Identify yourself. We don't have a lot of patience or time!"

A response finally came, the transmission weak and filled with static. "Don't shoot! We're coming in! We're force recon!"

"Ford, Mac, cover them," Lamar ordered.

"I see 'em," Ford said, gazing ahead cautiously. "Four of our ground apes if their IFF is real."

"Make certain they're ours!"

"Yes, Major," Lamar said. She stepped out, weapon at the ready. "Ford, keep them covered. Check 'em, Mac."

Private MacKinder scuttled to the four new soldiers, checking over their armor and systems. "They're ours," Mac reported after a moment. "Ground force recon."

"Get them over here with us," Mele ordered.

"Major, we've got faint movement indicators all around," Glitch reported. "Growing in intensity. The enemy's concentrating toward the sounds of this fight."

"We've gotta move," Mele said. "Everybody—"

"No can do, Major," Corporal Okubo said. He was kneeling beside the wounded Marine, working fast even as he talked. "Private Luk got hit bad. If we move this Marine, he dies."

Mele paused, looking over at the other figure lying near the medic, an enemy soldier. Her helmet providing air still concealed her face, but half of her combat armor had been pulled off and plenty of blood marked the skin suit worn under the armor. Mele could tell that Okubo had taken the time to at least stabilize her for a moment. "What about that one?"

Okubo managed to shrug while still working to save the life of the wounded Marine. "Might live if we move her now. I doubt it, though."

"Give me your recommendation," Mele said.

"We leave them here and I keep working on them." Okubo glanced at her for just a moment. "Ma'am, I've got to stay here or they both die."

The big picture. Focus on the big picture. She couldn't afford to let what might be the last medic in her forces be captured in order to save a single friendly life. And the loss of a single additional enemy life, while regrettable, wasn't cause to sacrifice her medic. This was war, after all. It was her job to win this fight, and every Marine and ground forces soldier was expendable when it came to that.

Mele glanced down at the wounded Marine.

To hell with the big picture.

"Okay, Corporal Okubo. Stay. Have you got a weapon?"

"Uh, a sidearm."

"Give." Mele held out her hand. "You'll be safer if you're not armed when they get here."

The medic paused one of his hands' work long enough to reach around, flip the quick-release fitting on the sidearm holster, and pass it to Mele.

"Turn on your medic badges," she ordered.

Okubo nodded quickly. Mele saw bright red symbols glow to life on his shoulders, on the forehead of his battle armor helmet, and between his shoulders on the back of his armor.

"Give us a good minute after we clear this spot and then light off your medic beacon, too. Understand?"

"Yes, Major."

"Good." Mele reached out to grip Okubo's shoulder for a moment. "Save them, and keep yourself safe, Marine."

"You got it. Thank you, Major."

Mele stepped back, her eyes sweeping what little could be seen of the surrounding area. Her four remaining Marines, and the four figures in ground forces armor. Only four. "Are you apes on your own?"

One soldier tried to answer, stumbling over the words. "Uh . . . we . . . ah . . ."

There were times for gentle methods, and there were times like this. "Spit it out, soldier!"

"Yes, ma'am! We're all that's left of our group. Corporal Singh was leading us, but he just got killed when they jumped us." A mix of sorrow, exhaustion, and despair made the soldier's voice sound weird, his words hard to understand.

But Mele got the important parts. "You're with us now. That's Corporal Lamar. Do what she says. Or what I say. Glitch, have you found a way from here to that place we were going to hole up?"

"Yes, Major," Sergeant Giddings said, pointing down the hallway. "That way."

"Lamar!"

"Yes, ma'am," Lamar said. "Ford!"

"Yeah. Point." But Private Ford didn't hesitate as the warnings on the Marine sensors grew more urgent.

The group of now only five Marines, counting Mele, and the four ground forces soldiers headed off down the darkened hallway for a short distance before Ford darted to one side into a narrow access passage. Barely five meters along that, he paused to flip open a panel, leading the way onto the stairs beyond it. Mele made sure the panel closed tightly behind her before following the others.

"Freeze!" Giddings said, his whisper sounding loud over the command circuit, one hand coming up to make the sign for the same command.

Everyone in the small group stopped moving. Mele felt herself breathing slowly and shallowly even though that sound wouldn't carry through the battle armor.

She felt the thump of feet passing overhead, along a hallway that crossed over the shaft holding the stairs, heading toward where the enemy patrol had been decimated.

Mele hoped that the enemy wouldn't simply fire when they got there and saw Corporal Okubo. That could happen. Their minds wouldn't register the red medic symbols glowing, instead showing them an enemy, and fingers on triggers would twitch. Oddly enough, AI-controlled weapons could do the same thing, ignoring clear signs that the target was a noncombatant, or even friendly, and firing anyway. Something to do with complex decision trees and options spontaneously collapsing, a code monkey had once told her. Humans probably accidentally shot their friends for different reasons, but the result was the same for whoever ended up being the target.

But the enemy battle armor should register the medic beacon. Hopefully. If Okubo had remembered to activate it while trying to keep both that Marine and the enemy soldier alive.

The tremors from the footfalls overhead fading, they set off again, reaching a landing with a door that led to another hall, then a room, and inside that a hidden access panel that allowed them to crawl into a maintenance corridor whose usual entrance had been sealed.

"Everybody rest. Lamar, post a sentry. Glitch, find me a link to Lieutenant Paratnam or Sergeant Savak or the *Saber*."

"What if I contact Gunny Moon?"

"Get me anybody!" Mele sat down, back against a wall, trying to plan what to do when she didn't know how many forces she had left or where they were, or how many enemies were left or where they were.

"Major?" Mac came by, pointing to the wall. "We've got live power outlets."

"Bonus." Mele plugged in her battle armor so the systems could recharge. "How can we still have power here?"

"Separate battery backups. There are different battery banks for the equipment on the facility, but since we pulled off what equipment we could and shut the rest down, there hasn't been any drain on the batteries since primary power went down. If we find a battery bank that hasn't been drained yet, we're good. I think these might be the facility stabilization systems."

"Facility stabilization? Any idea what happens when the batteries for those systems die?"

Private MacKinder shook his head. "I guess when the facility stabilization stuff shuts down, the facility goes unstable."

"Thanks, Mac," Mele said, knowing her sarcasm probably wouldn't register on the tired Marine.

A couple of minutes later, Corporal Lamar eased up toward Mele. "Major, my suit's reporting damage to your armor."

"Damage?" Mele remembered the enemy grenade, checking her side. "Yeah. Got nicked, but it didn't penetrate."

Lamar knelt to examine the damage, playing a dim light on it. "It could worsen if it's not repaired. We're out of liquid weld. Mac! See if there's any duct tape in that maintenance locker. No, wait! Check that maintenance locker for booby traps, then see if there's any duct tape in it."

"Got it." A couple of minutes later, Private MacKinder got the door to the locker open, rummaged inside, and then emerged with a partial roll of duct tape. "We're saved!"

"Shut up, you idiot," Lamar said, laughing, as she took the roll. She worked for a few moments, tearing off strips of duct tape and reinforcing the damaged area on Mele's armor. "There you go, Major. Good as new. Almost." Lamar paused. "I just thought of something."

"What's that?"

"What if someone made a weapon that homed in on duct tape?"

"That'd be the end of life as we know it," Mele said. "Don't give people ideas."

"I won't!" Lamar looked down at her arm, the limb hidden by the battle armor covering it. "I got a bad scrape once and Doc Okubo slapped some duct tape and gauze on it. Do you think he's going to be okay, ma'am?"

"Yeah," Mele said, trying to sound as if there wasn't any doubt of that. "As far as we can tell, the guys we're fighting are taking prisoners.

Okubo had his medic lights on and should have turned on his beacon as well once we were gone. He'll have been able to keep Luk alive, and be able to treat the other prisoners the enemy has taken, so that's sort of a good thing."

"Kind of funny a guy named Luk getting hit that bad, huh?"

"Well, he didn't get hit bad until now, and Doc Okubo was there to help him, so maybe his name still fits."

"I bet you're right, Major." Lamar looked about her as if the dark and the walls would yield to her vision. "I wish we knew where they were holding the prisoners. Maybe we could get to them. Free 'em with an all-out hostage rescue and recovery."

"The enemy won't be holding prisoners on this facility," Mele said, shaking her head. "They'll probably have taken the prisoners to the freighter. Easier to guard them there."

"Maybe we can find out for sure," Giddings said. He'd been listening, and began fiddling with controls on his equipment. "If Doc Okubo had his medic beacon lit off. Those have a lot of power to cut through jamming during a fight. If the enemy didn't remember to have him shut that off . . . yeah. There it is. Bearing . . . distance . . . that's got to be that ship. The prisoners are definitely on it."

"That's good to know. Not that we can do anything about it," Mele said. "The freighter will be a problem for the space squids. They can—" Memories from the fighting at Kosatka abruptly forced their way into her mind. "Oh, crap. Glitch! I need comms to *Saber* now! Get me a line! Anything you can find."

It took time. Giddings had to avoid attempts by the enemy to spot and trace his tries at finding an intact line out, and twice everyone had to freeze while enemy patrols passed close enough to create worries they might spot the faintest vibration from the Marines.

But finally Giddings gave her a go signal and Mele saw her comm light glow green. "*Saber*. Am I talking to *Saber*?"

The reply sounded wary. "*Saber* is the ship. You're talking to me. Who the hell are you?"

"I'm Major Darcy, commander of the defending forces on the facility. Who the hell are you?"

"Uh . . . huh? I . . . uh . . . Petty Officer Tork . . . engineering watch. Is a major like a lieutenant?"

"A major is like a commander—"

"I'm sorry, ma'am! But this circuit isn't supposed to link to outside calls. Oh, did you come in through the system status net? That shouldn't be active with only one ship out here. I'll—"

"Never mind! I need to talk to Commodore Geary. Right now. This moment. Before we lose this link! Can you patch me through?"

"I . . . I'll tell someone! Hang on, Commander!"

Waiting for the next several seconds took all of her willpower.

Rob Geary's voice came on the line so abruptly it startled her. "Mele? Is that you?"

"Yes, sir."

"You scared the hell out of one of my petty officers. Did you get my message?"

"Yes, sir! Listen, I've got to say this quick before we lose this link. We know the enemy has taken prisoners of some of my Marines and some ground forces soldiers. We've got indications that those prisoners are being held on the freighter. If that freighter runs, while it has some of our people as prisoners aboard it along with enemy soldiers trying to get out of here, can you stop it without killing our own people?"

He didn't answer for a moment. "That might be a problem. If the freighter was on its own, we could match vectors and take out parts of it, but even then we couldn't know if prisoners had been placed near any of those pieces of equipment to keep us from firing on them. If the enemy cruiser and destroyer remain as escorts, we'd have to make high-speed runs instead of matching vectors with the freighter. If we're moving that fast, it's very difficult to aim to hit just one or two particular spots on a ship, even if we did know exactly where on the freighter our own people are located and tried to avoid hitting those areas."

"What options would we have?" Mele asked. "Anything better than those two?"

"Unless I can make those two enemy warships go away, my options would be to risk killing some, or possibly all, of the prisoners in order to stop the freighter, or to let the freighter go. If the warships run and leave the freighter, I can try taking out its control deck or engineering, but if the enemy places prisoners in those locations, I won't be able to fire without killing them."

"That's it? There's nothing else you can do?"

"Mele, that's one of the reasons we carry Marines. To give us more options. Only I don't have Marines. You've got them all, and for good reason."

"Dammit, sir, I can't take that freighter! It'd be a death trap! As long as the enemy . . ."

"Major Darcy?" Rob asked. "Do we still have a link or did I lose you?"

"I'm still here." Mele hesitated, trying to sort through her thoughts. "Can you keep them off me?"

"I'm not sure what you—"

"If I capture that freighter, can you keep the enemy warships off me?"

A pause. "When?" Rob Geary finally asked.

"At the earliest, another twenty-four hours. How long is it until our reinforcements get here?"

"About three more days. It's four destroyers, Mele. From Eire, Benten, and Kosatka."

"Four—?! When did Eire and Benten join the war?"

"You'll have to ask your friend Lochan about that. I'm assuming he made it happen. We've also got Adowa and Catalan as allies."

For a moment Mele was lost for words. "Cool," she finally got out.

"That gives us superiority in space. Enough firepower to destroy both of the enemy warships. If the enemy warships try to escape, and I'm sure they will, they'll have to start running within thirty-six hours or the four new destroyers will be able to alter their vectors to cut across the star system and catch the enemy before they can reach the jump point. The new warships aren't broadcasting IDs, so the enemy might still think these are reinforcements for them. But that's only going to last so long before the enemy warships realize they're not getting the right answers from our new friends. I expect the enemy warships to bolt in about twenty-four hours, and I'll be chasing them when they do, trying to slow them down. So that's your timeline, Mele."

"Twenty-four hours," she repeated. "And they'll take the freighter with them?"

"I don't think so. It's possible the enemy warships will choose to sacrifice themselves to protect the freighter, but that's not what a careerist does when the chips are down, and the enemy commander has been acting like a careerist who wants to protect his own hide above all else. It's already too late for that freighter to escape with them. It accelerates too slowly. The only chance the enemy warships will have to escape is if they abandon the freighter, and the only chance the freighter will have is if it has hostages to prevent us from firing on it."

Mele nodded to herself. "Meaning we'll have a chance to capture and hold the freighter if we hit it after the enemy warships head for home. I can't set things up in less than nine hours anyway. Okay, we're—" Mele heard a rapidly repeated snapping sound over the circuit. "Commodore? Are we still connected?" Nothing.

"They spotted the transmission and spot jammed it," Sergeant Giddings said.

"Did they trace it? Do we have to move?"

"I don't think so, but we should move in a little while anyway."

Mele sat back against the metal behind her, thinking. "I need to talk to Ninja. How are your comms with the surface?"

"I can get you a link. It's harder for the enemy to spot that because they're not in the line of sight between us and the surface. When do you need it?"

"Five minutes ago."

Half an hour passed, while Mele tried not to scream at Giddings to get her the connection *now*.

It did give her time to think. There hadn't been any sign that the enemy soldiers were withdrawing to the freighter, which would be the only smart thing at this point. Whatever else she'd learned about the enemy ground forces commander, he or she wasn't stupid. They'd know they should be pulling back, and fast. So, why weren't they?

Maybe because they hadn't been told about the four new destroyers. Maybe because the enemy warship commander didn't want a lot of soldiers clamoring to be picked up before the warships bolted for safety. Mele had been warned about that as a private in the Marines back on the Old Colony world Franklin. *"Never count on the space squids. When it comes down to supporting the Marines or running to save themselves, the squids will always look out for themselves."*

Rob Geary hadn't been like that. She'd forgotten that some squids supposedly thought like that. Maybe they didn't. Maybe it was just Marines not trusting anyone else any more than they had to. But the enemy hadn't impressed her as being the sort to play straight with their troops. More like being willing to cut their losses anytime things looked bad.

If the enemy ground forces commander hadn't been told that everything was about to go to hell, they wouldn't realize how much the situation had changed for the defenders.

"Major? I got Ninja's line. Voice only."

"Great." Mele hit the alert command repeatedly to tell someone at the other end that she was trying to connect. "Hello, hello."

A familiar, and very youthful, voice answered. "Who are you? Where's your picture?"

"It's Aunt Mele," she told Rob's little girl. "I need—"

"Hi, Aunt Mele!"

"Hi. I'm calling on business. Where's your mom?"

"Just a sec! Mommy! Aunt Mele wants you to hack somebody!"

Mele waited for a few seconds that felt like minutes until she heard Ninja's voice, sounding worn-out. "I'm already hacking for all I'm worth, for what good it's doing."

"Can you—"

"No! I haven't been able to get in!"

"The freighter."

"What about the freighter?"

"Can you get me and several other people onto the freighter?"

Ninja's reply took a moment. "Right now?"

"No. About twenty-four hours from now."

"You mean physically? You mean the freighter the enemy came in on? You want to sneak aboard?"

"Yes!"

"I thought you had to stay on the orbital facility to defend it."

Mele shook her head before realizing that Ninja couldn't see the gesture. "Not anymore. We won. The soldiers we're fighting don't know that yet, though. Which is good. It gives me a chance to grab control of that freighter before they can use it to try to escape. The rest of my people on the station can hold out until the enemy soldiers have to surrender, which won't be long."

"Oh. Got it. So you need to get aboard the freighter. Yeah, I can do that."

"That's great!" Mele said. "I need—"

"Almost," Ninja added. "I can almost do that. It's just . . . it involves spoofing enemy sensors using a worm . . . but it's got to be perfect, you know? Any discrepancies and the sensors tag it and the enemy takes a close look using their eyes and . . . wait a minute."

"I haven't got a minute."

"Do you look as bad as you sound?"

Mele stared into the darkness, trying to come up with an apt reply. "Probably. We're a little short on mirrors, but that's probably just as well."

"What about your outfits? Your armor? Is that messed up?"

"You mean damaged? Yeah. Everyone's armor has damage at this point."

"What about the enemy?" Ninja demanded. "Does their armor have lots of damage on the outside?"

"Every one of them that I've seen," Mele said. "Why does that matter?"

"Because I can tell the worm to tell the sensors that any inconsistencies or anomalies they see are just damage to the armor! The sensors will still see things inconsistent with friendly armor, but it'll assume those things are because of damage because I'll tell them to do that! Why didn't I think of that before?"

"I don't know," Mele said. "How long will this take?"

"When do you need it again?"

"I need to hit the freighter in twenty-four hours. That's when our space squids say the enemy warships will have abandoned their soldiers here, but before the enemy soldiers have figured that out."

"Uh-huh. So you need the worm in time to insert it in the enemy systems and give it time to spread. Ummm . . . I'll try to get it to you in another couple of hours. Maybe."

Mele sighed, resigning herself to the need to wait for something she hadn't expected to have a chance at ever getting at all. "Okay. We'll try to punch a line through to you again in a couple of hours. Sergeant Giddings is giving me looks that say I need to end this call before the enemy fixes on us."

"I'll get you that worm, Mele. And stop calling my husband a space squid."

"It's a term Marines use to show their admiration for sailors. Honest. See ya." Mele broke the call, knowing that Ninja would understand the abrupt hang-up.

After spending another moment gazing into the dark to order her thoughts, Mele called over the local command circuit. "Giddings. Lamar."

"Right here," Giddings said.

Lamar hustled over, settling next to her.

"Alternate command circuit two," Mele said, waiting until both of her noncommissioned officers gave her the thumbs-up to confirm they were on the new circuit. "Here's the deal. Glitch has confirmed that the prisoners the enemy has taken are on that freighter. We can be sure of that. Once the enemy realizes that four destroyers just came in on our side—"

"Four destroyers?" Lamar blurted out.

"Yeah," Mele said, trying not to let fatigue and stress make her impatient. "Sorry I didn't tell you that. That'll give the space squids five destroyers counting our own, which I'm told is real good odds. But if that freighter heads for home with our people aboard as prisoners, the squids will face the choice of either trying to knock out the freighter knowing they'll probably kill at least some of our own people, or letting the freighter go to ensure our people don't get killed."

"That's all they can do?" Giddings asked.

"That's all they can do," Mele said. "Which means the Marines have to get the job done. We have to get aboard that freighter and take control of it before it pulls away."

"Five of us?" Lamar said.

"We've also got the four ground forces guys," Mele said. "Look, we don't have to control the whole freighter. We just have to grab their control deck and the power core controls compartment. Engineering control. We've practiced doing this, boarding freighters and taking them under our control. This'll be just like that."

"But there'll be all those enemy soldiers nearby," Giddings said. "Won't they come charging in to take back control?"

"We've got four more destroyers coming! Plus *Saber*. We tell those enemy ground apes that the freighter can't outrun those destroyers, which is true, and their escort warships are about to get blown away, also true, and if those ground apes maybe want to survive instead of dying futile and meaningless deaths, they'd better rethink things.

Commodore Geary thinks the enemy warships will bolt in about a day, leaving the freighter and all the enemy ground apes behind."

"Maybe they'd just surrender then," Lamar said.

"Maybe," Mele agreed. "Or maybe they'd load up in the freighter and force it to leave, knowing our squids can't shoot them up while they have some of our people aboard as hostages. We need to make sure that option is closed off before the enemy realizes they need it."

"Okay," Lamar said. "Yeah. Yes, ma'am. It'll be risky. But better than sitting back and watching our friends die. How do we get on the freighter? There're bound to be sentries and sensors watching for any threat to it."

"Ninja told me she thinks she can make a worm that'll fool the enemy sensors into seeing us as friendlies."

"Deception," Giddings said. "Yes. That's good. We'd just have to get the worm into their network."

"Can you do that?" Mele asked.

"I've pulled some net gear off enemy armor, so, maybe, Major, we can do that if Ninja gets us that worm."

"She's good, right?" Lamar said.

"I wouldn't want her going after my systems," Giddings said.

"But you said she thinks she can do it, ma'am? What if she can't?"

Mele tried to rub her forehead, her palm instead hitting the front of her helmet. "I'm open to ideas."

"How about if we Marines pretend to be guards and the four friendly ground apes we've got are our prisoners and we're taking them to the freighter—"

"We'd need five functional sets of enemy battle armor," Giddings said.

"Okay, so if the friendly ground apes pretend to be guards and we Marines pretend to be prisoners, we'd only need four functional sets of enemy armor," Lamar said.

"We haven't even got one," Giddings said.

"Can we capture any armor?" Mele asked. "Stage an ambush and strip the bodies?"

Giddings shook his head. "We could kill four or five of them, but getting functional armor off them that we could wear without looking like the walking dead? And without the enemy armor systems wiping themselves to prevent us using them? Major, what do you think the odds of that are? And we'd have to strip off the armor before an enemy reaction force got to the ambush site, and the enemy would see that we'd stolen four or five sets of armor and they'd probably figure we'd done that for a reason and—"

"Yeah," Mele said. "That won't fly. How about a diversion? Something to grab their attention so that even if the worm doesn't work one hundred percent we can still get to the freighter before they notice?"

"We'd need another element to handle the diversion," Lamar said. "Even with the friendly ground apes this group is pretty low on numbers. But if it gets confusing enough, and we can position ourselves to jump across to the freighter when the right moment comes, we might be able to get through before anyone realizes what we're doing. I mean, they won't expect it, will they? It's a little crazy."

"I'm going to be honest with you," Mele said. "It's a lot crazy. Until those new warships showed up to help us it would've been totally crazy. I need to get in contact with Gunny. Hopefully he's got enough left with him to manage a diversion. Hey, suppose about the time the diversion starts, we also make sure all of the enemy ground apes learn that they're facing five destroyers now, and their chances of winning and escaping have just entered a decaying orbit and will end in a big, ugly crater? Their own officers might not have been told, even if their senior commander got the word, and I bet he or she hasn't. Their squids might be staying quiet on that to avoid, you know, worrying the ground apes."

"Space squids and senior officers can be really considerate that way," Corporal Lamar said. "Present company excepted, of course."

"I doubt I'll ever be a senior officer," Mele said. "I've only gotten this far by sacrificing corporals whenever I needed to stage a diversion. Get me Gunny, Glitch."

"Yes, ma'am. But first we need to move."

"Okay. Let's try not to get caught and killed on the way to the next hiding spot. Lamar—"

"Got it, Major. We're moving again, boys and girls! Ford! Take point!"

They moved out behind a gloomy and grumbling Private Ford.

CHAPTER 13

"Living like a rat sucks," Private MacKinder complained as he crawled through a hole into a six-meter-long hall that had been sealed off at both ends.

"Try walking point every time," Private Ford replied.

"Shut up," Corporal Lamar said. "Mac, since you've got so much energy you can waste some bellyaching, you're on sentry."

Mele looked about the space, darkness shrouding both ends. The four ground forces soldiers had stayed mostly silent and now sat down together as if their last link to their unit would be lost if they were separated. "Are you apes okay?"

"Yes, Major," one answered. "What are we going to do?"

"We're working on that. Glitch, do you think you can get links from in here?"

"Yes, Major. There's a comms router that should be . . . yeah. Right inside this wall."

She stooped to look at the web of connections that he'd uncovered. "Sergeant, if I haven't mentioned this lately, you're doing amazing work. I don't know where we'd be without your skills when it comes to comms and systems."

Giddings perked up. "Thank you, Major. I'll get ahold of Gunny."

"Great. Do it and I'll make you a lieutenant."

"Major, why would you tell me I'm doing a great job and then threaten to punish me?"

"Fine," Mele said. "Do it and you can stay a sergeant."

That took another forty-five minutes. Mele spent the time going over the schematics of the facility, figuring out a path over that distance that would bring her group undetected to where they could get onto the dock in a place that would give them a shot at reaching the ship. They'd be heading toward the enemy's strongest positions, through areas the enemy must have mapped by now, and probably lined with sensors that would have to be spoofed or avoided and mines that would have to be spotted.

"I've got him, Major!"

"I need a diversion, Gunny," Mele said over a circuit that popped and faded and hissed as agile jamming fought agile frequency hops. "On the dock. So my group can get to the freighter."

"Okay, Major," Gunnery Sergeant Moon said, just as if this were a routine request for paperwork or something equally mundane. "Diversion. Where are you going to be?"

"We're going to come onto the dock on the right side as you face outward toward the freighter."

"So we need to kick up dust on the left side," Moon said. "How big a fuss do we want to make?"

"As big as you can manage. I need it at 0400 facility time. Can you get into position by then?"

"No problem, Major."

"If you can get another group in that part of the facility to assist you, tell them it's on my orders. We need to take that freighter, so we need as big a diversion as you can manage."

"Yes, Major. At least you won't have to jump to get to the ship."

"Say again?"

"You won't have to jump. They docked their ship. You can walk right on."

"I doubt we'll be walking the whole way, but that'll be a lot easier. Thanks, Gunny."

"No—"

"Gunny? Say again." Nothing. The comm light on Mele's suit glowed a steady red. "We lost the link," she told Giddings. "In about an hour and a half, try to get a connection to Ninja again. At that time, we'll also record my announcement for the enemy soldiers and figure out how to upload it to where it'll broadcast at the right time. But first, Sergeant, spend about an hour sleeping. That's an order."

She realized there was something yet to be done, getting up and moving quietly toward where the four ground forces soldiers were still huddled in a tired, dispirited clump. "Are you guys ready for duty?" Mele asked. "We've got an operation coming up."

"Another reposition, ma'am?"

"No. We'll be moving back to the dock area. We're going to attack the ship the enemy troops came in on."

The soldiers looked back at her, their expressions hidden behind the face shields of their armor, yet somehow conveying bafflement. "We're going to attack?" one asked.

"Yes. The prisoners they've taken from us are being held on that ship."

The ground forces soldiers perked up for the first time since they'd joined up with Mele's group. "We're going to free the prisoners, Major? Get 'em out of the prison?"

"Not exactly," Mele said. "We're going to capture the prison."

"The five of you? Ma'am?"

"No, we expect you to help. That'll make nine of us. Five Marines and four force recon. I think that's enough to do the job."

The ground forces soldiers hesitated, then all four straightened to attention again and saluted. "Yes, ma'am," the first said. "That's enough. Just tell us what to do."

Lochan Nakamura sat at one of the small tables in the dining area on the destroyer. Militaries mysteriously called dining areas "mess halls" for reasons he didn't care to speculate about. He slumped in the small, hard seat, his head in his hands.

He'd come this far. He'd succeeded in finding help, and not long ago had learned from Commodore Geary's message that Mele Darcy was still alive. But until these ships actually arrived at the world they were aiming for, Mele would still be in tremendous peril every moment. He might have gotten here just quickly enough to avenge Mele rather than fast enough to save her.

"Are you all right?" one of *Asahi*'s sailors asked, sitting down opposite Lochan.

He looked up, forced a tiny smile, and nodded. "I'm okay."

"Something's bothering you," the sailor said, taking a moment to look over his meal. "Have you eaten? It's a good meal today."

"Compared to food on a freighter, it's wonderful," Lochan said. "I just . . . how do you stand it?"

"Stand what?"

"We're here. We can see where we need to go. But it's literally taking days to get there, at a time when every second counts."

"Oh." The sailor nodded. "That does take some getting used to. We don't think in space ways, you know. Humans think, 'I can see that, so it can't be too far off.' But space isn't like that. You look outside and you can see forever. That's not an exaggeration. You're seeing things billions of light years away, and billons of years in the past. That's pretty neat, huh?"

"It's pretty hard to deal with at a time like this," Lochan said.

"It's a long way." The sailor pointed a utensil in a direction that must be toward the planet they were aiming for. "Not so long ago in our history, getting from one planet to another would take weeks or months. I think maybe years for outer planets. Being able to cover that distance now in just days is remarkable." He smiled sympathetically at Lochan. "Did you ever think that you're looking into the past when you look at one of the planets? Like the one we're heading toward. We're still about two light hours from it. So when you look at it, you're seeing that planet two hours ago. You're looking at history, things that already happened."

Lochan looked that way, seeing only the gray bulkhead of the ship. "History. Things that have happened. Too late to change. I'm sorry, but that doesn't cheer me up. Someone I care about may die before we can get there."

"That's difficult. We're doing all we can."

"I know. And I'm enormously grateful for what you're doing. That we have a chance to save my friend at all is because you were willing to help a distant neighbor in need."

"We all eat from the same iron pot, don't we? I was told people came to the stars so they could get away from other people. But there are always other people. You can ignore them, or fight them, or become their friends. I think we should be friends."

Lochan couldn't help a smile in return. "We should be friends. But you're a sailor on a warship. Your job is to fight other people."

"My job is to be ready to fight other people," the sailor said. "When I was a child, a woman came to our home seeking safety. Her husband beat her. My parents took her in, and sealed the door against the husband when he came looking. My parents didn't want to fight, but they wouldn't stand aside or refuse help to someone who needed protection. That's why I do this work. If we protect places like Glenlyon, we also protect my home of Benten. And when we protect others, we protect ourselves. Who we are, or who we wish to be."

"Your parents were wise," Lochan said.

"I didn't think so when I was younger!" the sailor said with a laugh. "But I learned. Do you have children?"

"No. That . . . never worked out."

"But you try to protect the children of others."

"Well . . . yes," Lochan said. "That's . . . the only right thing to do."

"So you understand why I am willing to fight for others."

"Yes." Lochan roused himself, thinking that he should eat something. "Thank you."

"If it is possible, we will save your friend. Surely, knowing that help is coming, they will stay as safe as possible until we arrive."

"You'd think so," Lochan said. "Unless you knew Mele. I'm afraid she may not be staying all that safe."

Lyn had taken the name Ninja for her hacking work long before she'd come to Glenlyon and even before she'd joined the small fleet that the Old Colony world of Alfar had maintained. Alfar's fleet had never figured out that Petty Officer Third Class Lyn Meltzer was also Ninja, but they'd discovered enough about her activities to court-martial her. Fortunately, a certain Ensign Rob Geary had recommended a simple discharge instead, not because he knew or liked Ninja but because he wanted to see her treated fairly, and the infractions, while embarrassing to certain officers, weren't really serious. (The infractions she'd been linked to, that is. She hadn't seen any need to admit to anything she hadn't been caught doing.)

When that same Rob Geary left Alfar for a new colony, Ninja decided to join the effort as well. She'd never told Rob that she'd come here not just because her options on Alfar were really limited and this had looked like an opportunity for a better future, but also because he seemed like someone worth knowing better. Even if it had only become a friendship, she figured a future with a dependable friend on a new world was better than one alone on an old, crowded world.

So here she was, hiding in a tent in a forest along with other people evacuated from the city, trying to put the finishing touches on the worm Mele needed so Ninja could finally make a difference in this latest fight, while her and Rob's daughter fended off visitors and brought energy drinks and candy to her work area whenever she noticed Mom had run low on those essentials. Normally the energy drinks made the still-a-few-weeks-from-being-ready-to-come-out child inside her kick with extra vigor, but as if sensing the urgency of Ninja's work, the kid seemed content at the moment to be squishing his mother's guts up against her lungs, giving only an occasional reassuring twitch to let her know he was okay.

She half hoped and half feared that he'd be like his father, idealistic and too willing to sacrifice for others. But at the least Ninja expected that kid to inherit something she and Rob had always shared, the belief that you never let someone else down when that someone was depending on you. As Mele was now depending on her.

If there'd ever been a time to dissolve into panicked despair, this was it. Rob up there risking his life again, herself exhausted from long days spent worrying about him and Mele while she hurled her hacking talents vainly against virtual walls that refused to offer any cracks, and hormones driving her body off-kilter. But Ninja had taken some deep breaths, willing herself into that creative fugue state where nothing existed but the challenge and the methods and the means. She'd never done drugs. She'd never needed them. There couldn't be any better high than this.

The worm couldn't be perfect, but it didn't have to be. It just needed to be able to convince the enemy systems that any flaws in it were the result of flaws in the real world. Like a martial art, using the enemy's strengths against it.

An alarm brought Ninja slowly back to awareness of the world about her. She felt sweat on her skin and heard the songs of native creatures that everyone called birds because that's pretty much what they were. "Ninja here."

"I know it hasn't been quite two hours, but have you got it done?"

the voice of Sergeant Giddings asked. "We can't maintain this link for very long."

"Yeah. Just finished. It won't take long to send. I've compressed the worm along with the unpacking program," Ninja said. "Sending." The bright send status line scrolled from one side to the other, ending with a green "complete." "Have you got it?"

"Hold on." Giddings's voice sounded hushed and hollow. Ninja could almost feel his surroundings in that voice, the dark and cramped hiding place that Mele's group must be using at this moment. "Yeah. It's clean. Any special instructions?"

"Just dump it into their systems. It'll do the rest on its own."

"Major Darcy says thanks and you're a wonder."

"Tell her I am a goddess," Ninja said. "I produce miracles."

"Major Darcy says she agrees."

"Good. Also tell her not to get her fool self killed. You, too, Glitch. Stay safe. I've done all I can."

The link ended, leaving Ninja to blink at the shadow patterns shifting on the top of the tent as leaves shivered in a slight wind. As if cued by her completion of her task, a hefty kick inside her caused her to wince. "Just wait a little longer," she said. "Believe me, I'm not any happier about that than you are."

"Mom?" Her daughter Dani looked in. "We good?"

"We're good," Ninja said.

"Will Aunt Mele be okay?"

"I hope so."

"I want to be just like her someday."

"Great. I'm going to do my best to talk you out of that. Can you bring me a candle?" There was one more thing she could do, and that was praying to her ancestors for any help they could give. Maybe, as some said, that wouldn't help at all. But maybe it would. It certainly couldn't hurt. And Mele and those with her doubtless needed all the help they could get, no matter the source.

———

"Freeze!"

Mele stopped all motion in response to the order called out by Sergeant Giddings.

Giddings advanced cautiously until he was even with Private Ford on point. "I'm getting readings on what looks like a sensor."

"Does it see us?" Mele asked.

"No, Major. I've got it doing constant resets. But this type of sensor usually comes matched with at least one mine. You see anything, Ford?"

Private Ford leaned to the side, gazing down the wall with his head close to it, playing his light along the wall. Like the rest of the facility after so much fighting, this hallway lacked atmosphere. In the vacuum, without air to diffuse the illumination, the lights had sharp edges, showing only what they directly fell upon and leaving pitch black everywhere else. "There's a bulge down there. Maybe a meter off? About waist height."

"Yeah. I see it. They planted the mine on the wall and matched its cover to the wall real nice. Any more?"

"Not that I can tell."

Giddings eased close to the enemy sensor, tapping into its controls. "Okay. It's linked to the mine, and only one is showing up. They're probably short on mines by now. I'm disabling the detonator on the mine, telling it to reset in ten minutes so it doesn't tip off the enemy they've got a problem."

One of the force recon soldiers spoke up. "Sergeant, check the ceiling."

"The overhead?" Giddings looked up, as did Private Ford.

"Something there," Ford said, pointing where his light had settled on a round object with a flat bottom. "The paint doesn't quite match."

"Sure as hell." Giddings glanced back at the soldier. "Do you know what kind it is?"

"The ones we found had spider-silk trip wires with current running through them," the soldier said. "Break 'em and the mine went off."

Giddings played a light down the hallway, moving it slowly around. "There they are. See those?" he said as gossamer-thin threads shone in the light. "We can get by them by going low."

Mele came forward far enough to see for herself. "Are you sure it's safe to go through here?"

"It should be, Major. We'll send Private Ford first, and if he gets through, the rest of us will follow."

"What?" Ford said.

"You can see the mine there and the threads there," Giddings said. "Go ahead. We'll cover you and watch for any other danger."

"But—"

"You've got a good instinct for this. I'm not worried."

"Great," Ford muttered. "You're not worried." He moved carefully, reaching the point where the spider threads glittered in Giddings's light, dropping down then to slide forward until past them. Studying the hallway beyond, Private Ford took slow, cautious steps for another few meters before pausing and looking back.

"Hold on," Mele said. "Glitch, can we use the link to this sensor to dump Ninja's worm into the enemy systems?"

"Um . . . yes, Major. This is tied back to the enemy command center, so it should work fine for that. But if we upload the worm to them now, it gives them more chances to spot it and neutralize it before we reach the dock."

"Ninja said it needed time to propagate through the enemy systems, though." Mele looked ahead to where Private Ford waited. "What's your recommendation, Glitch?"

He didn't answer for a long moment, then nodded. "We should load it in here. That'll give it time to spread through the enemy systems, and we don't know if we'll find another good load point between here and the dock. I think those two things outweigh the extra time it'll give their system watchdogs to spot the worm."

"Do it, then. Corporal Lamar, get the rest of our people past the mines, along with yourself. Sergeant Giddings and I'll follow."

"Yes, ma'am. Take it slow and easy, you apes. Mac, you go next with one of the ground apes, then I'll bring the other three force recons through with me."

"You guys look after the corporal, okay?" Mac told the soldiers. "She was at Kosatka, you know."

"She's safe with us, grunt," one of the soldiers replied.

Mele kept switching her gaze between Sergeant Giddings as he uploaded the worm into the enemy systems and the Marines and soldiers creeping past the enemy mines. Not that she'd have time to do anything if either one screwed up, but it was what an officer did in cases like this. What was that quantum thing someone had told her about, where when particles were watched they behaved differently than when they weren't being watched? Officer supervision of enlisted seemed to be based on the same concept. As long as you were watching, they'd somehow know, and things would turn out different.

"All done," Giddings said. "I think it went in clean, Major."

"All right. Go."

"With all due respect, Major, you should not be rear guard."

She hesitated. "You're right. Follow me when it looks safe."

Mele went perhaps faster than she should have, worried about the amount of time they'd spent in this hallway, but slowed as she passed under the spider-thread trip wires. Once on the other side, she used her light to illuminate the threads as Giddings came through the danger area.

"Up there," Corporal Lamar told Private Ford, pointing to a vent cover.

He tilted his head back to look. "What idiot came up with this route?"

"The Major."

"Oh. Uh. Okay." Ford was hoisted up about a meter to reach the vent cover and hook it back. He peered inside. "This is gonna be a tight fit in battle armor."

"It should take us undetected through an enemy threat area," Mele said. "It should be about a hundred meters until we reach the right vent opening to exit the tube. Watch for any sensors planted near openings we pass."

"Yes, ma'am." Ford wriggled inside the circular vent, followed by two of the force recon soldiers. Lamar went next, then Mele, followed by Sergeant Giddings, the last two force recon, and in the rear Private MacKinder.

The inside of the tube was as tight as Ford had said. Normally a human wouldn't have found it cramped at all, but in their battle armor the Marines and soldiers had a much tighter fit. They had to pull themselves along, pushing with their feet, trying not to create any more vibrations than necessary. Noise couldn't travel in a vacuum, but the structure of the facility could carry tremors for a long distance.

One hundred meters wasn't that far. An easy, quick walk. When crawling through a tight, dark tunnel, it was agonizingly long.

They finally made it to the vent opening they should exit through, dropping one by one into a compartment just large enough to hold everyone. "Rest here," Mele said, sitting down carefully to avoid making any betraying thump.

For a few minutes no one said anything as they tried to catch their breath and recover their strength.

"Why do they call it that?" Private MacKinder muttered.

"Why do they call what what?" Private Ford replied.

"Inching. I was thinking, we had to inch our way through that pipe there, and then I thought, why do they call it inching?"

"Because that's what it is."

"That's what what is?"

Sergeant Giddings interrupted the conversation. "Mac, you've got a dictionary in your armor systems. Everyone does. It doesn't take up much space in the memory. Look up 'inching.'"

"Okay, Sarge. Huh. It says an inch was an old system of measurement. There were twelve inches in a foot."

"Twelve in a foot?" Private Ford asked. "Everybody's feet are different sizes. How could you use that as a measurement?"

"I dunno. Hey, it says an inch equaled two point five four centimeters. That explains it."

"It does?"

"Yeah," MacKinder said. "You couldn't say we were two point five four centimetering our way through there. That'd just sound stupid."

"Yeah," Ford agreed. "But if you inch your way along far enough, do you start footing your way along? Like if you—"

"Shut up," Corporal Lamar said. "For the love of my ancestors, both of you shut up. Why out of all the Marines in this unit are you two among the survivors at this point?"

"Maybe we're lucky," Ford said.

"Or maybe I'm being punished for my sins," Lamar replied.

"Corporal," Mele said, "it sounds like everyone's rested. Our time margin is shrinking. We've only got an hour left to cover the remaining distance. Let's get moving."

"Yes, Major. On your feet, boys and girls. Ford—"

"Yeah, I know," Ford grumbled. "Take point. What're you gonna do if I get shot?"

"I'm going to feel real bad for maybe one second, and then I'm going to put Mac on point."

"There they go!"

Tired and half drowsing on the bridge of *Saber* as he waited for something to happen during the rough time frame that Vicki Shen had predicted, Rob Geary bolted to full alertness, gazing at his display where the vectors of the enemy warships were showing sudden, large changes. For days on end the enemy vectors had remained close to the same, maintaining their guard between *Saber* and the enemy freighter. But that was changing rapidly. "Give me an intercept vector. Bring the ship to full combat status. All weapons ready."

The general quarters alarm resounded through the ship as a chorus of eager acknowledgments answered his orders. Ready markers for all departments glowed green almost immediately, showing they were prepared for combat. Rob wasn't the only one aboard *Saber* who'd chafed at their enforced passivity.

"All weapons ready," Ensign Reichert reported.

Rob checked the vectors of the four approaching destroyers, still coming in hot, but much too far distant to have any impact on this battle.

The freighter hadn't moved and didn't show any sign of preparing to move. "They kept the freighter and their ground forces in the dark," Rob told his watch officers. "We would've seen preparations to leave, with ground forces going aboard along with their supplies."

"Why wouldn't they tell their own freighter?" Reichert asked.

"Because we would have seen those preparations and known the warships were getting ready to run. The commander on the light cruiser was willing to sacrifice the freighter and the ground forces he was supposed to be supporting to ensure we wouldn't have any advance notice."

"That didn't work, did it?" Lieutenant Cameron said. "Intercept vector ready, Captain."

Over the last several hours, Rob had shifted *Saber*'s orbit. While space itself had no up or down, whenever a ship was near a planet, "lower" always meant closer to the planet and "higher" meant being in an orbit farther from the world. Knowing that if the enemy warships fled they'd have to take a path through space toward the jump point for Scatha, Rob had positioned *Saber* higher than the orbiting facility and the enemy warships orbiting not too far from it, and in an orbital location that the enemy would have to pass not too far from when they ran. That pre-positioning meant that now the enemy light cruiser and destroyer couldn't avoid an intercept by *Saber* as they tried to leave orbit on their way to a jump point out of this star system.

Rob ran his eyes over the intercept vector, seeing nothing that looked wrong. "Execute intercept vector maneuver."

"Executing intercept maneuver," Lieutenant Cameron echoed as he entered the command.

Saber rolled and pitched up under the push of her thrusters, followed by her main propulsion lighting off on full to accelerate her onto a path that would catch the enemy warships as they fled for the only jump point that they had a chance of reaching. Rob touched the general announcing circuit to speak to the crew. "All hands, this is the captain. We're moving to engage. Our job is to slow down these two enemy ships so they can't reach the jump point they're aiming for before our friends can catch them. We need hits that damage propulsion and maneuvering. Do your best."

Finally. Finally. After the long period of enforced waiting, there was a wild exhilaration to the charge into action. Rob's fist clenched tightly as he saw the vectors steadying, *Saber* sweeping in fast to catch her prey.

Prey that still had deadly stings. But *Saber* could now concentrate on hitting the other warships since the Marines were going to handle the freighter, and if they failed, the remaining destroyers could easily overtake the slow freighter before it could escape. Even if *Saber* was knocked out, if she managed to slow the enemy warships in the process it would still be a win.

"Lieutenant Cameron, Ensign Reichert, I want an evasion maneuver that gives us the best chance we can get to avoid their last missile while still managing an engagement with either enemy ship. Preferably the cruiser. We don't want them getting away."

"Yes, sir."

Rob pulled on his survival suit, knowing that the odds of *Saber* getting holed were pretty bad.

"Got it, Captain," Ensign Reichert said. "This should give us a roughly even chance of evading the missile, and then bring us close past the front of the light cruiser's vector. Assuming he turns to engage us, that should give us a shot at his stern as we pass. Since they've just begun accelerating, like us, and we're coming in from above and behind them, the relative speed during the engagement will be only about one hundred kilometers per second. We're going to practically crawl past them, which should give us a decent chance of aimed shots."

"Excellent," Rob said.

"Captain," Ensign Reichert added, "this intercept will also give them good opportunities to hit us in return. There's no way to maximize our chances of a hit that doesn't also give them good chances to hit us."

"I understand. We'll have to accept that risk. What counts is us being able to slow them down." Rob approved the maneuver, trying to maintain the numb feeling that was holding back fear inside him. He'd done plenty of attack runs before, but when facing decent odds. This was the first time he was charging a ship straight in to catch the full force of a significantly stronger enemy formation, at a relative velocity so slow that a lot of hits could be expected on both sides.

"Fifteen minutes to intercept," Lieutenant Cameron said.

Rob touched another control. "Lieutenant Commander Shen."

She responded from her post in engineering. "Here, Captain."

"If I'm killed or incapacitated, and *Saber* can still fight, do all you can to slow down those two enemy ships."

"Understood, Captain." Shen spoke in an unnaturally calm voice, like someone trying very hard to sound composed when they weren't.

Rob wondered if he also sounded like that.

At five minutes before intercept, exactly when the old Earth Fleet combat manuals mandated, the two enemy ships cut off their main propulsion and used their thrusters to pitch themselves up and around so that their more heavily protected and armed bows faced *Saber* as it approached.

The bridge felt abnormally quiet, the only sounds those of the watch standers moving in their survival suits, the soft noises made by the equipment as it acknowledged commands entered, and the ever-present soft whoosh of the ship's fans circulating air through the ship. Then even the gentle sound of the moving air stopped as the ship closed off all vents and sealed her interior hatches in preparation for exchanging fire with the enemy.

One moment the two enemy ships were thousands of kilometers distant, seconds later they were within less than a thousand kilometers, then they were here close enough to exchange fire and *Saber* was twisting in the last-moment evasive maneuver and weapons were firing and Rob felt his ship rock under multiple impacts and then they were past between one eye blink and the next, *Saber*'s stern pitching up as her bow went down because of the way-too-close explosion of the enemy's last missile, which *Saber* hadn't quite evaded.

Red lights flared on Rob's display. Damage alerts.

"We've lost two of our pulse particle beams and number two grapeshot launcher, Captain."

"Damage aft, Captain. Cannot light off main propulsion. Checking for cause."

"Maneuvering systems compromised, trying to correct."

"Fire control reports primary systems took hits and are down. Backups are online."

"Engineering reports power core is stable, Captain."

Saber was temporarily out of the fight, unless the enemy changed his vectors to chase *Saber* to try to finish her off. But doing that would take time the enemy didn't have.

Rob listened to the damage reports with half his attention, knowing his crew knew what to do and would take the proper actions. They hadn't reported dead and wounded yet, for which he was grateful. But he kept the other half of his mind on his display as *Saber*'s damaged sensors tried to evaluate how much injury the destroyer had inflicted on the light cruiser.

The projected vector on the enemy ships showed them pitching their bows down and over to begin accelerating toward safety again.

But the enemy wasn't matching the projected movements.

"Estimate significant damage to the light cruiser's main propulsion," Chief Petty Officer Quinton reported. "His acceleration is consistent with one main propulsion unit being off-line. He's at half power for main propulsion. Their destroyer hasn't taken any damage, but he's staying with the light cruiser."

"That's doctrine," Lieutenant Cameron said. He was staring helplessly at the maneuvering display, unable to do anything with both the main propulsion and thrusters down. "All units are to stay together so damaged units can be escorted to safety."

"Captain, number three pulse particle beam is destroyed. We can't get it working again. Number one will take at least an hour to get back online."

Rob nodded before remembering that the weapons officer wasn't on the bridge. He touched the reply command. "We won't be able to reengage the enemy in less than an hour. How about the grapeshot launchers?"

"Number two got hit hard, Captain. I can't give you an estimated time to repair."

"Chief Quinton," Rob said, "any updates from engineering?"

"Lieutenant Commander Shen gave me an estimate of one half hour before we can light off main propulsion again, sir. Maneuvering thrusters are starting to come back as damage is repaired, so we should be able to stabilize this tumble within the next few minutes."

Lieutenant Cameron was already running estimates. "If we get propulsion back within half an hour and the enemy light cruiser remains limited in his acceleration, we'll be able to reengage them before they can jump."

Saber's part in this fight might not be over after all. Rob sat back, not wanting to ask the next question. "Do we have any casualty counts?"

"Six dead confirmed, five wounded, but that's a partial count and very preliminary," Lieutenant Cameron said. "Chief Austin can only tell us how many he's personally counted so far."

"Understood." Rob reached out and touched some commands on his display, seeing projected vectors change in response to his inputs.

The curve leading toward the jump point for Scatha that represented the path of the fleeing enemy ships had altered as their rate of acceleration was cut roughly in half. He asked the navigation system to assume the four new destroyers would change their vectors as soon as they saw the enemy ships fleeing. Another curve appeared, showing the four destroyers swooping in like deadly birds making a strike, their path swinging through space and meeting that of the enemy ships well short of the jump point. "Unless they manage to repair the propulsion on the light cruiser, we got it done," he said.

On his display, the marker for *Saber* herself spun away from her former track, reflecting the impact of the missile and other enemy weapons.

"We can still rejoin the fight," Lieutenant Cameron repeated. "If the estimates from engineering are right we'll be able to catch them again and join in the attack with our new allies."

Rob looked back at the lieutenant, and at the other watch standers. All were happy at that news. *Saber* had been hit hard, but she'd done some hitting as well. And she wasn't out of the fight yet. Her crew was ready to engage again.

He hated this. He didn't want any more of *Saber*'s crew to die. But they wanted him to lead them, and lead them he would. "Yes. Let engineering know that, Chief Quinton. If they can make their estimated times for repairs, we can help finish off those guys."

His eyes went back to the orbital facility where the battle was still under way. If Mele didn't manage to capture that freighter, *Saber* might have to deal with the less glamorous task of taking out that ship. And of trying to rescue Major Darcy and whatever was left of her defending force.

Somewhere outside, where the stars shone and infinity beckoned, the enemy warships might already be running for safety. If not now, then soon.

But Mele Darcy and her group were still trapped in the maze created to slow the enemy, working their way through the traps and dead ends and tight passages while also avoiding any more surprises the enemy had left. The pitch dark that existed anywhere lights didn't rest didn't make the task any easier, and they were already tired when they'd started out.

Mele had allowed six hours for her small force to make it undetected from where they were to a compartment granting access onto the dock facing the freighter. At the moment they were huddled in a side passage, their sensors reporting the vibrations from the movement of an enemy patrol on the other side of a wall that didn't seem nearly strong enough.

She checked the time again. Only half an hour remained. Six hours had seemed like plenty of time, but this wasn't the first enemy patrol they'd had to avoid, and there were more spots where enemy portable sensors or mines had been seeded. Just moving through the tight areas had taken a heavy toll on time and their endurance.

The signs of the enemy patrol faded, moving away at right angles to the path Mele's group needed to take. "Move out," Mele ordered.

They had to swing around a series of tight corners, drop down two levels, and make a final approach through what felt uncomfortably like a waste disposal shaft. Mele checked her schematics and saw that was exactly what it was.

Only ten minutes remained before the planned start of the assault on the freighter when she and the others finally crawled into the small compartment next to the dock and paused to rest. "Take a look, Corporal Lamar."

Lamar wriggled over on her stomach and eased open the access giving onto the dock, gazing outward. "Looks okay, Major. Plenty of enemy apes wandering around, but no sign they're preparing for an attack here in the very near future."

"Glitch, are you picking up anything?"

"There's a lot of activity out there, but that's to be expected."

"No indications the enemy is alerted?"

"No, Major."

"Let me take a look, Lamar." Mele took the corporal's place, cautiously scanning the dock. "Gunny was right. That freighter is docked. I guess they did that to make it easier to get to it themselves and get supplies off of it. But it also makes our job easier. Looks like two sentries at the main air lock onto it." She studied the rest of the dock area, seeing numerous small groups of enemy soldiers moving about amid a few piles of crates that must have come off the freighter. Even though she could only see the outside of their armor on the airless dock, none of the enemy soldiers acted as if they were alarmed. But as Mele watched their movements she could see the tiredness in them. Her people weren't the only ones who'd been pushed hard for too long.

She wriggled back from the access, looking around at her group. "Okay. We've got . . . five minutes until things start popping. Get ready. Glitch, how confident are you that Ninja's worm made it into the enemy sensor systems?"

Sergeant Giddings spread his hands. "I think maybe. That's the best I can tell you, Major."

"What about the announcement I recorded?"

"I fed it into the facility's emergency broadcast gear, which still has some battery power. You should boom out on all frequencies just before the diversion starts. We got maybe two minutes before we hear it."

"Not much time to get our breath back," Mele said. "Okay. When the diversion starts, we'll get out onto the dock and head toward the freighter like we're reinforcements for the sentries there."

"Major?" one of the ground forces soldiers said. "How about if the four of us are on the outside and you grunts are on the inside? Because our armor looks more like the enemy armor than yours does. That might help the worm's effectiveness in spoofing their warning systems."

"That's a good idea," Corporal Lamar said. "And if any of the enemy does detect that we're Marines, they might think we're prisoners and the four ground apes are our guards while they take us to the freighter."

"Yeah," Mele said. "Good idea. Once we're out there, all of us Marines hand our rifles to the ground apes. Keep your sidearms. If things go bad, grab back the rifles and head for that freighter."

"The announcement should broadcast in thirty seconds," Giddings said.

"Get ready, and follow me when I go," Mele said.

"I'm not going first?" Private Ford asked.

"Are you complaining about that?"

"No, ma'am!"

Mele knelt by the access, controlling her breathing, trying to blank her mind of everything except what was happening around her and what she'd need to do.

Oh, yeah. She'd forgotten one thing. "Corporal Lamar."

"Yes, Major?"

"Effective immediately, you're Sergeant Lamar. Battlefield promotion. Congratulations."

"Really?"

The blare of the announcement on all circuits cut off any reply that Mele might have made. She listened to her own voice speaking with calm authority and wondered that she'd been able to sound that cool after so many days of combat. "All enemy troops aboard this facility. This is Major Darcy, the Glenlyon commander. Your leaders haven't told you that Glenlyon has received major reinforcements to its space force and now heavily outnumbers your warships. There are destroyers from three different star systems coming to our aid, and to attack you. Eire, Benten, Adowa, Catalan, Kosatka, and Glenlyon are now allied and will bring their full force against you! Your own warships are abandoning you to your fates. Your mission is—"

The message disappeared into a barrage of static and randomly wavering musical tones. "They're jamming it," Giddings reported.

"As long as enough enemy soldiers heard it, it'll cause a serious dent in their morale and some temporary confusion," Mele said.

"And since the jamming is on all frequencies it'll prevent them from sending orders for a few seconds after—"

Through the structure of the facility Mele felt the shock of an explosion, followed by that of weapons firing. Her battle armor alerted her to combat occurring on the other side of the dock.

The small groups of enemy soldiers she could see had frozen in place when Mele's announcement began, and had stood rooted in place since then. Now as combat erupted on the other side of the dock, the enemy soldiers scattered like insects caught in the open, most running toward the fight. But before they got there, another barrage announced a second attack closer to the center of the dock.

"Gunny Moon must've found another group of ours that could help," Lamar said.

"Follow me," Mele replied.

CHAPTER 14

S he squirmed through the access, cursing the bulk of her battle armor, onto the deck outside, and stood up as Lamar followed, and
then the rest of the group. With all attention focused toward the two
attacks, no one seemed to have noticed them. She handed her rifle to
one of the force recon soldiers. "At a trot, as if we're going somewhere
on orders but not running or attacking or anything like that."

The small force set off, the five Marines in the center, the four
ground soldiers spaced around them. Mele kept looking around as they
moved at a fast pace, watching for trouble. The jamming cut off, but
Mele's broadcast had been stopped anyway once the diversions began.

A bigger explosion rocked the dock, the shaking apparent even
without the help of the battle armor sensors. Enemy soldiers were
rushing toward the left and center of the dock area to confront the diversions, which Mele thought were producing an impressive amount
of firepower. If she'd been the enemy commander, she'd have believed
an all-out assault was being launched against the dock.

They were two-thirds of the way across the dock when she saw trouble approaching at an angle, a single enemy soldier who changed course, veered to intercept them, planted themselves in front of one of Mele's soldiers, and gestured vigorously.

What the hell was the enemy ape doing? He or she seemed to be addressing Mele's soldier, but of course that soldier wasn't on the enemy's frequency so he wouldn't be hearing anything.

"I think whoever this is, is chewing me out for something I did or didn't do," the force recon soldier reported to Mele.

She didn't want a fight to erupt here, out in the open, where the enemy might spot it immediately. "Try saluting."

The force recon soldier stiffened to attention and saluted as if acknowledging the unheard orders and/or grievances being directed at her.

It didn't work. The enemy soldier seemed willing to keep going for hours.

Mele looked toward the sound of the fighting, which had begun to taper off quickly as the enemy pushed forward in superior numbers and her own diversionary forces faded away to avoid being trapped.

Enough. Mele drew her sidearm as she stepped next to the angry enemy soldier. The soldier hesitated as the barrel of Mele's weapon touched the enemy helmet at a weak spot, but Mele fired before the enemy could react.

As the enemy soldier was flung sideways by the impact of the shot, Mele grabbed her rifle from the soldier holding it. "Follow me!"

She ran, knowing the others would be behind her, seeing the two sentries at the freighter noticing and raising their weapons. Mele jerked herself to a halt, aiming carefully. She fired just as other shots went off around her. One sentry dropped, then as more shots came from Mele's group, the second fell.

Her armor's sensors warned of shots from the side as the enemy soldiers who had been distracted by the diversion realized what was happening and opened fire on Mele's group. But those shots were from much farther off, and Mele's group was almost to the freighter now.

She hurled herself into the air lock, shoving the fallen soldiers aside, hitting the emergency close control. Mele and the others huddled against the sides of the air lock as a flurry of shots followed them into the freighter and impacted on the inner air lock hatch.

The outer air lock hatch slammed shut, enemy projectiles rattling off of it like hail. "Lock this hatch," Mele told Giddings. "Lamar, get the inner hatch open."

Mele waited, tense, as Giddings worked the air lock controls. "I reset the lock. That'll hold 'em for a couple of minutes," he said.

"Inner door opening," Lamar said, her weapon already aimed toward the interior of the freighter.

A shocked-looking enemy soldier in a skin suit stood staring at them for only a second before Lamar smashed her rifle butt against his head and knocked him against the side of the passageway.

Mele looked up and down the passageway they were in to be sure no one else had to be dealt with immediately. "Section One with me. Sergeant Lamar, you know where to go. Don't let anything slow you down or stop you."

"Got it, Major. Come on, Section Two!" Sergeant Lamar ran aft, followed by Privates Ford and MacKinder, and two of the force recon soldiers.

Mele ran forward, along with Sergeant Giddings and the remaining two soldiers.

Unlike warships, freighters all pretty much had the same layout, their design driven by requirements that didn't vary much from ship to ship. And Mele had made her Marines practice getting around inside freighters every time one of them stopped at Glenlyon. Which hadn't been that often in the last several months, but enough to gain some familiarization with the deck plans. She knew the control deck, which was what freighters called their bridge, would be up forward and centered.

She didn't have to hesitate as the passageway split. Coming around a corner, she found two enemy soldiers in battle armor running toward them and fired before the startled enemy could, she and her force recon soldiers pumping rounds into the enemy faceplates until both soldiers fell.

Around another corner, down a short passageway, to the right again, and there was the hatch onto the control deck, centered in the forward bulkhead, sealed and locked. "Glitch! Get it open. You two," she told the soldiers with her, "watch that direction."

Mele turned to guard the other approach, her weapon at the ready. She heard one of the soldiers behind her fire.

"One enemy, no armor. They ducked back!" the soldier called.

"Waiting for reinforcements," the second soldier guessed.

"How are we doing?" Mele asked Giddings. "Do we have to blow it open?"

"Nah. Almost . . . got it." Giddings stood up as the hatch swung open, his weapon centered on the opening. He went through as Mele backed toward it.

"Come on," she told the force recon soldiers, waiting until the soldiers went through, then following. "Get it shut and locked again, then join me," she told Giddings. "You two guard it," she told the soldiers. "Don't let anyone through."

"No one's coming through that door, Major," one of the soldiers said.

Spinning, Mele faced the two-meter-long passage leading onto the control deck.

Instead of moving cautiously she ran the last two meters and hurled herself out onto the control deck, her rifle seeking targets.

Several civilian sailors stood staring at her, frozen in surprise.

Mele came to a halt against a control panel on the forward bulkhead, hoping that she hadn't inadvertently banged into one of the controls, her rifle leveled at the sailors. She set her helmet's speaker to relay her voice now that she was inside the freighter with atmosphere and people could hear it. "Who's in charge?"

One sailor hesitated as the others looked at him.

"You," Mele said, aiming her rifle directly at the man, whose eyes seemed to have doubled in size as he watched her. "I'm Major Darcy, Glenlyon Marines. I hereby take control of this ship in the name of the government of the star system of Glenlyon. No one will be harmed unless they give me a hard time. Where's your comm to the ship's power core compartment?"

"I . . . I don't . . ."

"Did you hear what I said about people who give me a hard time?"

One of the other sailors lurched toward a nearby panel, pointing. "That control."

Mele went to it, keeping her weapon pointed at the freighter crew members, who backed away as she advanced. The display there had glowing virtual buttons helpfully labeled with compartment names and functions. She pressed the one that said "engineering." "This is the bridge. Who's there?"

The reply came quickly. "Corporal La— I mean, Sergeant Lamar, Glenlyon Marines. That you, Major?"

"That's me. Any problems?"

"We had to plow our way through a few hostiles, but we're inside and the hatch is sealed. Oh, we've also got two freighter crew members in here, but both claim they know nothing about engineering and were just in here for some privacy."

"Pick a button that looks important and push it to see what happens," Mele ordered.

A few seconds later she heard a commotion over the intercom, then Lamar came back on. "Wow. That made her really angry. Or worried. She moved like a scared cat to keep me from pushing that button. Yeah, she's the engineer."

"Is she hurt?"

"Um . . . not much."

"Okay."

"Should I still push the button?" Lamar asked.

"NO!" Mele said, trying to put as much force as possible behind the word. "Do not."

"Major!" one of her soldiers called. "There's someone trying to force this hatch!"

Mele touched another control labeled "general announcing." "Everyone aboard this ship, this is Major Darcy of the Glenlyon Marines. We are in possession of the control deck and the ship's power core. Any attempts to force entry into either compartment will result in us destroying critical equipment.

"You should be aware that I'm saving all of your lives by capturing this ship. Glenlyon has achieved space superiority and would be moving to destroy this ship if we had not captured it.

"I want the senior officer aboard to contact me. I repeat, any attempts to force entry into the control deck or the power core compartment will result in critical damage to both areas, which would leave you all helpless as our destroyers arrive to blow you away. Contact me on the control deck."

Mele called back to her soldiers, "Are they still trying to get in?"

"No, ma'am! They've stopped."

"Keep an eye on it and kill anyone who tries to come through."

The ship's captain had finally found his voice, though it quavered slightly. "We'll do what we're told. We won't try anything." From the looks of him, he'd been running freighters for a long time, the sort of old hand that had more and more trouble finding steady work as younger officers were hired instead. He'd probably ended up this far out because he couldn't find a job closer to Old Earth. "We're not soldiers like you."

"I'm not a soldier," Mele said, her voice colder than she'd intended. "I'm a Marine."

"Uh . . ."

"We won't harm noncombatants," Mele repeated. She had kept her rifle aimed toward the captain of the freighter and finally moved it a little to one side.

"Control deck, this is Captain Horvath of the Hesta Peacekeeping Expedition," a man's voice said over the speakers on the control deck.

"This is Major Darcy," Mele said. "Are you prepared to surrender those aboard this freighter to me?"

"I don't have authority to do that," Horvath replied. "I need to speak with Colonel Busik, our commanding officer. That may take some time."

"How much time?"

"Half an hour. I've ordered my soldiers aboard the freighter to avoid taking any action until we receive commands from the colonel."

"All right," Mele said. "Talk to your colonel. We won't block your transmissions from this ship. But no nonsense and don't take too long. I've got three enlisted Marines in the power core compartment, and if they get nervous or bored they might start pushing buttons to see what happens."

"I understand. Are you aware that those members of your force that we have made prisoner are aboard this ship?"

"That's why we captured it," Mele said. "Do I have to emphasize that nothing had better happen to those prisoners?"

"We are not criminals," Captain Horvath said, his pride clearly stung. "We abide by the common rules of war. I wanted to ensure that you knew any actions you take to endanger this ship will also endanger your own captured personnel. I will now contact Colonel Busik."

Sergeant Giddings came onto the control deck and leaned against one of the seats bolted to the deck. "The hatch is locked, Major, and I reset the controls so only I can open it without forced entry munitions."

"Good. How are the ground apes doing?"

"Happy. They got to hit back at the bad guys. I feel real bad for anyone who tries to come through that hatch." Giddings looked around. "Man, they've got old gear on this tub. But they've kept it up well."

Mele had seen the crew's defensive reactions to Giddings's first ob-servation, and how they'd relaxed a bit when he added the second. "Are you the owners?" she asked the crew.

"Yes," one of the older ones answered. "We bought it on shares. That was when Hesta was free."

"Shhh!" another sailor tried to hush him.

"I won't be silent! That puppet government that runs things on Hesta now told us we'd been seized for not paying some taxes that no one had ever heard of. We had to do this, Citizen Marine! This ship is our lives!"

Mele nodded. "As long as everybody plays nice, you might get this ship back in one piece. We won't damage anything we don't have to, and Glenlyon isn't in the business of seizing property unless there's a good legal reason for it."

Sergeant Giddings indicated the controls. "Can you guys show us the situation in space?"

"If that's okay," the captain said, eyeing Mele warily.

She nodded, and the captain brought a display to life. "This is the situation in the region of this planet. You see . . ." He paused, looking stunned. "Those are the warships that accompanied us! They're leaving!"

"So they are," Mele said.

"You told us the truth!"

"Yeah, that happens sometimes. What's that there?"

"That's, um, your ship. The destroyer. The way it's moving, it must have been badly damaged. They don't seem able to control the ship."

Damn. Mele tried to block emotion from her voice. "What about your ships? The warships. Are they damaged?"

"It's hard to tell. We're a freighter, not a warship or a research ship. Our sensors can't . . ." The captain paused again. "Something seems to be wrong with the bigger warship. That's all I know."

Rob Geary had been in a fight, and hopefully had accomplished what he needed to. "Show me what's going on in the rest of the star system."

"The rest? There's nothing—" The captain had run out the scale on the display and stopped speaking as he stared. "Four more warships. Headed this way very fast."

"You didn't know about those?" Mele asked.

"Only from your announcement. We had orders from the warships. Keep our display on local region only. I . . . I guess they didn't want us to panic."

"Will they attack us?" another sailor asked, her voice frantic with worry.

"Not as long as my people are in control of this ship," Mele said. "So cooperating would be a really good idea. You guys got any coffee?"

Twenty minutes later Mele accepted a transmission to the ship from the enemy forces on the facility. The ground forces colonel who stared impassively from the display bore the marks of too many days with too little sleep aggravated by frustration and regret. "This is Colonel Busik, commanding officer of the Hesta Peacekeeping Expedition."

"Major Darcy, Glenlyon Marines," she replied. "I believe that you're Colonel Busik, but I don't believe that you're really under Hesta's command, and you and I both know your mission wasn't about keeping the peace."

"That's the official name of the unit," Busik said, glowering.

"All right. Call it what you want. Are you ready to talk?"

Colonel Busik inhaled, looking down, before raising his gaze to look at her again. "Major Darcy, I have been able to confirm the information that you broadcast. That your forces now have superiority in space due to the arrival of reinforcements, and that the warships supporting my unit are . . . conducting a tactical withdrawal."

"A tactical withdrawal? Is that what they're calling running away?" Mele asked.

"I see no sense in debating terminology," Busik said. "My request for an explanation from the warships supporting us has not been answered. I understand the situation. My forces have lost any means to withdraw, as well as our supplies. I have no wish to lose any more soldiers in this battle now that the outcome is our certain defeat. Will you negotiate in good faith?"

Mele nodded. "So far we've been trying to kill each other in a civilized fashion. I think we can also negotiate in a civilized way. Which is my way of saying that you and your forces have conducted yourselves honorably, so I have every intention of conducting these negotiations in the same manner."

"Good. I want to ensure an immediate cease-fire goes into effect for both sides. I've already ordered my soldiers to remain in their current locations and only fire if first fired upon."

Mele nodded once more. "Stop your jamming and I'll see to it that the same orders go out to my Marines and the ground forces soldiers under my command. I'd like to ensure that all prisoners taken by your forces are also not in any danger."

Colonel Busik frowned again, as if upset by the question. "They are not in danger. Order them to remain in place, though, until we arrange their official release."

"I'll do that," Mele said. "I'd like an accounting of prisoners as soon as possible."

"Of course. Do your forces have any prisoners from my unit?"

"I honestly don't know," Mele said. "My communications with the subunits on this facility have been intermittent. Once your jamming ceases I will order that I be immediately notified if any prisoners are held by any of my forces."

"Done. Do I have your word that negotiations may now proceed face-to-face without any danger to the participants?"

"You have my word," Mele said. "I'll meet your delegation at the main air lock to the freighter in one half hour."

"Good. I'll be there with some of my staff. No weapons. I give my word your safety and that of your representatives is also guaranteed." He paused to study her image. "They told us on the way here that this would be a walkover. That we'd be going up against amateurs led by a self-important corporal promoted far past her level of competence."

That sounded almost like something that Colonel Menziwa would say. Mele gave Colonel Busik a thin-lipped look. "When you're working for someone who lies to everybody, it's not really surprising when they also lie to you, is it?"

Busik nodded, some distress showing in his eyes. "I don't like to think that my soldiers died because of lies."

"But you know they did."

The colonel nodded again. "Yes. Busik, out."

Mele let out a long breath of relief. "When mercenaries choose the wrong employer, they pay an awful price. Sergeant Giddings, let me know when the enemy jamming stops."

"Yes, ma'am. I . . . it just stopped. All frequencies are clear. I can relay you through the freighter's systems so you've got a lot of power."

Setting her comms to broadcast to her entire force, Mele spoke as clearly as she could. "All Marines and Glenlyon ground forces operating on the orbital facility, this is Major Darcy. Thanks to your own guts and determination, as well as the support of the space squids, we've won. I am on the freighter, which we now control, and am negotiating the surrender of the attacking force, whose commander has agreed to immediately cease combat operations. All units are to remain in place until further notice, and cease firing unless attacked. I say again, remain in place and do not fire unless fired upon. Individual unit commanders are to contact me using the command net frequency to confirm your receipt of these orders, and to advise whether you are in possession of any enemy prisoners. Darcy, over."

Almost immediately her comm light came on. "Major, this is Gunnery Sergeant Moon. I understand your orders and will carry them out. The Marines with me have no prisoners. Moon, over."

"Major, this is Sergeant Major Savak. Understood and will obey. Three prisoners. Savak, over."

"Lieutenant Paratnam, Major. Orders received and understood. Two prisoners. Paratnam, over."

"This is Corporal Oshiro, Major. Understand orders. No prisoners with my group. Oshiro, over."

"This is Sergeant Karlal. My unit merged with the remnants of Lieutenant Killian's force. Orders understood. Five prisoners. Karlal, over."

"Corporal Rajput, reporting in. Orders received and understood. No prisoners with us. Rajput, over."

Mele paused before replying. "All groups, stand by for further orders. Darcy, out." They'd begun with about one hundred forty Marines and soldiers divided into eleven groups. Counting Mele's companions, there were only seven groups left. She wasn't looking forward to seeing the casualty lists, to seeing how small those groups now were, to knowing how many had died to make this victory happen. Colonel Busik's words came back to her. *"I don't like to think that my soldiers died because of lies."* At least she knew that wasn't true of those who had died defending Glenlyon.

But at the moment that was very cold comfort indeed.

"Main propulsion back online. Ready to boost at full," Chief Petty Officer Quinton reported.

"How're maneuvering thrusters?" Rob Geary asked.

"Online."

"Lieutenant Cameron—"

"I have the intercept ready, Captain. I've been keeping it continually updating."

"Send it to me." Rob looked over the solution. They'd be in a stern chase. Only the damage to the enemy light cruiser's propulsion gave

Saber a chance of catching the enemy again, nearly two days from now. "Do we have enough fuel cells for this?"

"Yes, sir."

"Execute."

As soon as *Saber* had steadied out on her new course, Rob stood up from the command chair, feeling stiff. "I'm going to sick bay, and then checking out the rest of the ship."

He left the bridge, walking carefully until his legs loosened up.

Don't look gloomy or sad. Grim. That was it. Grim and confident. Be a leader. Show you respected and grieved for the sacrifices, but were still strong and believed in them and were ready to lead them into other fights. That was what Rob thought the crew needed to see. He tried to show them that. Not because he wanted them to think more of him, but because he wanted them to know what he thought of them. They deserved the best he could show them.

Sick bay was a crowded shambles, Chief Petty Officer Austin working continuously to save the lives of the wounded, the bodies of those he couldn't save set aside. Rob gazed on it for a moment, not wanting to interrupt Austin's work. He was about to leave when he saw one of the wounded watching him, and instead stepped in, careful not to hinder Chief Austin. He spoke to those who were conscious, telling them all how well they'd done and how *Saber* was still in the fight.

Chief Austin finished working on one patient and paused, slumping with weariness.

"Is there anything I can do?" Rob asked.

"Stop sending me work," Austin said. "Sir."

"I'll try."

Rob went on to tour the rest of the ship, checking on the damage, and speaking with the still-healthy crew members, who all seemed eager to hit the enemy again, to make them pay for the losses they'd inflicted on *Saber*. "We'll catch them," Rob promised.

He found the weapons officer supervising attempted repairs to the knocked-out grapeshot launcher. "This is going to take a while, Captain, but number one particle beam is back online and ready to go," the weapons officer reported.

"Just give us a target, Captain!" one of the gunner's mates said as her comrades nodded their approval.

"You'll get one," Rob said.

Eventually he was back in his stateroom, where he sat down and stared at nothing for a while, alone where he could let his real feelings show.

"Hey, Doc. Glad you made it."

Corporal Okubo, who looked like he hadn't slept since Mele last saw him, turned and offered a salute rendered sloppy by fatigue. "Yes, ma'am."

She looked around the medical compartment on the freighter, where wounded Marines and ground forces soldiers from both sides lay in bunks, grouped by their medical status rather than their allegiance, then indicated the man standing next to her. "This is Captain Horvath of the Hestan forces."

"We've met," Okubo said.

"We're working out surrender arrangements."

"I'm sorry to hear that, Major."

Mele blinked. "They're surrendering to us."

"Oh."

"How are your patients?"

"Haven't lost any." Okubo gestured toward a Marine lying sedated in one of the bunks. "I told you if I stayed I could save him."

"What about the enemy ground ape you were also working on?"

"She's over there."

Mele looked, seeing the soldier, her face also slack with sedation. But alive. "Who else you got here? I'll get to everybody, but are there any of our officers and noncommissioned?"

"Captain Batra. Over that way. And Yoshi, Corporal Yoshida, over there."

"Good. Corporal Okubo."

"Yes, ma'am?" Okubo responded, trying to focus bleary eyes on her.

"There are two ground forces medics who came with me, one enemy, one friendly. They can handle things here for a while. Turn over with them, then sedate yourself. That's an order."

"Yes, ma'am."

Mele went to where a sentry stood. "You know Captain Horvath?"

"Yes, ma'am," the sentry replied.

"Your orders are to stay on your post, but not fire unless directly threatened with deadly force," Horvath said. "Do you understand?"

"Yes, Captain."

"This is Private Ford," Mele said, waving Ford forward. "He'll stand guard here for my people. Same orders, Ford. No shooting unless someone is trying to shoot you. Understand?"

"Yeah, Major. Can I talk to him or anybody else?"

"As long as you stay alert. No hugs."

"Got it, Major."

"You okay?" Mele asked Captain Horvath.

"Yes," Horvath said. "With your permission, I will check on my own wounded."

"Be my guest. I'm going over to talk to some of mine."

Corporal Yoshida looked at her anxiously when she stopped by his bunk. "Major, we got ambushed."

"I heard," Mele said. "What happened to Lieutenant Nasir?"

"They must have figured out he was in charge, because their first volley took him out, ma'am. He never had a chance."

"Damn." Mele closed her eyes for a moment before looking at Yoshida again. "How many others did we lose in your group?"

"Five or six. I think. From what I saw before I got hit. But some of those might've been wounded."

"Okay," she said. "We won. Did I mention that? Good work. We'll get you fixed up and back on duty in no time."

"Major . . ." Yoshida blinked back tears. "I did my best. I did. There were just too many—"

"I know you did your best, Yoshi. You did good. Take it easy, okay?"

A few meters away, Captain Batra lay on a bunk, his midsection immobilized. "Got it in the gut, huh?" she said.

Batra, his face noticeably thinner than it had been when last she saw him, looked at her, his lips twitching into an attempt at a smile. "Hello, Major. I heard we won."

"You heard right."

"You told me . . . when I'd done something . . . I could discuss your experience."

Mele paused to remember that conversation. "So I did. What is it you want to say?"

"That you were right, Major. And that I and my soldiers are fortunate you were in command here."

"Words are cheap, Captain." Mele leaned down to give him a questioning look. "Next time I'm at your base, are you going to buy me a drink?"

"I'll buy you a whole bottle. Old Earth booze."

"I'm going to hold you to that."

"How did you manage to capture this ship? I thought it would be very well guarded."

Mele shook her head. "Until our new friends showed up with a lot of shiny destroyers, any attempt to capture this freighter would've been stupid. We just would've been sticking our own heads into a trap and waiting for the enemy to lop them off. As long as the enemy warships were hanging nearby we couldn't have gone anywhere with this ship without being attacked immediately. All we could've done was hold out at the dock until a counterattack recaptured the ship. The enemy commander knew that as well as we did, so he had some guards around the dock, but didn't expect an attempt to seize the freighter. If the commander on that light cruiser had told him that major warship reinforcements had arrived for Glenlyon, the ground forces commander would've known the logic of capturing this ship had changed big-time. But he wasn't told, so he didn't shift his defenses accordingly."

"Betrayed by their own side! Maybe they'll want to get even," he added jokingly.

"Maybe," Mele said, then paused as a thought came to her. "Maybe."

"You said something about new friends and a lot of destroyers?"

"Yes. Glenlyon has been offered a part in an alliance of, uh, let's see, six star systems I think."

"Six." Batra smiled. "Good. I'd like to have the odds in our favor next time."

"Me, too. Excuse me, though, I need to go meet with Colonel Busik and get the surrender terms nailed down."

President Chisholm had the look of someone who couldn't quite believe they'd won the lottery, found the love of their life, and backed up an important file just before their system crashed, all on the same day. "Glenlyon knew we could count on you, Major."

"Thank you," Mele said, thinking that it looked like she really would remain a major this time. "I need to talk to you about the surrender agreement with the enemy ground forces. I held preliminary talks with their commander, Colonel Busik."

"What are they proposing?"

"They led with something they know they're not going to get. They want full honors of war, which would mean they agree to leave and we let them go, along with all of their weapons and equipment."

Chisholm laughed. "No, they're not going to get that!"

Mele cleared her throat. "Madam President, maybe we should consider it."

"What? Why would we agree to that?"

"Because they might agree to what we want. There are times," Mele said, "when someone throws a grenade at you, and you have a chance to throw it back at them before it explodes. This could be something like that."

The president eyed her, thoughts chasing behind her eyes. "Go on."

"These guys were hired as a unit from Old Earth. Hired by the puppet government on Hesta. Many of them brought families with them. They got to Hesta and found out things weren't quite as promised, and then they got sent to attack us, after being told a pack of lies about how weak and helpless we were. They were told this would be a cake walk, and it turned out to be a buzz saw. Then they got abandoned when their warships took off. They're not happy with their employers. Not at all."

"I find I lack sympathy for them," Chisholm said.

"The point is," Mele emphasized, "these guys are very unhappy with the puppet government running Hesta. And from my talks with them and with the crew of this ship, that puppet government is really unpopular on Hesta. It's got control of vital facilities, and the threat of intervention by Scatha, Apulu, and Turan. Without those things, that government would be gone."

President Chisholm nodded slowly. "What are you thinking?"

"I'm thinking that we use the people who attacked us as a grenade tossed back at the thrower. We let them go back to Hesta, but this time they'll be working for us. They show up at Hesta in the freighter, announcing that they left a garrison on the facility that they captured, they take Hesta's orbital facility by surprise and capture it, then they drop onto the planet and start breaking that puppet government."

"You want us to hire them?" President Chisholm shook her head. "My government, and the people of Glenlyon, would never agree to pay the people who attacked us."

"The payment would be granting them full honors of war," Mele said. "It wouldn't cost Glenlyon anything. It'd actually save us a lot of money because we wouldn't have to worry about handling a bunch of prisoners for who knows how long."

Chisholm stayed silent, thinking. "You think they'd agree to that? To attack their own former employers?"

"They got lied to, and their friends died as a result. They're not happy, and legally those lies could be considered a breach of their hiring agreement. They want revenge on those who lied to them, and they want to get back to Hesta to protect their own families. And," Mele added, "when the people of Hesta regain control of their star system, they'll know it was thanks to the people of Glenlyon. We'll have more friends out there who owe us big-time."

This time Chisholm took even longer to reply. "You're a very dangerous woman, Major Darcy."

"Thank you."

"Why would you agree to this? These enemy soldiers killed your people. Why would you want to let them go free?"

Mele sighed, feeling dark thoughts swirl inside her. "There are a couple of reasons. The enemy fought, well, honorably. They didn't commit any atrocities. I personally would like to see the people who gave the orders to attack us suffer for what they did, rather than punishing the soldiers. There's justice in using against them the weapons they sent against us, right? And last . . . the truth is, Madam President, I could stand up every enemy soldier in a line, and walk down that line shooting them one by one and watching them slowly die at my feet, and it wouldn't bring back one single Marine that died in this fight. Far better I honor those who died by acting with honor myself, and by ensuring that their sacrifice leads to safety for this star system and the people in it. That's what they fought for. That's what I want to do." She stopped speaking, embarrassed at stating her feelings so openly.

"I see." Chisholm nodded several times. "Yes. What about the enemy warships, though? Won't they pose a threat to that ship and the soldiers if we send them back to Hesta?"

"I'm told those enemy warships will never leave Glenlyon," Mele said. "Our new friends and allies are going to see to that. They are allies, right?"

"Tentatively, allies," Chisholm said. "Commodore Geary made some strong arguments in favor of accepting membership in the alliance. But a final decision hasn't been made."

"All right. As long as they help us destroy those enemy warships here. And if there are any other warships at Hesta, these soldiers we've been fighting have all the codes and passwords and everything else needed to get past defenses and get things done. The strings of the puppet government will be cut by the time they realize that their own weapon has turned on them."

"Free Hesta. Strike back at those who attacked us. And use the attack itself to pay for the retaliation." Chisholm nodded again. "That I could sell. I fully expect some members of the government to argue that we shouldn't let those who attacked us go free, but if you're arguing in favor of it, that objection won't have much force. Can you get Colonel Menziwa to back the idea as well?"

"You want me to convince Colonel Menziwa?"

"Yes. You two speak the same language."

Mele sighed again. "I guess it looks that way from where you sit. Okay. I'll get Captain Batra and we'll talk to her together."

Captain Batra wanted to get a haircut, shave, and new uniform before speaking to Menziwa, but Mele propped him in an adjustable bunk in his torn battle outfit and stood beside him as she called the colonel. Her battle armor was damaged, her helmet off, her hair and face probably a nightmare, so Mele didn't care what Batra looked like. Next to her, he probably looked ready for inspection.

Menziwa listened without commenting until Mele had finished outlining her idea. Then she focused on Batra. "Captain, are you aware of any atrocities committed by the enemy forces?"

"No, Colonel."

"When you were a prisoner, did you experience or observe any maltreatment of yourself or other prisoners?"

"No, Colonel."

"Did you and all other wounded prisoners of which you're aware receive all necessary medical treatment?"

"Yes, Colonel."

"Were you interrogated?"

Captain Batra nodded. "Yes, Colonel."

"Was any torture or other unlawful methods employed?"

"No, Colonel. Standard interrogation techniques. I told them nothing of importance, and I do not believe any other prisoner told them anything significant, but they did not respond unlawfully."

Menziwa sat back, thinking, her eyes going to Mele. "Major Darcy, your impression of Colonel Busik is that he can be trusted to honor any agreement made?"

"Yes, Colonel," she said.

"I assume there is no objection to my speaking personally with Colonel Busik."

"No objection at all, Colonel," Mele said.

"What was your impression of Colonel Busik's unit?"

"Professional. Well disciplined. Very good at what they did. We were lucky that external support arrived for us."

Menziwa looked at Batra again. "Do you agree, Captain?"

"Yes," Batra said. "I believe that Major Darcy's plan to defend the facility was the best we could have employed, and the actions of all of our soldiers and Marines were the best that any men and women could have provided, but our opponents were very capable, had heavy fire support, and outnumbered us substantially."

"I see." Colonel Menziwa tapped her desk, frowning. "Major Darcy, set up a call with Colonel Busik for me. I'll reserve any recommendation until after that call, but if what I've heard so far is borne out by my conversation with Busik, I expect to support the proposed course of action. Oh, one thing more, Major Darcy."

"Yes, Colonel?" Mele asked, wondering if Menziwa was finally going to offer open praise for her.

"I trust that before any formal talks are held you and Captain Batra will correct your appearances to that expected at all times of officers. Menziwa, out."

As the colonel's image vanished, Mele laughed. She couldn't help it. "I hate her," she told Captain Batra. "Excuse me while I check on the situation in space instead of taking time to wash and style my hair."

L ochan gazed at a display showing the lean, hungry shapes of the destroyers accompanying *Asahi*. "Accompanying" in space terms meaning about ten thousand kilometers distant. *Caladbolg*, *Gae Bulg*, and *Shark*. Without magnification the deadly vessels would have been invisible to human eyes against the infinite black and stars of space, both a reminder of how small the works of humanity were and how deadly those works could be.

"Hey." Freya Morgan walked up beside him and winked. "Interested in a little private recreation?"

"Ummm . . . sure," Lochan said. He followed her to the tiny stateroom she shared with one of *Asahi*'s officers, who was currently on watch. As soon as the hatch closed, Freya started checking something on her comm pad.

"There's a listening device," she reported, "but I've got it jammed for the moment."

"You really ought to find another way of asking me to a private conference," Lochan said.

Freya gave him an apologetic look. "Do I keep getting your hopes up? Or is it you're afraid Brigit will hear of it?"

"I . . . what's this about?"

"Something odd." Freya looked about her. "A couple of hours ago there was a conference of ship captains. I just happened to be aware of it, though I couldn't figure out a way to tap in before it ended, so I don't know what was discussed. What I do know is the conference consisted of Captain Sori, Captain Hubbard, and Captain Tanya the Wicked."

"That's . . ." Lochan spread his hands. "They were talking strategy or something. Tactics. There wouldn't be any need to include us in— wait. Did you say Captain Derian was part of that conference?"

"I did not," Freya said. "Captain Derian wasn't included."

Lochan stared at her. "What would they have been talking about that they didn't want Derian to know?"

"That's a fine question, isn't it? What is it our new friends and allies are hiding from us?"

CHΛPTER 15

"**W**hat the hell are you doing, Rob?" *Saber* was far enough from the planet by now for a conversation to be impossible due to the time lag as light itself required several minutes to make the journey between them.

Ninja's image looked out at him, exhausted and bewildered. "I thought we'd done our part. I thought you'd done what you had to. The other ships can handle the enemy. Rob, why are you risking your life again?"

She looked down. "It's because of them, isn't it? You know they'll go on to the fight without you. Rob, you're killing me. I know who you are. I know what you think you have to do. But please. Let this be the last time.

"I'm going to see what else I can do. Mele was able to get her hands on a lot of the enemy codes and passwords when their ground forces surrendered. I think I can crack into those two warships now. But give me a break, okay? Come home when this is done. I love you. Lyn, out."

She'd called herself Lyn instead of using her nickname. Rob closed his eyes, thinking, knowing the signal that sent. Ninja was absolutely serious about this. She wouldn't demand he quit this job. But she couldn't handle him staying in it.

And he couldn't blame her.

But even then, she knew he had to see this through, and was going to be by his side, in the virtual sense, when he did.

"Captain?" Lieutenant Commander Shen stood in the doorway. "Can we talk fuel?"

"Yeah." Rob called up the image of *Saber*'s path through space, a great arc ending light hours ahead where it crossed the projected path of the fleeing enemy warships. "We can make this intercept."

"We can. How low are you willing to go on fuel cell reserves?"

"How low are we talking about?"

"Captain, we had to use a lot of fuel cells while dancing with the enemy before this. When we catch them this time, we'll be at fifteen percent. That's enough to get home, where shuttles hidden on the surface will be able to haul more fuel cells up to us. But . . ."

Shen grimaced, looking to the side. "We'll be at fifteen percent fuel reserves, pretty beat up, some of our weapons out of action, even before we engage the enemy again. And then, when that fight is over, we'll be at less than fifteen percent, probably beat up some more, near four destroyers belonging to other star systems."

"You don't think Commander Derian would betray us, do you?" Rob asked, surprised.

"Not Derian, no. He's committed to repaying the debt owed to us from Kosatka, and I had time there to learn what kind of person he is. But the other three . . . I don't know."

"I thought you were acquainted with Bard Hubbard and Tanya . . . the Wicked. Does she have a last name?"

"Nobody uses it. Yes, sir, I am, but . . . I have to worry about what orders they might have." Shen shook her head. "I'm probably being paranoid."

"That's your job. Anticipate problems." Rob rubbed the back of his head as he thought. "Do you know anyone else on those new ships you could talk to? Someone who might be able to either reassure us or warn us?"

"I don't know. Earth Fleet was pretty big before it got really small really fast. Even the officers I know, like Hubbard, I don't really know. I've just heard their names and something about their reputations. But I can try."

"That'd be natural, wouldn't it?" Rob asked. "You seeing if there was anyone on those ships who was an old friend, someone you wanted to connect with?"

"It would be natural," Shen said. "Permission to proceed with that?"

"Granted. For the time being, I'm assuming that these ships are what they say they are. But it doesn't hurt to do a little checking with anyone you might know."

"And the fuel cell situation? You'll have to personally authorize going that low on reserves, and entering combat in that state."

"I'll authorize it," Rob said. "I'm reading the crew right, aren't I? They want to be in on the kill of those enemy warships."

"Yes, sir, they do," Lieutenant Commander Shen said. "You don't always have to give the crew what they want, but in this case I think it will be an important precedent that those ships be defeated with the active participation of *Saber*. Otherwise someone will always want to hang an asterisk on our defense of this star system, saying it was actually won by someone else."

"Yeah," Rob agreed. "Do you know what 'asterisk' originally meant?"

"I guess not."

"A little star. Literally a minor star. That's ironic, isn't it? Glenlyon is sort of a minor star, nothing special about it. But maybe we've been at the center of something really important."

Vicki Shen smiled. "Maybe we have been. Maybe someday your name will be in histories."

Rob surprised himself with a laugh. "If it is, there'll definitely be an asterisk next to it."

"**F**our hours remaining to intercept with the enemy warships?" Freya Morgan asked Captain Sori.

Lochan Nakamura, who always felt like an unwelcome intruder on the small, crowded bridge of the destroyer, stood uncomfortably to one side as Sori glanced at Freya. "That is correct."

"Would you be free for a private meeting?" Freya asked.

"There are preparations to be made before battle. Is the reason for this meeting an urgent one?"

"It could be," Freya said.

"I see." Sori looked from Freya to Lochan, then back again before facing the senior watch officer on the bridge. "I'll be in my stateroom. I expect to return within ten minutes."

She led the way off the bridge and to the small room not far away that held the grand name of Captain's Stateroom. There was barely room inside for the three of them, Sori taking the sole seat and gazing at them impassively. "What is urgent?"

"Meetings," Freya said. "Meetings that don't involve everyone they should."

Sori smiled slightly. "You're disturbed by the conference I held with the commanding officers of the two ships from Eire? Yes, Freya Morgan, my crew did detect your intrusion into our systems. Since you did no damage, I decided not to make an issue of what could have been interpreted as an unfriendly act."

Lochan had to admire the way that Sori had quickly shifted the burden of accusation from her actions to those of Freya Morgan, and done so using polite terms that didn't leave Freya grounds for an angry rebuttal. But he also couldn't let her dodge the issue so easily. "Holding meetings that are kept secret from representatives of star systems who are supposedly allies could also be interpreted as an unfriendly act," he said. "We're concerned about what that could imply."

"Do you accuse me of acting falsely toward you?"

She was good, Lochan admitted to himself, using respectful language to divert questions and use the questions themselves as a means to put her questioners off-balance. "No one is accusing anyone of anything. We're curious as to what issues were judged to not involve the representatives of Kosatka and Catalan, as well as Captain Derian."

"We're preparing for battle, Citizen Nakamura. You and Citizen Morgan are not combat officers."

"And Captain Derian?" Freya asked.

"*Shark* still carries damage from her last encounters with the enemy. We discussed means to honorably limit the exposure of *Shark* to further damage without insult to her crew and captain."

"That was the only matter discussed?" Lochan asked.

Captain Sori gazed at him. "Of course not."

He let some frustration show. "Captain, this is still a very new and very fragile alliance. Any hint of grounds for distrust or secrecy between us could break these bonds before they strengthen. Surely you understand that."

"What possible gain would Benten and Eire achieve by betraying Kosatka and Catalan?"

She'd neatly turned the question back on him. Lochan shook his head. "I see why you're in command of this force. Captain, Kosatka has been repeatedly attacked. So has Glenlyon, whose people I still feel an obligation to represent as I was asked to by Citizen Camagan. Catalan has been effectively blockaded. Put yourself in our places. We have every reason based on our experiences to distrust other star systems. We chose to trust Benten and Eire anyway."

"Despite the flaws and ambitions of Eire's leader," Freya added. "Lochan couldn't say that, but I can."

"Do you and the ships from Eire have orders of which Freya and I are unaware?" Lochan asked. "Please just tell us. We've risked a great deal by accepting your offers of help, and want to feel nothing but gratitude."

Captain Sori rested her chin on one fist as she studied Lochan and Freya. "Do you think we're a danger to your star systems?"

"There are people in our star systems who fear that. And our mutual enemies would like nothing better than to sow suspicion between us and break up our cooperation as quickly as possible."

"Let me put it this way," Captain Sori said, her eyes closely watching both Lochan and Freya. "Can you accept that the self-interests of Benten and Eire might also benefit Kosatka and Catalan?"

"What does that mean?" Freya asked.

"It means my ship, and those of Eire, will not turn around from here. Once we've defeated the force that has attacked Glenlyon, we have orders to continue on to Scatha and destroy any pirates or hostile warships we encounter."

"Scatha?" Lochan stared at the captain, then at Freya. "Why?"

"They're your enemy. Why do you need another reason?"

"Because you're risking your ships," Freya said. "What is my father up to?"

"Pirates," Lochan said, having seized on that word. "What about after Scatha?"

Sori looked at him for a moment before replying. "On to Hesta, then to Catalan, to return Citizen Morgan to her home in suitable style."

"Oh, my ancestors," Freya said with a sigh. "There's my father's hand. Even if he's disowned me he still wants a Morgan given all the pomp and ceremony he can arrange."

"And from Catalan?" Lochan pressed. "On through connecting star systems until you return back through Kosatka?"

"Those are our orders," Sori said.

"Pirates. Your other mission is to clear trade routes," Lochan said. "Benten and Eire derived a lot of income from the trade that has been flowing through their star systems en route to more distant stars in this region. That trade has been choked off by the actions of Apulu, Turan, and Scatha, including the pirates they've been sponsoring. You're going to sweep the stars of those pirates, and make sure everyone knows your star systems intend to keep those routes open from now on, using joint military action when necessary."

"Very succinct," Captain Sori said. "Yes."

"Why did you think Catalan would object to that?" Freya asked.

"It expands the conflict," Sori replied. "In the eyes of some. It expands the commitments of the star systems involved. Benten and Eire were willing to make such commitments. We had no sense that Kosatka or Catalan would agree at this stage, so the decision was made to take action using our ships."

"The conflict is already there," Freya said. "This also has the hand of my father on it. He wanted trade opened up, and didn't want to deal with any obstacles raised by Lochan or myself."

"The representatives from Benten also agreed," Sori said.

"You should have included us in this matter," Lochan said. "Yes, both Kosatka and Glenlyon were concerned primarily with active, ongoing attacks against them, but we've both suffered from the actions of Scatha, Apulu, and Turan that have been strangling trade."

"Catalan," Freya said, "has yet to face active attack, but the whole point of my mission was to open up free trade again."

"The decision was not made by me," Captain Sori said. "Time was judged critical. That's all I know."

"Why wasn't this brought up while we were at Kosatka?" Lochan asked. "I could've asked the government to sign on with this."

"How much extra time would it have taken for the government of Kosatka to debate and vote on that extra issue?" Sori asked him. "Especially as it would have involved more risk for Kosatka's lone warship? I judged it more important to have *Shark* with us when we reached Glenlyon, for the symbolism that would add to our mission, and for us to reach Glenlyon as quickly as possible in case our support was needed urgently. I believe that you must agree I judged right in those matters.

Even a single day more of delay might have been too long for the defenders on that orbital facility."

Lochan grimaced, but finally offered a reluctant nod. "You probably were right. As much as I would've preferred resolving that issue then, it would've been a big complicating factor. But now is different."

"How so? The government of Kosatka has not agreed to the larger mission concerning clearing trade routes in this region. That cannot be changed."

He offered her a thin smile. "Captain Sori, I am a representative of the government of Kosatka. The authority given me to represent the interests of Kosatka was not changed while we passed through my star system. I admit that's because no one thought it might need to be changed, but the fact remains. I can still make preliminary agreements and commitments in the name of Kosatka."

Sori's gaze on Lochan grew more intense. "Are you saying that you would be willing to commit *Shark* to accompany us? I admit that would please me. The increase in our firepower and capabilities, as well as the political impact of having warships from three star systems in this force, would be welcome."

"I'm saying that I'm willing to consider it," Lochan said. "If I'm allowed to freely discuss the matter with Captain Derian, and with the captains of the two ships from Eire. No restrictions. Full discussion."

She nodded to him. "I will authorize that. What of Catalan, Citizen Freya? You have no warship here, but if you can speak for Catalan as well . . ."

"I'm not sure I can commit to that," Freya said. "I'll sit in on Lochan's discussions, and see what's possible. As I said, Catalan sent me out to reopen the trade routes. This is what we want."

"What of Glenlyon?" Lochan asked. "Should we see if they want to send their warship, *Saber?*"

"It's unlikely that will be an option." Captain Sori turned to call up some data on her desk display. "This is what our sensors have reported on *Saber*. She took extensive damage while crippling the main propulsion on the enemy light cruiser. It was a brave and heroic attack, and accomplished its goal, but with that amount of damage I would be uncomfortable having *Saber* accompany us on jumps to multiple star systems even if she has sufficient fuel reserves aboard to handle such a journey."

"Yet you altered the vectors of this force to ensure *Saber* participated in our attack on the enemy," Freya said.

"They earned that," Sori said. "I will not deny them a role in that action."

"They should still be asked," Lochan said. "From my discussions with Leigh Camagan, Glenlyon has the same pride that afflicts any group of humans. They might not be able to assist in clearing trade routes, they may not want to participate even if *Saber* is judged capable of the mission, but they will want to be asked, to be treated as equals who'd be capable of contributing and carrying their share of the load."

"Would you extend that offer to them?" Sori asked Lochan. "As a diplomat trusted by Glenlyon, you're in a better position to do so than I am. If you do so, emphasize that we cannot wait around for a decision. We don't have the luxury of lingering at Glenlyon while the matter is debated here."

"If that's an accurate picture of how badly *Saber* was damaged," Freya said, "they won't debate it long. But, yes, I agree with Lochan that they'll want to be asked."

Sori stood up. "Then if this matter is resolved, I will return to the bridge. We have a battle to fight in . . . three hours and forty-five minutes."

"It's resolved," Freya said, "for now. But happy as I am to know I'll be returning home in style with a mission completed to the benefit of Catalan, I'd be happier if I'd known of it from the start. Trust begins at home."

"Many things begin at home," Captain Sori said.

"You're not going to get me started there."

"I was told to inform you at the right time," Sori added. "Since you were a most reasonable individual I did not believe that would pose any problems."

"A most reasonable individual? Who the hell told you that lie about me?" Freya demanded.

Sori waved one hand toward Lochan. "Perhaps it was a friend of yours. If you'll excuse me." She passed them, headed back to the bridge.

"Did you tell people that I'm reasonable?" Freya demanded.

Lochan tried his best to look baffled by the question. "Not that I . . . well . . . I might have said compared to your father . . ."

"That's a very low bar to cross, Lochan. Don't you think you should be putting in a call to Commander Derian? You need to get a feel for how he'd see participating in that trade-route-clearing mission. And, Lochan," she added with a warning expression, "don't think your government will take this decision lightly if you commit *Shark* to a long trip to potential battles at other stars. That's a big thing to take on yourself. You might be deciding your own future as well as that of Kosatka."

"I know," he said. "Someone once told me that if it's worth doing, what matters is that it gets done. She was right. I think this needs to get done."

"She?" Freya raised an eyebrow at him. "Was it that Carmen girl? Or Brigit?"

"Mele Darcy. The Marine."

"You know some very interesting women, Lochan."

"I certainly do. I'm going to make that call to Derian. Do you want to listen in on it openly, or would you prefer covertly tapping into it?"

Freya grinned. "Oh, maybe do it in the open just this once."

"Ten minutes to intercept," Lieutenant Cameron reported.

Rob Geary nodded, his eyes on the display at *Saber*'s command seat. The light cruiser and destroyer had continued to flee, the

JACK CAMPBELL

destroyer tucked in fairly close to the cruiser to protect it. The four new destroyers were coming in at them from well on the port side and just slightly below, aiming to hit the enemy almost on their beams. *Saber*, just to port and above the enemy ships, would cross their paths at almost the same moment as the allied destroyers, but coming in from behind and crossing ahead.

"Sir," Cameron added, "on current vectors *Saber* will engage the enemy almost a second after the four allied warships do."

"Captain Sori did that on purpose," Lieutenant Commander Shen said, sitting in the seat next to Rob's. "She's trying to ensure that her undamaged ships take fire from the enemy before we do."

"They'll have to go bow on toward Sori's force to face the stronger threat. That'll give us shots at their beams and sterns." Rob fought down a tremor of anxiety, the results of the last engagement haunting him. He didn't want another success purchased at that kind of price. "Did you find out anything that would indicate we can't trust our new allies?"

"Nothing," Shen said. "What was that message you were sent by them half an hour ago?"

"A copy of a message sent to the government," Rob said. "Inviting Glenlyon to participate in follow-on operations at stars like Scatha and Hesta to clear out threats to trade."

"You're kidding." Shen looked intrigued and alarmed. "Immediate follow-on operations? But *Saber* . . ."

"That's what I told the government. We can't. It's not an option given the damage to this ship and the low state of our fuel cells." He turned a wry smile on her. "The government will probably be grateful to hear that. It gives them a graceful way to decline to participate without turning down the offer to help get trade going in this region again."

"And yet . . ."

"Yeah," Rob said. "And yet. How crazy are we that it's a disappointment that we can't assist in that operation?"

"All sailors are crazy, Captain. All departments report ready for action," Shen said.

"You have to give the captain of that enemy destroyer credit," Rob said. "He could've run and gotten to the jump point before we caught him, but he stayed with the light cruiser."

"I doubt he was given a choice. The overall commander on the cruiser probably ordered him to stay. If he'd run he'd have been court-martialed as soon as he got back."

"Five minutes to inter—" Lieutenant Cameron's voice broke off abruptly. "What the hell?"

"What's that, Lieutenant?" Shen snapped.

"I'm sorry, I just—the light cruiser is dropping his shields. He's— here go the shields on the destroyer. Captain, both enemy ships are dropping their shields fast toward minimum strength."

"Are you sure of the sensor readings?" Lieutenant Commander Shen demanded.

"Everything looks clean on our end," Cameron said. "The enemy ships are dropping their shields."

"We haven't received any surrender messages," Shen said. "If they intended surrendering, they'd have sent those before dropping their shields."

Rob laughed, drawing surprised looks. "I think my wife just sent us a present. Using the codes our Marines captured, she managed to hack the enemy defensive systems and set their shields to drop just before we caught them."

"I've always liked your wife," Lieutenant Commander Shen said.

"Message from Captain Sori on *Asahi*!"

With only a few minutes left, Sori didn't waste time. "With the enemy vulnerable, my four ships will concentrate fire on the light cruiser. I recommend that *Saber* engage the destroyer. Sori, out."

"Ensign Reichert," Rob said, "set the enemy destroyer as our priority target."

"Fire control set to engage the enemy destroyer as priority target," Reichert said. "One minute to engagement."

The two enemy ships were using their thrusters to turn their bows toward the four allied destroyers, exposing their beams to fire from *Saber*. Their shields had bottomed out and not yet begun rebuilding. The light cruiser, its missiles expended, was badly outmatched by four destroyers. "These guys are toast," Shen whispered, smiling.

Rob knew his sight of the allied warships whipping past was the product of his imagination, since the action had occurred too fast for human senses to register. *Saber* came in immediately behind them, her remaining weapons hitting the enemy destroyer.

"Status," Rob said as *Saber* curved up and around for another firing pass.

"No damage to *Saber*, no hits on our shields," Lieutenant Reichert reported. "They concentrated their fire on the allied warships. I don't think they penetrated the shields on any of them, though. We got solid hits on the destroyer. He's lost some maneuvering thrusters and two pulse particle beams."

"How's the cruiser?" Shen asked.

"Evaluating . . . they hit him hard. Looks like he's lost almost all weapons and maneuvering control."

"Captain Sori is broadcasting, Captain."

Rob saw Sori's image, the captain from Benten appearing perfectly relaxed and confident. "Enemy warships, this is the commanding officer of *Asahi*. You are directed to surrender immediately. Power down remaining weapons and cease attempting to rebuild your shields. I repeat, surrender immediately or you will be subject to another attack."

"Private message for you from *Asahi*, Captain."

"Commodore," Captain Sori said, "I have directed *Shark* to assist you against the enemy destroyer on this next attack run. My remaining three destroyers should have sufficient firepower to eliminate the cruiser."

"Adjust vector to intercept the destroyer," Rob ordered as *Saber* reached the top of her loop and began angling back down again.

"Sir, the four allied ships were able to weave about faster to a new intercept than we could because of their approach vector. They'll hit the enemy again about ten minutes before we can."

"That can't be helped," Rob said, trying to think of a way to put the best possible gloss on the situation. "*Saber* will deal the final blows."

"Finish them," Ensign Reichert murmured.

"They haven't responded to the surrender demand," Shen said.

"Then we will finish them," Rob said.

The allied destroyers tore past the light cruiser again. Rob stared as the cruiser's forward section came apart, shattering into a swarm of broken pieces, and the stern section wavered off into space, out of control, lifeboat pods ejecting as the surviving crew sought safety.

The enemy destroyer staggered under the barrage from *Shark*, also veering off its former vector under the blows.

"Five minutes to intercept," Lieutenant Cameron said. "He's helpless, Captain."

"I know." Rob cast a look at Lieutenant Commander Shen. "We don't have any choice, do we?"

"Not if he doesn't surrender," she said, unhappy. "What a waste."

"Captain! Message from the surviving enemy ship."

The commanding officer of the enemy destroyer was in a survival suit with the helmet sealed, signs of damage visible on what could be seen of the bridge behind him. "I surrender my ship to you. I have no remaining working weapons, no maneuvering control, and most of my shields have been knocked out and cannot rebuild. I repeat, I surrender my ship and place the lives of my surviving crew at your mercy."

Rob hesitated for a crucial second, wondering why he felt a sense of recognition as the enemy captain spoke. He wrenched his mind back into motion, speaking loudly and clearly. "Ensign Reichert, disengage fire control targeting!" Rob said. "Do not fire on that ship!"

"Understand do not fire on enemy warship," Reichert responded. "Fire control system ordered to break lock on enemy warship. Weapons set to no-fire status."

Saber raced past the surviving enemy warship, but this time no weapons tore at the helpless vessel.

This fight was over.

O ne moment two groups of people were using the latest tools crafted by human ingenuity to try to kill each other, and the next the winning group was trying to save the lives of those they'd been trying to kill. If any aliens were secretly watching humanity, Rob thought, they must be having a hard time understanding what they were seeing.

"Do you have enough life support?" he asked the captain of the surrendered ship, which turned out to be named nothing except D-11.

"It won't be comfortable, but we'll manage," that officer replied. He was out of the survival suit, in a part of D-11 that had restored atmosphere. "I guess Rob Geary turned out to be the better captain."

Rob shrugged. He'd never really liked Charlie Forez when they'd served together in Old Colony Alfar's fleet. Charlie had been the sort who knew all the right people and kept his eyes fixed on his next promotion. But Rob also wasn't interested in gloating over having beaten him. "I thought you were doing well at Alfar. Why'd you come out here?"

"Alfar was downsizing," Forez said. "Even someone like me didn't have many chances. But these guys offered me a command."

"Sure." Never mind what "these guys" wanted him to do. They'd offered him a command. "Keep us informed of your medical and life support needs. My people are installing monitors in all of your systems. Please don't mess with any of those. We need to know the status of all of your equipment at all times. I'd hate to have to fire on your ship again," Rob said, "but I will if it seems my own ship might be in danger from your actions."

"Hey, not a problem! I'll let you know as soon as we're ready to be taken under tow. It's great seeing you again, Rob!"

Rob ended the call, feeling a headache coming on. Even after losing his ship in combat and his crew suffering a lot of casualties, Charlie Forez was still schmoozing his way through life.

Never mind what aliens thought of human actions. He himself had a lot of trouble understanding people sometimes.

Rob sat in the grandly named wardroom of the *Saber*, because as not-really-that-large as it was, the compartment was nonetheless large enough for several displays to have been set up facing him. On those displays he saw Captain Sori of the *Asahi*, Captain Hubbard of the *Caladbolg*, Captain Tanya the Wicked (what was her last name?) of the *Gae Bulg*, Captain Derian of the *Shark*, Lochan Nakamura, and a woman named Freya Morgan representing Catalan. The five warships were close enough for the virtual conference to be in real time.

The captain of the surrendered enemy warship was not present, of course, but the fate of D-11 was first on the agenda.

"Who gets the ship?" Bard Hubbard asked.

Rob waited to see what the others would say.

"We're in Glenlyon star system," Nakamura said. "This is space that belongs to Glenlyon."

"But not everything in that space belongs to Glenlyon," Tanya said.

"Glenlyon should have it," Freya Morgan said. "For two reasons. One is simply practical. How is anyone else going to get a badly damaged warship home to their star system? The other is longer term, a matter of generosity, and recognition that Glenlyon has borne the brunt of a nasty fight here."

Captain Sori nodded. "I agree. There is another factor that you didn't mention. The success of Glenlyon's malware intrusion caused the enemy ships to lose their shields just before combat, ensuring our victory was much quicker and less hazardous to our own ships. For all the reasons given, I believe that the ship should be considered a prize for Glenlyon. What is your opinion, Captain Derian? Kosatka has also suffered serious harm from attacks."

Derian smiled. "Kosatka would've lost *Shark* if not for Glenlyon. We owe them a warship. I agree with Citizen Nakamura and Citizen Morgan."

"Will Eire's captains make this an issue?" Sori asked them.

Hubbard shook his head. "I felt an obligation to bring up Eire's interests. But I can't deny the other arguments. Tanya?"

"I'm good," she said. "We have no way to get the hulk home. Glenlyon can have the prize. I'm sure the prime minister of Eire will be happy to be able to tell others how generous Eire was in this instance."

"He'll find a way to bring it up fairly often for a while," Freya Morgan agreed.

"Thank you," Rob said. "I wasn't looking forward to a fight over that."

"I think you've earned a break from fighting," Captain Sori said. "Commodore Geary, have you heard from your government regarding the clearing-of-trade-routes mission?"

"Yes," Rob said. "Glenlyon extends its regrets that it is physically unable to participate in the operation due to damage to its only warship. We're also very low on fuel, so even without the damage the need for us to return to our world to refuel would slow you down by at least a week. However, there's an issue you need to be aware of if you're going to Hesta. The freighter that brought the invasion force against our orbital facility should be leaving dock soon to return the surrendered troops to Hesta."

"You're sending them back?" Tanya said, surprised.

"With all of their weapons and equipment." Rob grinned at the reactions to his statement. "The enemy forces were hired from Old Earth by Hesta's puppet government, actually Scatha pulling the strings in this case, we're certain. They believe their terms of employment were violated, and agreed to take employment with Glenlyon for a single mission in exchange for their release with all of the arms."

"What's the mission?" Freya asked.

"They're going to try to overthrow the puppet government and allow Hesta's people to govern themselves again. From what we've been able to learn, they'll have a high chance of success, especially since they should achieve total surprise when they hit the puppet government's forces."

"We will not engage that freighter if it is encountered," Captain Sori said, nodding. "It should be well behind us, though. Our ships should sweep Scatha space of any threats to it before the freighter arrives there, allowing it to transit Scatha's space safely and jump to Hesta, which we will have also swept of threats by that time."

"If Glenlyon helps free Hesta," Freya said, "you'll have Catalan's warm thanks."

"What exactly are you going to sweep out of Scathan and Hestan space?" Rob asked Captain Sori.

She made a dismissive gesture as if the task wasn't of any concern. "Pirates. Any merchant ship carrying weapons or extra propulsion. They won't be able to fight us or escape us."

"What about warships?" Rob said. "Scatha isn't just going to sit and watch you do that."

"They might have no choice but to sit and watch," Bard Hubbard said. "We put together what our different governments have seen of warships heading outward from Earth and the Old Colonies, and have a pretty good handle on what Scatha, Turan, and Apulu must have been able to assemble to date. Bouncing that against their losses, they don't have much of anything left."

"They bet the farm on their attacks on Kosatka and Glenlyon succeeding," Commander Derian said. "Instead, their attack forces were almost wiped out. There is the destroyer that got away from Kosatka, but that was beat up so badly that if we encounter it we won't have any problem finishing the job."

"In addition to that destroyer, there might be a corvette or two left to Scatha at the moment," Captain Sori said. "We're authorized to deal with them in response to Scatha's attacks on Eire."

"When we're done passing through Scatha," Tanya the Wicked said, "they won't have anything left to mess with anyone else. And good luck to them finding the money to keep hiring new ships and mercenaries after that. They won't be able to extort from any more merchant travel through other star systems."

"Win-win," Freya said. "We ought to do this kind of thing more often."

"I thought that was the point of the alliance," Hubbard said. "I didn't get the impression this was a one-off and then we'd all get back to glaring at each other."

"I'll do all I can to make it long lasting," Lochan Nakamura said. "No other star systems should suffer as Kosatka and Glenlyon have. There are a lot of details to work out, but I think we can manage that now that our governments have all experienced the negative sides of not having anyone watching out for the interests of everyone."

"Never underestimate the ability of people to mess up a good thing," Freya said.

"I didn't say it wouldn't involve a lot of work," Nakamura replied. "Commodore Geary, in the discussions I've had with your president, she seems to have become much more enthusiastic about the alliance than when we first spoke."

"She was concerned about outsiders coming in to coerce us," Rob said. "Which is understandable concerning our recent history."

Captain Sori inclined her head toward him. "We'll be heading in different directions soon, but I am looking forward to further opportunities to work with you and Glenlyon's forces in pursuit of common interests."

Rob hesitated, not knowing what to say, and not wanting to lie to these officers who'd helped save his home. The gazes of the others on him grew curious, though. He had to say something. "I . . . hope that Glenlyon will be a strong partner in future endeavors. I . . . can't say at this point what my personal role will be, but I'm sure whoever does work with you from Glenlyon's forces will do very well."

After a few more rounds of mutual farewells and hopes for the future, the others ended the conference, their displays blanking until only that showing Lochan Nakamura remained. "Commodore Geary, Mele Darcy is my friend, and you're her friend. I can sense there's some uncertainty about your future. Is there anything I can do?"

"No," Rob said. "Mele's not going to be happy that you didn't stop by to see her."

"She's not going to be happy if anything adverse happens to you."

"That's true." Rob shrugged. "I made some tough calls. Those decisions could haunt me once I get my ship back to the orbital facility. But I don't think I could've done differently."

"I see." Nakamura nodded slowly. "For what it's worth, Mele admires you as an officer."

"She admires you as well."

"She saw something in me that I didn't see. That's strange, isn't it? No one knows more about what we think and feel inside than we do, and yet those outside of us sometimes see us better than we ourselves do. Good luck, Commodore."

"Thank you. Hopefully we'll work together again."

Nakamura's call ended as well, Rob went to check on the status of the preparations to tow the captured warship.

It was time to go home, no matter what waited there.

CHAPTER 16

Mele Darcy stood in her repaired battle armor on the dock of the orbital facility, her remaining Marines and the surviving force recon ground soldiers in ranks behind her. All wore their armor on the airless dock, making them appear much more menacing than if they'd simply been in uniform. Visible against the stars were the shapes of two destroyers on final approach to match orbits and dock. *Saber*, coming home, and the captured enemy ship that might one day also join Glenlyon's forces if it could be repaired. Mele's forces were both an honor guard for *Saber* and a guard for the occupants of the captured ship.

Civilians who didn't work on the dock had been banned from it until the prisoners had been processed. That was the justification Mele had used, anyway. She was a little tired of hearing wails of distress from returning business owners as they took in the damage to the facility from both the fighting and from the defensive modifications Mele's forces had made.

"I just inspected the compartments prepared for holding the prisoners before they're transferred down to the planet," Gunnery Sergeant Moon reported. "Everything is ready, Major. We were given a count of one hundred twelve prisoners from the surviving crews of the enemy cruiser and destroyer, but I'm ready for one hundred twenty just in case the space squids had trouble counting."

"Good," Mele said. "Who's in charge of the guards on the compartments?"

"Sergeant Lamar. I figured she could use the experience."

"It never hurts. Sergeant Lamar, how's life as a senior enlisted?"

Penny Lamar sounded bemused when she answered over the command circuit. "It's a little confusing, ma'am."

"How so?" Mele asked.

"Well, when I was a corporal, the sergeant was always telling me to do things. I got that. Made sense. But now I'm a sergeant, and I haven't got a corporal to tell things to do."

"We should fix that," Gunny Moon said.

"We are kind of short on corporals," Mele said, thinking. "Private Ford."

Ford's response sounded both professional and wary. "Yes, Major?"

"You're now Corporal Ford. Congratulations. You're assigned to Sergeant Lamar. Sergeant Lamar, you now have a corporal to tell to do things."

Saber's docking seemed to take forever, the ship gliding closer and closer until a final nudge from her thrusters perfectly matched the vector of the facility's dock and grapnels locked the ship in place.

The quarterdeck hatch opened and Rob Geary came onto the dock wearing a survival suit, looking about briefly before walking to Mele.

They exchanged salutes. "Congratulations, Major Darcy," Rob said to her.

"Congratulations, Commodore Geary," Mele replied. "I've got orders to head down to the planet once your ship was docked. I think half of Glenlyon's industry leaders want my head for messing up their orbital facility. How about you?"

"The same. I guess we're going to be called to account for our sins."

"Yeah," Mele said. "We should've just lost so we'd be celebrated as martyrs. Want to come have a drink while we wait for the prisoners to be processed?"

"I need to watch the captured ship as it docks," Rob said. "Responsibilities, you know."

"What's the name of that tub, anyway?"

"The D-11."

"Really? That's . . . inspiring."

"Yeah." Rob sounded tired. "We are fighting for the right side, Mele."

"I know," she said. "I just wish the right side would stop fighting us."

The city looked like it had never been temporarily abandoned. It was hard to believe that life had restarted here so quickly after the evacuation during the attack on the orbital facility. Rob stood on the sidewalk for a moment to look around before walking into the government building.

He and Mele were in their dress uniforms, making them stand out. Rob could feel the gazes of others on them as they walked to the office of President Chisholm.

"How's Ninja?" Mele asked.

"Fine. Happy that I'm back safe, and happy that you're back safe."

"Is she leaving it up to you?"

"Yes, but . . ." Rob rubbed the back of his neck with one hand. "She also made it clear I need to think about her and the kids when I decide."

"Fair enough, I guess," Mele said. "I'm glad my life's not that complicated."

"Really?"

"Really. I'm a very simple soul living a very simple life."

They reached the president's office, the secretary outside gesturing them to wait, then almost immediately beckoning them on and opening the door.

Rob led the way as he and Mele walked into the office, hearing the door close behind them, and stood at attention before the desk of the president. Chisholm's office, once famous for how few decorations and pictures it contained, had acquired a few landscapes and starscapes on the walls. But otherwise it still felt like a place the occupant saw as a temporary home, something that Rob realized brought him comfort.

"Sit down, please, both of you," President Chisholm said, gesturing to the chairs facing her desk. She had the look of someone carrying out a difficult task.

Rob sat, trying to keep his movements slow and easy to hide his inner tension. Mele sat down in the other chair.

Chisholm sighed, rubbing her face with both hands. "We won. I'm sure you've already heard about some of the reaction to what you two did during the most recent crisis."

"Yes," Rob said.

"I was ordered to save that facility," Mele said. "I did."

The president lowered her hands, gazing at them. "The amount of rebuilding and repair is going to be substantial. The businesses that cheered you on for your brave defense of the station suffered from choking fits when they got a good look at the, uh, alterations done to defend the place. Nonetheless, you're a hero to the people of Glenlyon, Mele Darcy."

"I did my job. I'd rather people remembered those who didn't make it." Mele pointed to Rob. "And I'd rather they remembered those who also made the victory possible by their actions."

"That's the problem, isn't it?" Chisholm looked at Rob. "The man who didn't act. The ship that waited."

"That's grossly unfair," Mele insisted.

"I know that. Rob, you probably won't be surprised to hear that Council Members Kim and Odom both wanted to hold a formal inquiry in which you'd be expected to answer for your actions, or lack thereof. I don't mind telling you that I let them know that had better not happen. For your own peace of mind, during the events in question

I asked both of those council members if they wanted to sign on to orders requiring you to attack, and both of them found reasons to avoid doing that. They knew as well as I did, and you did, that such an attack would have been a disaster. But they wanted to be sure only you would be held responsible. I didn't permit that, and if they push me, they know I'll make sure the public learns of it."

"Thank you," Rob said.

"I'm protecting myself, too," Chisholm said. "You know that, don't you? As long as portions of the public see you as being to blame for the lack of action, they won't demand that I be held personally accountable for nearly losing Glenlyon's link to space. But if you get up in front of an inquiry it will become obvious that the government accepted your decisions and shares in the responsibility for them."

"Doesn't it matter that I'm happy with what he did?" Mele Darcy asked.

"It does," the president replied. "Though many credit your friendship for that. But your public statements of thanks for the support provided by *Saber* and her commander and crew have done a lot to damp down any public sentiment against Rob Geary." Chisholm leaned back, rubbing her forehead with one hand. "The former hero of Glenlyon is, in some eyes, now the guy who lost his nerve, who held back when he was needed the most. If you'd charged in and gotten yourself and your ship blown to pieces, they'd be celebrating your heroism, and never mind that the enemy would've captured our orbital facility and started dropping rocks on us until we agreed to let them run this world. You've seen my public statements. *I'm* giving you full credit for our victory."

Rob nodded again. "And I've seen the reaction. They think you're praising me to cover your own back."

"Right. Though they can't make that claim in the case of Major Darcy." Chisholm picked up a stylus, looked at it, then tossed it down again. "I'm not perfect, Rob. I play the game as well as I can. But I know the value of someone who comes through when I need that kind of person. That's been you. That's why I want to protect you this time.

But it's hard to convince some people that not being a hero was the most heroic thing you could've done."

"What are you going to do?"

She didn't answer for a moment, frowning down at the surface of her desk before glancing at Mele. "I know whatever happens to Rob will produce a response from you. Please hear me out before you make any statements. Rob, Kosatka rightly considers you to be a hero. Have you considered going there? Before you answer, I promise that if you do, I'll make it clear to Kosatka's government that any favorable treatment of you will be regarded as a personal favor to me that will be generously repaid. Not that Kosatka would probably need any such assurance. You'd receive appropriate recognition there."

Rob hesitated. "My family thinks of Glenlyon as home. So do I. And . . . I know men and women who died defending Glenlyon. Some of them died following my orders. I don't want to leave behind my home, and the sacrifices that others made for it."

"Rob, I want you to stay here, but I can't keep you in command of Glenlyon's space forces. I'll face a vote of no confidence if I do, and I don't think I could win that vote."

"I understand."

"The hell you do!" Chisholm glared at the door to her office. "My falling on my sword wouldn't make any difference to the outcome! Glenlyon will probably need you again. But if I'm forced to relieve you of command, and of command of *Saber*, you'd have every right to tell Glenlyon to go to hell the next time we're in trouble."

"Rob Geary isn't the only one who'd be telling you to go to hell," Mele Darcy said in a deceptively mild voice. "I need to know that I and my Marines will be fighting for a government that respects us and our sacrifices. I won't act against the government if you dump Rob, but I won't serve it, either."

"Mele—" Rob began.

"Sorry, boss. No."

Rob did his best to keep his voice steady. "It's not about me. It shouldn't be about me. Others gave their lives for Glenlyon. That was expected of them, demanded of them. Why should my career, my reputation, be regarded as more valuable than the lives others gave?"

"You'd make a lousy politician, Rob," the president said. "Or maybe a great one. I don't know. I do know that Glenlyon needs people like you, so I'm glad that you intend remaining here." Chisholm picked up the stylus again and began tapping it lightly on the surface of her desk, watching its movements. "I've got an option. To your detractors, it'll be seen as a demotion, as punishment. That will satisfy them. But I think it's a very important job, and in the long run perhaps the most important job you could do."

She set down the stylus and nodded toward a star chart on one wall. "You chewed me out when I hesitated to commit to the alliance. Once I talked to Nakamura and got a look at the preliminary agreements, I realized that you were right. But it's just a start. The alliance agreement, in its very provisional and vague current form that Glenlyon has agreed to, doesn't establish a single space force or fleet. It does call for each member star system to contribute resources to the common defense if called on." Chisholm looked over to meet his eyes again. "I can appoint you to that. There'd be some travel involved, to places like Kosatka and Eire and Benten, but you'd still be based at Glenlyon. You'd also not be in a command position. This wouldn't be a combat job. Your task would be liaison and coordination, setting the stage for a common defense fleet by agreeing to joint procedures and rules. You'd be more of a diplomat, helping to turn this new alliance into something enduring."

President Chisholm rested both of her hands on her desk, speaking slowly. "I'm not going to sugarcoat this, Rob. While you'd officially remain a commander in rank, you'd be in a staff position that gives you no command authority. Everyone will notice that. You've made some extremely tough command decisions and made them well, and your reward will be a public slap in the face denying you any more opportunities at command."

From somewhere, a sense of self-mockery rose to help Rob cope with the idea. "You could've sugarcoated it a little."

Chisholm smiled, but her eyes remained wary. "That sounds like the sort of thing Major Darcy would say."

"Major Darcy," Mele said, "isn't happy that Commander Geary is being treated this way, like a bone being thrown to those unhappy with the fact that miracles don't happen because we wish for them. Commanders who make hard decisions should be rewarded."

"So should politicians who make hard decisions," Chisholm said. "Can you make that happen? I know you're aware of history."

"No good deed goes unpunished," Mele said.

"Exactly. I can't change people, Major Darcy. All I can do is try to herd them in the right direction. And I don't pretend to always be right about which way that is. Rob, will you take this job?"

Rob exhaled slowly, looking down at his hands tightly clasped together in his lap. "It's important, isn't it? Hesta is going to be free again, and Scatha is getting a face full of the surprise attacks its been handing out to everyone else. But that's not going to end this. This alliance will have to hold together."

"Commander," Mele said, "all you have to do is ask, and I'll draw a line in the sand over this."

"No," he said. "I'm not sacrificing *you* for my career."

President Chisholm snorted. "Major Darcy is very safe. If she came out against my actions, I'd be the one whose career was likely to end. And there'd be substantial public demand for her to sit in this chair."

"My turn to say no," Mele said. "I don't want your job, I couldn't do your job, and I won't take your job."

"You're probably the smartest person in this room," Chisholm said. "Rob, if you demand it of me, I'll go to the mat for you. But I'll most likely lose. A majority of the council will insist that they've lost confidence in you."

"Because he made the right decisions," Mele said.

"Because he made the right decisions."

"This needs to be done," Rob said. "The job you're offering. Who does it if I don't? And . . . Mele, you know how Ninja feels about me being in combat. She'd never force me to avoid my duty as I saw it, but it's very hard on her. I've been sacrificing my family, in a way, to get these jobs done. What we're talking about now is just my career. Any military officer who isn't willing to sacrifice their career for the right reasons doesn't deserve to be a military officer."

"I can't deny that," Mele said.

"Maybe I should take this offer because I've paid enough of a personal price," Rob added. "I don't need any reward for what's been done in the past other than knowing my family is safe, and that I did what I could to make that happen."

"I'm not offering you a vacation," Chisholm said. "There are likely to be some hard decisions and negotiations. We have to make a new system for ensuring we're safe." She looked at the star chart once more. "When we came out here, I think all of us hoped that sort of thing wouldn't have to be called for anymore, that there'd be enough room and resources that everyone would leave everyone else alone. But that's not how people work, is it? I disliked the excess of rules in the Old Colonies as much as anyone, but it turns out we need some rules. Enough rules to keep safe those who want to follow them, and other rules for how to deal with the ones who won't follow the rules and see their fellows as sheep to be sheared."

"Sheep?" Mele asked.

President Chisholm gave her a crooked smile. "From my own family's history, Major Darcy. Why I fear those in authority who have no allegiance other than to themselves. A long time ago my family was kicked off of their land and exiled to another place far away because those in authority who were sworn to protect them preferred to have sheep on that land. The sheep produced a much higher profit, you see, than did the men, women, and children who'd lived there for many generations. The attacks on Glenlyon have proven that we need to be part of something bigger than ourselves, but I want to be sure that something doesn't also turn into a threat. It needs to be something we can trust, and that's why I want someone I can trust helping to create it."

"I understand," Rob said. "I accept the offered position. Mele, I'm good with this."

Chisholm sighed with relief. "Who should be given command of *Saber*?"

"I recommend that command of *Saber* be given to Lieutenant Commander Shen, and that she be promoted to commander."

"I'll make that happen. We'll put off the change of command for a month so it doesn't look like we're kicking you off of *Saber*. If anyone on the council complains, I'll tell them that there are, um, sailor things that need to be done before you can turn over command. What about the new ship?" Chisholm asked. "We don't have a name yet, and it'll be a while before the damage to it can be repaired, but we have to think of a captain and crew to help get that ship in shape to help protect this star system."

"I'd recommend Lieutenant Cameron," Rob said. "He's sharp. He'll have a steep learning curve as commanding officer, but I think he can handle it."

"Good." Chisholm looked at Mele. "Major Darcy, have I mentioned how much you frighten me?"

"Not yet today," Mele said.

"Will you stay in command of the Marines?"

Rob saw Mele look at him, and nodded. "I think you should. You're a damn good Marine."

"We want to expand the Marines," Chisholm added. "At least two hundred. To start. And as promised you will remain a Major. We're supposed to offer up some defense resources to the new alliance, forces designated for common purposes. I was thinking of formally committing the Marines to that."

"You want to take the Marines out of your control?" Mele asked.

"No, Major, I want to make the Marines a force that thinks in terms of defending this alliance, not just Glenlyon. You see, this alliance isn't a grouping of star systems. It's a grouping of shared values. That is what the Marines will be committed to defending."

"I'm still unclear on this," Mele said. "Usually when someone gives up military resources they give up their least valuable assets."

Chisholm laughed. "Of course they do. But not in this case. Your Marines are too valuable. They're exactly the sort of small, elite force that could be corrupted. Not by you! But you'll be replaced someday. You'd be amazed how quickly traditions and policies can be undermined by men and women with clever minds, clever tongues, and no principles. I don't want Glenlyon's Marines to become like those ancient Praetorian Guards. I want them to stay apolitical no matter what happens. Assign them to the alliance, and they'll be committed to the common principles of the star systems in the alliance rather than get involved in local politics. I told you that you frighten me, Major Darcy. You're the sort of person who could take over a world if she wanted to. I don't think you ever will, because you're too smart to think running a world is like running a military unit. But you're creating the sort of force that could take over a world if it was led by someone else."

"So," Mele said, "I'm doing my job too well."

"Exactly. Just like Commander Geary. Those jealous or worried about either of you will be happy to see you committed to duties with this alliance. They don't realize I'm committing you to those jobs because I want that alliance to be both strong and not a danger to the star systems that belong to it."

"You're either a really, really good liar, or you really mean that," Mele said.

"I'm a better liar than I should be, but I do mean it," the president said.

"Okay." Mele looked at Rob. "I guess if we're both doing stuff with this alliance, we'll still be working together."

Rob nodded, smiling at her. "I can still keep an eye on you."

"And I can keep an eye on you for Ninja. She's going to be happy. You won't get a parade, though."

"I'd rather have what I fought for," Rob said, "and I didn't fight for a parade."

Lochan Nakamura stepped off a shuttle and onto Kosatka's orbital facility, surprised by how strongly the feeling of coming home struck him. His heart must have joined his head in deciding that this place was now "home."

"So you're finally back," Carmen Ochoa said, smiling. She looked thinner than he remembered, except in her middle abdomen, signs of lingering strain around her eyes, but otherwise Carmen didn't look as if she'd changed.

"You didn't have to come up and meet me," he said, looking around. "This place is a mess."

"You should have seen it right after the battle," Carmen said. They walked past the security post that had stopped them on their first arrival at Kosatka years ago, the guards waving to Carmen. "Kosatka has a lot of cleaning up to do, but we've got new people and new shipments of material coming again."

"Trade is coming through?"

"Yes." She shook her head at him. "That's probably what saved your butt, Lochan. When we heard that you'd taken *Shark* along with those other ships on a grand tour of other star systems, there was a lot of drama. How dare he decide that on his own! But then more freighters started showing up, talking about how the pirates had been cleaned out, and gradually you became the guy who helped break the blockade of Kosatka."

Lochan shook his head in reply. "I just helped convince people. Others did the work."

"Sure. You'll have trouble convincing people on Kosatka that you don't deserve some credit. I saw the report from *Shark*, about all of the pirates destroyed at Hesta and Scatha and Kappa and other star systems. You've been in a lot of battles now."

"I've watched a lot of battles," Lochan said. "Other people fought them. I'm glad they did some good."

"No doubt of that! This world is growing again. There are even people beginning to move into Ani." She looked down the hallway, her eyes suddenly darker. "That's going to be strange. Seeing Ani as a living city instead of a battlefield."

"Things must have been rough," Lochan said, pausing to look at a display showing the planet below them. "I feel horribly guilty that I wasn't here."

"Slacker," Carmen said, smiling at him even though the darkness lingered in her eyes. "Rushing off to help bring into existence the alliance of free star systems that offered Kosatka our first hope in a long time. When you could have stayed here, picked up a weapon, and died very quickly."

"I might not have died quickly," Lochan protested. "Even Freya called me dangerous, you know."

"Freya," Carmen said. "I want to know more about this Freya. Brigit would never say much."

"Brigit? How is . . . uh . . ."

This time Carmen grinned. "Pretending she's not waiting for you to get back. Don't meet her assuming anything, but if you play your cards right she just might want to get to know you a lot better."

"Really?" Lochan laughed. "I suppose it was inevitable that sooner or later I'd meet a woman who didn't want to just be friends. And speaking of friends, my closest friend, how are you doing?"

"Still getting used to not being at war," she said, leaning against the bulkhead and smiling. "See these clothes? Like something you'd wear if you're not worried about being shot at. I spent so long in camouflage I was uncomfortable wearing something that didn't conceal me."

"What have you been doing?"

"During the fighting I, um, collected intelligence."

Lochan let her see that he could tell how much she wasn't saying. "You weren't hurt?"

"No. Dominic lost part of a leg, but he's got a prosthetic and he's on the list for a regrow." She smiled again. "Yes, we got married."

"Congratulations. What have you been doing since the fighting stopped?"

She shrugged. "I was offered a position with the new Combined Intelligence Office, which was created to be an independent voice from the Integrated Intelligence Service."

"Really?" Lochan asked. "What position?"

Carmen looked embarrassed. "They wanted me to be in charge."

"Seriously? You took it, right?"

"No," Carmen said, shaking her head, her mouth set in a stubborn line. "I'm not qualified to run an office like that. I told them to hire my old boss Loren Yeresh, and they did. He'll be good at it. A strong, independent voice."

"Then what have you been doing?" Lochan pressed.

"I've been taking care of things the First Minister wanted done. Just occasional work, really. That's okay. It's given me time to be with Domi. He's planning on staying with the defense forces, because he says our kids are going to grow up not worrying about someone invading their homes."

"Kids?" Lochan asked, letting his eyebrows rise.

"Not yet," Carmen said, patting her midsection. "But on the way. I took some convincing, because of . . . Mars. But Domi was right. Kids represent hope. We're going to give ours a safe, free world."

"I wanted to talk to you about that," Lochan said. "Are you going to be able to travel?"

"Of course I can travel. I'm a Red. It takes a lot to knock us down."

"Carmen, I don't know how much you've heard about the alliance, but it's all preliminary. There are going to be a lot of negotiations to make it into a lasting deal. There are a lot of issues to resolve between star systems that want the alliance to be strong enough to protect their interests but don't want the alliance to be too powerful."

"That sounds tough," Carmen said, eyeing him.

"Someone with experience in conflict resolution might be very useful," Lochan said.

"You're offering me a job?"

"Carmen, it's the job you came out here to do. Isn't this your dream? To ensure that this region of space doesn't become a vastly bigger form of the humanitarian disaster that Mars turned into?"

"Yes," she said, "that's my dream." Carmen looked to the side, blinking away tears. "I'll need to talk to Domi. But I think he'll be happy with the idea. It'll make Kosatka safer, and I won't be facing any personal danger like when I was, um . . ."

"Collecting intelligence?" Lochan asked. "Part of my job, our job I hope, will be trying to set up something that won't fall apart as soon as the immediate threat is dealt with. Apulu, Turan, and Scatha have been knocked back on their heels, but might lash out again as they become increasingly isolated out here. Even after that threat is dealt with, though, there are longer-term concerns. Freya Morgan is worried about what's out there beyond the current frontier."

"Do you mean aliens?" Carmen asked.

"No. It's about those colonization missions run by corporations that went way deep in search of habitable planets far from any government that might tell them what to do. Or what they couldn't do. She thinks the way they were set up is much too likely to produce dictatorships. If those oppressive governments combine to support each other, our alliance might face some powerful opposition when we finally run into them."

"I see." Carmen gazed toward deep space. "Our job's not done."

"The most dangerous part of it may be done."

"Maybe." She looked back at him and smiled. "Welcome home."

EPILOGUE

Admiral John Geary looked up as Captain Tanya Desjani walked into his stateroom aboard the Alliance battle cruiser *Dauntless*. "Am I late for something?"

"I would've called if you were late," she said, offering him her data pad. "I was reading."

"What about? Tactics or ship maneuvering?"

"Very funny. History." Desjani placed the pad on his desk so he could read it. "An unpublished manuscript sent to me by your grandniece."

"Personal Memoirs of Mele Darcy, General, Alliance Marines," he read. Geary frowned in thought. "Darcy. She founded the Alliance Marines."

"You know that, huh?"

"Yes. The Gearys have a tradition of toasting the birthday of the Marines every year. Apparently there was some tie between my family and her."

Desjani laughed. "Apparently? You don't know the reason? That she and your ancestor Robert Geary were close friends? That he commanded her in action more than once?"

"Commanded her?" Geary took another look at the screen. "I knew he served for a while, helped organize the Alliance fleet, but I never heard about him having combat commands. Rob Geary is honored in the family as the founder of our line on Glenlyon, and because he established the tradition of the family rendering service to Glenlyon and the Alliance."

"Nothing about him being a major hero of the pre-Alliance wars?"

"A major hero?" He shook his head. "Is that what General Darcy says?"

"Yeah." Desjani sat down facing him, her eyes studying Geary. "According to her, he made tough decisions that hurt his career, didn't consider himself a hero, and rarely said anything about what he'd done."

Admiral Geary laughed. "I admit it sounds like my apple didn't fall very far from that ancestral family tree. I guess that's why the family doesn't have stories about what he did. He didn't want that."

"He should have let his descendants know. You should read this," Desjani said. "Find out what he did. You've asked your ancestors for help, for advice, more than once since I got to know you. And you've told me that you felt as if they did offer some very good advice."

"Maybe Robert Geary knew more tactics than I've ever given him credit for," Geary said, looking down at the device once again. "He was good friends with Darcy, though? I guess that explains why one of Rob's daughters was the black sheep of the Geary family. She joined the Marines instead of the fleet."

Desjani smiled, the expression shifting to something questioning. "Have you ever heard the name Ochoa?"

"Ochoa? I don't think so."

"My ancestor, from the same time as Rob Geary. She's mentioned in that."

"Rob Geary was friends with your ancestor?"

"I don't think they were that close. I think they might have met through mutual friends like Darcy. But it's definitely my ancestor Carmen Ochoa. Funny to realize that she knew your ancestor."

Geary stared at Desjani. "I guess fate wasn't ready to bring our family lines together at that point."

"I guess not." She stood up, touching the comm pad. "Read it. According to Jane Geary it remained unpublished because Darcy expressed herself and her feelings about events and people very candidly. It felt like the unvarnished truth to me, except that Darcy always downplays her own actions."

"That fits if Robert Geary liked her."

"Jack, do you ever wonder if this was all planned out by something greater than ourselves? That we're all playing roles in a story fate set into motion long, long ago?"

"More often I feel as if fate is making it up as it goes along. One thing I do know. What we do matters. I guess that came down in my family from Robert Geary. It doesn't matter what plans fate has, we struggle to do what's right anyway."

"That's come down in my family, too," she said. "Though it was a bit jarring to learn that Carmen Ochoa was a Red like those Martians we encountered at Old Earth. My family had managed to bury that little bit of history."

"I'd guess that Ochoa wasn't like one of those Reds," Geary said.

"You're right. That's a safe bet." Tanya Desjani tapped the reader. "Give this a read. Find out where this story of ours started."

"Right now I'm wondering where it's going to end."

"Let me know when you figure that out."